Praise for Alexa Colette's

Stripped

"To say this book was good would be an understatement – it was kick ass and a bag of chips on top. ...As a new to me author she tick all my boxes with very descriptive language and with a clear structure to the plot – I was loving the little side stories that she used to gel the plot together while opening me up to a whole slew of characters that were just as easy to hate as they were to love."

~ *Erotic Horizons*

"I enjoyed this story so much that I went back and reread it after reading it once. The characters just jump off the page, and I could picture each one clearly."

~ *Coffee Time Romance & More*

"I've read about many amazing women in urban fantasy, but this is the first time I meet a stripper-bouncer-half werewolf-witch-friendly-crossbow sniper who is experiencing some serious memory issues. Impressive, isn't she? But Alexa wasn't the only super heroine in this novel; the author did some significant ass kicking too—with her writing of course."

~ *Pagan Culture*

"Ms. Colette grabs her readers from the beginning and keeps a tight hold to you until the end of the book, where she leaves you begging for more. She has created a world unlike any other. The pace is fast and the action is unforgiving. Her character descriptions were just enough to leave the reader wondering and searching their own imagination. The scenes were off the chart, as in out of this world. As a reader you will never expect the suspense, the drama, and the thrills. Throw some side stories thrown into the mix, and some steamy sex, and you have a read unlike any you've ever experienced before."

~ *Long and Short Reviews*

Stripped

Marcia Colette

A Sאᴅħאıח pʊðlıŝħıחɡ, Lᴛð. publication.

Samhain Publishing, Ltd.
577 Mulberry Street, Suite 1520
Macon, GA 31201
www.samhainpublishing.com

Stripped
Copyright © 2010 by Marcia Colette
Print ISBN: 978-1-60504-745-4
Digital ISBN: 978-1-60504-640-2

Editing by Anne Scott
Cover by Kanaxa

First Samhain Publishing, Ltd. electronic publication: August 2009
First Samhain Publishing, Ltd. print publication: June 2010

Dedication

This book is for my growing list of fans and visitors to my blog whose encouragement has been amazing. Also, to the lovely women of Naked Scriptorium who are always there for me whether it's in my writing life or celebrating the fabulous moments in my personal one—hint hint. To my newest supporters, the Clayton Pack, you guys are the best. Hugs on top of hugs to my incredible editor, Anne, for believing in my story and helping me to make it better. You rock! To the wonderful Magaly Guerrero, thank you for the info on the witch's ladders. And last but not least, to my aunt for being a voracious reader. Thank goodness, Grandma passed that trait on to both of us. Fingers crossed that there are less "Sponge Bob" moments with this one.

Chapter One

Thick, hazy smoke and bright lights hid the faces of the drunken men as they cheered and hurled obscenities. As soon as empty beers mugs clapped on tabletops, hands raised to flag down X-rated waitresses for refills. The music thumped hard enough to break through my chest. Despite the painful noise, the degrading banter stayed with me. They didn't have any right to yell and whistle at me like some nickel whore.

This must have been a nightmare. Like the kind you have when you're dreaming you're naked on stage and you wake up realizing it was only in your mind.

One problem: I was partially naked, on a stage, and even my mind wanted to hide under a rock. Not funny at all, considering I had no idea how I had gotten here.

I dared to shift my eyes to the right. They landed on a gold pole stretching from the stage to the black-painted ceiling. Just as I thought. No amount of pinching would wake me from this horror.

Colored lights radiated overhead, heating the center stage. I knew how a hamburger under a heat lamp felt. I stood in the middle of the waxed hardwood floor while two more strippers danced at opposite ends of the stage. The music hit an ear-blasting crescendo and the dancers tore off the tops of their striped prisoner uniforms. Two pairs of boobs jutted out at the same time.

If there was a cue, I missed it. My behind wasn't dropping a thing for these bums.

Pain bit into the side of my big toe. Tight straps nearly strangled it to numbness. I glanced down, pulling my bent knee inward. A very naked knee at that. Someone had strapped a pair of five-inch, black stiletto heels around my bony ankles. It was a miracle I remained standing in these things.

My hands clung to both edges of the tiny policeman's jacket. A black thong rode up my butt crack like floss through teeth, no thicker than the straps on my heels. Something sat on my head, holding my wavy black hair down. Reaching up, I pulled off a policeman's hat with a bright, shiny badge pinned in the center. Gee, why didn't that surprise me?

"Come on, baby," a man yelled at the edge of the stage. Between the missing teeth and the long stringy hair, I would rather kiss a donkey's crap-filled ass than go near that creep. His hand thumped the small round table, sloshing beer from his mug. "Come on, sugar. Blast me with those cute little tits y'all got hidin' under thar."

How I had sunk to this level, I didn't have a clue. In fact...I didn't have much of a clue about anything. Not my name, where I had come from, or family. It was all...gone.

Men loitered in every nook and cranny of the seedy saloon. Some shoved shot glasses in their mouths while others gulped their beer from frosted mugs. A long bar stretched across the back wall where a half-dozen patrons waited for the bartenders to fill their orders. One of the barkeeps finished putting foam-dome touches on a beer before placing it on a tray covered with shot glasses and more mugs, and handing it off to a scantily dressed waitress. Then again, "scantily" was an understatement. She wore a V-neck outfit that covered up the areolas of her bulbous boobs and stretched down to barely cover her crotch. Another similarly dressed waitress made her way around a crowded table. I got a look at her fishnet pantyhose with the rest of the V riding up her ass and out to her shoulders. A man at the table slapped her on the bottom before smoothing his hand along her reddening butt cheek.

I didn't know which was grosser—the outfits or the way these men degraded the women.

An image in the mirror behind the bar caught my attention. From this distance, my reflection showed me standing on the stage with my one hand tucked under my jacket ready to flash the room. Only now, the other two strippers stared at me like I had lost my mind. The dark-haired one nodded for me to take it off. I shook my head. She'd need a crowbar to get me out of my last shred of dignity.

My feet staggered backward. On the way, my elbow clipped the pole. Panic began chiseling away at my nerves. The men sitting closest to the stage pulled their heads back, faces twisting in bewilderment. That made two of us.

"Boooooo," a man shouted. "What the hell's wrong with this girl?"

"She's probably on something."

"Mr. Wiggly will straighten her out."

"Fuckin' whore!"

A scotch tumbler flew across the stage. Shattered glass and whiskey spilled everywhere. One stray piece sliced the top of my strangled toe.

Why that no good, son of a—! Stiletto heels or not, I marched to the end of the runway, fisted the man's shirt in my hand and lifted him from his chair. His eyes went wide. His rapid heartbeat thumped loud enough to reach my ears and his pupils dilated. I'd have him crapping his pants in about...three...seconds...

I paused.

I had lifted him straight up out of his seat with his feet dangling about four feet off the floor. My bony arms hardly strained a muscle. Something in the back of my head screamed I should be accustomed to this kind of strength, but I wasn't.

Nonetheless, someone needed to let this inebriated jerk know he couldn't get away with things like that. I yanked his sour-smelling face within an inch of mine. "Next time you throw a glass on this stage, you had better damn well hope it kills me."

I let him go before he stuttered through a pathetic response. The man dropped onto the rickety table, smashing it to pieces and startling a group of onlookers.

The blaring music stopped—finally—and everyone came to a standstill. All eyes were on me. If I didn't feel comfortable a few minutes ago, I sure as hell wasn't feeling it now.

I zipped up my police jacket, turned on my stilettos and marched—slipped once—my thong-clad behind out of there. I threw open a pair of blood-red curtains, leaving collective "boos" at my back. Butt cheeks flapping or not, I didn't care. Depending on how many times I had stripped without realizing it, these jerks probably had grown accustomed to seeing my ass in the breeze.

Click, click, click.

I didn't turn around. I knew the other girls had followed because my instincts said so. In fact, my instincts seemed more heightened than usual. But then again, I didn't know what usual was nor did I remember.

The miniscule print in the corner of a movie poster was as clear as a message on a billboard. My ears captured conversations behind closed doors. The toxic smell of alcohol-laced perfume pinched my nose from trails left minutes—hours—ago. There were at least four different types on the air, meaning at least four different people had passed through this hall and brought a horrible stench of incense with them. My nose picked up a few more scents, making it nine fresh ones in the last few minutes and numerous ones in the last couple of hours. Stale dust settled on my tongue from the blowing air conditioner that hadn't been cleaned since the owners had it installed.

I passed more than a half-dozen girls, giggling and wearing some sort of X-rated getup. There was a nurse, a scantily dressed princess and someone who looked like a dominatrix. What kind of striptease freak show did I belong to?

The rust orange hall tickled my mind with familiarity. I had a general idea of what lay behind each of the doors. None of them interested me except for the last one on the right. An announcer's voice boomed through the walls, muffled but audible as he apologized for my slipup and introduced the next act.

Tender hands warmed my shoulders. "Keisha, honey, what's wrong? You can't just leave the stage like that."

Keisha? I didn't know this woman, so she had no right putting her paws on me. I threw her off and whirled on my heels. "Don't *ever* touch me again," I snarled.

Redness brightened her made-up cheeks. With her long curly hair, thick lips and high cheekbones, she was very pretty. If only she would sandblast some of that crap off her face, a decent guy might take notice. She stood an inch taller in her heels and had boobs that would keep a set of sextuplets happy for months. When I tried to pull her name out of my head, I drew a blank.

Grabbing my shoulders, another woman shoved me into a rack of hanging clothes. "Get a grip, Keisha. Don't make me get

Paul to put your ass back on straight. You ruined our act."

I wanted to snatch each of her long blond hairs from her scalp. Who cared if she had a few inches over me? I'd be more than happy to blacken both of her baby-blue eyes. Better yet, I'd tear that prisoner's hat off her head and shove it far enough down her throat to feel like a stomach staple.

I dug myself out of the clothing rack just in time for "Drop It Like It's Hot" to blare over the speakers. How apropos for what I planned to do.

Narrowing my eyes on the chick, I slugged her with a right cross. That pop to the chops registered up and down the hall. She staggered backward into the rust orange wall.

Snagging her thin neck between my fingers, I yanked her to her feet. "If this Paul person has answers, then get him." I shoved her hard enough to crack the back of her head against the wall.

Now that our little alpha-female power display was over, I wanted answers.

I stalked down the corridor and stopped in front of a burgundy door with a gold star glued to the front. The familiarity surrounding this place came through like a bright light from the heavens; only this place had more to do with hell. My mind traveled into the past where I recalled a beige locker with a Harley Davidson sticker on the front and someone else's initials carved on the lower right corner.

Although I couldn't be sure, I'd bet anything it was mine. Perhaps some of those answers I wanted lay in there.

Slapping my hands on the door, I burst inside.

Chapter Two

A line of half-naked women either sat in front of mirrors painting their faces or stood around adjusting their bare-minimum costumes. Not one in the bunch seemed to care that they were about to strut their bony asses or jiggling boobs in front of a group of a perverted drunks. This was their thing, and at some point, it had become mine.

None of this registered. Not my name, where I was born or my favorite color. I didn't even know if I had a favorite food. Many questions like how I got here and where exactly was here continued to plague me. What had I done to deserve this?

I'd come looking for answers but began to doubt I'd find them here. These women were doing what they were told, and my missing history wasn't a part of their program. I had to relax.

Be cool, whoever you are.

Easing through the room, a tremor worked across my shoulders. If I had to go into an amnesic coma, why couldn't I wake in a more dignified setting like a college campus? Knowing nothing about my circumstances and having my pride stripped away made me more livid and scared than being on that stage.

"Keisha," a woman said, making her approach. She reminded me of a mid-nineteenth-century madam with her tight corset and boobs spilling over the front. "Darling, you look pale. Is something wrong?"

I stopped her advance with a talk-to-the-hand gesture. "Back off. I don't know you from a real fairy or a fake one."

As I stormed past her, I couldn't help catching a glimpse of myself in the mirror. I had almond-shaped, dark eyes that were remarkably like my mother's. How I knew that, I don't know.

Call it another feeling. Without the heels, I was of average height and slim. Heck, I had a rather nice figure, somewhat athletic. Unfortunately, I needed another cup size—or two—in the boob area if I wanted to be in the same league as the other strippers. What the heck made me stripper material? Then again, those drunkards couldn't tell a tit from a bowl of ice cream with a cherry on top.

My skin amazed me to the point that it dusted off a few cobwebs in my brain. I had an olive or mulatto complexion because of my Native American father and African American mother. That was what the voice in my head said and I was going with it. Most people referred to it as "high yellow". I think. I looked more like cappuccino. More cobwebs began to clog up the memory passage until it fizzled away.

I was a stranger to myself. That notion churned my stomach in such a way that I thought I'd lose my lunch right there. I just wanted this to make sense, like a person misplacing their keys and suddenly remembering where they had put them. Why couldn't it be that easy for me? Unsettling didn't begin to describe the not-knowing of how or when I had gotten here.

The "madam" clapped her hands and shouted, "Everyone out! Now!"

Through the mumbles and scowls, the strippers gathered their things and made a line toward the door. She stopped one of them, mumbling something about getting this Paul person and my having a fit. That crazy woman had no idea.

Some things came back, a few disjointed images and weird feelings. But that was the problem. I didn't know who or what to take as gospel. Dammit, I hated being confused like this.

Pulling away from the mirror, I went to the row of beige lockers lining the wall. I noted each name before stopping at the masking tape that had *Keisha* written in black marker. That was what everyone called me. In the corner was a small sticker of a Harley Davidson motorcycle.

"Dear..." The madam kneaded her pudgy fingers and blinked with the innocence of a child up to no good. "Why don't you sit? Paul's usually good at calming you girls down before and after a show. He'll—"

I tore off the door to my locker. Literally. My fingers remained wrapped around the knob while I stared with my jaw agape. Wow, was I strong. This might come in handy, other than tossing drunkards around a bar.

I let the bent metal clatter to the floor. Inside, I found a pair of jeans, an ivory shirt and an emerald green bra. I unzipped the police jacket and dressed in a hurry. Whoever this Paul guy was, I didn't want to meet him like this.

Just as I had finished buckling my pants and grabbed my shirt, the door burst open. A man stood there with shaggy hair touching his shoulders, a light-brown goatee and hazel eyes. He looked rather average with the dirty jeans and a plaid shirt with the sleeves rolled to three-quarters length.

"Hey, baby." He sauntered into the room, his eyes fixed on me. "What's shaking? Frankie says you're having a bad time."

"You're Paul?" I kept a tight grip on my sweater. I needed my hands free for whatever came next, which meant forgoing pulling it on and losing sight of the enemy.

The enemy? Talk about a survival-of-the-fittest attitude.

"I see." He reached for his back pocket and pulled out a syringe. "Don't worry about this. It's just a something to calm you down. We're worried about you. Aren't we, Dottie?"

My eyes widened. Was that how they kept the women under control? They used drugs to soften us up before we went on stage? Damn them. Thank goodness I had missed my dose or I wouldn't be standing here right now. But the question was, why hadn't they given it to me before I went out on stage? Did they think it would sour my act?

The madam nodded and plastered a gentle smile on her face, lifting the mole above her cheek. "That's right, sugar. We only want what's best for you."

Paul continued across the floor, uncorking the syringe and squirting an arch of clear fluid in the air. "You're feeling a little disoriented, huh? A slight headache?"

Well, now that he mentioned it, perhaps a little nauseous too. But I wasn't talking. Instead, I backed into the wall behind me. A mental voice screamed to fake my fear and that was what I did. My eyes widened, head shaking while my hands felt for the cold wall. Perhaps I did this a little too well.

"I'm sorry," Dottie said, coming from the other side. "I should've listened better when you said you weren't feeling good."

"Shit, Dot!" Paul glared. "You knew she was like this and

you didn't tell me?"

"She said it was a little headache is all and wanted to dance tonight. I even checked the incense by her dressing mirror to make sure it was full. How the hell was I supposed to know it would lead to this? She won't remember anything, right?"

"Shut up."

It was time to leave. I threw the sweater in Paul's face and followed it up with a slug across the jaw. The syringe scraped my forearm when he went down. Dottie grabbed my other arm, but I jerked her forward and smirked.

"You don't want to do that." I slammed her with a left cross.

Paul grabbed my ankle. Blood trailed from the side of his nose. He spat another clot onto the floor. Using my free leg, I kicked him across the bridge of the nose, knocking him out cold.

I traipsed over to where Dottie had shrunk back and towered over her. "You're going tell me what I want to know. There won't be any of this what-if-I-don't bullshit. You *will* talk to me."

She nodded like a bobble-head doll.

Chapter Three

Dottie told me things, but unfortunately, there was this trust issue standing between us. The part that intrigued me the most was how the workers at Trixie's Tricks had found me sitting in the back corner of the bar about eight months ago, looking confused and sick. They had taken me in because they found out I had "certain skills" that came in handy. Dancing wasn't one of them. Bouncing vagrants out the door was. Looked like my instincts were on the mark after all. The dancing came up because guys wanted to know if I stripped as well as I fought. This was only my third week on the stage as the main attraction.

My doubts about Dottie had surfaced when she said it had never occurred to anyone to report me to the police or dig deeper to find out where I had come from. The saloon's owner, Robert Gamboldt, only cared about what he got out of me while I was there. Gathering my senses would mean losing his cheap labor.

According to my fake license—Dottie had it made up when they couldn't find my ID—I lived in an apartment on the east side of Battle Rose, Arizona. How I had ended up in a town with two thousand desert urchins, your guess was as good as mine. While driving down the road with the hopes of finding answers at my so-called home, everywhere I looked there was desert, tumbleweeds and cacti. A steer's skull with the jaws clacking together wouldn't have surprised me.

Going to the police sounded like the smart thing to do, but I didn't know how to find them. Not only that, after seeing Paul with the hypodermic, Trixie's staff probably dealt out drugs like candy. The cops would think I had come off a bad drug trip or something. The minute they called Trixie's, Dottie and Paul would have me up on assault charges to cover their asses. Memories or not, I needed to get out of this town.

It took some doing, but I found my two-story apartment building and parked just below my window. When I got out, I glanced at the second floor.

A niggling feeling told me someone else lived there. In the past hour, I had learned to pay close attention to my gut. Looking around the parking lot, I tried to jog memories of my roommate owning a car. Perhaps I'd know if she was still there. Nothing came to mind other than me driving this beat-up 1987 Honda Civic with a busted-out passenger window. Thank goodness for clear plastic. Rope held one of the rear doors on and the pungent exhaust fumes made me sick. The pay at Trixie's must have sucked if this was what my cash bought me.

When I reached the second floor, I unlocked the door and pushed it open until it bumped against the wall. My eyes needed a second to adjust from the lighting on the open balcony to the darkness in the apartment, but when they did, turning on the lights was unnecessary. I made out colors and angles of furniture and objects around the room. Two rag magazines lay on the two-seater table near the window. A lava lamp sat on a small table in the corner. Stains marred the worn carpet and thickness saturated the air.

I stepped inside.

Something covered my mouth.

My hand went out, stopping my assailant from stabbing me with an incoming syringe. Man, I hated needles.

My elbow jabbed a set of bony ribs. The woman grunted and her grip loosened. I moved forward to keep her off balance. I shoved my hip into her side, grabbed her arm and launched her over my shoulder. Still holding her wrist, I twisted it backward and plowed a right cross into the woman's face.

After leaping off her still body, I closed the door and flipped the light switch. The brightness burned my eyes the way the odor from a busted tailpipe rifles through your car's vents. At first it bothered me that it took a few seconds for them to adjust. Thank goodness there wasn't another person waiting or they would've had the jump on me.

That wasn't right. I'd have to get my eyes checked when I got a chance. It hurt as much as the pungent scent coming from the vents. Speaking of which, the air tasted like a pack of cigarettes and rotten garbage.

My assailant had long black hair and a small scar just above her lip. She had dressed for bed wearing a black baby doll with a red-kisses pattern throughout the silk material. She was probably the roommate, though she really could've been anyone. Attacking me certainly didn't make her my friend.

She moaned and her head rolled to the left. She'd come to soon.

I ran around our small one-bedroom apartment and collected plenty of cord to use for bindings. Once I had her situated, I began going through the apartment looking for anything that might clue me in to my past.

Other than clothes, some money and a bunch of business magazines, I found nothing. My "roomie" had a chest filled with adult toys and a collection of men's underwear. I closed the trunk and washed my hands. Heaven only knew what kind of diseases that skank left sliming up the walls of that thing.

"Hey," the woman shouted from the other room. "You in there, Keish?"

I backed away from the bathroom counter and stormed into the other room. "My name isn't Keish or Keisha. Call me that again and you'll swallow some teeth until you get it right."

A smile splayed her face. "Relax, hon. We're only trying to help. Dottie called and said you had one of your fits. That you needed your medicine. They're real strict about—"

"Got any money?"

Her face contorted. "What for?"

"Money, bitch. You're a stripper, so I know you got some."

"You do too." She lifted her chin toward the bedroom. "You keep a lock box in the bedroom closet on the top shelf."

I found it where she said. Unfortunately, none of the keys on my key ring opened the lock. Frustrated, I slammed the metal box against the bathroom counter until the top bent enough for me to get my finger around the raised edge. One good yank and I tore it off the hinges. Man, I loved this strength.

Inside were a couple hundred dollars in cash, a credit card with the name Keisha M. Walker on it and a matching birth certificate. Great. I closed my eyes and repeated, "My name is not Keisha."

I dumped everything from the box into a suitcase. A bunch of clothes went on top. Anything that might lend a clue to my past. I packed in record time. Items clanked and rattled inside, but I didn't care. I wanted my real life back, no matter what it took to get me there.

As I left the bedroom, I stopped by the woman on the floor. "What's your name?"

"My what? Geesh, hon, you sure got whopped across the head pretty hard."

"I asked you a question. Or did Dottie tell you what I did to her fingers when she wasn't forthcoming?" I hadn't done anything, really, but the fear in her eyes said she bought into the lie. Bully for me.

"Joy. Joy Rockwell. I've been here for the past two years."

I started for the door.

"You'll never get out of Battle Rose," she said. "Paul's on his way. He and Sammy are going to fix you up real nice."

"Who fixed me up to begin with? Who was I when I arrived in this dusty little pit of hell?"

She shrugged despite her hands tied behind her back. "All I know is that I get a nice chunk of change for letting you stay with me. See if I ever do anything for Paul again, you little shit. We should've dumped your ass beside the road."

"How long have I been here?" I wanted to make sure Dottie wasn't lying.

A deep throaty chuckle. "What diff—"

I narrowed my eyes, yearning to tear her throat out and use it as a patch. Unfortunately, that would defeat the purpose of getting any information. I could always beat her into the ground if I had to take it to that level, though I'd rather not. I needed my strength for getting out of this armpit town.

Something on my face made Joy gulp. "Just after Valentine's Day eight months ago. I know because your arrival ruined my vacation."

"I'll cry a bucket of tears for you." I started for the door again.

She said something more, but it went over my head. I'd been stripping in that bar, bouncing people out, and doing God only knows what else with those people. Did I have a boyfriend or boyfriends? Any STDs or abortions? Did I limit my sexcapades to men? The possibilities were endless. Unless I dunked myself in a vat of scalding water, nothing would ever take away the feeling of knowing those mongrels had touched me.

Joy was right about one thing. Getting out of this town would be tough. Everybody knew everybody and with the strip joint being the biggest draw, there was no telling how well they knew me.

I didn't know where to go or how to get there. Everything prior to when I had "awakened" on stage was gone. All of it erased. Though I didn't have any answers, I was damn well going to get them.

Within two hours of driving, I pulled my Honda off the road and into a trailer park. Cars were parked in front of the dilapidated trailers like a junkyard parking lot. One more wreck-on-wheels wouldn't make a difference. Battle Rose was just a bad memory at this point.

With some time to breathe, I started going through the things I had collected from my apartment. Right away, I noticed I had a thing for collecting business cards. It was like I had kept every damn card known to mankind. Some had to do with various computer and maid services, while others were for accountants.

One of them belonged to a plastic surgeon in Phoenix. On the back, someone had penciled in an appointment for eight a.m. on Tuesday. Yeah right. I tossed that one out the window. After seeing those chicks with the grapefruit-sized boobs, horrific thoughts went through my mind of them stretching my A cups to D-sized volleyballs.

The second business card belonged to a real estate agent with a Boston address. Why in the world would I keep this? If I wanted to buy property here—hell to the no—then I'd go with someone local.

But I owned property...somewhere. Boston perhaps? In a weird, disconnected way, it made sense. I pictured a large house, almost too big for one person. A red schoolhouse on the corner of a residential area. There was a sign out front, but no matter how hard I tried to hold on to the memory, the name never cleared.

That wasn't the end of my reminiscence. A college wasn't

far from there. I pictured myself carrying a black backpack on my shoulder and going to class. I must have been a student in my past life. That was better than being a stripper in my present one.

The memory feed snapped off. At least it confirmed that I was more than a piece of stripper candy.

Chapter Four

My growling stomach woke me. It took a moment for the fog to clear from my brain and remember that I had driven about two hours last night before pulling into a trailer park to sleep off the early morning hours. Instead of heading to the local diner, I filled up at a gas station, bought a road map and started on the road again. Bottled water and two packs of Twinkies sustained me the rest of the day—I got lost—until I had reached the Cactus Bowl Motel.

"That'll be forty dollars," the desk clerk said with a deep southern drawl.

Forty dollars for a two-story roach motel in the middle of a dust bowl? I fingered the credit card with my fake name on the front. "You take credit?"

"Ma'am, do we look like we just got in from the Dark Ages?"

Gee, I don't know. I glanced around the lobby of the one-star motel. A rundown couch had patches of orange-colored foam poking through and duct tape keeping other spots together. The thirteen-inch black-and-white TV sat on the other side of the L-shaped counter with a piece of foil wrapped around the rabbit ears. Dust swept across the floor every time wind blew the door open. Let's not forget the old-fashioned slide pad used to imprint the credit card. It sat next to the calculator that doubled for a register.

Did he really want me to answer that question?

I slapped the card onto the counter and watched him imprint it. Then I asked the stupidest question of all time. "Is there a place where I can get computer access?"

His droopy eyes and scooped neck remained frozen. He pointed at the window facing the road. "See that sign in blue with the L symbol and pointing down the road? That stands for library. But today is Saturday. That means the library is closed all day today. And would you look at that? According to my watch, it's close to dinner. They're especially closed around this time even on the weekdays."

A smirk slid across my face. This jackass had better be thankful I needed a room for the night. I fought the urge not to stab him in the throat with my credit card for being such a jerk.

"You got ID?" he asked. "I need it for ver-if-i-cation purposes."

Time to see if this fake driver's license stood up. Maybe I should rethink the stabbing part and aim for his eye instead.

Reaching inside the black kidney purse I had found in my locker last night, I pulled out my wallet again. I flipped through every section of the billfold. Pieces of paper, old receipts, coupons. What a mess. There was no way I was like this in my past life. I couldn't be. I had become the complete opposite of everything I stood for. Memory loss or not, I knew it.

The clerk traded the license for the guest registry. Once I signed it, he checked the signature and handed everything back including the key to room eleven. Once I put everything away, I traipsed out of the office. With a little luck, I'd never see that weasel again not even at check out.

After parking next to the cess—er, uh—swimming pool, I left my car there instead of driving it around to the backside of the building where my room awaited. I hiked up the stairs and decided to break in to room twenty-four in case someone I didn't want to see came looking for me in room eleven. Using my unnatural strength, I forced the window open. Other than mine, less than half of the rooms had occupants. Perhaps that meant there would be half the number of foul-mouthed morons too.

The room needed some serious airing out. Before I put anything down, I scoped out every inch of my accommodations. Old cigarette smoke irritated the inside of my nose. I picked up the remote and noticed some*thing* or someone had chewed off part of the buttons. Grimacing, I tossed it on the sagging bed with the polyester comforter. Lord only knows who had touched that thing. When I went into the dressing area to wash my hands, I found brown mildew at the base of the faucet where it connected to the bowl. More mildew had taken up residence on the tiled floor next to the shower stall.

Damn. I thought they would have at least provided a bathtub. Then again, what was I complaining for? I'd think twice before using it anyway.

Once I finished my sweep, I sat on the bed and searched through my suitcase. I had close to a thousand dollars in cash, some pictures of me having a good time with the other strippers—a few too embarrassing to mention—and more receipts.

Oh God! The idea of letting those mongrels have a touch for money made me push the suitcase away and hug myself. How many times had they caressed my skin? How long and how hard had I worked to get this money? Did I do favors on the side? Dammit, I wanted to know.

I spent the next few minutes hunched over and holding my head. When I started rocking back and forth, I forced myself to stop. Going loopy was a luxury I couldn't afford.

After a *very* long, *very* hot shower and munching on a slice of cold pizza I had delivered from the only pizza joint in town, I sat on the edge of the bed wearing a scratchy towel tucked around my chest. The scent of old cigarettes and alcohol on the carpet made me nauseous again. Thank goodness for socks because I didn't want to think about what might have stained the carpet. After putting on my same clothes, I lay on top of the slick polyester comforter and dozed off the second my head touched the pillow.

Gravel crunched.

A car pulled up to the backside of the motel and woke me. I bolted upright like a soldier at attention. Brakes squealed to a stop. Car doors popped open and closed. I jumped from the bed and went to the window.

A beige pickup had parked on the opposite side of the lot. My insides trembled as thoughts slowly returned to me. Unless the jerks from Trixie's Tricks had a crystal ball for radar, there was no way in hell they should've found me.

A woman got out of the passenger's side. She had to be in her fifties with her puffy cheeks and a worn look around her eyes. Gray dusted her curly blond hair. Her husband, I presumed, struggled getting out of the driver's seat. I smiled to myself, thinking his plump belly might have had something to do with it. He tipped his straw cowboy hat up on his head and slid his arm around the woman's shoulders. She adjusted her cotton sweater before smiling and kissing him.

Thank God. My tension released with a heavy sigh. They weren't here for me. They were here to call it a night under the starry sky. I leaned forward and watched them disappear around the side of the building. They seemed like a nice-enough couple. What I wouldn't give to be in their shoes.

That was a reality check. I'd let myself fall asleep in a place I knew nothing about. That could've easily been Paul and his goons parking down there and blocking off my escape.

It was time to go.

I packed the one suitcase I had and headed down to the seventies lobby to check out. This place was a trap waiting to happen and I didn't want to get blocked in.

I slammed my palm down on the metal bell. The door behind the counter opened, and the same smarmy dude swayed toward the desk. His silk shirt was half-undone with thick curly hairs matted across his chest, coarse enough to scrape the grease out of a pan. Ick.

A whiff of the marijuana reeking from the back office had wrinkled my nose. Great. This guy had probably spent the last few hours getting high.

"I'm checking out." I slapped the room key on the counter. "Where's the registry?"

The man ran a finger down his jungle-haired chest. "Why ya want to leave, sugar? I might have something for ya?"

I was too through with this man. I smacked my hand down on the counter to keep from reaching across and snagging him by the collar of his cheesy disco shirt. Glaring, I snarled, "Get me the damn registry."

He snorted and shook his head before handing me the book. I signed it and tossed the pen over the counter.

The fax machine on the far counter came to life.

Wow. This guy had a fax machine. Obviously, his technology priorities were a bit skewed.

The rollers began spitting out a picture of someone. It got as far as the eyes and bridge of the nose when I recognized it as me. My fingers began tapping, hoping it would signal him to hurry up before he noticed the blown-up photo from my driver's license. If my drumming annoyed the hell out of him, even better. At least he would be glaring at me and not the fax. The slimy attendant busied himself with getting his calculator to print out a receipt. Unfortunately, his fat-finger-itis forced him to start over twice.

He tore off the receipt and handed it to me. "H-h-here you go."

"Thanks." I snatched it from him and walked out the door. My legs itched to run to the car as fast as possible, but I didn't want to give him any clues that something had me on the run.

I made it all the way to the airport in Lubbock where I parked my car in the garage and pretty much kissed it goodbye. Halfway across the parking lot it dawned on me that I had no idea where I was going. I just knew I needed to get far away from here.

"You can go anywhere you want to in the great state of Texas," the clerk said. "There's Dallas, Houston, Austin, Fort Worth—"

"Stop!" My fingers gripped the counter while I forced myself to dig through my thoughts.

The clerk mentioned Austin. I didn't want to go to Austin exactly, but there was something about that name that threw up a red flag with fireworks. *Austin.* Dammit, what was so special about that place? My subconscious stomped around like a petulant child, yelling, *No! No! No!* The city wasn't special, but rather the name.

I met her eyes. "Austin is familiar, but it's not right exactly."

Her eyebrow arched. "How exactly?"

"Not sure. It sounds almost like another city I've heard of. A place that *is* familiar to me. But..."

The clerk tipped her head. "Ma'am? Are you okay? Maybe you shouldn't fly."

A rounder woman approached the other woman from behind. She had a more authoritative look about her. Her confidence came through with her lifted head and penetrating stare. "Can I be of assistance?"

I shook my head. Her eyes said "challenge". I don't know why that word popped in my head, but it did. Something about this woman made me lift my chin in an effort to be the "bigger" woman. To meet her confrontation eye for eye, demand respect without voicing it.

The woman's demeanor softened. "Ma'am, if you're sick, we can't allow you to fly. We have rules against that."

"I'm not sick," I replied.

"There's a first-aid station—"

"I'm fine."

My clamped jaws weren't fast enough to catch the words blurting from my mouth. My gut said someone had spent years worth of brainwashing on me to discourage the use of police, doctors and even first-aid stations. But that couldn't have been at Trixie's because I wasn't there that long. It was another one of those illogical instinct things that willed me to follow along.

Images flooded my brain of a horrible wolf attack. Lips peeled back from a set of drooling, serrated teeth. A growl as loud as a lawnmower blocked out my screams. I was practically a baby when that monster attacked me. He grabbed hold of my...baby brother? I remembered the fear, the horror of the hellish nightmare. The rabid, oversized dog had torn my baby brother from my grasp. I got mad and went after the monster. That was when he dropped my brother and snapped his jaws at me. Somehow—the images moved in a blur, too fast for me to comprehend—he locked his jaw on my foot.

Wolves packed enough of a bite force to break through the leg of an elk. That allowed them to become skilled hunters whenever it came to taking down their prey permanently. I didn't know if the monster had applied that much force, but it was enough to break skin and possibly my flimsy foot.

I screamed. As a helpless five-year-old, that was about all I had in my power to do.

"Ma'am?" The authoritative woman closed her hand on the back of mine. Worry filled her eyes. "Are you okay?"

A tear trickled down my cheek. When had I started crying? I wiped it away and cleared my throat. My breathing came fast and swift like someone had untied a plastic bag from around my head. I glanced over my shoulder to make sure no one in the ticket line saw. These people would think I was a basket case.

"No," I whispered. "I'm fine. I just need to get somewhere safe. Austin's too close. I need to go farther."

The other attendant handed me a tissue. I thanked her with a nod.

The authoritative woman leaned close. "Is it a boyfriend,

honey? Because God knows we've all had our share of knuckleheads."

Wish I had thought of that. I stifled the smile about to bubble to life on my face. The woman had offered me an out and I took it. "Yes. He's been...forcing me to do stuff. I finally got away and now I want to leave. For good."

"What about the police? Do you want us to—?"

I shook my head. "No. I think he pretty much owns the police in Battle Rose. I don't know how far his hands reach and I don't want to take any chances. I want to go home. I even took his money and stuff to pay my way. That's why I don't want the police, if I can help it. Look." I dug into my pants pocket and pulled out that lousy Keisha M. Walker ID and her credit cards. "I'm not a complete thief. Some of my money is in here too. I can pay. Honest."

The woman studied me a few seconds longer before waving me down to a closed section at the end of the counter. Her long fingernails began clicking across the keyboard with spot-on precision. "If you're not interested in where you're going, there are a bunch of flights leaving the airport. I can put you on any one of them."

If it weren't for the counter standing between us, I would have hugged her. "My memory is a little shot. My ex kept me drugged most of the time."

"What?" Her face turned to rage, though not aimed at me. "Girl, are you sure you don't want to call the police on this fool?"

I shook my head. "No. I just want to leave. Slip out of town unnoticed, if I can help it."

She muttered something under her breath while her fingernails went on their tapping crusade again. "Well, since you're not inclined to Austin, how about Atlanta? A same-day flight is a little cheaper than anything else I'm seeing. Plus, it's big enough for you to get lost in."

Boston. I couldn't explain why it popped in my head, but it made sense. My gut screamed to be there even though the rest of me didn't know why. So far, it was the only thing on my side.

I lifted my head high. "I'd like a ticket to Boston."

My brain chose that moment to flood me with more images. There was a Giant Dig—or was it Big—and the Salem Witch Trials weren't far from the city either. Contrary to popular belief, you'll find more witches living in New York or L.A. than you would there. Their subway system was the oldest in the country even though you had New York's system, which was more expansive. Good Lord, I recalled the fishy smell hovering in the air around Chinatown. I had walked those narrow streets many times with my friends after work. After seeing plays or shows in the Theater District, my friends and I had camped out at Legal Seafoods to dissect what we had seen. We'd spend an easy three hours there if we weren't careful, forgetting that I had to get back to...to...?

The images disappeared.

The woman smiled. "Okay, then. Let me bring up the prices."

I waited like a child dancing with glee on Christmas Eve.

The woman stopped typing. "It's twice the price to Boston."

I slapped Keisha's credit card on the counter. "I'll take it."

"The only thing is you'll have to sit for a couple of hours. The earliest flight out that isn't full won't leave until six in the morning. It makes a stop in Dallas where you'll change flights, but that's it."

"Doesn't matter. I'll take it."

Happiness filled me from head to toe. I was on my way. The only problem was...what would I do when I got there?

After going through security, fatigue rotted my senses and left me with one hell of a headache. I wandered over to the wall and found a chair a few gates down from mine. I had completely lost track of time. The only thing I knew was at least two nights had passed since my awakening at Trixie's. A quick search of my bag, and I found a watch. I fixed it to sound off an hour before my flight left. If I missed it, then I'd get a rental car and drive my butt there. No way in hell was I spending another day away from the only place that held some sense of familiarity to me. I chanced a nap without worrying who might get the jump on me and drag me back to Trixie's. After spreading my jacket over my front, I drifted off.

A hand touched my arm. I bolted awake.

Paul shushed me to silence.

Chapter Five

Paul sat *so* close that onlookers must have thought we were lovers about to make out in the middle of the airport. My heart thumped so hard the vibrations clogged my throat. His nose appeared red and swollen, but he cleaned up nicely. Well, nicely was still a matter of opinion.

Another man sat on the other side. With the way he stared and the smile brightening his face, he must have known me too. Dark brown hair brushed just above his massive shoulders. Though I wasn't one for cowboy hats, the deer-hide color did him justice. Light blue eyes matched the blue plaid of his button-front shirt. He looked like an honest-to-goodness cowboy cover model.

"Hi, darlin'." Tenderness came over in the cowboy's low voice. "We're here to take you home."

Unbelievable. "How did you...?"

"Robert gave us the go-ahead to purchase some tickets to get through security. He's not at all pleased about it."

"Robert, the bar owner?" I shook my head. "Where the heck would he get that kind of money and who the hell are you?"

"Aw, sugar."

He reached for my cheek, but I pulled away. If that man tried to touch me again, he'd find my teeth embedded in his knuckles. My face must have said as much because he dropped his hand to his lap.

"It's Sammy. You and I were gettin' really close right before you left and all."

"Oh, *really*." My pissy mood kept me from being afraid. Given I didn't trust these two, I should've run screaming. Instead, I crossed my arms and slumped in the chair. "How did you people find me? No. Let me guess. It was that nasty little weasel of a clerk and Keisha's credit card, wasn't it?"

Either I had witnessed something in my previous life and Gamboldt wanted to keep me quiet, or I had done something to make me invaluable. Whichever it was, Gamboldt had authorized two tickets that probably cost him a couple thousand dollars to bring me quietly back through the security gates. This guy must have wanted me something bad. Far be it for me to please the king pimp when he was probably the one who gave Paul the drugs to keep me sedate.

A smirk splayed Paul's face. "Yes and no. Yes for the clerk, but no for the credit card. We had a hunch that obviously paid off. There's no use hiding from us, honey. We know you too well."

"We need you to come quietly." Sammy stood while pulling me up by my arm.

I slit my eyes at him. "You need to take your hands off me."

"We're not doing this, Keisha. Not here. Now you need to come home where you belong."

I yanked my arm away from him. Paul seized me from behind.

"Hey! Hey!" A security guard sauntered down the hall. He held the walkie-talkie up to his mouth and mumbled something about backup at Gate Six. "Is there a problem here?"

Paul released me and held his hands up in defense. "No problem, Officer. Just helping my little lady up out of her chair."

"Mm hm." The security guard waved me over to his side. I grabbed the handle on my suitcase and did as he said. "You okay, ma'am? I got a report that you were being harassed by someone."

A report? From who? There was hardly anyone in the airport. "Uh. Yeah. Those two right there." I pointed them out to be sure.

Paul's shoulders tensed and his fingers curled into fists. He took a step toward me, but Sammy captured his arm. They knew an airport was the last place in the world anyone would want to start a fight.

Sammy reached in his back pocket and pulled out his ticket. "Sir, we're trying to get to Boston. That's all."

Boston? Damn. But at least it proved that town meant

something to me. I could've gone anywhere, and somehow, they knew I'd go there.

The security guard waved his finger between us, but he addressed Sammy. "You three are traveling together?"

"Yessir."

"Are not," I grumbled. "Yes, I know them, but there's a reason why I was trying to get away from them." Lying had occurred to me, but if they had any pictures to prove me a liar, say a photo with all of us being best of friends, then I'd look like a fool.

Two more security guards made their way down the hall like they meant business. Although one had more paunch than the other, neither seemed to be in the mood to deal with problem flyers.

"What's going on, Chuck?" the bigger belly of the two said.

"We've got a little trouble," he replied. "I think we need to have a talk with these gentlemen about airport etiquette."

Lord have mercy, I had to look away and tightened my lips to keep my grin to a minimum. From the corner of my eye, I spotted the nice lady at the ticket counter who had sold me my airline ticket. Smiling, she nodded her head while purchasing a coffee and a bagel at one of the various cafes scattered throughout the airport. I mouthed a thank-you to her.

"But what about our tickets," Paul shouted. "Now, look here, man! We've paid for these here tickets and we're gonna use 'em."

"You'll use them," Chuck said. "Just not on this flight. I'm sure the airline can accommodate you on another one. But if you really want to be difficult..." He unsnapped his gun and rested his hand on top of the handle. "We can make this as hard as you want to. It's all about cooperation."

Paul's eyes hooded with such a fierce scowl that it would send a dog whimpering in the opposite direction. That man hated me with every ounce of his being and then some. Too bad I remained unfazed by his grandstanding. Judging from Chuck's deadpan expression, he remained unmoved too. The security guard signaled for both of his colleagues to lead Sammy and Paul away.

Paul yanked his arm loose when the security guard went to grab it. "Get your hands off me!"

Chuck's fingers curled around his gun, still leaving it in the holster. "We're just going to sit and have a long talk in the security station about airport protocol and how to handle the situation when a lady isn't into you."

I gnawed my bottom lip to fight off a smile.

Chapter Six

The trip was smoother than I thought, but it didn't stop me from looking over my shoulder. When we landed in Dallas, I ran to find my connecting flight and sat in the waiting area with my back against the wall to deter any surprises. With my eyes on my surroundings and twitchy nerves about to break me out of my skin, I refused to use the bathroom, thinking that Sammy or Paul might catch up with my flight and try to corner me in there. So, I pinched my bladder and waited until the plane took off and the pilot killed the *Fasten Seatbelt* sign. Who would've thought the skies were friendlier than the ground? With the afternoon sun burning bright, we touched down in Boston before one. The people shuffled down the aisle like the walking dead headed for the next meal. I could've jumped out the emergency exit and kissed the tarmac.

When I opened the door of the cab in the taxi line, I couldn't help remarking on the hundreds of different scents that infiltrated my nose. Some of them smelled hours old while others had been there for days. One particular scent—cheap cologne—must have come from a regular because there were more than a dozen spots stretching from one end of the seat to the other. Either that or a bunch of people walked around wearing the same crappy toilet water.

On the other hand, perhaps the driver was entertaining some chicks on his off-duty time. Hmmm? That curled my lips into a tiny grin.

"Ya getting in, lady, or what?" He motioned with his hand while his arm lay across the back of the front seat. "'Cause I ain't got all day."

After coming from a small town where a drawl reigned

supreme, my ears struggled to comprehend his tough-guy accent. I tossed my bag in the backseat and watched where my foot landed on the dirty floor. There were less filthy areas than others. My toes had some space between the gum wrappers and food containers squashed under the seat.

Once inside, he sped away from the curb.

We jerked to a stop. Horns blared on my left-hand side. I threw myself against the door on the right, clutching the handle. The action didn't scare me. It was the sound. Man, was my hearing sensitive.

"Fuck you!" my cabby yelled. He flashed his middle finger out the window. "I'm tryin' to drive he-ah, you moron!"

The horn blew from behind again.

The cabby jerked the car forward again. "Screw you." He peeled off fast enough for me to grab my suitcase and plaster my back to the leather seat. His finger flipped the switch on the meter. "Where ya goin', lady?"

I hadn't thought that far ahead, but given his frame of mind I dug through my bean purse and tossed a fifty over the seat. I didn't want any hassles from him. "How about you drive me around the Boston area until my fifty runs out? I'll decide after that whether or not you're worth another fifty-dollar tour."

He shrugged. "Good enough for me."

It wasn't long before my money ran out and I had to cough up another twenty to get me out of the rougher areas. I think he planned it that way, the jerk. Still, all of that driving around didn't do anything for my memory. Nothing looked familiar. I wanted to extend the search out a little farther, but I had already paid twice the price of a rental car for a cab ride.

"Let me out at that hotel on the corner." I had a little over six bucks and some change left on my seventy-dollar investment.

"Here?" the driver asked. "You sure this is where you wanna stay? Don't get me wrong or nothin', but not all of Fenway Park is a good area. Let me take you back up to Copley. The hotels there are much better."

My eyebrow arched. "At the rate you drive and all this afternoon traffic, it'll cost me another ten bucks. As it is, you've already got your tip by me not asking for change."

He stopped at the light, one block from the Lansdowne Hotel. He lifted his eyes to me via the rearview mirror. "You sure you're a tourist or something? I only ask because you seem to know how to handle yourself. Most folks don't."

I had a snide remark in mind, but I traded it in for picking the man's brain instead. "What makes you say that?"

He shrugged. "Just sayin' is all. Although, you don't sound like you're from around here either."

"Then where do you think I'm from?"

"I don't know. Northeast, maybe? I've never traveled far from Boston, ya know? But you certainly ain't no New Yorker either."

I don't know about that, my brain threw out like a quick reflex. Perhaps I had lived in Boston, but something said I wasn't originally from here. Until my gut steered me wrong, I had to believe I was a Boston implant and not a native.

The cabby dropped me off at the corner like I had asked. One look at the Lansdowne Hotel and I understood why he had reservations about this place. The gray stone face needed a good scrubbing to clean the slimy mold from the cracks and crevices. Paint peeled from the red shutters. Looking at the rusted hinges hardly holding some of them in place, I'd say nobody had cleaned them in years. My trepidation didn't stop at the building. People walking up and down the sidewalk kept their heads hung low. A few blocks down the prostitutes had come out a little early to play with some of the cars stopped at the light. Short skirts, four-inch heels and low-cut blouses were the garments of choice. Next to the hotel, a homeless guy sat in front of another brick building with bruises dotting the crook in his arm. He lifted his gnarled fingers up to passersby, begging from money. Half his teeth looked like miniature tree stumps after a termite infestation.

I lowered my gaze and blinked. How could I see with that kind of clarity? I lifted my head and made note of the same features, only this time I picked up a mole just above his shaggy mustache. Again, I lowered my gaze. My eyes were capable of zeroing in on objects that went beyond the normal 20/20 vision. But...that was impossible.

I shook my head and went inside the hotel.

At least the owner had kept up this place better than the last hotel where I stayed. The furniture came up about two decades and there was a computer sitting behind the barred check-in desk. I prayed those brass bars were part of the décor and not meant to keep the occasional robbers out. Other than a faux terra cotta tiling and large windows, there wasn't much to see.

A sign pointed to an elevator at the end of the hall. The closet-sized door opened and metal accordion bars slid into the wall. Two people stepped out dressed normally except for the Buddha symbol on the woman's brown T-shirt and the guy's overgrown hair reminiscent of the hippie era. Both of them wore flip-flops on a chilly day and the bottoms of the overly bell-bottom pants had shredded to mop consistency.

The people who stayed here were unusual to say the least.

The guy stopped and stared at me. A smile bowed his lips. "You here for a room?"

I nodded. "You own this place?"

He slipped his arm around his lady friend. "No. We're just managing it."

"Good enough. I'll need two nights and I'm paying with cash."

The girlfriend tipped her head as if to look around me before making her way to the desk. "Where's Leonard? He's supposed to be manning the desk."

Her boyfriend ran a hand through his brown messy hair. "Your guess is as good as mine, babe. That's Sonya, by the way, and my name's Frank." He offered his hand.

I didn't know how to respond to that other than to meet his handshake.

"Okay." He finished pumping my hand then he walked around me and through the door marked *Manager Only*. While Sonya disappeared out a back door, he began tapping across a computer screen. "I hope you're not looking for a fancy room or anything because they're all pretty much the same. This computer is about the fanciest thing we have and it's about four years old."

My gaze traced the metal bars again. "How's the crime around here?"

Laughter burst from the upper level and echoed down to the first floor. A well-dressed man wearing a slick gray suit descended the staircase with a blond woman on his arm. A turquoise, wraparound dress swayed at her knees, brightening her blue irises. Neither one of them looked like they belonged here. Since they didn't have any luggage, I failed to understand what had attracted them here.

They stepped off the staircase, expensive shoes clacking across the floor as they made their way to the front desk. A weird scent touched my nose. It was almost the same for both of them. Despite her putrid perfume and his vulgar cologne, there was an underlying scent of...pheromones?

Oh. Well. That answered the question about why a well-to-do couple would come here. They had just finished having sex. With a platinum ring on his finger and a gold band with a shiny, one-karat diamond on hers, they were married all right. Just not to each other.

I stepped aside to let them go ahead of me. Strangers at my back left me vulnerable to possible attacks. The man smiled and thanked me before signing the receipt Frank had slipped under the bars.

The front door slammed open. The junkie from next door stormed into the hotel. He curved his lips in a hideous smile that made his rotted mouth look like a dark, haunted forest with jagged limbs jutting in different directions. His yellow eyes bulged like a wild animal about to lock his jaws on some succulent meat.

"I came for my soup, Sonya. You said..." He tightened his eyes before swaggering across the floor and pointing a grimy finger at me. "I saw you. You were looking at me. You want a piece of this fine body?" He ran his filthy hands up and down his chest, sliding them toward his crotch where he grabbed hold.

"My God." The woman turned her head into her companion's shoulder.

The door to the front desk/manager's office opened. Sonya put on a huge smile as she approached the junkie. "Billy, what did we say about bothering the patrons? You can't be in here when we're conducting business." She cupped his elbow. "Come on. I'll bring you around back. And if you're good, maybe I'll make you some of my miso soup."

"Get off me!" He shoved her hard. Sonya landed on the floor against the back of a chair sitting in the lobby.

"Hey!" Frank burst out of the office and went straight to his girlfriend to make sure she was okay. "What's wrong with you, man? She's pregnant for God's sake!"

Pregnant?

Billy shoved Frank before he could finish helping Sonya to her feet and she dropped to the floor. Billy's eyes turned wild and dangerous. Before the hotel manager reacted, the junkie pulled a knife and began waving it in the air.

"You want a piece of this?" When he jabbed the knife at the two adulterers, the woman screamed and ducked behind her so-called knight in shiny armor. Spittle dripped from his slimy lips. "Give me your money, playboy."

"All right. All right." The guy reached inside his jacket for his wallet and began counting the money like he only intended to part ways with some of it.

Billy snatched it from his hands. The junkie jabbed the knife toward the woman and got another shriek out of her. "What about you, bitch? Give me the purse! Now!"

Hands shaking, she extended the purse in his direction. He snatched it and pulled it up his arm. I couldn't help the smile that lifted my cheeks. He looked ridiculous with an expensive bag hooked around his shabby shoulder.

He turned to me. That was his first mistake.

"Billy, stop it!" Sonya started to pick herself up again, seeing as her husband didn't get the chance to help her last time. "You've taken this game of yours too far this time."

This time? This was normal for him? Wow. The hippie couple really went out of the way with the humanitarianism if they'd let him get away with it before.

The junkie didn't listen. He started straight for me, his wild eyes thirsting for more.

I had not come this far to let some junkie rob me. When he waved the knife toward my face, I jerked my head back to keep him from slicing my nose. A urinated breeze billowed from his filthy coat. From his rotted smile, I guess he'd expected a scream out of me. This just wasn't his day, only he hadn't realized it yet.

Billy slashed the knife at me again, his momentum carried him through. I threw up my arms to defend myself. The knife sliced across my wrist. Pain came through sharp and quick like a giant-sized paper cut.

When he tried to straighten up, I wrapped my arm around his neck in a headlock. I ran backward, slamming his head into the counter. When I pushed him away, blood leaked from the top of his forehead above the hairline. He touched his scalp and pulled away, blood coating his fingers.

"You bitch!"

He ran straight for me again. You would've thought this fool had learned his lesson.

I threw my forearm up to block him, and my fist caught him in the throat. Billy staggered backward, coughing.

It was time to go on the offensive. I drew my fists up to protect my face and hunched my shoulder. I threw a right cross to his cheek, followed by a left hook. My legs dropped me to a crouch position. My foot swept out, knocking his knees from underneath him. I spun into an upright position with my fist drawn and ready for another counterattack.

Billy remained on the ground, dazed and hardly able to hold his head up. I dropped my fists, grabbed his ankle and dragged him out onto the sidewalk on his back. Nasty as he was, I'd need some serious hand sanitizer to get rid of that smell.

When I returned, Mr. Adulterer stood there with his hands on his hips, scowling. "He still has my wallet."

I glanced over my shoulder, watching Billy the bum roll over on his stomach and struggle to get to his knees. "Guess you had better go get it, huh? At least before your wife finds out you've been entertaining company." Lifting my chin, I walked right past him and his lady-of-the-afternoon and picked up my purse. "Now. I needed a room for two nights. Preferably one that comes with soap so I can clean that junkie's scent off me."

"Are you kidding?" Frank started across the room with Sonya in tow, but had to stop before the adulterers ran him over as they traipsed out the door. "Those two days are on the house."

This wasn't exactly what I had planned, but I'd take it. Far be it for me to look a gift horse in the mouth.

"Sorry about Billy too," Frank said. "He gets a little outrageous, but never anything like that. He must be tripping on something. We do our best to help some of the homeless around here, but there's only so much we can do. The rest is up to them."

Funny he should mention homeless. Looks like I had come to the right place.

"You didn't tell us your name." Sonya leaned against the counter while her boyfriend went around back and pulled a pair of keys from a small box against the back wall.

Again, with the name thing. Couldn't they just leave well enough alone? "I have one, but it's not mine."

She blinked. "Not yours? Then whose is it?"

"Someone else's. I don't know who I am."

Sonya's jaw hung. She closed her mouth, but opened it again as if to say something but not quite sure what. She finally settled on one word. "Oh."

Chapter Seven

Frank and Sonya practically glued themselves to me. He insisted on bringing my one suitcase to what he claimed was the best room in the house. It was...adequate. Nothing special. It had a full-size bed, a dresser that almost stretched the length of one wall, and a small table in the corner with two chairs. The room wasn't very big, but it was clean. Well...as clean as it could be anyway. My sensitive nose picked up every scent that had ever walked into the room. There was a heavy stench of bleach on the air, implying someone had recently picked up a bit. Perhaps a bit more than usual. What they were trying to hide, I didn't want to know.

An hour after sitting in my room, Sonya came up with a bowl of miso soup and some homemade breadsticks on a tray, thinking it might help me feel more at home. When Frank arrived with a large knit blanket, I knew they had lost their minds. All I wanted was to sit down and watch the twenty-four-hour news channel for anything that might jog my memories.

A knock came to the door during the evening. I rolled my eyes. Based on the hoodlums who frequented this place, the only people who knocked were Frank and Sonya. Everyone else settled for screaming and slamming doors.

I crawled off the bed and answered it.

Just as I thought, Sonya stood there with a saucer of cookies and a glass of milk. She must have mistaken me for a kid—not that I had a problem with that. I stepped away from the door to let her inside.

"I hope I'm not intruding," she said. "You asked about cookies for dessert. I found some mix stuffed in the back of the cabinet. This pregnancy thing has given me a crazy cookie-dough craving."

I pointed at her flat belly. "Your first?"

She nodded. "We weren't planning to have any kids until Frank finished his doctorate in chemical engineering and we moved out of here. Managing this hellhole makes it easier to save money."

I took the cookies and the milk from her, and set them on the nightstand, but I couldn't peel my eyes off them. Something told me chocolate-chip cookies were my favorite. The only difference was Sonya's cookies were smaller than my normal ones. I didn't have cookies every night. Only on the most challenging ones, although I wasn't sure why my brain thought this. Someone brought a tall glass of ice-cold milk with three large cookies on a plate. I never finished all of them and it didn't bother the person who made them. No, I take that back. She made them for the entire house and stashed a few away for later.

For the life of me, I dug through the vision trying to get a face and maybe a name. *Come on. Let me see more.* The only thing I made out was a white apron, thick forearms and wrists, and a slight limp with each step, barely noticeable unless you watched her for a while. She was an African American woman, but not once did my vision pan to her face. Her name was as empty as Billy's morals.

"You okay?" Sonya's voice came through, tearing me from my thoughts.

I took a breath I had no idea I was holding. "The cookies."

"Oh." Her large smile forced her eyes closed. "Yeah. They're one of the few luxuries Frank won't fight me on. We're trying to lessen our dairy, egg and red-meat intake."

"I'm not talking about the cookies." I sat on the bed, pulling my legs off the floor. "They reminded me of someone, but I don't know what she looks like."

Sonya sat on the bed next to me. "You know...Frank and I have a friend, Manish. He's a hypnotherapist. Maybe he can help."

I shook my head. "Nobody's picking around in my brain. Sorry."

"But if—"

"No. I have a feeling it's too dangerous in there." Dangerous because Gamboldt's people preferred to keep me drugged out of my mind. Not like I'd tell her that.

Sonya slouched. "How much of the visions do you remember?"

"Hardly enough to get me anywhere."

Today's events had worn me out. Between flying half the day from one part of the country to the other, driving aimlessly around town to get a feel for the layout and getting into a fistfight with a junkie, this day had pretty much gone to the entire dog kennel. Although my dreams hadn't yielded much, perhaps tonight I might get lucky and find myself with names and places from my past. Anything had to be better than this damn not-knowing.

The best thing that had happened was Frank and Sonya giving me a free room and not asking to see ID. The more I followed what little clues I had and the closer I got to the truth—fingers crossed—the more cautious I grew. Though I had heard a couple of police cars scream by just outside my window, hiding in a lowlife place like this where nobody cared made it easier to get lost.

Sonya fidgeted with her fingers. Her gaze pressed at my back, following me as I got up to pace by the window like a caged animal. "What about going to the hospital or the police?" She shifted on the bed, tucking one ankle underneath her long, wrinkled skirt, a nice change from her jeans. "They might be able to help you, you know."

My fingers pushed the curtains aside and allowed me to stare three stories below. Cars traveled up and down the street while the number of whores had doubled in size. "I can't."

"Why not?"

"Suppose I'm wanted for murder?" Her silence suggested she hadn't thought about that. I certainly had. All those hours spent in the air left me with plenty of ponder time. I turned away from the window and leaned against the sill. "I'm not about to pretend like you and your boyfriend didn't witness what happened in the lobby. I could've killed Billy with my bare hands, if I wanted to."

"Okay…?"

"You're okay with that? Killing your junkie friend?"

She shook her head. "That's not what I meant. I'm just saying that you *could have* killed him. Could have. You didn't. You protected us. That says a lot about a person."

Believe me that wasn't my intent. I did it to protect myself. If Billy had gone after me first, then Sonya would've never found herself on the floor. If he had gone after the adulterers first, same outcome. In the end, it was about me. That was a good reason to be naïve about my skills and how I used them when provoked. Someone should paint a big *J* on my forehead for jerk.

Sonya lifted off the bed, the hemline on her skirt falling around her ankles. She stood clutching her fingers. "If you're looking for a job, we could use some help around here. Frank had to fire the last guy because he left his post one too many times for a drink."

That was sweet of her to think of me. "Thanks for the offer, but this is temporary. I'm getting my real life back, one way or another."

She nodded. "I understand. But if you change your mind, you know where to find us. The door's always open for you." With that, she left the room.

Fatigue gnawed my bones to the point that I wanted to collapse on the floor. After a hot shower, I did. Only on the bed.

A quick leap, and I tucked and rolled into a standing position. Behind me a set of bushes rustled from where I had sprung.

Wow. That was pretty cool. A grin lifted my cheeks right before I darted into the woods.

I continued through the brush, ducking under tree limbs and hopping over large rocks. Stray twigs scraped my bare legs. The coppery smell of blood reached my nose.

Someone was hunting without any regards to what their carnage might bring, opening up our existence to the human race. At least that mongrel didn't belong to our group. After all, we were paid to hunt the hunters.

A black timber wolf the size of an Irish Wolfhound, Dane, led the way while the rest of us followed. No one dared to push ahead of him or challenge his leadership. Another black wolf hurried to his side, staying close enough to make sure his beta position remained intact. More bodies moved in. Blond, brown, red wolves. An entire sea of fur running wild and free. I ran in human form at the rear of the pack, holding the second most important position. I watched our backs with my fingers clutching a crossbow and ready to fire at a second's notice.

Other sets of feet trampled the thicket floor, and not a human voice to go with them, which added to the creepiness stalking the woods. Stopping to see who else was out there other than us would be stupid. Instead, I picked up the pace in record time. Twigs and dead leaves crackled somewhere on my left, followed by heavy breathing on my right.

Dark fur swooped in front of me, sprinting in time to my strides. Enemy wolves had gotten the jump on us. They knew I was the weakest in rank, which was why I ran at the rear. It made sense to come after me first. Their plan was to herd us just like a group of deer.

I'd have to show these bastards not to underestimate a human hybrid.

When I darted to the left, another wolf swooped in, blocking me from the front. I turned right.

I ran alone, my pack gone. *Uh-oh. Not good, Lex. Not good at all.*

A black wolf caught up to my side. I turned to sniff the air. A set of jaws with a large canine head came straight for my face like a fist. I pulled the crossbow between us and fired.

A knock woke me from my adrenaline-filled nightmare. I lifted my head from the mangled pillows and sheets, wavy hair falling around my shoulders. I leveled off the last of my hammering heartbeats and wiped the sweat from my face.

"Who is it?" At first I thought perhaps the knocking had come from my dreams or was the last of my pulse throbbing in my ears.

"It's Sonya." Her voice was low and muffled. "Can you come downstairs? That jerk Mr. Cramer filed a police report about someone stealing his wallet. The cops want to question everyone involved."

I glanced at the clock on the nightstand and noticed the golden sunlight ready to burst through pulled shade. "Huh? What for? We didn't take it."

"I know. But he's raising a big-enough stink and even threatening to sue."

Son of a bitch. I slammed my fist in the foam pillow before throwing the covers back. "Give me ten minutes."

"Okay."

I threw my legs over the edge of the creaky bed. My elbows rested on my knees while I smooth my hair back with my fingers. I knotted them behind my head.

What was the dream about? Think, girl, think. I clawed through my thoughts, pulling everything out of them. There were woods, animals, and...something...

I called myself Lex, or at least I think I did. But what did it mean? It might have been one of those stupid metaphorical dreams where water or fish meant pregnancy. Nonetheless, that was one scary nightmare I didn't want to revisit. I was running in the woods with wolves and I called myself something like...a human hybrid? Or did I? None of it made sense. If it were real, I wouldn't be sitting on this bed and sweating like I had run a three-legged race in the Boston Marathon.

I hauled myself off the bed, took a quick shower, dressed and made my way downstairs.

Two cops stood in the lobby, one taking notes on a pad while the other stared toward the building next door, probably looking out for Billy. He must have been absent from his post or they'd have had him handcuffed and asking us to ID him.

The cop with the notepad looked up and pointed his pen at me. "Are you Ms. Keisha Walker?"

My heart pounded. Their presence scared me. Not in the sense they looked intimidating or anything, but there was something about their uniforms and badges that bothered me. I wanted nothing to do with them or their authority.

I nodded. "To the best of my knowledge."

"Look, ma'am, either you are or you aren't."

"And that's what I'm trying to tell you. I..." Screw it. I turned toward the staircase about to leave. "How about I get my ID and just show it to you?"

"Stop right there!"

I froze. I didn't know if anyone else had heard that. It was the same click in the Lubbock Airport when the security guard had unclipped his sidearm.

Lifting my hands, I turned, hoping my ears weren't that good. The cop who stood by the window wasn't there anymore. He had made his way toward me.

"Look." I tamped down the fear in my voice. "I'm just going

upstairs to get some ID."

"You signed the registry as Keisha M. Walker," the cop with the notepad said. "Kind of weird that you used your middle initial, don't you think?"

"No. So?"

The closest cop rested his hand on his unclipped sidearm. "Ma'am, I'm gonna have to ask you to turn around and put your hands on the back of your head."

"Noooo," Sonya whined. She rushed to my side, worry filling her wide, innocent eyes. "She hasn't done anything. You guys said you were here because Mr. Cramer wanted to file a police report."

"We are."

"Then what are you arresting me for?" I asked.

"There was a report filed about eight months ago for a missing woman. Her name was also Keisha M. Walker."

"So?"

"She was found dead in the middle of the street with an arrow through her chest."

Ohmygod. I was a killer after all.

Chapter Eight

Something screamed for me to run as they handcuffed and loaded me in the back of the police car. Although my stolid face and limp demeanor may not have shown otherwise, I wanted to fight, to run, to hide. Instead, I did as I was told.

It was like my mind had broken into two different voices where one said to get the hell away while the other said remain calm. For some reason the calming voice sounded male and a lot more human than the other grittier one. In fact, it gave me instructions the whole time while ignoring the frightened one that said I should make a break for it. I thought it was some guy from my past, but a name never came through. Even weirder? He called me Angel.

Perhaps my name was Angel Lex or Lex Angel.

Oh hell, no! Both of those sounded so stupid they almost cracked my stoic persona with a smile. I was in the back of a police car, for heaven's sake. What was there to smile about?

I sat cuffed at the desk of Detective Roy Konoval. He left me there while he went to check something out.

People yelled over each other with their Beantown accents while papers and folders waved in their hands. The phones rang every few minutes with an average of one ring before someone picked up and shouted into the mouthpiece. Very few of the cops seemed to believe in manners and they didn't say goodbye before hanging up. The criminals they brought in weren't any better. Each one wanted a phone call, their public defender or something from the snack machine. Who would've thought a pack of powdered donuts would make someone want to lose control? It did when a guy went ballistic with his cursing and tried to run his head into the vending machine instead.

I minded my own business, although I had a hard time not looking over my shoulder with my back turned about sixty degrees to the rest of the room. Call me crazy, but I had this *thing* about being on my guard in unfamiliar surroundings.

The smell of thick coffee corroded my nose, but it was nothing compared to how many detectives walked by with a cigarette stench fanning off their clothes. The combo fed my nausea. My coughing fit convinced one of the detectives at a neighboring desk to get me a cup of water. It didn't help that he smelled like tobacco too.

"Two packs a day will kill you." I wiped the corner of my mouth with the back of my hand.

The detective stared. He was your average white guy with light brown hair, a chin that stuck out a little too far and crow's feet at the corners of his cornflower blue eyes. "Excuse me? How did you know I smoked two packs a day?"

Good question. It was as if I had smelled it from a massive repertoire of scents lying dormant in my brain. When an odor touched my nose, it pulled out a scent and matched whatever was closest to it.

I played stupid and shrugged. "I don't know. A guess."

His mouth turned downward as if to silently spite me. "Anyway, do you need a tissue or something?"

"No. But it would be nice to get these handcuffs off."

He pointed over my head. "You'll have to ask him."

Detective Konoval was a large man. I suspected he'd been a football player long before his hair had turned salt and pepper. He had a soft-spoken voice whenever he talked to me, but didn't hesitate to raise his voice to match those in the office. A ketchup stain dotted his brown-and-maroon-striped tie, although he wore a pair of smoke-gray slacks with a blue shirt. The faded wedding band implied that after years of marriage his wife probably didn't care enough to examine his wardrobe before he left the house. Though I couldn't tell, I bet he was a happily married man.

"This is an interesting case." He slapped a folder down on the desk. After reaching in his pants pocket, he pulled out the keys to the cuffs and released me.

"What makes you say that?" I rubbed my sore wrists.

"Because your fingerprints aren't anywhere on the weapon.

In fact, there aren't any fingerprints at all. That means the killer probably wore gloves."

I relaxed in the chair. "Are you charging me with a crime? If so, I'd like to have a lawyer present."

"Let me guess. You'd like to hire that lawyer friend of yours."

Shrugging, I shook my head. "I have no idea who you're talking about."

Konoval leaned forward and opened the folder. He lifted the papers at an angle, which kept me from reading them. "Matthieu York of Lesher, MacMillan, and Goldstein. He was in the running for partner the last time I checked."

"And...?"

"Why don't you tell me about the Crescent Inn?"

I stared at him. "You mind telling me where you're going with this?"

"Your parents called, *Ms. Phillips*. They wanted to know how you were doing. They're really excited about seeing you again."

"Great. Where are they?" I twisted in my chair to see them in case someone pointed at me. Seeing them might jog a few memories. Unfortunately, nobody skirted around desks in the busy office with their gazes pinned on me and their faces beaming. Everyone remained engrossed in their own issues like tracking down leads and processing criminals like me.

Konoval shook his head. Sighing, he leaned forward and folded his fingers together on the desk. "*Ms. Foster*, I'd like you to take a lie detector test."

In no mood to play his entrapment games, I turned back to the lying bastard. "Is my name Foster or Phillips? Where do I live? When can I go home?"

"As soon as you tell me who murdered Keisha Walker and stole her body from the morgue before the autopsy."

Holy shit. Regardless of what I remembered and what I didn't, there was no way I'd do something like that. I just couldn't. Could I?

This man confused me more than ever. I wanted to lean across the desk and slap some sense into him, but went for a pointed stare instead. "I told you everything. I don't know who Keisha Walker is, let alone how bodies walk on their own.

Someone gave me that ID and the credit cards. They said that's who I was."

"And these people work at a strip bar called Trixie's Tricks in Battle Rose, Arizona."

"Yes."

Konoval sat back in his seat. His folded fingers transferred from his desk to his belly. "There's a Battle Rose, but there no Trixie's Tricks. I've had it checked out."

"That's impossible." I didn't know what to say or do despite hysterics creeping up my back like a granddaddy longlegs. I gulped. "I was working as a stripper there. There has to be a name on record for the utility bills and stuff. They took everything from me that was a clue to my past, stuck me with some stripper persona and made me do things I don't remember doing."

"Like what? How can you say they did anything if you don't remember?"

"How the hell should I know? This is secondhand information. I woke up while on stage during a Snoop Dogg song."

"And yet, you remember the name of the bar."

"Yes."

"And the name of the owners."

"Yes."

"The name of the dancers."

"Not all of them."

"And yet you don't remember your own."

Why that no-good son-of-a-smooth-bitch. He deliberately riled me up to sound like a fool. My story was filled with more crap than a horse's shit bag. I knew what had happened to me and there was no damn way he could shake up my mind about that. Foolish as it might sound, that was my story and I was sticking to it.

I folded my arms and slouched in my chair. "Fine. If you want to pin a murder on me and say that my story isn't worth the air I used to spill it, then get me a lawyer. I'm not talking to anyone else until then."

Frank and Sonya wanted to help, so I used my one phone call to ask them to find me an attorney. I thought about calling up the lawyer Detective Konoval had mentioned, but something about having a string of names in the company title meant more dollar signs than I had to my name. Correction: I had no money whatsoever because the cops had confiscated my credit cards and cash. I'd be lucky if I got anything back.

Monica Hardcourt agreed to take my case, which had me at a loss since I had no money. It took the woman a couple of hours to get her behind down to the police station to figure out this mess. If I'd had more money to offer, perhaps it would've moved her faster.

Still, I couldn't knock the woman on her expertise. Once she heard my story and read the police reports Detective Konoval had on file, she went into action with getting me off. For now. The hook the cops had in me was more like a bent paperclip at best. We got a hearing where the bail was set and Monica signed for it, which shocked the hell out of me. I was racking up one heck of a bill from her.

Monica pushed her black-trimmed glasses up her pert nose. When we stepped out of the police station, a heavy wind whipped around her blond, wispy hair. "It was a bad arrest. The police asked to see the registry without a warrant. Mr. Cramer and Mrs. Kimsey lied to the cops about what had happened when Billy Weisman stole the wallet." Not once did she look at me. She went to the corner and lifted her hand to hail a cab.

I stepped in front of her. "What does this have to do with Keisha Walker being dead? I didn't kill her. Don't you think I'd remember something like that?"

"No fingerprints on the weapon or at the crime scene. No witnesses either. The only evidence the cops have is your missing person's report filed after the murder, and you having Ms. Walker's fake ID and credit cards. Had it not been enough to convince the judge, we'd be having a very different conversation and your bail would be a lot higher." She cursed as a cab zoomed past us. Frustrated, she tried hailing again.

"Which brings me to another question. Why set the bail so low for something like murder? Shouldn't I have—"

She shook her head. "They haven't charged you with murder. Yet. They don't have enough for a conviction, but they're going in that direction. These charges are just for having a stolen ID, credit cards, and assault and battery."

"Assault and battery? On who?"

"Billy."

"For crying out—" I threw my hands in the air before folding them over my chest and shaking my head. "That freakin' junkie threatened everyone with a knife and I get charged for kicking his sorry ass. Un-fucking-believable."

Monica held her hands up in defense. "Calm down, okay? The next step is to push the amnesia issue to get the charges completely dismissed and destroy any chance of the DA connecting you to Ms. Walker's death. We can consult a psychologist to provide expert witness testimony. Not only that, we need to hire a private investigator to find this Trixie's Tricks place. Also, a background check to make sure you're not—"

"I'm telling you I didn't kill anyone. If I need to take a lie detector test to prove it, then I will."

"All in good time. First, I'd like to have both a physician and a psychologist examine you. Then, we conduct our own lie detector test and see what happens."

"I didn't kill anyone."

"I know. I heard you."

"But do you believe me?"

Monica lowered her hand long enough to give me a few seconds of her attention. "I do. Look, if you have amnesia and we can trace the forged license back to that bar, then you might stand a good chance at being cleared of all the charges. Better yet, if we got someone like Mr. and Mrs. Hill to vouch for your whereabouts at the time, it would—"

"Mr. and Mrs. Hill? Who are they?" I wish the name had brightened a bulb in my head, but it didn't.

"Charles and Flora Hill. You mean the police didn't tell you?"

"Tell me what?" I shouted. Several passersby cringed at the sound of my voice. Some of them gave me a scathing stare. Ask me how much I cared when Monica and the police knew something about my past that I didn't.

"Ohmygod." She stormed past me and stepped off the curb as if to throw her body on the hood of the next cab. With it being this late in the evening, most people were either on their way home or having dinner. "We can talk on the way."

"No, dammit." I stepped into the street and yanked her around to face me. "I want to know now."

She paused. "Charles and Flora Hill are your employees. They're the ones who filed the missing person's report on you."

"My employees?"

"You own the Crescent Inn. It's a nice-sized bed and breakfast just a short drive from Boston University." A taxi slowed. Monica nudged me backward to give her some room to step back on the curb. "That's why Detective Konoval was questioning you earlier. He didn't buy your amnesia story, although your answers were enough to make him tread more carefully with this case. The real Keisha Walker's murder is still unsolved."

The murder charges didn't come as a surprise. Unfortunately, the rest of it was a letdown heading straight for disaster. "I take it my name isn't really Foster or Phillips."

"He was fishing. If you answered to both names, then he would've assumed you were trying too hard at the amnesia thing. It's Alexa Simone Wells. Look, just get inside and we'll talk on the way."

Monica opened the door and shoved me toward the pleather backseat of the cab. After my last cab ride, I didn't want another one. Hell, I could hardly afford it with the bill this chick would soon drop in my lap. "Where are we going?"

"To meet the Hills. Nobody's told them, yet, so I'm sure they'll be dying to see you again."

I hope she meant that metaphorically.

Just as the cab was about to pull away from the curb, another one blocked its path. The cowboy hat stunned me to silence. Monica continued to talk at my side, but I never heard a word. I watched Paul and Sammy exit the car and start up the stairs of the police station.

Dear God, I had missed them by a few minutes. Even worse, they knew *exactly* where to find me. Perhaps that joke I had made about them having crystal-ball radar wasn't too far off the mark.

Chapter Nine

I breathed a little easier when we arrived at the Crescent Inn, though I wasn't ready to drop my guard just yet. For all I knew, Sammy and Paul were waiting inside.

Still...

The inn was like something out of a long-lost memory or dream. It reminded me of a little red schoolhouse. Instead of vinyl siding, real wood adorned the beautiful tertiary-level home with white shutters on each of the windows. During the daylight hours, those two large trees must have provided plenty of shade in the front yard. A chilly autumn breeze nudged the porch swing sitting at the far end. Between the bushes and the flowers wilting in the flowerbed, I bet this place was gorgeous in the spring and summer. Even on a semibusy street like this, it had more quaintness than the other surrounding homes combined. If anything, it accented the charming neighborhood.

Monica accompanied me to the front door. In a way, I didn't want her to follow me because this was something I had to do myself. However, she was there. Depending on how this turned out, I might need her to vouch for me.

"Let me ask you something." I opened the whining storm door. "Is this why you decided to take my case more seriously? Because you knew I owned this place and I didn't?"

Monica adjusted her glasses. "I won't lie to you, Ms. Wells. I'm a lawyer, which means I have fees. I took on your case because I thought it was interesting. Whether or not you could afford my services was a close second. Like you, I have to eat."

I nodded. "Fair enough. Honesty is a good thing these days."

I couldn't knock the woman for that. She offered up a

service I needed. If she thought my pockets weren't ripe enough to foot her bill, then my case would've been in the hands of the public defender. For both our sakes, I hoped this place had some cash reserves stashed away.

I raised my hand to knock on the door, but muffled laughter stopped me. Good old-fashioned fun lurked beyond those walls, my instincts said. Easing to my left, I peeked through the window and a set of ivory-laced curtains on the inside.

A dozen people sat around a spread fit for King Henry VIII. An enormous brown-sugar glazed ham sat in the center with a charred crisscross pattern scored into the skin and pineapple slices stuck in place with toothpicks. To one side was a large pasta dish decorated with olives, cherry tomatoes, celery and other colorful vegetables I couldn't identify. Another leafy green salad sat near the end of the table while corn on the cob and a mound of mashed potatoes sat at the other. Someone left their seat for a small table at the far wall. They came back with a roll and a small bowl of soup. Who knew what else they had in there that I couldn't see?

A tall African American woman entered the room through a swinging door. She looked to be in her late fifties, if not early sixties. She carried a third tray with finger-food desserts like cheesecake and chocolate covered...something or rather. As she set the tray down, a tuft of her silver mane slipped into her face. Her flower-print dress fit a little snug around her stacked midsection. She cleaned her pudgy fingers on her white apron and spoke to the crowd. They lifted their heads in a reverent manner, nodded and chowed down on their food. For a woman who stood a couple inches taller than me, she carried her weight pretty well. Before she strolled away, she said something to her guests that left them hunched over in laughter and a few spitting up food.

The milk-and-cookies image filled my brain again. She was the one who had brought them to me. Her name was Flora Hill.

"Excuse me," a voice said, starting my heart. "You lost or something?"

I yanked away from the window, thrusting my back against the cold, red siding.

A young couple, around my age, strolled up the last few steps. The way they held hands and the smiles on their faces made me envy what they had. It would've been nice to have a companion to go through this horror show with me.

Another man bounded onto the porch behind them, carrying a camera case in hand. "You guys gonna stand there all day? Flora's going to have our asses for being late for dinner." He bypassed the couple, yanked the door open and went inside.

"You ladies coming too?" the man asked.

"Sure am." Monica started ahead of me.

My stomach knotted. Flora hadn't seen me since I walked away from this place, leaving her and her husband, Charles, to run it alone. Granted, they looked like they hadn't done half-bad, but it still wasn't right in my book. Suppose they held it against me? If I were in their shoes, I would be pissed. For once, I wished my instincts or feelings would just shut up.

"Close that door!" someone shouted from the dining room. "You guys are gonna let all the heat out. What do you think this is? Summer?"

A smile penetrated my lips. Flora's tone tugged at old memories and feelings, warring to be brought to the forefront of my brain. Unfortunately, all I had of her were milk-and-cookie memories.

The inside of the B&B left me in awe. Hardwood floors with a Persian rug led to an angled staircase. On the first floor, there were two rooms on my right and one on the left. All of them had French doors with lights shining behind the curtained glass and into the hallway. Through a window, I noticed a large backyard and a house with a porch light. Textured waves coated the pale blue wallpaper. While the room closest to my right took on a Victorian theme with the darker shades of red and cream, the dining room on the left had cream walls with a blue and gold country flair.

The people in front of us had hurried into the dining room. I wanted to slip in unnoticed and explore some more with the hopes of jogging a few memories, but I knew Flora would prefer to see me. After all, she had a right to.

I turned to Monica. "Can you wait here? Please? I need to do this, but I'd rather do it alone."

She shrugged. "Sure. I'll wait in the lounge."

I'd rather she go home, but unfortunately, she was my insurance in case this meeting went farther south than geese.

"That's fine. I'll only be a few minutes."

The clatter of silverware, dishes, and voices filled the air. This may have been a B&B, but Flora ran it like Big Momma's house. Just as I thought, more food sat on a long serving table off to the side making it easy for people to fill up their plates. Dessert trays and baskets of rolls and cornbread took up most of the surface while glass pitchers of ice tea and juice took up the other end.

The kitchen door burst open on a spring hinge. Flora carried a large porcelain kettle of steamy hot soup. Vegetable beef, by the smell of the carrots, celery and potatoes. Damn, I loved my heightened senses. My watering taste buds and growling stomach did too.

"Coming through." She waited while a guest moved a chair from her path. "Watch your feet if you don't want a pot of...hot..." Staring at me, her words trailed off.

Her hands trembled, sloshing the soup against the sides. The kettle slipped from her grip. I raced across the room and dove with my hands outstretched to keep it from crashing onto the floor. I landed on my stomach, knocking the wind from my lungs. Blazing stew sloshed out of the bowl and landed on the backs of my hands. All in all, it was a good save, thanks to my quick reflexes. With my fingers burning from the hot porcelain, I let out a screech. I pushed the kettle onto the floor and flapped my scorched hands.

"Oh my God," Flora breathed. Her gaze stayed on me as I got to my feet. I picked up the kettle by the handles and placed it on the side table. Once I was clear, Flora yanked the towel off her shoulder and wrapped my burned hands in it. Her wide eyes remained square on my face. "Is it really you? I'm not having a reaction to my high-blood-pressure medication, am I?"

A timid smile pursed my lips. "Not that I know of. But if you mean—"

She yanked me forward in a hug that threatened to squeeze the air out of my lungs. Her large boobs left me with enough tunnel vision to get a close-up view of her floral print dress.

"Charles! Our baby girl has come home." Sobs rocked her chest. She tore me away to get a good look at my face then jerked me back into her arms with another suffocating embrace. Smacking kisses pressed into the top of my head. "Girl, I could shake the mess out of you for what you put us through! Why in the world did you run off like that?"

"Like what?"

Heavy footsteps walked down the hall behind another spring-loaded door. It opened with a long outstretched arm holding it in place.

"What are you fussin' about woman?" the man said. "I can't even work on the furnace on the count of you...yellin'..."

His jaw bobbled and eyes widened. He was just over six feet. Fuzzy gray hairs on his head and a thick mustache placed him in his mid fifties to early sixties. Underneath his blue plaid shirt and sagging jeans, I bet anything that he had the body of a weightlifter back in the day, but age had caught up to him. He was darker than Flora's golden brown hue.

"Good Lord." The color had drained from his face. His fingers brushed his mouth in disbelief, eyes unable to look away. "Don't take this the wrong way, honey, but is it...is it really you?"

I half-smiled. "We've already been through that, but yes. I'm as real as it gets."

"Charles Emerson Hill," Flora chided. "Now you stop acting like you don't know our baby girl. Come give her a hug."

He let go of the door and stepped closer. Color began coming back to his shocked face. "It's just that...she's been gone forever. All those flyers and stuff. The police. Why didn't they call us? They brought you here, right?"

I shook my head. "A cab brought me. There's a lawyer in the other room. I've uh...gotten into a little trouble." I winced, hoping that went over more smoothly than the criminal way it sounded.

Charles leaned his fist on an oak armoire. "Does it have to do with the money you stole and the drugs?"

"Say what?"

Flora undid the apron from her waist and handed it to Charles. "Would you mind finishing up here, dear? I'd like to talk to Alexa before you scare her off."

I started past Charles when he reached his hand for mine and stopped me. His fingers tightened around my seared hand and he lowered his gaze. Something warred inside him. He didn't know what to think of my being here. That made two of us. To offer a little bit of reassurance, I cupped the back of his hand and offered up a friendly smile. He lifted his eyes to me with a tentative grin.

I didn't know if he had bought it, but if it was enough to get that much of reaction out of him, I'd take it.

With Flora holding the door, I followed her into the hall. Right now, I had too many questions stirring my mind. The main one being, what did stolen money and drugs have to do with this?

Chapter Ten

Stepping into the lounge through the French doors was like stepping back in time to one of those English periods where they wore frou-frou gowns. The couch didn't have the bulk of a modern-day couch. Instead, it had a heart-shaped back trimmed in dark rosewood. The same went for the curved legs with the clawed feet. A fire dancing beneath the rosewood mantle kept the room at an even temperature. Across the way, books ranging from the classics by Jane Austen to darker ones written by L.A. Banks stood with the spines out in the built-in wall shelves. A huge Persian-style rug covered the floor from one end to the other.

The only thing that looked out of place was a string of feathers hanging from the top of the bookcase. Weird. It made me feel uneasy, though I couldn't put my finger on why. Perhaps the ugliness of it bothered me.

Monica sat on a chaise lounge enjoying a plate of sugar cookies from the small table next to her. She placed a hardcover book in her lap and lowered her glasses. I thought she was going to sit on the couch and twiddle her thumbs while waiting on us. Instead, she had made herself at home.

Monica shoved the cookie in her mouth before dusting off her hands and hurrying across the room to introduce herself to Flora.

Just like any perfect, humble hostess, Flora laughed and waved her away. Flora took the wingback chair while Monica and I went for the couch next to it.

I told them everything I remembered, minus the part about the weird dreams and my strange heightened senses and uncanny strength. Monica took notes to keep us from having this same conversation again in her office tomorrow. That was a nice weight off my shoulders because given the choice, I didn't want to repeat it.

When we got to the part about my working at the strip bar, Flora shook her head in disappointment, refusing to believe it. Thank goodness someone thought what I had been thinking all this time. There was no way I'd choose a life like that.

When Monica left, a veil had peeled back and allowed me to breathe again, to soak up my surroundings. I didn't know this place as home, but I sensed something oddly familiar about it.

Charles brought me downstairs to the finished part of the basement where I had a large studio apartment. It didn't jog my locked memories. All the extra furniture and boxes piled up didn't help either.

I blew a coat of a dust from a picture on my chest of drawers. When that hardly made a clearing, I used my fingers to clean it. There was an older man with bushy eyebrows who had his hand around an African American woman. The guy looked white, but there was something different about him. I held up the picture to Flora. "Who are they? More friends of mine?"

Chuckling, she unfolded her arms and sauntered farther into the room. "No, baby. Those are your parents. Avery and Selena Wells. Speaking of which, don't you think you should call them? They spent weeks over here. Months, in fact, looking for you. They even called that sweet friend of theirs, Wesley Dane, to help."

"Wesley?" I placed the picture back on the dresser.

"He prefers Dane. Not sure why, but from what I understand, he's a close friend of the family. He helped you guys out of a jam once. Now what about those parents? You callin' them or should I?"

"Not yet, Flora. Please. There are...things I need to do before they know I'm here."

"But I don't understand. Don't you want to see them?"

"I can't miss what I never knew I had." I picked up another picture. At least five women and one guy in a photo taken in front of a large picnic area with children playing in the background.

Flora shook her head. "You must've fallen and bumped your head pretty hard. I'm making a doctor's appointment for you tomorrow morning."

"But—"

She lifted her hands and shook her head like she didn't want to hear it. Might as well quit while I was ahead. "It's either that or you call your parents. Putting them through another day of heartache isn't fair and you know it. I don't care what kind of amnesia you have. Either you go get yourself checked out or I have them make you."

She had me on that, the devious old...innkeeper. Sure, I wanted to meet them, but I also wanted to wait. Until I got a grip on all this and made sure there weren't any repercussions from Paul and Sammy, I wanted my loved ones as far removed from this mess as possible. Like any fiercely protective daughter, I took it upon my shoulders to keep them safe.

I placed the second picture on the dresser. "Fine. But you could at least tell me about the drugs and stolen money. What did I do that has Charles so skeptical about me?"

Flora sat on the creaking full-size bed, sighing as the weight came off her feet. "There were signs that led up to your disappearance. Twenty thousand dollars was stolen from the cash reserves. Not only that, you started acting weird. Like you walked around in a daze most of the time. With the missing money and the changed behavior, the police assumed it was drugs. They asked us if we wanted to press charges on the money laundering, but we refused. We knew there had to be more to it."

There was. However, it had more to do with what she wasn't telling. I folded my arms and leaned against the chest of drawers. "What else? Something's bothering you and you know it."

Flora paused. "This didn't happen in just one day. It happened over a few weeks. If Charles and I had confronted you earlier—I mean really confronted you—we might have stopped this. We didn't—" A tear leaked down her cheek.

My heart cracked. Sadness sliced into my gut and heaviness knotted the pieces together. I rushed to her side and dropped down on the bed beside her. My arm went around her large shoulders. It was a little awkward with her height, but I didn't care. I just didn't want her to be upset for no reason. "Please don't tell me you and Charles sat here all this time blaming yourselves. What you did or didn't do might not have changed anything."

Flora wiped away the tear and patted my hand. "I know, baby. But it's not just that. It's been such a strain on us for the last few months. I was scared we might lose the place."

"Lose it? How?"

"Well, maybe not lose it. But let's just say our luck was headed in that direction. That money could've fixed a lot of things around here. And let me tell you, Murphy's Law has been alive and well. The washer and dryer stopped working within a month of each other. We had to buy a new air conditioner and hot-water heater. The plumbing—"

"But I'm here now."

Half-smiling, Flora took my hand off her shoulder and smoothed it on her lap. "I know you are. I also know it's going to take time to get back into the swing of things. I still think you should call your parents. Maybe your sister and your friends. Well...some of your friends."

I chuckled. "Not all of them?"

"Not that Ramona woman. She's a little wild, if you know what I mean. I swear that woman must buy her clothes at Prostitute & Company."

I laughed. Hearing her frankness had warmed me enough to forget about her sadness. She must be a championship people watcher.

Flora stood and placed her hand on her hip. "And while you're at it, you should think about contacting that lawyer friend of yours. I'm sure he'd love to see you safe and sound."

Confusion tightened my face. "You mean Monica?"

"No, honey. It was something like Matt. Anyway, the police had named him as a suspect in your disappearance. He was cleared of the charges though."

"A friend, huh?"

"Yup. From what I understand, you two had a thing going on. Since you kept him from us, Charles and I thought maybe you two...got together and all. You know. Eight months gone. Plenty of time to...I don't know...have a baby and—"

"Whoa!" I jumped off the bed waving my hands. "Hold on, Flora. If you're suggesting I did this to hide a pregnancy—"

"I'm not suggesting anything. But the thought had crossed our minds and the police's. Stolen money, strange behavior and

65

a well-dressed man coming up to the house who we'd never met. What would you think?"

Unfortunately, she had a point. Since I couldn't recall any of this, all I had to go on was her word.

Flora started for the door. "It was better than thinking you had gotten mixed up with drugs. That's why Charles and I didn't want to press charges on you. If you had run off to have a baby, then we can understand why you did what you did."

"But I didn't."

She stopped at the threshold and lifted her head over her shoulder. "Maybe. Until you get yourself checked out by a doctor, I'm willing to believe just about anything."

That made two of us.

After the exam, nervousness gnawed at my insides while I waited for the doctor who said he wanted a second opinion on something. I sat on the table with the paper crinkling under my every move. Even if I breathed, I swore the stupid tissue paper had a crackle fit. A draft had slipped down my back from the opening in my white gown with the pale blue diamonds, freezing my nipples to points.

That doctor had had his hands all over me and I'd hated it. Every time he touched, images of those perverts at the bar flashed through my mind. When he went to do a breast exam, I slapped his hand away twice before I finally sat up and declared he had gotten enough of a feel. When he asked me for a stool sample, I suggested he skip that part of the test. At that point, he asked a nurse to come in and assist him with the rest of the exam. I don't know if that was done for my benefit or his. In fact, the old fart should've had her in there in the first place. My blood and urine had made it to the lab, so what more did he want from me?

I pinched my nose for the umpteenth time to keep the antiseptic from corroding my nasal lining. It hurt like sandpaper on a burn. Talk about a drawback to heightened senses. It made me queasy and fed the throbbing between my temples. I just wanted out of here.

I hopped off the table, pulled on my clothes and headed out the door. If anything turned up disturbing enough for him to call me, I'd handle it from there. In the meantime, I couldn't deal with this anymore. The back of my mind said this was a mistake. The only reason why I hadn't questioned it until now was that I had done it to ease Flora's mind. Good for her, but bad for me.

When I left the hospital, I got off on the wrong floor and ended up in the garage. Thank goodness, I spotted the main street. My shoes clicked on the pavement of the parking garage. Among the sea of cars with every other row separated by a concrete half wall, there was silence. Traffic echoed from the streets surrounding the underground lot, horns blowing and brakes squealing in the distance.

Gray skies greeted me as I emerged from the concrete dungeon. Moisture scented the air. The wet, tart taste touched my tongue. It wasn't exactly sea mist as much as smog.

I started down the street.

A block away and my shoulders tensed. With all of these people on the street, I couldn't help feeling like someone was stalking me. Somewhere my subconscious knew what it felt like. If this had anything to do with my dream about those wolves, then stalking was second nature to me.

I glanced over my shoulder. The same pedestrian heads bobbed, but none of them made eye contact. I continued to the next block before stopping at the corner for another look-see. Nobody made eye contact. If they did, they didn't maintain it.

However...there was one person. A few of the people on the street wore scrubs because we weren't that far from the hospital. But a woman with a red curly bob and chipmunk cheeks flashed her hazel eyes at me. Not once, but five times while I waited for the light to change. Either she was gay or wanted something.

The light changed. The pack that had formed at the corner started to cross. I went with them because I wanted to give this woman the benefit of the doubt.

A half a block later, I descended into the subway, paid with my pass card and hurried down a second flight of stairs. Instead of heading for the subway platform to wait with the rest of the commuters, I ducked behind the staircase into the shadows.

Ms. Redhead had followed. She lifted her head, glancing around like a frantic woman who had lost her child. Or in her case, lost her target.

It was my turn to do the stalking.

Chapter Eleven

She clutched a vial of blood in her hand. "Reveal."

I lunged for her. My feet moved faster than I commanded, startling me a bit. Nonetheless, I went with the flow and snatched her from behind. My hand covered her mouth and I locked her free hand behind her back.

Two people saw me, but from their unconcerned gazes, I bet they thought we were in some sort of weird lover's hold. Instead of indulging their fantasies, I ushered the redhead behind the staircase and into the shadows.

Grabbing her neck, I pinned her against the wall with one hand. I made sure nobody followed after a quick glance over my shoulder. Unfortunately, the platform started getting crowded with more people flooding the stairs and escalator. Talk about a time crunch.

"What do you want?" I seethed.

With her pinned a few inches above me, the muscles in my arm strained and grew tired. Her toes hung a few inches off the ground. Blood filled her face while she sputtered to breathe. Her hands grasped mine, struggling against my hold. The blood vial with my first initial and last name slipped from her curled fingers as she clutched my sleeve. I let go of her and caught the vial before it hit the platform and shattered. The woman slid down the wall and coughed.

I turned the vial repeatedly, examining it and making sure it was my name. "You got a sample fetish or something?"

The woman coughed. "No. But I know you shouldn't have gone to the hospital."

"What business is it of yours?"

Her long fingers rubbed her throat. "I work there. In the

lab. Anything coming through that looks questionable I try to steal a peek."

"Why?"

"Because I'm a lab technician with a specialty in microbiology." She coughed again. Using her hands, she crawled up the wall until she stood eye to eye with me. "I'm also a witch."

"A witch, huh."

"Yes. I was headed to your room to get you out of there when I saw you leaving on your own."

"And you followed me."

"I was wondering why you showed up at the hospital. If you had a problem you would've been better off going to the black market for answers."

"There's a black market?"

She nodded. Her hand fell away from her reddened throat. "Almost every major city has one. Trying to find it can be a bitch though."

"What does this have—"

"You're a supernatural. Perhaps a shapeshifter of some sort—I don't know. But I saw the results of your blood tests and it wasn't exactly human."

My thoughts began to swirl, not one of them coming together to form a cohesive question. Could my visions with the wolves in the woods be...? It sure would explain my heightened senses and strength. But how was it possible? There was no way I was a werewolf. No freakin' way. If so, then why would my dreams portray me as a human running with wolves? It didn't make any sense and neither did she.

The witch reached in her pocket and fished out a pack of cigarettes. "I had to change the results on your blood tests, you know. I could lose my job." Her timidity had faded, strength returning to her voice. She lifted her chin to me, challenge in her eyes.

Unbelievable. How dare this woman think she could beat me? A grin bowed my lips. If nothing else, I had to give her credit for being bold. However, I was the alpha bitch in these tunnels and the sooner she realized that, the less of a chance I'd throw her onto the train tracks.

Although I was ready to assert my authority, there were

larger things at stake. "Forget about your job being on the line right now."

"I can't."

"Well try." I glared at her, daring her to spite me again. "You followed me when you could've stopped after I left the hospital. Why?"

Her face relaxed. She took out a lighter and lit the end of her cigarette.

"There's no smoking in here," I said.

"Bite me." She blew out a puff of smoke. "No one can see us back here and I doubt they'd really care other than to bum one from me."

We were off on another tangent. I dragged us back to the question at hand. "You were saying? About witches and black markets and stuff?"

"Members of the supernatural community have formed a tight-knit group around here. We have sentinels—so to speak— placed in certain parts of the city. The hospitals, the police stations, libraries. You name it. That's how we cover for each other. That's how we stay hidden in plain sight among the humans.

"Supernaturals are small in number, because we don't have access to things like druid doctors or vampire nurses. For that reason, most of us die due to infections or sickness. So, to help combat that problem, we started stationing our kind at hospitals in case a supernatural got scared enough to go to one. We monitor their treatment with the hopes of finding an opening to sneak them out of the hospital before anyone is the wiser. Just don't let it happen again, okay?"

I folded my arms. "You're one of these sentinels, huh. You got a name?"

"Pippa." She took another drag of her cigarette, igniting the burnt ambers at the end. "I like working in the lab and acting as a sentinel. When I'm not doing that, I teach at our coven house."

I closed the distance, stopping my face inches from her smoky breath. "And just what do you plan to do with me?" I raised a finger as she took a drag of her cigarette. Her cheeks puffed out, holding her smoky breath. "If you even think about blowing that crap in my face, the next cigarette will be smoked out of a hole in your throat."

Although Pippa met my eyes, she lowered them and turned her head to the side. This was a bold witch. She didn't back away, and yet, she knew her place in our invisible hierarchy. Good. She might leave with just a few bruises on her neck.

"I'm not planning to do anything with you." With one hand shoved in her coat pockets, she rested her back against the wall under the staircase. "You're a stray, aren't you?"

"What do you mean?"

"A stray. A shapeshifter without a group. You must be a rare one. A mermaid, perhaps? No. If that were the case, then you'd have a lot more mercury in your system. You're something else."

"Suppose I told you I was a werewolf?" I took the plunge with that because I didn't want to believe it myself. She didn't laugh me down, so I was screwed. Damn.

"Not buying it." She puffed her cigarette again. "Parry Casabianca would've found you by now."

"Who's he?"

"The leader of the Boston Pack. A group of psychos if you ask me. You can ask any supernatural around town. He doesn't take kindly to other wolves intruding on his territory. His people roam the city all of the time looking for trouble. You're lucky you haven't been here long enough for them to find you or we wouldn't be having this conversation." Pippa sucked down another eighth of an inch of her cigarette. "If you don't mind me asking, why did you go to the hospital to begin with?"

"I was blackmailed into going." That wasn't far from the truth. When Pippa's eyes bulged, I threw up a hand and smiled. "Relax. It was for a good cause by good people."

"In case you're wondering, your CAT scan turned out normal."

"How did you—"

She laughed. "I took a look at your chart. You bumped your head it says. Something about amnesia."

It was now or never. Either confide in this woman or take my chances on my own. If I was a werewolf, it made sense to trust her more than anyone else, including the doctors. Perhaps there were answers to my past at this supernatural black market.

"It's true." I shoved my hands in my pockets and kicked a crumpled cup. "I can't remember anything beyond the last few days."

Pippa stared at me. She flicked her cigarette onto the track.

Rolling metal against metal in the distance caught my attention. It was then I realized I stood closest to the tracks with no way to prevent her from pushing me off the platform. I shifted, putting her on my left and the tracks on my right.

My ears opened up to the train charging down the tunnels. I stepped out a little farther and scanned the crowd. None of them noticed the train headed this way. They continued standing there like a bunch of zombies looking at the people across the way on the other side of the tracks. Some read books while others flipped through magazines and newspapers. Everyone seemed impatient, huffing and checking their watches.

"What are you looking at?" Pippa asked.

"The train's coming. Can't you hear it?"

She shook her head. "No. But are you serious about the amnesia? Like it's not a lie to get out of something?"

"No."

"That would explain why you went to the hospital."

"There's a lot more about me you don't know." And I wasn't sure if I was ready to get into all that. If what she said about the supernatural community wanting to keep their existence from the humans was true, then I was poised to start a witch hunt if Detective Konoval slapped me with a murder charge.

Stepping out of the darkness, Pippa turned her head toward the tunnel entrance. A line of travelers formed on the subway platform, each taking a position where they thought the doors might open. "That's the train."

"I know."

"Yeah, but I didn't hear it the first time."

"Maybe it's because I'm like you said. A supernatural."

Pippa turned her face to mine, not giving up an inch. She beamed like a child ready to break open a treasure chest to get to the goodies inside. "Cool. You really are a werewolf. Oh man. What else can you do? You gotta place to stay? Between me and my coven sisters, I'm sure—"

I held up a hand to stop her. "I've got a place. In fact, I own it. What I really need right now are my memories back. Unless you know how to pull them out of me, I've got nothing to talk about."

Pippa paced around me nibbling on her knuckle. "I'm not sure what I can do, but know of people who can help. Is there a way I can reach you?"

I hesitated to give her the address to the Crescent Inn because I didn't trust people I just met. However, since she had seen my chart with the inn's address on it, there wasn't anything I could do to stop her from finding me.

I smiled. "I'm sure if you dig deep enough, you'll get it without my help. But do yourself a favor. Don't mess with me. Either you can help or you can't. I've had enough people screw with my mind over the past few days. Trust me when I say today is not your day."

The train slowed as it approached the station. The roaring engine made it impossible to tell if Pippa told me to go screw myself or not. I wasn't about to stick around and find out. I turned...

...and found myself staring down the narrow shaft of an arrow with a red bull's eye in the distance. A leather guard curled with the inside of my fingers, protecting my hand against the taut bow. My shoulders strained, building up the pressure for a high-impact release.

I had stepped into another vision.

Chapter Twelve

"I'll whack you with a silver spoon if you don't pull tighter on the bow." Wesley Dane leaned close to my back.

He was a tall man with long toned arms and legs that filled out his clothes. He had a large smile that stretched across his too-tanned face. His eyes were dark like the back of a beetle and his black, wavy hair had a few flecks of gray. You had to be close to see them. His large fingers slipped over my hand closest to the tip of the arrow. Heated breath steamed up my ear while he checked my aim.

Annoyance seeped inside me. I didn't need him to show me that. I knew I had the target in my sights long before he confirmed it. Even better, if he had let me use my crossbow instead of a long bow, I would've shot the target before he opened his mouth.

I couldn't understand why Dane and my father treated me like such a baby. They were so freakin' overprotective. They needed to chill out. Better yet, teach me something like knife throwing or hand-to-hand combat. Perhaps they never thought I'd get that close to werewolves. Being a hybrid, they had better get over it and fast. My scent was like delicious pot roast slamming you in the face when you walk through the front door. That was what Dane and the rest of his werewolf friends said.

"You and Dad are always trying to get me to do boring stuff." I huffed with my eye still on the target. "When do I get to do other stuff like go out hunting with you guys? I'm old enough. I'm sixteen."

"And still a pup whose head is probably on her junior prom and not on her prey."

I grinned. "What's the difference?"

"Jail time, if it's not self defense." He let go of my hand, but remained close to my shoulder. "Now keep your eye down the length of the arrow. Picture it—"

Snap. The arrow impaled the bull's eye less than an inch from dead center. Not bad for a first try.

Dane's jaw hung. It turned into a smile when he stepped back to stare. "Okay. That means practice is over. Want to try a moving target now?"

A hand yanked me back. The train roared by, missing me by inches. My heart became rabid like a wild animal pounding to get out of its cage. The car sped down the tracks, gaining speed by the second to the point I couldn't make out the blurred faces on the other side of the windows. Pippa's hand rested on my shoulder.

"What the hell are you doing?" She shouted just as the last car sped by. "Kill yourself on someone else's time."

I yanked my arm away from her. "I'm not into suicide, thank you. I had another vision."

Her visage remained incensed, but instead of pitching another verbal fit, she cooled her face. "You're weird, you know that?"

"Look, I'm trying to get my memory back before whoever kidnapped me decides to do it again. For all I know they might be trying to kill me to keep me quiet. So, if that makes me a little crazy, too bad. I never asked you to follow me." I turned to leave.

"Where are you going?"

"Use your snooping skills to figure it out. I've got another lead to follow." I pushed through the remaining travelers and headed up the staircase.

Back at the inn, I used the computer in the office to look up Matthieu York's office number and address. If this guy and I had a past that the police and the Hills knew about, then perhaps he'd clue me in to it.

"He's with a client now," the secretary said. "May I ask who's calling?"

"His girlfriend." I don't know why I said that, but perhaps it would go further than being a regular client who only had business ties to him. I wasn't ready to give up my name yet because first I wanted to make sure he wasn't pissed at me. Eight months is a long time to go AWOL. I got lucky with the Hills, in that they were happy to see me. The last thing I wanted to do was to fool around with my luck.

Click. Lousy chamber music came on the line. Now that I had his attention, I prayed the right words would come out of my mouth.

"Hello. Matthieu York speaking."

I went blank. Damn. I'd been waiting for this moment for the past twenty-four hours and here it was. I couldn't think of a thing to say. Shit.

"Hello?"

"Uh…" A gulp slipped past the tightness in my throat. "Hi. It's…it's a friend. Look, after everything I've been through, I'd rather not say. Hell, I don't even know if I can trust you."

He paused. "Oooookay. Can you at least give me part of a name? Some initials, maybe?"

Think, dammit, think. "A friend of yours disappeared a few months back. I have information on how to find her."

He paused. Springs creaked as though he had sat up in an expensive chair. His ass must be as wide as a truck for that to happen. I bet he weighed about three hundred pounds with a hundred of that being gut and he had a receding hairline as far back as it would go. Whether or not that was a true memory, I couldn't say.

"Who is this?"

"It doesn't matter. Finding your friend does. Or did I make a mistake?"

"Not yet."

"Good. Do you have any room in your schedule?"

Again, the chair squeaked from his end. "How about I leave it up to you? You come whenever you have room in yours and I'll make sure you're accommodated."

I hung up. My heart thumped hard enough to register from my ears to my shaky knees. Nervous didn't begin to describe what this guy did to me. Other than listening to what others had said about him I had nothing to go on. Flora spoke well of him, but she also said it wasn't until after meeting him that I had disappeared. As much as I hated to say this, I had to see this guy. If he was the reason for my memory loss or had even an inkling about my stripper days at Trixie's, then he wouldn't just pay. I'd kick the change out of his ass.

With a population this big, midafternoon was just as busy as rush hour. People walked at a hurried pace, some carrying briefcases while others had satchels. A herd of students strolled down the sidewalk, their voices carrying until a squealing cop car drowned them out. More cars zoomed back and forth down the street, a horn blaring at a group of people bunching into the street at the corner, waiting eagerly for the light to change.

Somewhere in the far reaches of my mind, I knew I used to be one of these people. Flora said I had split my time between teaching bioinformatics classes during the weekdays and computers science classes at night and on the weekends. The bed and breakfast was a part-time venture. Every morning, I got up at 6:30 to grab breakfast before the guests, then hurried to catch the subway up to Sullivan Square. Flora hated that I worked an average of twelve hours a day, but it was about to pay off right before my disappearance. We had enough cash in the bank that one more year of my workhorse determination would have had us sitting pretty. The plan had been for me to quit my jobs, and help Flora and Charles take care of the inn full-time. My departure, the missing cash and needed repairs had set us back by about three years.

Yeah, someone was going to pay for this all right. If Matthieu wasn't that "someone", then I'd find who was.

The size of his law firm left me stunned. The office was located in a corner spot of the Quincy-Kale building on Berkley Street, taking up half the entire floor. From the elevator, I couldn't take my eyes off the glass entryway into the office with the gold lettering hanging just above the receptionist's black granite desk. York's name wasn't listed there. However, when I stepped into the office, I noticed his name on the wall among several others. A leather sofa and chairs sat by the window with a great view of the city from ten floors up. The semicircular shape of the lobby allowed only one entrance to the back where office doors lined the walls.

The receptionist was a nice-looking African American woman wearing an earbud attached to her lobe. While she spoke into the mouthpiece, I approached the counter. At least I had her for a witness in case Mr. York tried anything.

The receptionist hung up and folded her fingers into a steeple. "May I help you?"

"Yes. My name is Leslie Austin. A friend of mine recommended that I come here. I don't have an appointment, but I'd like to see Mr. York. We spoke on the phone earlier."

"He has an appointment right now. And he's pretty full for the rest of the day. May I ask what sort of business you have with him?"

Thank goodness I had rehearsed a story on my way here. I had even dressed the part by wearing a snazzy gray pantsuit. "I'm having a lot of trouble with a contractor I hired to finish remodeling my restaurant. The guy made a horrible mess of everything and I'm worried I'll have to put off the opening by at least six months. I need a lawyer to help me figure out my options."

Smiling, she lowered her head again, fingers flying across keyboard. "Mr. Goldstein is also available. He's very good with small-business lawsuits."

"No, thank you. I'd rather speak to Mr. York. I trust my friend's judgment."

Gesturing me toward the black couch, she said, "Have a seat. I'll check on Mr. York's availability. But it could be a while. As I said, he has a pretty full schedule this afternoon."

"I'll wait."

Chapter Thirteen

Twenty minutes turned into two hours. I should've just walked away at that point, perhaps left him a note or something. Unfortunately, the receptionist got a good look at my face and could probably describe me to York right down to my black and silver earrings. All I wanted were answers to a few questions, and each time I came close, it turned out to be a pain in the ass. Literally, in this case. I had to get up and stretch my legs several times or end up with pressure sores on my butt.

Six people entered the office, and all of them had left. Surely, York needed to take a leak at some point? Then again, he might have walked right past me, and I wouldn't know because his face was a mystery to me. Hopefully, his memory was better than mine.

A woman showed up with her two rotten kids. Their screaming, running around and whining had worked a nerve on the side of my head. Once in a while, the mother would lift her head away from a magazine long enough to scold one of her miniature brats with a thirty-second timeout.

Annoyed, I sauntered to the window to gaze ten stories below. York must have gotten hit by a case of Alzheimer's and forgotten about me sitting in the waiting room. If it weren't for the kids from hell and their defeated mother, the wait wouldn't have grated on my nerves by the second.

When she and her little hellions received her summons to the back, fury ripped through me. I glanced at the receptionist who held a hand against her earbud, busy with another call. Everyone had something to do except for me, and my growling stomach couldn't stand waiting any longer. Flora had said she'd kill me if I missed dinner, and from the look on her face and the way she waved her spoon, I believed it. Not to mention that woman was a culinary goddess.

With the receptionist preoccupied, I gathered my things and headed for the counter. Making a scribble motion with my hand, the receptionist handed me a piece of paper and pen without looking. Guess it was commonplace for those without an appointment to leave a note and storm out of the office.

A scent tickled my nose before I finished the first sentence. A touch of male musk flooded my mind with images of the dewy loam and pine, deer, and a bubbling brook. It was almost as strong as a men's cologne, except this was much more wild and reeking with sexuality.

A tall, gorgeous man emerged from the other side of the reception counter and slapped a folder down.

I couldn't pick my jaw up fast enough.

He had a set of dark eyes and jet-black hair that glistened under the sunken ceiling lights. Broad shoulders covered by an expensive gray suit made him even more staggering to the eyes. Putting a hand on his hip, the jacket opened, revealing a slim waist and flattened stomach. I'd bet my life savings that he had abs like cobblestones and a butt tight enough to sprain your wrist if you tried to slap it. If it weren't for this being a lawyer's office, I'd swear he'd stepped out of *GQ*. Yes, for a white guy, he wasn't bad. In fact, I could've melted in the palm of his hand.

"Janet, can you get in touch with IT? I need my trial notes on the shared drive and..." His focus went from the receptionist straight to me, glaring.

I swallowed.

Hooding his eyes, he sauntered around the large receptionist area. "I know you."

I couldn't move. Something about the challenging look on his face and the way he stalked toward me, I had my first deer-in-the-headlights moment. If I moved an inch, he might lash out, snagging my neck in his hands and cracking it in half with a single jerk. All that beauty and yet a monster hid underneath. Everything about him screamed predator.

"You came here for me, didn't you?" he asked.

"Uh..."

"Yes." The receptionist stood up and gestured toward me. "This is Ms. Leslie Austin. She's been sitting here since—"

"Matthieu York." He offered me his hand. "But you can call me Matt. It's nice to see you again...Ms. Austin."

My fingers turned into icicles, clutching the gold pen in my hand. When the tip started quivering, I put it down and backed away from both him and the counter. I needed to get out of here. His presence alone made it hard to breathe, hard to think.

"I have to go," I whispered.

"Wait."

Yeah right. I shoved the door open and barreled down the hallway toward the elevators. Something about that man scared the hell out of me. He was a dangerous beauty if I'd ever met one. Every inch of my body said so, and I'd learned to trust my instincts more than anyone I had met in my nightmarish journey. They screamed for me to get out. Run while I had the chance.

I jammed my finger on the down button, praying the elevator would arrive before that crazy man did. I never should've come here.

A hand clamped around my wrist, whirling me about-face.

Matt pressed his nose within an inch of mine, gutting me with a glare. "Where the hell have you been?"

"Let me go."

"Not until you tell me why you're here, Ms. Lex 'Missing Person' Wells. What the hell is going on? What happened to you?"

I stopped struggling.

He called me Lex. Not Alexa.

That name flooded my mind with images. They blurred as they slipped from my mental fingertips in no particular order, slamming into me like information overload. If the images weren't enough, the emotions tore my insides to pieces. Anger, fear, lust, happiness. All of them. The questions trailed right behind them at such a fevered pace that I only latched on to a few of them. Like, was he the one who'd sent me to Battle Rose? Had he mucked up my memories? Who was he and was this part of some elaborate plan?

The last image scared me. It was Matthieu York standing before me wearing no shirt and a gorgeous hairless chest radiating sexual fire. When he fixed his dark eyes on me, the feral animal lurking behind them had turned gentle and warm. My stomach clenched as the back of his smooth hand caressed my cheek. Something inside me had linked with him on more than just an intimate level. Crazy as it sounded, I felt like I had found my lifelong mate.

A cold tear slipped down my cheek. I tried to blink it back, but it was too late. Another one slipped down the same trail. My heart slammed back and forth, threatening to break free. If my bowels broke free, I'd never live it down.

"What did...?" My ears hardly recognized my airy voice. "What did you call me?"

Matt narrowed his eyes. "What are you talking about?"

"I don't..." The bright lights began dimming around me although I swore my eyes remained open. "I don't...know."

Darkness sucked me under.

Chapter Fourteen

Voices mumbled near my head. Something about water and keeping this quiet. I wanted to open my eyes, but they were too heavy for me to lift. Almost drug-like. Smooth fabric covered my front, blocking out the cold air of the room. I forced a moan from my lips to let the people in the room know I was still alive.

"Did she say something?" A female stood somewhere beyond my closed lids.

"She moaned." A heated hand touched the back of mine. "You in there?"

That was Matt...but I knew by his touch. Scary.

Pushing my eyelids open took some doing, but I got them to rise to a half-closed position. I tried looking around the room, but *his* handsome face took up most of my view. With a soft leather couch underneath me, he sat by my hip, dabbing a cool cloth on my brow.

"She's awake." He lifted his head over his shoulder. "Janet..."

The receptionist handed him a glass of water. Nutball that I was, I thought it was for him until he lifted my head for a drink. The cool water soothed my cracked lips and sandpaper throat. I wanted more, but I choked on one gulp too many. Matt handed the glass back to the receptionist and wiped my lips with the cloth.

"You still with us?" he asked.

I nodded.

"Good. Janet, would you excuse us for a moment. Ms. *Austin* and I need to talk."

"But sir—"

"If anything comes up, I'll let you know. In the meantime, if you could reschedule the rest of my day tomorrow, that would be great."

She sighed. "Yes, sir."

A door opened and closed. I leaned to the side to make sure she had left. We were alone in his office, a situation I bet had happened before in my previous life. If so, I wished to God that I knew what we had done. Although, if it had anything to do with sex, that memory was better left alone. Considering my state of mind, I didn't want to think about getting it on with a guy who was a stranger to me.

"You mind telling me what all this alias crap is about?" Matt snorted. "And where the hell have you been all these months? For that matter, why didn't you come to me when you got back? Do you have any idea how long I've been looking—"

I cupped my hand to his mouth. Wow, did he have soft lips. Were most men like that? Strangely enough, I had this eerie feeling my hand had been there before. My stomach lurched a second time before my cheeks filled with warmth. Forcing myself to sit up helped calm me. I needed some sense of control and conversing in an upright position was a good start.

Matt's jacket sagged to my lap. That was sweet of him, though he could've used my coat. Marking me as his possession, perhaps? Nah. Even though it was the first thing that came to mind, that couldn't be it. It made no sense.

He loosened his tie and scooted farther down on the couch. The invisible weight pressing on my personal space had lifted. It was as though he had read my body language and knew it was the right thing to do. I couldn't help staring at him, nonverbally asking for confirmation on that. Of course, he didn't answer, other than to maintain eye contact. I broke away first by swinging my feet down on the carpeted floor.

"Where's my purse?" I asked.

He pointed at his desk. "You can hit me if you want, but I went through it."

I continued to take in the abstract art on the ivory walls. A large bookcase was in the corner with books that overflowed to a nearby table. Behind his oak desk and leather chair was a fantastic panoramic view of the city that mimicked the one I had seen from the lobby. Based on the line of headlights dotting the bridge and not going anywhere, rush hour was in full swing.

Opposite the view was another window that stared into the hall of his law firm.

"How did you get me here without anyone, other than Janet, knowing?" If he was smart, he'd understand my meaning behind that question. I wanted to know who else knew I was in his office in case things got out of control.

"You passed out, so I carried you through the back door. Bringing you through the waiting area would've had people whispering left and right. As it is, one of our law clerks has a mouth like a geyser. I had to threaten her with unemployment to shut her up."

"Thanks...I think."

"Now if you don't mind, would you answer my questions for a change? Like where have you been? You disappeared off the face of the earth for months and out of nowhere you show up at my office."

Forget his questions. I wanted to curl up on this couch and sort through the memories that had plagued me in front of the elevators before I passed out.

Speaking of which, what was up with that passing-out crap? I don't pass out. There was a tough-girl aspect of me that refused to believe I had fainted like some 1950's B-movie actress. In my gut, I knew there was a way to prove it, but I couldn't figure it out just yet.

I leaned forward with my elbows on my knees. "Look, I don't know you from Santa Claus. So if we've met, then you have one up on me. My memory is gone. I've got nothing for you. Had it not been for getting arrested and finding the Hills, I wouldn't be here now."

He grinned. "Yeah, right. If this is some sort of game, you—"

"Look at my face. Do I look like I'm kidding? Why would I go through all this, if I didn't have something to protect? Namely, my own ass. I've spent the last few days getting away from a hellhole in the backwater region of Arizona. Do you think—"

"Not even your name?"

"Like I said, I've got nothing for you. Just bits and pieces from my past that are more like passing thoughts. I need to know what happened to me and make sure it doesn't happen again."

A puzzled look knitted Matt's eyebrows. "Are you saying you've been gone all this time because you've been suffering from amnesia?"

Did he not just hear a word I said? I remained straight-faced, refusing to answer him. He was a lawyer. He'd figure it out.

Matt went to his desk. His finger slid around the rim of a mug still steaming with hot coffee, based on my acute sense of sight and smell. "So...you don't remember anything. Like how we met and what happened after that."

"You tell me. What happened after that?"

Matt yanked his tie from around his neck and tossed it over his shoulder. "It was at an estate auction. The Garridans owned several antique and consignment shops around town. Their idiot accountant messed up and left them in one hell of a financial bind. They had to auction off half of their assets just to make ends meet. You showed up because you wanted to see if there was something to salvage for your bed and breakfast. Um...you didn't buy anything because I kept distracting you. Er rather...more like hitting on you." Pinkness flushed his dimpled cheeks. He lowered his head.

"Did you succeed?"

A devilish smirk stretched into his eyes. "More than you'll ever know."

Oh God, just kill me now. I wanted to die. What in the world had possessed me to sleep with a guy I hardly knew? Had it been a one-night stand? My gaze dropped to the floor while I allowed momentary heat to flood my cheeks. *Hmmm...? I wonder if I was any good in bed? No. I can't ask him that.* Besides, it wasn't important. Understanding how he was relevant to my life was.

Matt chuckled. "Anyway, you said a close family friend with some ties to money had bought the Hill's bed and breakfast. It wasn't doing too good. Financially speaking. The Hills had some health problems to complicate matters, so they couldn't take care of the B&B like they used to. Occupancy had dropped to less than fifty percent, which made it impossible to afford the mortgage. Anyway, your friend bought the place and turned it over to you as owner and manager. And if you don't mind me saying, that's one hell of a nice family friend. You took charge, renamed the B&B, and gave it a new image to bring it into the twentieth century. Since your knowledge of the business was nil, you asked Charles and Flora to stay on. They were delighted and the rest is history. Any bells ringing yet?"

I shook my head. "But at least it corroborates some of the stuff that Flora told me."

"You had a full-time job at one of the community colleges around here too. As a comp-sci instructor. In fact, that job brought you here to Boston from upstate New York. Did she tell you that?"

I nodded. It was one of the few things that didn't come with my fleeting memories.

He grinned. "I guess this means we won't be picking up where we left off."

"No, we won't."

Matt pushed a small black button on the wall. A spring-loaded door popped open. He reached inside the closet and pulled out a long overcoat. "We should go."

"Go where?"

"You're staying at your inn, right? Not a hotel?"

I grabbed my coat and purse from his desk. "Where are we going?"

"Anywhere but here. It's not safe."

"And you are? For all I know, you could be the person who dumped my butt in that strip bar in Battle Rose. Not to mention, probably sent your goons all the way up here to Boston to find me. Is that why you told Janet to cancel everything on your schedule? To bring me back yourself?"

Matt started for the door. "Could you at least try to trust me? If I wanted to hurt you, I had about ninety-three chances already. Your being unconscious was number one to ninety-two."

"Then take this as a pity party if you want. But if these last few days are a clue as to what's to come, I've got more than enough reason to not trust anyone."

"Here's a question. How did you know to come back to Boston if you've spent all this time on the other side of the country with amnesia?"

I reached inside my purse, fished out the real estate agent's business card and handed it to him. "Before you say anything, I've already called the phone number. It's been disconnected."

"And the address?"

"That was on my list of things to do after I visited you."

Matt lifted my coat from my arm and held it open for me. "Then by all means, let's go."

"Just like that?" I slipped my arm into the sleeve.

"Yes. You see, you're not the only one who's a skeptic here. I was the prime suspect in your disappearance and it didn't help that your friends and the Hills said they saw me with you on several occasions. We were dating a few weeks before you vanished. To the police, that was enough for them to get a search warrant for my condo. I could've lost my job because of you."

I glanced around his office. "You poor man. May my good tidings of humiliation, stalking, abduction and murder rain down on you and give you the same joy they've given me."

Growling—literally—Matt stepped around me, eyes taking a moment to drill into mine. I had to replay the sound in my head to make sure it was real. Though he didn't appreciate the cynicism, there was no way he could compare his situation to mine. He'd had a few days of discomfort while I'd had months of it, and still no end in sight. I had every right to be more pissed than him. He knew it or he would've mustered up more than a stupid growl.

Matt filled his bag with his laptop, a couple of files and his cell phone. One more check of his desktop computer and he motioned me toward the door.

I stepped into the hallway first because I wanted some space between us. In fact, I wasn't sure if I wanted to be around him. Regardless of what we'd had in the past, everything had changed. Until I figured this mess out, my life, in every facet, was on hold.

After Matt locked up, he led the way down the hall to the reception area. A pencil-neck man stood and offered his hand to Matt, but we brushed past him heading for the doors. Janet stood, leaning over the counter.

"Mr. York?" she said. "There's a message for you from—"

"Slip it under my door," he replied.

"But what about—"

"Take another message."

We continued down the hall in silence until we came to the

elevators. Matt slammed his thumb on the down button. Eight elevators and this stupid building didn't have one that stopped on this floor when we needed it. It figured.

I checked my watch, noted the time and said a silent prayer. Flora was going to kill me for missing dinner. Although I had only known her for a day, something made me hold the Hills close to my heart. My respect for them wasn't just because they were old. It had more to do with honoring those who'd come before me and benefiting from their years of knowledge and experience. Instincts said it would be unwise on my part to neglect the guidance of the old guard.

The elevator behind us chimed. When the doors opened, an older couple exited. A guy with liver spots dotting his forehead and cheeks smiled at Matt. I stepped in the half-full elevator first.

Matt reached around me and shook the liver-spotted guy's hand. "Nice to see you, Mr. Streiber. We'll have to do lunch some time."

Oh brother. Here we were in a hurry and he wanted to make a lunch date. One thing. I had yet to figure out why the haste.

Chapter Fifteen

As we walked across the underground garage, I noticed Matt kept his eyes on his surroundings. He scanned the rows of cars as he turned his head from side to side. I couldn't be sure, but I bet he made a mental note of every footfall, crack and drip that echoed across the decks. Funny thing was, I heard them, too, and even pinpointed which floor they came from.

Matt held out his key ring to disable the alarm on a black Grand Cherokee. He opened the back door and tossed his things inside. "You said something about stalking when you were in my office. What did you mean by that?"

"Two guys followed me from Battle Rose a few days ago. I thought I had lost them in the Lubbock airport, but apparently not. They turned up at the police station last night while my cab was pulling away. Why do you ask?"

"Because I can't smell through metal."

"Huh?"

"If I had, this musty bastard wouldn't be alive now."

"Who?"

Matt raised his hands and stepped away. A gun stuck out of the door, aimed at his chest.

Hands slipped around me, pinning my arms to my sides. I should've screamed, but I didn't. That would be too much drama and probably please our assailants. Moreover, I got what I deserved if I forgot to use my heightened senses to their fullest.

The guy with the gun motioned for Matt to move to the back of the SUV. My assailant dragged me by force, leaving my heels to scrape across the pavement. Another car pulled up behind us, blocking Matt's SUV in. Two more guys got out.

Matt kept his hands up. "You okay?"

"I'm fine. Though I can't say the same for the guy who's holding me."

"Shut up!" My attacker let go, shoving me toward the car's open passenger door.

That was a huge mistake on his part. Once again, he was one of those morons who just didn't realize it yet.

I turned and smiled.

When he came at me again, I threw the back of my wrist into the gun to get it away from me and slammed my foot on the side of his knee. He screamed and grabbed his leg. I followed up with a right cross and an uppercut to the jaw that laid him out on the pavement. A muffled click of an open door caught my attention. Two more guys had gotten out of the car with their glares on me.

An uproar followed. Matt overpowered his guy, picked him up like sack of beans and hurled him across the hood at the car's driver.

When the other guy dashed toward me, I jumped out of the way with roadrunner speed, twisted with my arms outstretched and shoved him into the back of Matt's SUV. He smacked into the glass headfirst, leaving a crack in the rear window. When he grabbed his head and stumbled backward, I yanked a fistful of hair and rammed his face into the window again. More glass cracked under the blow.

I looked to Matt and shrugged. "I'll pay for that—I swear."

He replied with a grin, but it was short lived. The guy he had tossed over the hood of a car was up, so he had his hands busy with him.

The guy whose head I had rammed into the window staggered on his feet. I decided it best to help him to wherever he was going. With the back door still open, I grabbed him by the back of his jacket and waistband and shoved him inside. He smacked into the closed door on the other side. I jumped into the driver's seat and shifted the gear into neutral. We weren't going anywhere until this car was out of our way and since they had parked on a slight incline, I needed gravity to lend a hand.

It did. When the car started to move, I got out and gave it a bit of a shove for good measure.

Glass shattered from a nearby car and an alarm whooped throughout the garage. After leaving one of our limp assailants across the back window of a nearby vehicle, Matt raced to the SUV.

"We gotta go!" He ducked behind the steering wheel.

I barely got my door closed before he skidded us out of the space in reverse. He flipped the gear into drive just as our attackers' car plowed into the cement wall near the stairwell.

Two more guys hurried between a set of cars and stopped about three car-lengths in front of our path. One of them pulled a gun.

I shrugged. "Does he not see this SUV?"

"Apparently not." Matt slammed his foot on the gas and screeched the tires. The windshield cracked twice from the gunfire. I ducked before Matt could pick up speed.

Both men dove out the way. We fishtailed into the back of our attackers' crashed car, but continued around the corner to the next level.

"You know those guys?" he asked.

I shook my head. "Not a clue. You?"

"Same here. You were telling the truth about that stalking thing. Do I even want to know about the murder you mentioned in the same sentence as the stalkers?"

"Probably not."

Matt skidded to a stop when we reached the automatic gate. He lowered the window and flashed a badge about the size of a credit card in front of a black panel. Thank goodness, we didn't have to dig up a couple of dollars for a parking fee. We didn't have time to count change if these fools were coming for us. The gate lifted open. The SUV burst out onto the street to the sounds of blaring horns. I had to grab the dashboard to keep from flying into it.

"You done showing off?"

Matt grinned. "Not unless you are. Those were some nice moves back there. I'm guessing you don't remember where you got those either."

"Nope. They just...seemed like the right thing to do. Survival of the fittest, if you know what I mean."

"Believe me, I do."

My thoughts went back to Dane coaching me in archery. I had a feeling he had done more than show me how to shoot with bows and arrows. My fighting skills had to be due in part to his teachings. Boy, would I like to know where to find him because I'd love to have another lesson right about now.

Matt brought us to a hard stop at the light. "This never would've happened had you listened to me about going to the Garridans' house."

I stared at him. "If you're going to start pointing fingers, at least have the decency to wait until I get my memory back and can properly defend myself. Who the hell are the Garridans?"

When the light changed, Matt didn't get very far before he had to slow again due to cars clogging the street. "They're are Roma. Magical Roma, from what I understand."

"What's a Roma?"

"They're Gypsies, but prefer to be called Roma."

"And...?" I knew nothing about Gypsies and magic, and if I did, I didn't anymore.

"Their businesses went south, which forced them to sell a few items to pay off their debts. I met you at the first auction, which was held on fairgrounds just past South Weymouth. That one had gained a lot of interest. Too much, in fact. Subsequent auctions were by special invitation only on their property. Until they had sent one to an acquaintance of mine, I'd never heard of them."

"Why would you?"

Matt proceeded through the intersection, bouncing us across a couple of potholes. He stayed on the bumper of the car in front of him, slipping through the yellow light. "How much of your memory is gone?"

"What does that have to do with what I asked you?"

"Everything. You see, most supernaturals tend to keep their ear to the community. You know. To keep track of what's going on. Not everyone knew the Garridan Roma were magical."

"Magical. Yeah, you said that." A grin bowed my lips. Why would an educated guy like him believe in something as fictitious as magic? Perhaps he hung out in Salem hunting one too many witches like Pippa.

Then again, what woman lifted more than twice her weight and didn't have a muscle to show for it? Whereas she might get a whiff of a man's cologne, I smelled soap from Matt's shower, fine traces of his sports deodorant and a cheeseburger with ketchup, pickles, onions and bacon bits on his breath. Even with the windows closed, conversations of passersby came in so clear that I could've been walking right next to them. From blocks away, license-plate numbers and letters were crystal clear. None of this was normal. What had happened to me went beyond the laws of physics. Perhaps that was why he brought up that thing about the Garridans being magical Roma. They might have had something to do with giving me whatever strange powers I had.

Matt continued. "Acute senses, incredible strength. The first time we met, you didn't fall into the submissive role the way I had expected. There was this...arrogance about you. Like you were going to stand up to me without causing a scene. We would've gone after each other's throats had it not been for people passing by with their freakin' cotton candy and balloons. Of all the times to meet a human hybrid."

I crossed my hands for the time-out signal. "Back the truck up."

"Huh?"

"You know what I mean. You had me when you mentioned acute senses, but then you lost me far enough into the conversation that a lighthouse couldn't point me in the right direction. Human hybrid? Is that what people call me?"

We came to the next light and stopped. Matt stared at me for what felt like minutes. "You're not faking this amnesia thing, are you?" When I opened my mouth to yell at Sir Deaf-N-Dumb, because he obviously hadn't heard me the first one hundred times, he raised his hand to silence me. "You're part werewolf. I spotted you in the crowd at the fair because of your scent."

All thoughts left me scrambling for something to say. Instead, I sat there staring at him like he had a hand sticking out of his ear.

Matt half-shrugged as if fighting through momentary discomfort. "I'm a full-blooded werewolf."

"Uh-huh." I leaned back in my seat.

The need to put some distance between us had overwhelmed me more than wanting to know the truth about my mysterious past. This was *so* not the history I wanted.

Clutching my purse, I threw open the door and jumped out of the SUV in the middle of downtown Boston. I zigzagged around dozens of cars to make it to the sidewalk. Without looking back, I found a sanctuary in the form of the subway system.

Just when I was starting to somewhat like that guy, he had to go all shock factor on me. If he had been a part of my love life, then perhaps forgetfulness was bliss.

Chapter Sixteen

With everything going on, I started keeping a journal the second I got back to the B&B. If anything happened to me, I wanted there to be documentation. I had even emailed a copy to the Crescent Inn's General Questions email address.

Flora walked in carrying milk and a saucer of chocolate-chip cookies just as I started journaling my meeting with Matt. She had given me several addresses I'd set up over the years, including my work one. All five of them had received a copy of my diary. Too bad, I couldn't recall any of my passwords to get me in to check my eight months of emails. Then again, that might be a blessing in disguise.

"How did it go with that nice lawyer friend of yours?" Flora's voice came just over my shoulder. "I notice you haven't spoken to him in the last two days because you've locked yourself away in this office."

I turned my attention from the screen. My innkeeper stared me with sincerity masking her pudgy face. "You mean Matt? I thought you didn't like him."

"In all honesty, Charles and I didn't like him...at first. Face it, baby. When you went missing, we thought for sure he had something to do with it. Your friends had met him and didn't like him either. We automatically assumed he was a bad apple. But after you were gone for a month or two, he came here asking about you. Said that you and him were...well...intimate."

I turned my attention back to the laptop screen because I didn't want her to see the heat warming my cheeks. "He said we were, but I don't...I mean..."

"We're grown folks, honey. I know what you mean. The point is he could've been one of these fools who showed up once and never returned. He called at least once a week and visited about three or four times, claiming he just happened to be in the area. Charles even caught him sitting out in his car watching the front of the place one time. He sort of freaked my hubby out. Charles tried to get him to come inside, but he wouldn't. Just started the car and left. Like I said, he's a nice guy, even if he's a bit strange."

I turned away from the screen to say something when I noticed another string of feathers hanging in the corner of the room from a shelf. I pointed at it. "Don't take this the wrong way, but what's up with the ugly mobiles?"

Flora glanced over her shoulder. "Oh, that. They were gifts from a nice couple who stayed here a couple of months ago. Said they were good-luck charms. Considering what we've been through, we take all of the good luck we can get."

One of the first things I'd do when I got this place back on its feet was burn those things in the backyard. They made me nervous and I didn't like being nervous.

The more I learned my way around the Crescent Inn, the more it felt like home to me. Somehow, this place had imprinted itself on my subconscious, making it easier to identify with every inch of the twelve-bedroom inn. A solid foundation of determination, pride and hope stood before me. Charles and Flora had started this fifteen years ago with the motto "A home away from home with a family away from family". I was a part of that family. Even though it was my job to protect the business, in a way, it protected me. In a weird sense, it had become my personal den.

Although I didn't want to believe Matt's werewolf story, I couldn't deny the possibility. I was my own proof. Every time a patron passed me in the halls, if I closed my eyes and concentrated on their smell, I knew what they had eaten or whom they'd had contact with. My eyes had no problem with reading the titles on the book spines even though I stood about twenty feet away from them in the library. Twice, Charles had caught me standing at the bottom of the stairwell listening to the conversations from the top floor. He had given me this look like I had lost it.

I even tested my strength by moving huge dressers and cabinets without breaking a sweat. When I dropped a sock behind the dryer, I simply shoved it out of my way, retrieved the item and pushed the appliance back in place. Had it not been an industrial-strength dryer, which normally required industrial strength to move it, I wouldn't have given it another thought. I had enough evidence to wonder if the silver-bullet theory was plausible. The jury was still out on that because the sterling-silver flatware did nothing to me. Although, Matt also said I was half werewolf...whatever that meant.

Close to midnight, I sat on my bed wearing a mint green tank top and a pair of matching pajama bottoms. I had found some of clothes among my possessions that Flora and Charles had boxed up. They insisted I take a room on the top floor because my studio apartment in the basement had gone through a bout of water damage and needed some serious remodeling.

A howl beyond the inn's walls jarred me from my book. I lifted my head and looked at the closed curtains.

That couldn't be...? Could it?

Why was I so quick to believe I'd see a werewolf out there and not some stray dog roaming the streets?

Because I was just that curious.

Easing off my bed, I went to the window, opened it and stuck my head out. Ey-ya! A cold gusty wind slammed into my front, hardening my nipples against my thin tank top. Had I known it was this cold, I would've wrapped myself in a comforter.

From the third-story window, I made out six cars parked in the small lot, tree limbs swaying on the breeze around the edges of the property, a privacy fence separating our property from the one next to it and an alley between the fence the B&B. Just to the rear of the property line was a small two-bedroom, single-bath home.

If Matt was out there, he hid himself well.

On second thought, not that well. An enormous black wolf stepped into a sliver of light passing through the backyard. How I knew it was him, I couldn't say. Turned out my instincts were right after all.

He. Was. Jaw-dropping. Gorgeous. Looking very much like the timber wolves I had researched on the Internet, Matt wore a thick black coat that begged me to run my fingers through it. Wagging his tail high as a show of dominance, he watched me with the same human eyes that I woke to two days ago after passing out at his office.

I ducked back inside and closed the window. I had my shoes in one hand and my coat hanging on my arm when my free hand rested on the doorknob to my bedroom.

My gut tugged at me. *What are you waiting for? Go to him,* it said.

I felt funny about doing that after having jumped out of his SUV. He'd called the inn every day asking for me, and I'd told the Hills to tell him I wasn't in or was busy with a customer. No wonder he decided to change. Talk about getting my attention.

I'd needed time to sort through my thoughts. Perhaps he understood because this was the first time I had heard a howl in the neighborhood. I bet anything that was his way of saying, you've had your alone time, but now it was time to get back to business. I'd buy that. Still, he might be mad at me for leaving and tear me apart once I got down there.

My jets had cooled. I put down my shoes and coat, and eased toward the window again. My fingers clutched the curtain while I peeked over the windowsill.

Matt stood in the darkness with his head tilted, nonverbally asking what was wrong or why didn't I come down. If he wanted me to reply in wolf-speak, he was out of luck. I was half werewolf and didn't respond to the full moon. On second thought, he didn't operate according to folklore either if he was in wolf form now.

I looked up at the sky and noticed there was a crescent moon outlining the shadows of thick clouds. Now I knew where I had gotten the name for the inn.

Staying here would leave me in the dark and my curiosity in annoying limbo. Going down might loosen something hidden deep in my mangled brain. Whether Matt represented good or bad news, I needed to know more, and he might be the only one to lead me out of my mental fog.

Enough of this back-and-forth junk. I had my shoes and coat in hand—again—and hurried out the door.

Flora had shown me where she kept the spare keys. I crept out the back door and onto the porch. If Matt was truly a werewolf, it wasn't a good idea to show him off in the front of the building in case someone happened by.

A gust of chilly air rippled my pajama bottoms around my ankles. Note to self: *look to see if I have a long wool coat in storage tomorrow.* Several twigs cracked. My heart swelled as I raced to the side of the wraparound porch and leaned over the railing into the alley.

The cold steel of a gun silencer lifted my chin. I threw my hands in the air and eased back. The gun followed, exposing an extended arm, a chest, and finally...a head.

Great. Another replay of the garage scene.

"Do you have any idea what we went through to find you?" Paul kept the gun trained on me.

Holy shit. I swallowed the tremble I knew would come out of my voice. "The same you went through to get past security in the Lubbock Airport."

Man, I hoped my sassiness wouldn't cost me a bullet to the cheek. Paul didn't scare me as much as what his boss might have planned for my next routine. There was no way in hell I'd go back to turning tricks at Trixie's.

Paul shrugged, grinning through his excess facial hair. "We would've grabbed you sooner, but we saw that you had caught up with an old friend. The boys in the garage were clumsy. They took little ol' you for granted. We didn't. That's why I'm still standing behind this gun."

"We?"

The back door opened. Sammy stepped outside onto the porch. The wind brushed his brown hair across his sullen face. Why he looked tortured now, I didn't understand. It wasn't like he was the one who had to go back to stripping for dollars.

"Hey, sweetheart," he said, lips trembling into a tentative smile.

Okay, perhaps he was just weird like that. I chose to ignore him and pour my attention on the guy with the gun instead. "If you shoot me, you'll have a hell of a time explaining it to Gamboldt."

"He gave us permission. After all, it cost him more than he was prepared to pay, but he wants you, Keish. What can we say? Robert misses his favorite."

Oh God. Please don't tell me that sick son of a bitch had his hands all over me like a bottle of Jack Daniel's at a whiskey convention.

"That's a pretty large B&B to get lost in," Paul said. "You stayed out of sight most of the time, making it easy for Sammy to slip in as a houseguest. Thanks for the favor."

"Don't mention it. I mean it."

Paul waved the gun, motioning me down the stairs. "Let's go princess. Your vacation is over."

A throaty growl resonated from the shadows like the vibrating engine of a Harley Davidson waiting for the green light. Matt stalked away from the bushes with his ears flattened against his head. Black lips peeled back, revealing a set of serrated white teeth, dripping with spittle. From this distance, he looked about the size of an Irish Wolfhound or a Great Dane. But something about his wolfish appearance made him more menacing. Judging from Sammy's and Paul's bulging eyes, they agreed.

The gun began to shake in Paul's hand. "What the hell is that?"

"A family pet. And in case you haven't figured it out yet, I'm family."

"Shit."

Paul pointed the gun at Matt. I leaped over the railing and tackled him to the ground. The gun exploded, bullet slamming into the grass next to the wolf. Matt's growl turned into a ferocious bark that threatened to wake the neighborhood. Forcing Paul onto his back, I straddled his waist and plowed my hand into his throat. My fingers clenched his windpipe. I yanked the gun from his other hand and tossed it somewhere over my shoulder.

Paul struggled under my grip, hands clutched around my arm. "What the hell...?" He coughed.

I smirked, loving the fact that I had his life in my clenched hand. "I'm something you don't want to mess with. But then again, I think you already know that."

Sammy made a move for the steps. Matt jerked his head around, pouring all of his ferocity on him. The bar bouncer froze, his hands going up in defense.

The light on the Hills' front porch clicked on.

"Shit," Sammy spat. "We're out of here."

Paul sputtered. "I'm not—"

"Now!"

With my attention on the Hills' house, Paul backhanded me across the cheek. The force knocked me onto the cold, wet grass, a stark contrast to the burn on my face.

A series of barks erupted from Matt. Paul scrambled to his feet and dashed down the alley toward the front of the inn. Matt charged after him.

The Hills' door opened and Charles stepped out with a shotgun in his hands. "What's going on out there?"

"A midnight stroll." Sammy closed the distance and offered me a hand. "She tripped and fell."

"Fell, huh?" Charles scowled. "You better not have pushed her."

"N-no way, sir. Honest."

Shotgun or not, Charles was old and my responsibility. I didn't want to see him hurt while trying to defend me. So, I let Sammy win this round.

I glared at him before dusting off my hands and taking the one he offered. "I'm fine. Just clumsy."

"Mm hm." Again, Charles drew his gaze across both of us. "It's late. You two, go on back in the house and try not to disturb the rest of the guests."

"Charles," Flora said from somewhere inside the small home. "Who's out there?"

"It's nothin'." Charles flicked his hand at us. "Just these two kids out here causing trouble."

"Trouble? Which ones?"

"Alexa and Sammy."

The front door opened a second time. Flora appeared behind Charles, buttoning the top of her housecoat. She pursed her lips and shook her head. "Tomorrow, young lady, we're having a talk about fraternizing with the guests. It'll only get you in a mess, and you know it."

Fraternizing with what? Him? I wanted to say something, but the best I mustered was a sputter. It was too late and Charles was right. The longer we stayed out here, the more of a chance someone else would spot us. Although witnesses were my friends, they could also be a detriment if Robert Gamboldt was willing to let me, his so-called "most valued asset", take a bullet.

Charles nudged his wife back inside. "Let's go, honey. I'm sure they get the point."

Once their door closed and the light turned off, I put a few feet between Sammy and me. "I want you out of here. All I have to do is—"

"They're watching from the window." He stared over my shoulder. "Let's just go back inside and play it up. You know as well as I do that if we stay out here, they're going to think something's going on."

As much as I hated to admit it, he had a point. The only good thing about Charles and Flora watching was that Sammy couldn't try anything. Once we got inside, all bets were off and I'd be more than happy to try something first.

Chapter Seventeen

Sammy had a room on the second floor. As much as I didn't want him anywhere around me, he'd paid for a full night. Throwing him out this soon would result in questions from Charles and Flora that I wasn't prepared to answer. They didn't know about Sammy working at Trixie's and I wanted to keep it that way. Besides, Charles might get pissed enough to throw the bouncer out, ruining a good chance to question him. The only question I had was how that jerk had slipped by me.

"We need to talk." Sammy got that much out before I shoved him into the lounge.

"Later. Stay here." I closed the doors on him nearly clipping his nose off in the process.

Going to the front doors again, I undid the locks and stepped out onto the porch. I didn't want him anywhere around me unless Matt was there too. Even though his werewolf form took some getting used to, I'd take my chances with him because...? Well, I didn't know why exactly, but there was a little light in my head that flashed the word "trust" whenever he was around. That was more than I could say for Sammy and Paul who'd made it clear that my place was in the Battle Rose hellhole.

Matt loped down the sidewalk. When he spotted me on the porch, he quickened his pace. A pause while he crooked his canine head, then he finished closing the distance. He hadn't expected to see me standing there safe and sound. Unfortunately, "safe and sound" was relative, as he'd soon find out.

I crouched in front of him, my hand smoothing the soft fur on his head. For a vicious and wild animal, his silken pelt was a beautiful contradiction. Holding his snout in my hands, I urged him closer to run my nose through his coat. Resist as I might, tender kisses flowed from my mouth, smacking against the side of his head. His luscious heat poured into my hands. God, did he feel good.

"You comin' inside?"

Sammy's voice jarred me from my ecstasy. He had better be lucky I wasn't a werewolf like Matt or I would've torn his leg off at the knee.

Matt lifted his head over my shoulder and growled.

I placed my hand on top of his snout. "Don't. He's here because it'll take too much explaining if I throw him out."

"Save your breath, babe. I doubt the dog understands."

Ooooo, if he only knew. I had a feeling that growl wasn't because Matt didn't trust him. I think it had more to do with warning Sammy to keep his distance from me. A territorial thing, so to speak. How I knew that, I couldn't say, but that was the impression I got.

Stepping between both of them, I motioned my lovely wolf into the B&B. Matt twisted his head in a quick snarl as he passed Sammy. Yup. It was a territorial thing and I was pretty much a piece of land. We'd have to talk about that when he got his voice box back.

Once I had everyone gathered in the lounge, I took the couch with Matt sitting on the floor next to my legs. When he smoothed his wet gums and luxurious pelt against my knees, I stared. Perhaps it was the doggy thing to do, but he knew damn well he didn't have to put on any airs for Sammy. We had nothing to prove to this guy because he wouldn't be staying.

Sammy rested his butt in the matching Victorian chair, leaning forward with his elbows digging into his knees. "How long are you planning to hole up in here? You know we're going to bring you home, darling."

That southern drawl pricked my nerves. Nothing against southerners, but listening to his voice made me want to puke. "I'm not going anywhere with you. But as long as you're on my property, you're gonna level with me."

"Sugar, I don't know what to tell you."

Matt growled. Sammy stared, wide eyes not missing a beat.

I couldn't add anything more to that, but I certainly tried. "You had better say something. Otherwise I might let him have you for a midnight snack."

"Keish—"

"Robert Gamboldt. Who is he? What does he do? Why does he want me so—"

"I told you, I don't know." Sammy sighed and slumped in the chair. "Robert Gamboldt paid us to keep an eye on you. He doesn't give reasons. Although he'll give me a cracked skull, if we don't get you back."

"Don't sit there and tell me that I'm such a damn good ass-shaker that he'll spend thousands of dollars to get me under his thumb again. That's bullshit and you know it."

Sammy shook his head, staring at an invisible spot on the floor. "You're not like the other girls. Robert brought them to the bar for reasons he didn't share with the rest of us. At times, he'd send them away for a few days and then they'd return. Usually, it was for a week or so. They'd never say where they've been other than doing some extra work on the side for Robert. But you? You were different."

"How so?"

"Robert was really mysterious about you. Hell, he's being cryptic about why he wants you too."

A moan left Matt's mouth. I rubbed his head while my instincts interpreted the question on his canine face. "What did Robert say exactly?"

Sammy glanced at Matt again with guarded eyes as if readying himself to run in case the "dog" wanted a midnight snack. "Something about you being important. That you were like a daughter to him." He paused, a somber look penetrating his face. "He also said he'd make our lives miserable until we got you home. We've been in this business long enough to know he's not screwing around."

It sounded like Gamboldt was running some sort of business on the side with all of the women at the bar. They knew what was going on. My best guess at this point was the bar had to be a front for something else. It wasn't like I was about to return there to find out. My curiosity wasn't *that* piqued.

"So if one of his star strippers goes missing, he sends you and Paul with a small battalion to bring me back. How much is he paying you?"

"Now hold on, sugar." Sammy hunched over his knees with

his focus on me and Matt completely forgotten. "It's not like that. Believe me. I'm not in this for the money. I'm in it because I want you safe."

"Safe? Is that what you call letting me perform on stage in front of a bunch of drunks while they're slipping their nasty fingers into my panties to drop off a wrinkled dollar?"

"Keish—"

"My name isn't Keisha—it's Alexa. Get it right."

He rubbed a thumb against his forehead. "Alexa then. Honey, you were never in any danger there. I promise. Don't you remember me sitting at the other end of the bar every night when you—"

"What the heck makes you think I remember anything? Did you not get the foot memo I left across Paul's nose when he tried to drug me?"

"I only want you in one piece. We were an item, you know. You were the first girl I ever thought about getting serious with. You think I'm just going to let you go like that? I love you."

That was something new and different. And scary too.

Ohmygod! That's why he'd had such a forlorn look in his eyes that one time. At the Lubbock Airport, a smile had slipped onto his face when he saw me. It also made sense that they'd send him to bring me back. When a guy confesses his love for you, it made him do crazy things. So to speak. How stripping was good for me, I had no clue. Of course, that also meant that I...

Oh God.

"I think I'm gonna be sick." I slumped against the cushions. "Just tell me one thing. Tell me we used protection."

A startled smile bowed his lips. "Of course. But—"

Matt leaped to his feet and charged Sammy. I threw myself onto his back before he snapped the man's leg off. While Matt's ferocious barks filled the room, Sammy's yelling added to the madness. I had to claw at Matt's hide, snagging skin and fur to keep him from tearing the guy apart.

Sammy had climbed into the chair with his fist drawn and ready to pound Matt into the floor. The odds were two to one against Sammy. Matt's thick muscles and sheer force left me sliding across the carpet on my burning knees. He had better be lucky I had enough superhuman strength to hold him down or this would have been a different story involving animal control and euthanasia.

"Get out of here!" I put a chokehold on Matt to keep him still. That wasn't enough to calm him down. Whatever Matt and I had, it must have been something *really* special. I needed Sammy gone before my strained muscles gave way. "Move, Sammy. Get the fuck out or he's going to tear your heart out."

Sammy jumped and tipped over the Victorian chair as he fell on his backside. He scrambled to his feet and dashed out of the lounge. Thank goodness he had the sense enough to close the doors behind him, although I doubt that would've stopped Matt from going through the glass to chomp into a piece of that ass.

"Stop it, Matt!" I tightened my chokehold. "I'll throw you out of the window before I let you wake up this house with your barking."

His last bark came across like a yelp. He whimpered under my grip. Slowly, his body began to relax, compacted muscles easing down underneath me. It was a good thing. He had stretched my limbs to their limit. Ten more seconds of that and he would've gone through the French doors anyway.

A door clicked from somewhere on the first floor. Damn. I bet Charles and Flora had heard the commotion.

Panic kicked my butt in gear. I snagged the nape of Matt's neck and hurried him to the door. There was no way I was letting him go just yet. I cracked open one of the French doors and peeked around the edge. At the end of the hall, a tall shadow that looked like Charles stood in front of the window. A turn of the knob and the door opened.

I dragged Matt out of the lounge and jetted across the lobby to hide in front of the stairs. "Keep your mouth shut or both of us are sleeping in the streets tonight. You hear me? Now get your behind upstairs."

Matt took the steps faster than me, but even in human form, I didn't have a problem keeping up with him. A moment of a shock came over me when he stopped on the top floor, right in front of my door. That doggone mutt had traced my scent.

I snorted. "Uh-uh. There's no way in hell you're coming in my room."

Matt put on his puppy-dog eyes and tuned in to the whimpering channel.

"What kind of fool do I look like? You tote your ass in there and I'll—"

A lock from one of the doors across the open landing clicked.

Another bout of panic shot through me. Fumbling with the key, I jammed it in the lock and hurried inside the room. Matt stood in the hall staring. When the knob turned on room 3-A, I cursed myself under my breath. We had a No Pet policy in place. One look at Matt, the unfriendly "dog", and heaven only knows what sort of problems I'd have.

Clenching my teeth, I flagged him inside and closed the door. I peeked out the peephole in time to see an older man's head swiveling from side to side. I leaned against the door.

"You give me one ounce of trouble and I'll mount your muzzle on the wall." I turned, ready to give him a piece of my mind. Something about that wagging tail and goofy mouth hanging open, I bet he enjoyed every second of my agony. "You come anywhere near my bed and you'll lose a testicle."

After dropping my coat and kicking my shoes across the floor, I marched to the bed and climbed under the covers. Oh, how I wished it were that easy to get Sammy's confession out of my head. It was another good reason to make sure I bathed with a scouring pad come morning.

Chapter Eighteen

Tired of my empty grumbling stomach, I finally rolled my butt out of bed in a semicoma. After throwing on a pair of sweats and a zip-front sweater, I headed downstairs for some quick hellos while piling a bunch of food onto two plates. Flora gave me that "we have to talk" warning while flipping extra pancakes on the griddle. I nodded once before flying out of the kitchen with a large breakfast tray and returned to my room on the top floor. Knowing her, she probably thought one of these plates belonged to Sammy. Can I get a hell-to-the-no?

"Damn that smells good," my bed said.

Son of a... A tremor ran through my arms and I nearly dropped the plates on the table.

Matt crawled from underneath the bed wearing nothing. My eyes bulged at all his glory and then some. Toned muscles rippled across the upper half of his body, each of them moving with every nonchalant step toward the table. Arms, shoulders, chest and stomach. All of it left my jaw hanging until my mouth filled with enough juice to force me to a gulp. He didn't have the bodybuilding physique, but it made a woman count her blessings that she had witnessed a man gorgeous enough to walk off the cover of a sexy magazine. With the dark eyes and matching velvet hair, I wanted to drag him into bed and explore his luscious body. What puzzled me the most was his eyes weren't on me. They were on the food.

"Interested?"

"Uh..." I shook my head out of the gutter. "For heaven's sake! Put some clothes on? This isn't the Playgirl mansion." I snatched up the small glass coffeepot and began filling it from the bathroom sink.

He laughed. "I'm a werewolf, remember? I spend a lot of time in wolf form where nudity isn't optional."

"Whatever. I still think you did it on purpose."

"What can I say? I'm just trying to do my part to jog your memory. Guess it didn't work. Do you mind if I start without you? I just hate to see good food go to waste."

"Dive in. Half of it's yours anyway." I exited the bathroom, shoved the pot under the coffee drip and started the brewer.

By the time I turned around, a third of Matt's plate had disappeared in syrupy residue and grease. He chugged another slice of bacon before I made it to the other side of the table where he sat with the top of his butt exposed through the spokes of the chair. When my head began to tilt sideways for a better look, I shook it back to the upright position. He'd love to know I was checking him out and would probably hold it over my head again. Humph. Like I'd give him the satisfaction.

"You'll have to excuse me," he said, holding a slice of toast. "Changing forms burns a lot of calories. We eat about three times the average person."

"In other words, you'll want me to go downstairs and get more."

He shook his head. "Stay right where you are. You look cute in that pink sweat suit. Even cuter when you're sleeping."

"Salmon, thank you very much." I planted my hands on my hip.

Matt swooped out of the chair and scooped me off my feet. I pushed against his hardened chest, legs flailing to no avail.

"Put me down," I demanded.

"No." He marched to the bed and dropped me on the mattress. "You're staying right here. After everything you've been through, it's about time someone catered to you. I'd be more than happy to fit the bill."

"Not when you're making sexual innuendoes, you aren't."

A grin dug dimples into his cheeks. "You liked it before. Besides, I have to make up for lost time."

"*Noyoudon't.*" I scrambled to the other side of the bed.

Matt grabbed my ankles and pulled me back. The more I fought, the more he seemed to think that this was some sort of game. I clawed at the sheets and pillows, trying to get away from him. He finally hopped onto the bed and wrestled me onto my back. His lower half snuggled against mine, hardness bruising my thigh.

Okay...now what?

I lay there staring into his eyes. He did the same. I bit my lip to keep the urge to kiss him at bay. Boy was that a losing battle. When he lowered his head, eyes closing, I knew I had lost.

His lips touched mine and the kiss turned explosive. Passion ran wild inside both of us with the way we explored each other's mouths, drinking such heavenly juices. His lips were soft and smooth. They didn't look that thick until I kissed him on the mouth and filled myself with complete ecstasy.

The moment his hand slipped under my shirt, anxiety ran rampant through my knotted-up belly. I shoved him back and sat up.

"What's wrong?" he asked.

It was then that I *really* noticed his naked body still kneeling between my legs and his heated member fully erect and ready to go. I had to catch my breath, and it had nothing to do with passion. This was a full-blown panic attack. Images of those creeps at the bar flooded my mind like a California mudslide. Muck, mire, disgust. The pain would come in the aftermath of realizing I had survived everything while my memories lay in ruins.

I scrambled away from him and pulled myself to the foot of the bed. "I'm not ready to go where you're going."

"I don't understand. We were... You..." He started again. "We were practically a mated pair before all this. Just you and me. The only thing we never did together was run free. Which is probably a little harder for you considering your human form."

"Are you telling me I was able to change? Like into some bipedal half wolf?" Skip the bar creeps. Lon Chaney came to mind.

Matt shook his head. "Not like that. Man-beast form is a sign of insanity. It's not possible to hold that form without having a few screws loose. When we change, we go all the way. You, on the other hand, don't change. You have the heightened senses, strength, and some speed on your side, but that's it."

"Oh."

Matt pushed himself into a sitting position. "Don't be sorry either. If it takes having to win your heart a second time around, Alexa Wells, then I'll be more than happy to work just as hard again. You're worth it."

That jerked a tiny smile into my cheek. Whether or not he had said that to me before, it was a good thing to hear. Unfortunately, I didn't have time for romance. I needed to get Robert Gamboldt and his hoods off my back before reentering my life again. Compared to the one I'd had at Trixie's, I'd take this one in a heartbeat...even with an infatuated werewolf.

"By the way." Matt returned to his plate, bit off half a slice of bacon, then pointed the remainder at me. "If you think I'm sharing you with that lovesick boy toy of yours, guess again."

Oh my God. Was that not the pot-and-kettle situation? I snatched a pillow from the bed, marched across the floor and whopped him across the back of the head with it. "Smart ass."

He laughed. "And while we're at it, you shouldn't be sending a werewolf mixed signals like that."

"What signals?"

"Which do you think? Not only did you come to the front porch last night, but you marked me the way a wolf would with your kiss. *You* came onto *me*. I assumed you were ready for the next step."

I stared. Like I remembered what life as a half werewolf was like. "I was...just enjoying your fur. It's as soft as goose down, in case you didn't know. Who could resist running their nose through something like that?"

Matt arched a single eyebrow in disbelief. "Whatever. Right now, it's not important." He jammed a fork into a pile of scrambled eggs and brought it up to his mouth. "You never mentioned the name Robert Gamboldt when we spoke."

I pulled the chair away from the table and sat opposite him. "You never gave me a chance to tell you everything, remember? You hustled me out of your office."

He swallowed and wiped his lips. "Nevertheless, I know that name because his face shows up in the newspapers around town every once in a while."

"Wait a minute. Are you telling me that bastard lives right here?"

"Somewhere, yes. His charitable donations are legendary."

"Well, where the hell is he? What are we sitting around for? We should be going downstairs and rousting Sammy's ass out of bed to show us where he lives."

113

"Not possible. Your ex slipped out of the house about an hour after you fell asleep. I saw him leave through the front door and get into a pickup. I'm guessing someone convinced him that kidnapping you from the house was a mistake and that it might be easier to nab you on the streets."

Great. I couldn't believe Sammy had left like that. Matt was probably right about him rethinking his kidnapping methods. After seeing my tight relationship with the Hills and the "guard dog" we had on staff, taking me from here would be more of a headache than it was worth.

"But you know where we can find Gamboldt, right?"

"I called my personal assistant after you went for breakfast and left a message for her to find his address. She'll call back, but my cell phone is in my car and it's parked two blocks away. In the meantime, there's something else you should know."

"What?"

"Remember that business card you gave me? The one with the realtor's address on it that brought you to Boston?"

"Yeah. What about it?" I sipped my orange juice.

"I've spent the last few days tracking him down. He was killed in a hunting accident. Someone shot him in the head with an arrow."

I choked on the tangy sweetness.

First, it was Keisha Walker. Now, it was some real estate agent I couldn't recall. If the police put both murders together with the only common denominator being me, my ass was going to the electric chair.

Chapter Nineteen

It took some maneuvering to get Matt out of the B&B without any clothes. I had to sneak into a guest room and rifle through their clothes until I found something to fit him. Once dressed, he wanted to jump out of the window from the back of the building because a three-story drop was nothing to a werewolf. Despite my image of him splattering across the pavement like an egg, he did it anyway.

Matt's assistant was good. She had found an address for Gamboldt and left it on his voice mail. Unfortunately, her efforts were in vain. His address amounted to an office the size of my bedroom back at the inn with the only occupant being a fax machine and a wastepaper basket. Oh yeah, there was a secretary. Either she was too old and decrepit for this job or a narcoleptic who had this habit of dozing off during questioning. It didn't matter because her hearing aid only caught every third word. Her head fell back just as we were getting somewhere, gurgles rifling from her ancient throat. I wanted to drop a penny in her mouth to wake her from her coma, but Matt slapped my hand away and settled for shaking her awake instead. When all was said and done, we walked away with several brochures of Gamboldt's charitable organizations. The man was very generous with his money, but I suspected that had to do with him needing a diversion from his other nefarious deeds. Like kidnapping, for instance.

"It doesn't make sense." I lowered a plastic-coated map on my lap and watched the sign for Kingston speed by on our way back to the city. Trees whipped past the window, including a small cross and flowers signifying someone had died. "For a guy who likes to donate to the children's hospitals and orphanages, what does he get out of owning a strip bar in the middle of Battle Rose, Arizona? Where's the venture capitalism in that?"

I threw my hands into the dashboard and reared back in my seat. The bumper of the car in front of us came too fast at our windshield.

"Matt!"

He slammed his foot on the brakes. The SUV fishtailed between both lanes, forcing another driver to lay on their horn. The tires tore up the grass median as they slid closer toward the center. Matt yanked the wheel back to the right and crossed over the dashed line. He pulled onto the shoulder and threw the gear in park.

Matt's knuckles clutched the steering wheel, the bones about to break through the skin. His shoulders and chest heaved, his thumping reaching my ears without the need of a stethoscope.

I touched the back of his tightened fingers. "Is there something you need to tell me?"

"Sorry."

"That wasn't what I was looking for. Thanks though."

He glanced over his shoulder, looking at the opposite side of the road. "My pack lives down this way. I should've been more careful about paying attention to the road instead of looking at the traffic on the other side."

"I'll give you the 'more careful' part, but what does the traffic have to do with anything?"

"Red, beat-up Impala with a license plate I know all too well. I hope they didn't see my truck. Otherwise, they might decide to follow just for the fun of it. They know I don't come down here often unless I'm summoned by our Pack Alpha, Parry."

"The local pack prick?"

Matt half-grinned. "Parry Casabianca is an old-fashioned bastard who's very much set in his ways. He doesn't run our pack. He owns us and never lets us forget it."

It sounded like Pippa was right about him. Until now, I had forgotten that he was the leader of the werewolves and Matt's overlord. "Then why stay?"

"Because strays aren't allowed in our territory, which is all of Boston and the suburbs. If I break away, I become a stray on foreign land. Some of my pack would love to hunt me to gain favor with Parry. We're territorial like that."

"I guess so."

That explained why I thought the Crescent Inn was more like my den and didn't like anyone bullying me on it. Sammy and Paul were a threat, but what really pissed me off about them was they had come on my land and endangered everything I held dear. I would've thrown all I had into fighting them off.

"In case you were wondering, that's why I tracked you the way I did back at the fair."

I shook my head. "I don't understand."

Matt closed his eyes and shook his head. He shifted the SUV into gear, checked his rearview mirror and pulled back onto the road. "I thought you were a stray wolf. That's why I confronted you at the fair. Of course, you don't remember that. Anyway, I was going to tell you to clear out of Boston territory. The guy I was with, another member from my pack, wanted to do other things with you. I told him to back off and claimed you as my pet."

"Excuse me?" I would've planted a hand on my hip, but it was hard to do considering I was sitting in the passenger seat and it would've had less of an effect.

A smirk bowed the corner of Matt's mouth, digging a dimple into his cheek. "It was all for show. You didn't know it at the time, and I knew you wanted to skewer my balls regardless. So, I pulled off my bad-boy act and it was enough to scare the hell out of you. I thought you'd leave right away, but you didn't. Instead, you rejoined your friends just outside the Garridans' auction tent. We spent the whole time following you around."

"More like stalking, I bet."

"Yeah, you could say that. But it was with good reason. You smelled like a bitch in heat with cream filling."

A glare narrowed my eyes. Had I heard what I thought I heard? "You know, if you're trying to win friends and influence people, you should quit now or forever hold your teeth."

Chuckling, he switched on his signal and passed a slow-moving midsize car. "What can I say? You smelled delicious. But that wasn't the reason I was following you. I had never smelled anyone who was part werewolf before. Your scent is amazing. It still is."

"You're still losing friends."

"Then understand this. Parry would rather have two wolves fight to the death to settle a dispute than try to break them up. He's a purist fuck who drinks, eats and pisses too much, and doesn't have a problem with selling drugs on the side. He had a great Internet business going until he sold it. When he got bored, he took up growing marijuana in the basement as a hobby." Seriousness flooded Matt's face, his eyes hooded. He remained quiet as though gathering his thoughts before speaking. "If Parry finds out you're here, he'll kill you, Lex. I won't let that happen. He sees humans as nothing more than a means to an end. There's no telling what he'd do if he found out you were a human hybrid."

I said nothing. Supremacist jerks like Parry had a special place in hell, which surprisingly gave me some comfort. However, what he did to Matt by planting the worry in his eyes, bugged the hell out of me. I didn't want him hurt on my account. "I'll give you a reprieve on that losing-friends stuff. For now."

"That reminds me." He unclipped his cell phone and flipped it open. "Luz should've called back. She was looking for supernatural connections between Garridan and Gamboldt."

Both of us held two pieces of a puzzle and we needed to know if—how—they fit together. Matt hadn't known about my connection with Gamboldt and I never would've known about the Garridans had it not been for him filling me in. It was a long shot and not very clear-cut. If those two had dealings in the past, then maybe we'd find out what Gamboldt wanted from me now. That was better than just showing up on the man's strip-bar doorstep and hoping he'd tell me everything over a spot of noonday tea.

Which reminded me to check my watch. Did Monica have something planned for me? She'd rifled off a list of things we needed to do before my court date, but I couldn't remember them. "Do you know Monica Hardcourt?"

"The name's familiar. Why do you ask?"

"I was wondering if she was any good. The cops think I had something to do with the death of Keisha Walker because they found her ID on me. So, Monica is representing me."

"*What?*" Matt's eyes darted from right to left, looking from one mirror to the other before he changed lanes again. "Why the hell didn't you tell me?"

"I didn't get much of a chance until now. Truth be told, out of sight out of mind. Anyway, you might want to have your contact cross-reference Keisha Walker with Gamboldt, Garridan and anybody else you can think of."

"You know, this just complicates the hell out of things. Supernaturals don't do jail like they don't do hospitals. We work alongside humans or use them as a means to an end. The supernatural world has been living in secret for millennia and we'll do everything in our power to keep it that way. Even if that means paying someone off to kill you before you go to prison."

"Good to know." I leaned against the door just as a headache banded across my forehead with this new piece of you're-so-fucked information.

After grabbing a bite to eat—he was hungrier than me—we traveled to Newton to visit Matt's contact. He hired Luz Gonzales to handle highly sensitive research instead of giving it to one of the paralegals in his office. From what I understood, Luz was some sort of psychic who understood the implications of certain "special" projects he gave her. If he handed them over to the law firm's paralegals, a straitjacket and a Thorazine drip might be in order for him. It was better if someone understood where he and a few of his supernatural clients were coming from and knew how to use the right scrutiny to get answers.

Luz lived in a large apartment building with the luxury of a small pool and garden area on the fifth floor. Strange, but at least it was a nice place to go if you wanted to smell fresh flowers, barbecue or simply sit under a tree with a good book.

When we reached the seventh floor, Matt gave the door one knock before he pressed his nose to the frame. He didn't take the huge whiff I had expected.

"What's wrong?" I asked.

"Can't you smell it?"

"Smell what? I've never been here before."

He arched an eyebrow at me before trying the knob. It opened without a hitch. That wasn't good. Nobody in their right mind would leave a door unlocked, whether in a big city or suburbs.

Matt went inside first and I followed.

Dimness blanketed the apartment and the heavy air pressed against my chest. It was stale and musty, but...something else lay underneath it. I couldn't place the scent, but my gut told me it was familiar. How was that possible when I'd never been here before? At least, not since my return to Boston.

Matt went to the window and yanked on the shade. Light spewed into the room.

A corpse lay on the couch.

Chapter Twenty

Luz lay with her arms frozen straight in the air and her palms pressed outward as if to fend something off. Her eyes had gone gray and empty, matching her ashen skin. Her mouth was open like she wanted to scream, but couldn't get the words out. She had black curly hair splayed about her head, about twice the thickness of the average person. It was the only thing left alive in this lifeless place. Even the fish in the tank by the window had floated to the top of the water.

Matt knelt by her body and combed his fingers through her thick mane. His thumb brushed across her corpselike forehead.

Sadness came over me. Not for the pretty woman whom I didn't know, but for Matt. "I'm sorry."

Blinking the glaze from his eyes, his lips gummed together before answering. "She was a good friend. One of the few I trusted."

I opened my mouth to say more, but Matt stood. He rushed to the window, twisted the locking mechanism, and shoved the pane open. He filled his lungs, but a choking cough cut him off.

"You okay?" I asked.

"Can't you smell it?" He placed his sleeve over his mouth and continued coughing. "There's no fresh air. It's stifling. Like...it's alive and wants to strangle us."

I shook my head. "I don't get it. How can stifling air kill anyone?"

"The air is nothing more than a conduit." He rushed to another window and slammed it open. "This place has been cursed."

Oh. This was my first curse, so what did I know?

I couldn't take my eyes off Luz's body. The smell my mind

identified with was death. I had caused death more than once—I think—to know that scent. Perhaps I was responsible for killing both Keisha and the real estate guy after all.

"We should go," I said.

Matt stopped running around frantic and stared. "We have to call the police."

"The police? No way. I'm already the prime suspect in one homicide, potentially two. I don't need the police asking what brought me to the scene of another one."

"Did you touch anything?"

I glanced around the small, stuffy apartment. "No."

"Good. I'll call the cops. You go wait in the truck and stay out of sight."

He got no argument from me. I started for the door.

Something like a combination of both physical barrier and a sinus pressure stopped me. When I tried stepping into the hall, an invisible weight came down on my neck, shoulders and head.

"Matt." I touched the doorway, but my hand slid down the side and I dropped to my knees.

Wood creaked with each step as he approached me. He didn't get far either. Matt's reply came in a strangled gasp. He fell on his side with a thump. So much for getting help.

On hands and knees, I shoved my head through the entryway, weight drawing down my shoulders and extending toward my lower back. Using everything I had, I crawled through the heavy, invisible barrier surrounding the entryway and collapsed in the hall. There, the air was normal and I filled my lung volume with every ounce of it. Once I had my fill, I reached through the heaviness again and hauled Matt's limp body through.

The spell barrier snagged his lower half, putting me in a game of tug of war with his body.

"Matt." I strained, pulling on his shirt until threads tore along the seams. "You have to help me."

I braced myself with my foot against the wall and heaved with everything I had. He wasn't heavy so much as something was trying to keep him inside that death pit of an apartment.

He moaned. One of his hands slapped against the floor. His body lightened up. Whatever force held him in that room had lost part of its grip. Or he had regained some of his.

With his upper half lying in the hall, I reached down and snagged the waist of his jeans. Matt was of little help due to his groggy condition. Had it not been for his back moving with each deep breath, I would've sworn he was dead. I continued to haul his limp body into the hall. Lying on the floor, Matt rolled over and sucked in a deep breath.

Panting, I slump against the opposite wall. "What was that?"

"It's what killed Luz. Probably more potent to kill her faster." While propping himself up, he stared down the length of his body and back into the apartment. "Son of a bitch. When I get my hands on the bastards who did this..."

"What about the cops?"

"I still have to call them."

It figures. "But if the air got to her, won't it do the same to them?"

"I don't know. If the person who did this is smart, it'll only affect those with a hint of paranormal abilities. The chance of a witch or a vampire being on the police force and getting the call is nil. Even if I'm wrong, it'll teach the sloppy bastard a lesson about leaving spells behind for untargeted humans. It'll be their mess to clean up. They'll have some explaining to do if humans succumb to their magic."

In the short time I had been with Matt, I'd learned one thing. Humans could be a more effective weapon than teeth and claws when using them against a supernatural enemy. Even if the Boston Pack knew about me, they wouldn't dare bring their war to my B&B where there were plenty of human witnesses around. Perhaps that was my reason for owning the place.

Hours later, Matt and I sat in a diner contemplating our next move. He had joined me down the street just as I finished off a cup of hot tea. His steak with russet potatoes, green beans and a basket of rolls arrived minutes after he sat. I couldn't tell if he ate out of anger or simply enjoyed eating for no reason other than hunger.

The police investigation didn't turn up any foul play, but they thought it was strange that Luz died the way she did. It looked like suffocation via carbon monoxide poisoning, but the time it took for her rigor mortis to set in made no sense. Her body had frozen in time. Plus, the gas would've leaked to the other floors and more people would've died. Everyone else in the building remained unharmed.

Matt had planned to ask the few friends in his pack for an alibi, but it ended up coming from the one place nobody ever suspected. Gamboldt's secretary called and left a message on his cell making sure he received all the information regarding Mr. Gamboldt's charitable organizations during his earlier visit. Kind of ironic and convenient, if you ask me.

Matt cleaned his lips and tossed the dirty napkin on his plate. "That's the bastard's way of saying he's watching us. Not to mention he probably doesn't want to get a man like Parry hounding his ass about his precious werewolf lawyer."

I pushed my half-filled, second cup of tea. This was getting more complicated by the breath. "Robert has to be a supernatural. It's the only thing that makes sense in terms of his being able to track me."

"Which begs the question of why he doesn't show up here and now."

I shrugged because I didn't have an answer for that. Finding out what kind of supernatural he was might hold the answer.

Matt made room for his laptop on the table and booted it up while continuing to speak. "It could also mean that he's found a way to tap into our world and have supernaturals working for him. Remember, the guy is a millionaire. Just like everyone else, we need money to survive too. Enough money will certainly pay for the power he needs."

I folded my arms in front and leaned on the table. "What are you doing?"

Matt tapped away on the keyboard before turning it toward me. "One reason why I hired Luz is because she keeps copies of everything in her database. Even when she has news for me, it comes via a phone call and an email. I'm hoping she had the chance to send one."

She had.

Hola Matt,

Robert Gamboldt is a slippery son of a bitch, but I managed to find something on him just searching through my own circles. It turns out he's a psychic of sorts, but I have a feeling he's a rare one because even my contacts weren't sure. However, they warned me to stay out of his way because he's bad news. In fact, one of them specifically said, "Whenever something happens and you're left feeling like you've lost a sense of time, check the room to see if he's around. Then, run like hell." I also found out he was seen with an older woman, but nobody knows her name. The few who've passed close enough to her sense something earthy, yet powerful. But that's it. The only earthy supernaturals I know of are necromancers, voodoo priests, witches and cunning folk. I'm sure there are more, but I can't even begin to figure out how to contact any of those groups for confirmation. You might want to use your werewolf muscle to force that one because I have a feeling a simple psychic like me won't get anywhere.

I hope this helps, amigo. And before I forget, you owe me a beer at the next Patriots game. Don't make me come find you. ;-)

Adiós,
Luz with the clues

I could've kissed Luz. Just hearing that letter made me wish I had a chance to see her and thank her for her help. I hated never getting that chance. Damn, Gamboldt. Damn him to hell. She'd risked her life to get us this information. One way or another, I'd see to it that her death wasn't for nothing.

"Let's go about this another way." The pads of my fingers smoothed the surface of the table in small circles. "There was a woman at the hospital who said she was a witch. In fact, she followed me into the subway where I threatened her to leave me alone or else. She was the one who initially told me about your pack."

Matt stared straight ahead with a frown knitting his brows together. "What were you doing at a hospital?"

Oh great. As if I hadn't broken enough rules in the preternatural secret code. "Flora threatened to call my parents if I didn't get my head checked. I'd like to meet them, but I can only take so many shocks at one time."

"Their timing would suck too."

Matt pushed his food aside and tossed enough money on the table to take care of the tab. Keeping mostly to his own, he gathered up his stuff and we left the diner. Something was turning those wheels in his head. I had a feeling it had to do with a new resolve to help me and to make sure someone paid a price for Luz's death. At least, I hoped that was the case.

Once inside his SUV, I unclipped Matt's cell phone. "I don't remember her name off the top of my head, but I keep a journal of everything that's happened to me since last night. I'm sure I typed it in."

Matt reached across the seat without looking and folded the cell phone down on my fingers. "Wait a minute. Just how much did you put in that diary of yours?"

Oops. I forgot to tell him about that. "Pretty much everything. About you being a werewolf and me being half. I had to. If something bad happened to me again, I wanted a frame of reference or at least some breadcrumbs for someone to follow. I even added in that stuff about Trixie's and stripping in case my memory went AWOL again."

"Are you sure you want Flora reading all that? I mean...she's going to think you're nuts and probably call your parents anyway. You realize that, don't you?"

"Do we have a choice? If we go back to the inn and get the information ourselves, someone might trace us there and find a houseful of bait to use against me. I love the Hills, which is why I want to limit my contact with them as much as possible. Luz was one too many people killed in this. I don't want any more if I can help it."

Matt pulled his hand off the phone. "Good thing I've got plenty of minutes."

I took that as yes and dialed the number.

Flora answered on the second ring, but it took her forever to find her glasses. Matt and I would reach the inn by the time she pulled up the email for me. I motioned for him to start the engine in case it came to that.

"Let me see." Flora hummed a tune. "Honey, are you sure you're feeling okay?"

"It's just a dream journal. Honest." I wished I had listened better to Matt and thought this thing through. When she came to that part about me stripping at a bar in Arizona, she wanted to stop reading and fax me a copy of the journal. That would've worked if Matt had a fax machine in his glove box.

"Here it is." Several clicks came from Flora's end. "Her name was Pippa. Honey, I don't think it's wise to be writing about stuff like this. What happened to the sweet young lady I used to know?"

"I'm still the same person. Honest. Just that the doctor at the hospital suggested I keep the journal because it might help me with my amnesia."

"Don't you think it's time you called your parents? Baby, keeping this kind of secret from them isn't good. At least call your friend Mr. Dane. He was just as sick with worry as everyone else."

I dared to glance at Matt. This was one conversation I hoped his superhearing didn't catch. After the way he'd acted around Sammy, I didn't want to feel like I had to explain myself when I didn't have the memories to do so.

Of course, I was wrong. His fingers clutched the steering wheel while he stared straight ahead. When Matt turned, he glared. I pressed my hand to the mouthpiece. "It's not what you think. He's a family friend, from what I understand."

"Whatever."

I rolled my eyes and took my hand off the phone.

"By the way..." A chair or something moved on the other side of the phone. Flora must have stepped away from the desk. "You got a funny fax this afternoon. The letterhead says House of the Muló, which is owned by Brody Lennor."

"Sorry. Never heard of him. Is there—"

"I had thrown it away thinking it was just some lousy advertisement coming through. Now that I see you have this thing about going to an auction in your journal, maybe it isn't."

My thoughts paused for a breath. Flora wouldn't bring that up unless she had good reason. I lowered the phone and pressed the speaker button for Matt to hear, too. "Do you still have the fax?"

"Hold on a sec. I was just pulling it out of the garbage." Paper rustled in the background. "It's an advertisement for another auction they're having tonight in Nashua on Maynard Ave. The last time you got information about an auction, they sent it by special courier. Young lady, why didn't you tell me you're messing around with magic and witchcraft and stuff? I'd stay away from that junk if I were you."

Matt and I shared a dumbfounded look that only lasted a few seconds. Realization slipped onto my face, straightening out my knitted brows. Romas were the only ones having auctions these days and they had this thing for me being their guest of honor. Was it possible that Brody Lennor was a Roma too? Either these guys were stupid and thought I'd go quietly or they had something else on their minds. Perhaps they wanted to talk, although I would've preferred an invitation from the Garridans.

"Is that it?" I asked.

"Pretty much. Oh my Lord!" An ear-piercing scream wailed from Flora.

"*Flora?*" God help me, I wanted to go through the mouthpiece to get to her. Helpless, I had the phone in a stranglehold while screaming into it. "What's going on? Talk to me."

"Lord, have mercy. Lord, have mercy." Flora's prayers ignited into panic again with huffs coming over the phone followed by cries. "Charles!"

"*Flora!*" I'd never forgive myself if anything happened to her. *Please, God. Don't do this to her. Not her.*

A loud clatter jarred me away from the phone. Either feet or someone's body shuffled in the background. Flora's screaming tore a hole in my heart. I swore if anyone had hurt her, I'd beat the hell out of them.

I turned to Matt, pleading with him instead of speaking the words. Tears filled my eyes, ready to spill. He must have read my face or I did a good job with my unspoken terror. Matt threw the gear into reverse and peeled out of his parking space.

Chapter Twenty-One

The auction fax had burst into flames in Flora's hand and burned her all the way up to her elbow. I doubt it had anything to do with the fax machine. One of the guests had managed to put the fire out before it burned the rest of her dress. Somehow, compensating our patron for his entire stay just wasn't enough.

By the time we arrived in the ER, we found Flora resting in a private exam room with Charles standing at her side. I wanted to hug her, but her sleeping, scrunched face and the layers of bandages covering her arm told me not touch her.

Charles half-smiled. This incident had aged him ten years with the tiredness in his eyes and sadness weighing down his cheeks. When I touched his shoulder, the best he mustered up for me was a pat on the back of my hand.

I was responsible for this mess. If I hadn't gone back to the Crescent Inn, whoever did this would never have gotten Flora. Those damn auctioneers would pay for this. I'd shove their merchandise so far up their asses that it would make their tonsils look infected.

"How is she?" I swallowed through my tight throat.

Charles sighed. "As well as can be expected. It could've been worse. Thank the Lord someone was around when she started screaming. If anything had happened to her, I'd...I'd..." He shook his head, unable to say more.

I embraced him. I knew exactly how he felt. Both of us loved that woman, though he loved her with all his heart as only a husband would. In the little time I had known the Hills, they were like extended family. I wouldn't sit around and let some bastard get away with harming them. They were pack and I was the Alpha wolf. I'd be more than happy to put an arrow into anyone who messed with us.

An anger-fueled tear slid down my cheek. I quickly wiped it away when I released Charles and pulled out of our hug. I didn't want him to see me cry, although I was sure the telltale sign of matted eyelashes gave me away.

Charles took a deep breath that filled his chest. He nodded with a smile that was for his reassurance instead of mine. "She's gonna be all right, sweetheart. I'm sure of it. In fact, the doctors want to keep an eye on her blood pressure and stuff, so she's staying the night. It was a little high when she came in, of course."

"Of course." I stared at her before slipping my hand in hers. My thumb smoothed across the back of her pudgy knuckles. "If there's anything you guys need, just let me know. I don't care what it is, Charles. Does the B&B have health insurance for you guys?"

His smile remained in place as he slipped an arm across my shoulders. "Of course. You've taken good care of us."

"And what about—"

"Now don't you worry." Charles gripped my shoulders and turned me to face him. "The only thing she needs right now is rest. I'll make it back to the inn a little later and take care of things. At eighty percent capacity, it's a good reason to keep steaming ahead, you know?"

"You mean nobody is there watching over the guests?"

"Not exactly. After you disappeared, we went ahead and hired an assistant to work part time. She's one of those college kids who needed some extra money on the side. Anyway, she's with the guests right now."

Boy, this was a huge setback. Even worse, I couldn't just run out there and find the people responsible for this while our bread and butter sat in the hands of some college kid. Unfortunately, that auction was tonight. If I wanted answers then I needed to be there to get them.

A knock came at the door. Matt stuck his head inside the room and smiled, motioning for me to come out with a tilt. I excused myself and followed him.

"What's going on?"

He stared at the closed door. "I wasn't prying or anything, but I overheard that the doctors are going to keep her. It's that bad, huh?"

"If you mean by her high blood pressure, this is the first time I'm hearing about it. Or rather, the first time since my amnesia problem."

"Yeah well, I've been thinking. You do what you have to do. Let me worry about going to the Lennor auction."

My stomach dropped to my shoes. "Are you insane? What happens if they get to you too?"

"That's just it. I have an entire pack backing me. If anything happens, I have no doubt that Parry will go through the entire Roma world to get me back. Trust me—they're more scared of him than I am of them."

"How will—?"

"I'll leave word with my friend Tate that if anything hap—" Matt stopped just as a few nurses walked by from one direction and an orderly passed in the other. "If I don't check in with him in a couple of hours, he'll sound the alarm."

I shook my head. "I don't know about this, Matt. Suppose something bad happens to you? Luz is dead. Flora is hurt. I just don't want...I can't..."

I closed my eyes before a fresh batch of tears embarrassed the hell out of me. Between my quivering stomach and the lump in my throat, it was a miracle I held it together. During the little time I had known him, Matt meant something. He had done more than his share to see me through this. I couldn't ask him to take another dangerous step on my behalf.

Matt took me into his warm arms, hugging me tight. I stiffened at first because I hadn't expected it and in a way didn't want it. Once he crushed me to his chest, my rigidity melted away. Being in his strong embrace wasn't half-bad.

"Nothing is going to happen to me." He nuzzled my hair. "Right now your place is with your B&B. Flora's blood pressure will skyrocket if their pride and joy goes downhill because nobody stepped in. I know how much you love them, so don't pretend like it doesn't matter. It does."

I pulled away to see his face. "I can go with you, you know. Another few hours away from the B&B isn't going to hurt anything."

"Maybe not. But if an auction like this is what got you into trouble the first time, then it makes sense to send someone in your place. I can't think of a better person than a lawyer. Not only that, if this invitation went out to enough people, they'll be stupid to try anything with that many people around."

I hoped he was right about that. For his sake more than mine.

Running this place by myself made me appreciate the Hills more than ever. Flora had a list of emergency phone numbers with notes listed by each of them in case something happened. I was sure she'd never expected anything like this, but who would argue about it being an emergency?

We even worked out a schedule for the next couple of days. After that, I placed a call to the cleaning service to do the guest bedrooms and handle the laundry. The college freshman, Heidi, took care of all of the secretarial tasks, including booking outings with specialized tour companies and more reservations that came through.

Even with all of the help, the B&B took me to task. I thought about putting in an elevator for all the trips I made back and forth, climbing up those stairs. Not to mention one of the guests spilled a bottle of wine on the carpet and wanted me to clean it up or their entire world would come crashing to a halt. An hour later, they dropped chocolate-covered strawberries and whipped cream in bed. Another guest cranked up the TV, which turned his door into my punching bag for two hours straight, yelling for him to lower the volume. Even the other guests advocated for me to throw the jerk out. Then there was the older couple who didn't know how to work anything including the shower, the television, the alarm clock and their automatic coffee maker. One would think they shouldn't give a rat's ass about coffee at eleven o'clock, but they wanted to be prepared for tomorrow morning.

I made my first real managerial decision. Of the group we had, the last guest was scheduled to leave in three days. After that, no more guests. I didn't want another person hurt under my roof until my chaos was resolved. It was time both Charles and Flora took a few days off too.

The inn's guests kept me hopping without any hopes of calling Matt. Well, that wasn't going to work for me. I demanded the time by slamming the door to my office and picking up the phone. Unfortunately, he had left three messages on the answering service, asking me to call him back. I tried twice, but his cell-phone service tossed me into his voice mail. According to his message, he couldn't find the auction that was going down in Nashua as the fax had indicated. Too much of it was burnt to get the correct address, other than the street name.

I left a message for him to call my room directly when he arrived at the front door so I could let him in without waking up the house. The phone rang about an hour later. I dropped my John Saul book on the nightstand and picked up the receiver.

"It's a bust," Matt said. "Don't get me wrong. They've got some pretty nice merchandise here. Want me to pick you something up?"

I smiled. "See if you can find me a twenty-four-karat diamond ring and I'll upgrade your room."

He chuckled. "What? I can't spend the night with you again? Or is that the upgrade?"

"No. Your upgrade is from the second floor to the third."

He laughed. "Just for that, I'll bid on that sixteenth of a karat ring."

I licked my tongue at the phone. "Are you going to tell me what happened once you found the place or do I guess?"

He sighed. "I told the guy at the door that I was representing you. Anything they had to say to you, they had to talk to me first."

"Wow. That's brave of you."

"Don't pick. Anyway, he stepped aside and let me in. He also said it would be a while before someone spoke to me and that I should enjoy the show." He paused. "Hm. Looks like they're stalking me again. Trying to figure me out."

"What?" I sat up. "Get the hell out of there! What's wrong with you?"

"Relax. If they wanted to try something, they would've by now. And if they're smart, they're using someone who's good with auras to scan everyone coming through the door. I'm pretty sure they know what I am by now."

"And that means?"

"They know not to mess with one of Parry's werewolves. While he might be a bastard in every sense of the word, he's also a psychopath. It works in our favor in situations like this."

"Then the Lennors probably aren't going to talk to you. Think about it. They're waiting you out. Not only that, but it's the Garridans we want. Not these guys. Supposed they're *too* scared to talk to you?"

As much as I hated to think about it, his trip to Nashua had backfired. They didn't want Matt, they wanted me. Whether or not they had information to share, we'd never know unless I made an appearance. Come tomorrow, I just might have to do that.

"Maybe you're right. So, how are things going at the inn? People running you ragged yet?"

"What do you have remote viewing or something?"

He laughed. "Call it a guess."

"Um...there *is* something." I folded my arm, the one holding the phone, and leaned back in a stack of pillows. "Monica called. They moved my court date. It's two weeks away."

"Damn," Matt muttered. "You still have your journal?"

"Yeah. Why?"

"Print me out a copy. I want to know everything that's happened since you've been back. I'm pretty sure Monica will do her job, but..."

"It's more important that I get the charges completely dropped than spend even one night in jail."

"Something like that. Look, I'll be there soon. Okay?"

"Okay."

I understood his sense of urgency now more than ever. If he didn't want me in jail, the same might be true of Gamboldt. Busted memory or not, I knew things about him that he couldn't afford to leak out. He'd use everything in his arsenal to get me back. Which meant, more pressure on my shoulders to bring this to a close. I had two weeks to do it, which wasn't nearly enough.

After hanging up with Matt, I headed downstairs to the office and found the extra copy of my computer journal. I sent it to the printer, and just to be on the safe side, I forwarded a copy to Matt's email address. Luz had taught me that it paid off.

Once I finished, I turned out the light and started out the door.

A force threw me backward into the room. I crashed into the two chairs before slamming into the desk. Pain pierced my skull and twinkling stars flooded my vision. Damn that hurt. Using the surface of the desk as leverage, I staggered to my feet.

An elderly gentleman, one of the guests, stepped into the

room with a smirk on his face.

"What the hell?" I tripped over my feet with the first step.

"You should've declared the inn closed sooner." The man waved his hand over his shoulder. The door closed behind him. "My sincerest apologies regarding your innkeeper. A friend of Mr. Gamboldt had cursed anything associated with the Lennors from showing up on your property. I bet Brody's so-called auction was to warn you about us. That would've confused you and made things harder than they need to be. Besides, Mr. Gamboldt has been worried about you."

"You son of a bitch." I backed into a bookcase with my heart pounding in panic mode. "Who the hell are you?"

Shaking his head, he smiled. "I'm Mr. Gamboldt's butler, Thomas. Since the Garridans want to wash their hands of this, I've come to take you home."

The screen saver went black, putting the two of us alone in the dark. A sliver of light shone through the end of the closed curtain. If that was meant to scare me, he needed another gimmick.

My eyes came to life. I made out the pieces of the broken chair and the smooth edge of the desk. My ears opened up to the surroundings and the noises beyond the walls. Outside, crickets chirped and a car sped down the street. A creak from somewhere above my head caught my ear's attention. I looked to the ceiling, listening carefully to pinpoint the sound while my gaze picked out all of the divots on the surface.

When I brought my attention back to the rest of the room, Thomas stood inches from me. When I lifted my arm to defend myself, everything went black. Unconsciousness hit me hard.

Chapter Twenty-Two

Hot damn. What a set. Ever since I got back from vacation, the guys have been dropping money left and right. Not to mention the new thongs that Dottie had given me with the tassels along the front worked wonders.

I made my way back to the dressing room flipping each of the ones and fives between my fingers. I loved the slick surface of a crisp ten-dollar bill. A few of those had ended up in my G-string tonight. As the amount increased, my heart tripled in beats. A huge smile dug into my cheeks. Some of the fools even gave me a little extra for my comeback.

The stories ranged from me being sick to a family emergency. What a bunch of dumb fucks. Like Paul said, I'd just needed a little time was all. Stripping is a tough business. Eventually, you get burnt out just like you would with any job.

Too bad I couldn't remember a damn thing about it. According to Paul, my clumsy ass passed out while sporting a 104-degree fever. Thank God, it wasn't during one of my sets. The doc said it had hiked up to 105 degrees and scared the shit out of everybody. He said my amnesia was due to the fever. I began throwing fits and running down the street screaming like a fucked-up whore on a bad acid trip. With all the kickboxing I had learned from TV, I kicked a couple of asses and worked my way down to Mexico. Paul and Sammy came after me. Was that sweet of them or what?

Whatever I'd done during my rampage, it had scared Paul into keeping a damn good eye on me these days. Shit, I could hardly take a pee break without his cowboy ass following me around and stuff. That was only half of the new changes.

A mandate had come down on high from the pimp daddy

himself, Robert Gamboldt. He'd spoken to Dottie about sending me to another club in Albuquerque for safekeeping. Shoot, if he planned to send me to New Mexico, then I wanted a little cash in my hands first. I must have fucked up something bad on my fever trip for Robert to send me out of the state. I had at least a week left for them to get things ready for me, so I wanted to rake up as many dead presidents as possible because it might take a while for those Albuquerque pussies to warm up to a new face. A stripper has to eat too, you know.

I bumped open the dressing room door with my hip.

"Hey, Keisha." Several of the girls acknowledged me in unison with either a waving hand or nod of the head.

"How did your set go, girl?" Candy gave me a high-five.

"That motherfucker was off the chain." I scanned the room and noticed that she and several other girls were dressed alike with the feathers mounted on top of their heads, gobs of makeup and glitter on their cheeks and eyes, and *Moulin Rouge* beaded corsets. "You guys finally got the Vegas showgirl act together? Deeeee-ammmm!"

"Oh yeah." Elaine cupped my shoulders and smacked a kiss on my cheek. She leaned her five-nine frame forward and hugged me tight. "I wished you had called me, little sister. You know good and well that half of us would've gone after you. We don't leave a team member behind."

Tiffany snorted and adjusted her bright red lipstick. "Speak for yourself. I don't care what any of you say. She's not one of us. Ain't nothing but a place-filler as far as I'm concerned."

I narrowed my eyes on her. "At least you're putting the lipstick on the right cunt lips."

Tiffany was second-in-command because she "commanded" more money than anyone else on stage. She was the bar's main draw. Ever since my tips started catching up to hers, the slut had been hassling me at every turn. Nothing I did was good enough for that silicone D-cup bitch. *I'd give anything to tear that black ponytail from her head. Maybe punch out her green eyes while I'm at it.*

"Ignore her." Elaine guided me to my seat on the other side of the dressing room. She took the stool next to mine and smiled. "You sure you're all right, sweetie? You've...you've change since you've been back."

"Really? How so?"

She shrugged. "You're acting...I don't know. Weird, maybe?" She must have read something on my face because she leaned closer and gripped my hand. Her long fingernails dug my skin. "Don't get me wrong or nothing. I saw your first set and it was great. But it took you until the third set to really loosen up. You're usually on the ball the minute your foot hits the stage. The only reason why I bring it up is because Paul's been watching too. You know he's gonna ask. Not to mention, I'm sensing something strange about you. Like you've been living another life or something."

"Girl, please. Use that psychic bullshit on those others fools 'cause I'm not paying for that reading." I turned on my stool, keeping my upper body between the vertical lights lining the mirror. "Anyway, it's only because I've missed a month of work. It takes some time to get back into the swing of my jiggly things."

She giggled. "Honey, if you wanted some PTO, you could've put in for it. You've worked here more than six months as both a bouncer and a stripper. Trust me, you had the time."

"Are you shitting me? I probably used all that up with sick time alone. Even after I got back, that damn bug kept me down for the last three days. I don't even remember you visiting me."

Elaine turned to the mirror and touched up her lipstick. "I still don't get why Paul wants you in New Mexico. It's not like you're...you know. Like the rest of us. You can't read minds and stuff or see the future. Ain't no way you can really blackmail anyone. Besides, it won't hurt to keep someone who's somewhat normal around."

I didn't know what I had walked into when I came here all those months ago. Actually, I didn't walk into anything. I remembered sitting at the back of the bar, watching the girls shake and swing their asses on stage. I couldn't recall how I had gotten there, but Dottie sat next to me and said I should watch and take some notes. After all, I couldn't stay unless I found a way to earn my keep. Not only did the girls strip, but they did other things on the side like psychic readings and stuff. Robert rented out their services for big parties that usually involved really important people. They'd come back with presents and gifts and all sorts of things. I couldn't go because I wasn't special like that.

Well...not exactly.

I earned my keep as a bouncer at first because I had beaten up a couple of the guys for getting rowdy with the girls. It hyped up the crowd to see a little thing like me whoop some manly ass. Patrons started handing me tens and twenties without my having to drop a stitch of clothes. After that, Paul had the girls teach me how to pole dance because he thought it would bring in more money. It did. That was why I was such a threat to Tiffany without having one ounce of silicone plumping my tits.

"Seriously." Elaine turned her attention to the mirror and began dabbing her nose with face powder. "What the hell is in Albuquerque anyway?"

I shrugged. "Whatever I did on the other side of the border, it might get back to Robert. You know how he is about things coming back to him and threatening his other businesses on the side. Trust me, Elaine, this is for the best. I'm sure of it."

I knew that was a lie before it left my mouth. A nagging feeling said there was more to my life than this. In what previous life, I wondered, did I allow someone to have this kind of control over me? Unfortunately, I had trouble recalling a good part of those days. My shit-for-brains drew a blank at anything that might have happened to me before Trixie's. For now, it didn't matter. Until I got my fucked-up finances together to pursue other things, I'd hang around this joint and do what I did best. Dance my ass off.

"I know. It's just that...I'm gonna miss you, hon."

"And you think I won't miss you?" I smiled.

The door opened.

Paul entered with the enthusiasm of a five-year-old being dragged off to church. Even his light brown hair and goatee looked a little ragged around the edges. Most guys would perk up if they entered a dressing room full of strippers. Not Paul. He had seen enough naked asses during his ten-year stint to know that they all shared the same purpose. Making money.

He checked his watch and shouted, "Vegas Bitches, you're on next. Get your shit together and let's go. And make sure you guys hit up the banker in the back corner wearing the big rock on his ring finger. I want a good reading on him because we're doing a private party for him tomorrow."

Several, including Elaine, leaped off their stools and joined the clicking heels heading for the door. As always, whenever we had multi-girl acts, women whined about misplacing parts of their costumes or they accidentally messed up their makeup. The cursing started seconds later as two of them forgot something that made their showgirl outfits complete. With it being Paul's job to corral the cows, the women knew he meant business and wouldn't leave until everyone trickled out the door.

He turned his attention on me. "Keisha, you're on bouncer detail with Theo and Sammy for the rest of the night. Brad called in sick."

Elaine snorted. "If that pussy calls in sick one more time, you might as well put her on permanent detail with them."

"Don't you have somewhere to be?"

Pouting, she grabbed her feathered headgear. Leaning forward, Elaine planted a kiss on my cheek and left the room.

With all the girls gone, Paul sauntered into the dressing room and stood behind me. He leaned close, putting his hand on the counter and blocking me on one side. "You all right?"

"Fine." I turned a bottle of astringent up on a cotton ball and began cleaning my makeup. "A little tired, maybe."

"Then I'll get Jimbo to whip you up a cup of coffee. Maybe a sandwich too, since you're looking a little thin these days. No more stage. Got it?"

"Whatever." I tossed the spent cotton ball and reached for another. The strong astringent clawed the inside lining of my nose. I couldn't recall the last time I was this fucking sensitive.

Paul pulled away and leaned his backside against Elaine's makeup station. He rubbed his goatee. "I just got off the phone with Patty in New Mexico. It's set. You're done at the end of the week. Dottie redid the schedule, so you're going to Jasper's Jungle to dance the stage there. It's a little smaller, but it has a nice crowd. When the ski season opens, things will really rock."

I stared at him. "Where the hell does Robert get the names for the bars? Couldn't he come up with something more original like the Crescent Inn Saloon?"

Paul's eyes enlarged. A swallow bobbled his Adam's apple.

Now why would a name like that have such an effect on him? After all, it was just a name. The way his skin had paled, you'd think it was his mother's name.

His eyes narrowed, scrutinizing me again. "You sure you're feeling okay?"

I shook my head before cleaning the last of the makeup off my face. "You're weird, you know that? You must be sucking too much of Amelia's sour patch juice." A few days ago, three of us had exited through the staff-only door to find his face buried in her carpet in the flatbed of his truck.

"Hey, I'm asking the questions here, Keish. I need to know if you're okay."

"I'm fine! Just a little tired because I did three goddamn sets tonight and now you're asking me to bounce people out of a bar. How the hell do you think I feel? Given the choice, I'd rather dance one and you leave me the hell alone."

Crossing his arms over his chest. "You sure about that one last set?"

"If I have to say it again, I'm going to tear your damn ears off and use them as a megaphone."

"Okay then. You're up right after LaRonda. I'll tell Sammy to cover your post. Although I'm sure there's something else he'd prefer to cover." Paul winked before leaving the room.

Boy, did I hate that man sometimes.

Although I adored Sammy to pieces, something must have happened during my bad trip that put out the fire in my heart for him. Then again, I wouldn't call it fire, exactly. The sex was good and that was about it. Nevertheless, I felt as though I had left a piece of my heart with someone else in Mexico.

Chapter Twenty-Three

Come one in the morning, I got my second wind. Once I cleared it through Paul, I put on my cowgirl outfit and waited just behind the stage, clutching the red velvet curtain. More money more money more money.

Jubilant applause welcomed me onto the runway. Being the only strip bar for a hundred miles, dozens of salivating guys crowded around the stage while those less interested continued with their pool game on the far side of the bar. Others hollered from tables, flapping their money in the air, knowing I hadn't done anything yet. It never failed. A woman didn't have to do much to get these dipshits turned on. That included the middle-aged bastard to the far left of the stage with his hand stuck down the front of his pants, massaging his bulge.

Note to self: if he touches me, sanitize the spot with bleach before going to bed. That was assuming I didn't beat the hell out of him first. That motherfucker had better be dropping a twenty in my G-string or I'd break his arm.

Maggie finished picking pieces of her mermaid outfit off the stage before scampering away. She gave me a high-five and slipped behind the curtain. I planted my feet in front of the pole, waiting for my music.

Closing my eyes, I went into my badass persona and masked my face with a stolid gaze. When Cher's "Just Like Jesse James" piped through the speakers, I went into action. The black chaps would go first, but I had to time it right or all of my clothes might be on the floor by the middle of the song. As a teaser, I whirled around and bent over with the bottom of my ass cheeks flapping in the breeze from my Daisy Duke shorts. Just like clockwork, the crowd went wide. The sick bastards practically begged me to take their money for a closeup. Taking my time, I removed the belt with the fake guns first. A quick wink and more bills came out.

Near the back of the room, my eyes met Sammy standing at the corner of the bar. A huge grin plastered his face. Shaking his head, he lowered it. He was the first to critique my cowgirl routine and enjoyed every slobbering minute of it. When we started showing interest in each other, I'd warned him that he'd never make me his little mulatto cowgirl. He still hadn't, but I owed him this much for chasing me down after someone slipped a mad-dog mickey in my drink and had me acting a feverish fool in Mexico.

About two minutes into the song, it was time for the shorts to go. The moment I let them slide down my legs with my ass bent to the crowd a second time, the dumb-fuck perverts whistled a second wind of wild wolf calls.

The folded money hanging off the straps made my thong look more like the infamous banana skirt. Halfway through my number, I slipped some of the bills out, bent over and dropped my stash in my boot. Numerous guys showed their appreciation in the form of more five, tens and several twenties.

Jerk-off at the far left of the stage waved a twenty-dollar bill at me. Fuck. I didn't want to take that bastard's money. Unfortunately, the last guy I skipped over caused the bar more problems than necessary.

I danced to where he sat, leaned forward to make sure the bastard got a glimpse of the small breasts hiding behind my leather crop-top vest. Of course, his bloodshot eyes zeroed in on his target. When his hand reached forward, I pulled back and shook my head, keeping my smile in place. Dropping to all fours, I crawled in front of him, leaving the spot above my right hip open for him to insert the cash. A string of drool slipped down his chin.

What a nasty fuck. If this guy didn't get the torture over and done with, I'd pitch him out of the bar myself.

When his rough finger slid between my skin and the elastic thong, I turned my head to keep from gagging.

"Get your hands off her or I'll beat your ass into the next act."

Hold on. That didn't sound like Sammy.

Rotating my head to the jerk-off, my eyes traveled to

another man standing beside him. He had bushy eyebrows with a few wiry grays dotting his temples. From the stout chest, thick arms, and the long fingers he had wrapped around the jerk-off's neck, he looked like he meant every word of his threat. Very few wrinkles marred his face and his barely noticeable crow's feet hung in the corners of his eyes. Then again, it could've been the intensity in his face playing tricks on me. Those frown lines alone were deep enough to plant a garden on his forehead.

Another man came up to the other side of the jerk-off. He had wavy black hair, dark-tanned skin and dark eyes. Something about his face reminded me of a rich playboy—not that I recalled ever meeting any. He looked like the type who had put on muscle just to fill out his clothes. His white tee shirt with faded jeans and a gleaming silver buckle on the front made him fit in around here, but the shiny black cowboy boots sold him out. They were too new to imply he was a local. This dry desert land would've roughed them up by now. Both of them were out-of-towners and out of their league.

Their scents touched my nose.

Images of running through loamy woods, smelling of fresh pine after a light rainfall, flooded my senses. They scared the hell out of me, especially the rich playboy. His powerful scent flooded my mind with scenes of wolf packs hunting in the woods and devouring their prey. Gunshots rang out in my head and the wolves went down. More wolves converged on the scene and attacked the ones consuming the fresh meat. A severed human hand flopped onto the ground. One pack of wolves attacked the other ones while they tried to dine on human flesh.

I yanked my thoughts from the horrific images. They left me more nauseated than the jerk-off massaging his Vienna sausage. One look at the playboy and our gazes met. There was something so primal and fearsome behind his eyes that my queasiness turned to panic saturating my veins and flooding my senses.

"You promised me you wouldn't cause another scene, Avery." The playboy stared a warning at his friend.

"Fuck off, Dane." Avery pointed at the jerk-off. "You can't expect me to sit back and watch another piece of shit like this degrade my little girl."

"Little girl?" I remained stuck in my crawl pose, too busy

and too frightened to move. "Dane?"

Why would they say that? I knew nothing about these people and yet...something. My conscience went to war inside me. They were figments of my dreams that had come to life. There was no way they were real. Unfortunately, my gut said otherwise. I knew these men, even though they scared the hell out of me.

"Hey!" Someone shouted from the other side of the stage. "What the hell's going on with the show?"

"Yeah, man," another chimed in. "I paid good money to see the whore dance."

"Whore?" Avery whipped around. Dane placed a hand on his friend's shoulder that did nothing to stop Avery's mouth. "Motherfucker, that's my daughter you're talking about. I'll whoop your ass across this stage."

"Seet yer ass down, ya In-jin!" This came from one of the tables in the middle of the floor.

"Oh, *hell* no. You just earned yourself a meeting with my totem pole."

Avery flipped several tables to get to the man who had opened his mouth. The waitresses shrieked and glasses shattered into thousands of pieces. He went through the bar-room floor like a person walking through a wheat field, pushing tables and chairs like pieces of straw. I've seen strength before, but this guy had plow power backing him.

Just like me.

I shook the thought from my head.

Another man jumped on his back. Avery reached around and snatched up a handful of hair. He peeled the guy off and slammed a fist across his jaw. The man stumbled backward and crashed into a table. More shrieks and more busted glasses.

When he got to the guy who had slandered me, Avery yanked him out of the seat, leaving his legs to dangle underneath him. He whipped the man around and sent him flying into a nearby wall. Pictures and rusted horseshoes fell to the floor.

Before Avery could turn his back, a full-blown bar fight broke out. Chairs, tables, glasses and people went flying throughout the saloon. I remained on the stage, too exhilarated by the brawl to move. It wasn't every day someone fought over little ol' me. Ain't no way in hell I'd miss this.

Sammy grabbed my hand. "Come on, sweetheart. I need to get you out of here."

Dane snagged his forearm. "She's not going with you."

Sammy yanked away. He came up fast with a fist, but Dane caught the curled fingers and did a quick move that locked Sammy's hand behind his back.

"Don't you dare." I leaped off the stage.

Going into my kickboxing stance, I delivered a roundhouse kick across Dane's right cheek. He stumbled backward and loosened up on my bouncer boyfriend.

"Come on!" Sammy waved me to him.

Together, we worked our way through the rumble of flying beer mugs and smashed chairs.

A heavy weight tackled the two of us to the sticky floor. I got to my feet and started again. However, I noticed Sammy wasn't at my side. Turning around, I found him on the floor with Dane perched on his back. The stranger gave me a look that wavered between rage and confusion.

I froze. Something in the look warned me to stay put and my instincts demanded I listen.

Rough hands grabbed me from behind. I bucked and kicked as they pulled me backward through the crazed melee. No matter how much I kicked and screamed, he wasn't letting go. When he stopped, I tried to use the chance to run. No such luck. The motherfucker tossed me over his shoulder like an old rug.

Dane got to his feet and whirled Sammy around. He slugged my cowboy hard enough to knock him unconscious and lifted him into a fireman's carry.

Avery and I weren't the only ones who had amazing strength. Speaking of which, the scent alone gave away the person toting me out of the bar. It was Avery.

Two sheriff's cars skidded across the gravel parking lot with sirens squealing, and red and blue lights reflected off the front windows and door of Trixie's.

My kicking and screaming continued until that son-of-a-bitch Avery dumped me on the ground and raised his hands over his head. Damn, that hurt. I aimed my scowl at the no-good son of a whore for treating me like that. It was no wonder I had run away from home. No matter what, I sure as hell wasn't going back.

Max and Jethro leaped out of one car while Cy and Loni got out of the other. All four lawmen and lawwoman had their guns drawn. Sad to say, I knew them by name because they frequented the bar. It didn't matter that Max had a girlfriend and five kids under the age of eight or that Jethro and Cy each had a wife and three kids between them. Even Loni enjoyed an off-duty drink while watching her skank-ho girlfriend, Pamela, dance. Still, the Battle Rose police department wasn't complete without all-brawn-and-no-brains Johnny.

Speaking of which, I began to wonder where he was.

The front door slammed open and a body stumbled backward across the stoop. The heel of his boot clipped a rock the wrong way and the cowboy landed on his ass.

He spat out his toothpick along with a clog of blood. "Goddamn bastard."

That answered my question. That cheap chump must've sat in the background where I couldn't see his behind. If I had, I'd probably tell his five-foot girlfriend, Effie, so that he'd spend the rest of the week with his head ducked low from the black eye she'd give him. The last time that happened, he was the joke of the town.

Fury burned Johnny's eyes as he hauled himself to one knee, irate enough to go for another round.

"Ease up, part-nah." Sheriff Max steadied Johnny by the arm. "Are you a drunk or an off-duty deputy right now?"

Again, Johnny spat on the curb. "Shoot. I'm a deputy."

"Good. Then stand your ass up and fall in line or you'll fall on the wrong side of the line. I ain't got no time to be disciplining my own people when we've got enough trouble as it is."

And just like that, the punk got off. As for the rest of us, we were going to jail.

Chapter Twenty-Four

Locked up like a common criminal. Who would've thought this shit? All because those freaks had to start a bar fight.

I sat on a cold bench while two other strippers paced around our cell. Bonnie was caught cracking a glass over someone's head while Donella started helping herself to a few wallets during the fight. As for me, I was trying to flee the scene of a crime in their eyes. Those crazy bastards forgot to notice my thong-clad ass slung over someone else's shoulder at the time.

Welcome to the fools of the Battle Rose Sheriff's Department. Barney Fife would've looked like the Chief of Police compared to these morons.

A pair of keys rattled with each footstep clapping down the hall. Loni appeared in front of our cell. She continued to jumble the ring of keys in her hand until she found the right one and used it to pierce the lock.

A jail in the twentieth century should have better technology. But in this backward town, they were lucky to have four deputies and one sheriff. Ironically, they made sure there were enough cells to go around, including gender-specific wings.

Loni unlocked the door and slid it back on the track. The other two strippers leaped to their feet mumbling their relief.

She held a hand up and stopped them. Her index finger turned to me. "You. Out."

"Me?" My face crooked with confusion. "Why not—"

"Look, Keisha. I don't have time to give you a blow-by-blow, okay? You're free to go."

Donella snorted. "I bet she wants a blow all right."

"Shut up, skank!" Loni cracked her baton against the bars. "Any more lip, and I'll make sure your stay is more uncomfortable than it is now. Let's go, Keisha. I ain't got all night."

No matter how disgusting that sounded, Donella was right. If Loni thought I'd do her in exchange for letting me out of jail, she might as well throw my ass in solitary confinement. That bitch wasn't getting anything from me.

I continued down the hall, walking close to the wall while keeping an eye over my shoulder. Although I doubted Loni would do anything, many of the girls had returned to the bar in the past with stories of how they got their tickets reduced to warnings thanks to her. Given the disgusting choices, I'd just pay my fine or do my time—thank you very much.

I waited for Loni to unlock the gate at the end of the hall. While I kept my eyes on her short, curly hair, she never wavered from her duty. However, she needed her stripping-ho to dye those gray roots or they might take over the rest of her blond curls.

I came to a dead stop in the main office. Standing behind the spring-loaded gate was a gorgeous hunk with ink-black hair. But even with his back to me and wearing a pair of tight jeans and a dark gray tee, I knew he wasn't from around these parts just like those freaks who had tried to kidnap me. This guy looked too clean and smelled of sophistication. In fact, he smelled rather scrumptious. His wild scent reminded me of running through the woods too, even howling at the moon. I bet he was a real animal in bed. Heaven knows, I'd love to test-drive his stick.

When he turned and smiled, his dimples pierced me like a shot to the chest. His eyes were dark and endless like a mysterious black hole. Now I understood the meaning of getting lost in someone's eyes. The high cheekbones and toned muscle woven around his upper arms nearly did my thirsty libido in. Never in my life had anyone made me this horny. Not even that little cutie pie, Sammy.

Still, I needed to play this up right. For all I knew, those rumors about one of the cops running a brothel out of this place were true. With this out-of-towner stepping in here, they probably wanted to cut him some sort of deal.

"What's going on?" I planted my feet on the floor and folded my arms over my chest.

"You're free to go." Max flipped through papers on his desk without bothering to look up. "Loni, go ahead and return her belongings."

The female deputy snickered. "What belongings? She came in her one strap of clothing shy of a birthday suit."

Boy, would I love to give something to "suit" that bitch. Like a black eye. Since they were letting me go, I figured it was best to play nice. But that didn't stop me from eyeballing the heifer.

Five minutes later, I didn't bother with goodbyes. I walked my behind out of the sheriff's station and across the parking lot. I stopped before the road and stuck my thumb out. These losers knew me well enough to give me a lift, although I didn't trust them to not finger the goods. I just prayed it was by someone who'd give me a ride back to my place and not theirs. The only tricks I'd turned were the ones on stage in front of a crowd. I wasn't about to start something new on the side.

"Where are you going?" The cute guy had followed me out of the station and stared. "You're free to go and you want to hitchhike back to town? Are you nuts?"

I turned, gravel cracking under my heeled feet. "Say again?"

He pointed at a silver car parked on the side of the building. "That way. Hell, Lex, you're lucky I remembered where to find you."

This man must have smoked himself a big one on his way here. "I ain't goin' with you, man."

"Excuse me?"

"You heard me. I ain't goin' nowhere with some guy I don't know. So while I appreciate you gettin' me out of the jail, my thanks is all you'll be gettin' tonight."

The cutie hunk tilted his head as he stalked toward me. A handsome smile triggered the dimples in his cheeks. My heart swooned again. Hell, it tripped over itself just looking at him.

He rolled his eyes. "We don't have time for this. We have to go."

"I said I'm not going anywhere with you. Do I have to spell it out?"

"No. I get it...Keisha."

The man launched himself at me. I kicked and barely got off a scream when his hand clamped down on my mouth. He lifted me off my feet and hurried toward his car.

I couldn't believe this shit. Here I was right out in the parking lot of the sheriff's station getting kidnapped. Who would've thought? And if I expected those idiots behind the brick wall to give me a hand, I doubted they'd halt their doughnut break to give a damn.

The man threw me against the side of his car. I took that as an invitation to run.

He snagged my arm. Before I had a chance to duck, he had his fist wound back, paused like he had second thoughts and plowed straight into my face. Pain seared my cheek before darkness dropped around me.

I bolted awake.

Rope seized my wrists and legs, holding me in place on a bed. The harder I pulled, the more they dug into my flesh. Lifting my head, I noticed some sort of wraparound dress on me. That fucker must have fitted me in it and tied it off at the side above my right hip. How gentlemanly of him. I moved a tad, and felt a pair of silk underwear sliding against the material.

What the fuck? Underwear too?

Where this should've been a room, it opened up to the rest of a cabin with a log railing separating my loft area from the lower floor. Looking between my bound ankles and the spokes of the banister, I made out a television sitting on top of a stand. There was an opening on the side where the banister angled downward from the loft. Farther into the room, I noticed a seating area with a fireplace, a front door and a kitchen on the other side. Cherry wood beams spanned the ceiling with more lining the walls.

A door opened. Wind gusted into the cabin, fanning the curtains and loose papers throughout the room. I lifted my head higher to see who had entered. Darkness and crickets gave me a good idea of how late—or early—it was.

"You awake?" The voice came from somewhere downstairs.

I laid my head on the pillow and stared at the ceiling, refusing to answer him. He could kiss my biracial ass.

Footfalls thudded up the stairs. The man's head bobbed into view. His dimpled grin didn't melt me this time. Nothing about his smile was enough to wipe the anger out of me.

"You're pissed." He placed a grocery sack on the

nightstand. "We're going to be here a while, so I bought some soap, deodorant and things like that. I hope you're not picky."

"You sick fuck. You can't keep me here."

"Now that's a change in language." He clicked his tongue and shook his head. "I don't know what it took for you to come back to your senses the first time, but I plan to stick it out until they make another appearance."

"I *am* back to my senses, you jackass. You're the one who's out of them."

The mystery guy slid his fingers around my wrist, checking my rope burns. His finger continued to slide across my skin. What should've taken seconds felt more like minutes with his baby-soft touch. Who would've thought a full-grown man had the skin of a newborn? It made no sense.

Hovering over me, he leaned across and did the same to the other hand. I almost lifted my hand to help him, but I changed my mind and made it look like I didn't want him touching me. It certainly wasn't hard to pull off.

His eyes panned from the ropes to my face. A smile bowed his lips. "I care about you. A lot. If I didn't, I wouldn't be here now."

Perhaps, it was time to use a little female-coochie magic. A smirk slipped onto my face. I began squirming in a slow, sultry way like the girls had taught me how to do on the pole. A small moan left my mouth. My neck lifted, exposing my flesh to him, offering it up as an appetizer.

The guy licked his lips. His eye traveled from my throat to the coned tips of my nipples poking through the dress.

I bet this guy was as hard as a rock. Just like all of the other suckers, he was mine. "What's your name, Sugar Daddy?"

He swallowed, then took a deep breath before he opened his mouth. "You know my name. It's Matt."

"Mmmmmm. Mine's Keisha. Would you like a piece of candy, little boy?" I pushed my hip up as far as possible with my legs and hands bound. Guys usually nodded their stupid heads like greedy-ass puppies. Then they'd drop an easy ten or twenty between my G-string. This fool was no different.

Matt's hand traveled up my side before sliding down to my hip. A finger slid just over the waistband of my red silk underwear. I had to admit, the guy had taste. He lowered his body to mine, hovering over me. His hardness pressed into the side of my thigh.

His cheek brushed close enough to mine that I thought about biting off his ear to get his attention. Instead, I offered up my tongue along his earlobe. Good Lord was this bastard soft. It wasn't just his hands, but every inch of his body. On the flipside of that, I sensed wilderness about him. The way his hands traveled along my front, feeling me up, he had awakened something feral inside me, desperate to break out. He gripped my clothes as if to tear them apart, but uncurled his fingers and backed off. Why he didn't go for it, I didn't know. This man was pure animal. I just needed to drag it out of his sorry ass.

"It's all yours, baby." I continued my seductive squirm underneath him. "You know you want a taste. It's like slicking your tongue around a piece of taffy. Softening it up until you can jab it with a quick lick. The candy shop is open and waiting for its first customer of the evening."

The drunken lust that had filled his eyes drained out. He lifted his head to me and narrowed his gaze. Instead of finishing, he crawled backward off the bed.

"What the hell?" I smiled. "You lose your nerve or something?"

"No." Matt straightened the front of his packed jeans before turning his back on me and starting down the stairs.

"Hey, man!" Panic set in. Dammit, I'd been close to getting him to loosen up these ropes. "Where ya goin'?"

The back of his head stopped bobbing halfway down. He kept his back to me. "As tempting as it is, I don't want *you*. I want my Alexa back."

"Alexa?" I laughed. "Who the hell is that? I bet that tramp-bitch can't measure up to this."

"She doesn't have to, to get my attention."

He lifted his head over his shoulder. The wilds that flooded his demeanor had turned to something dangerous like a predatory lion. There wasn't anything sexual about it. This had more to do with rage. The maniac sent a shiver through me.

"I want the Alexa I know," he seethed. "I'd rather have her turn me down than some skeezer who uses sex to get the upper hand. Sorry to disappoint you."

Why that no good, son of— "Fuck you, limp dick. You stupid, whiny boy scout—get the hell out of here. I don't fucking need you."

I yanked and pulled on the ropes. It pissed me off that I couldn't break free to beat the shit out of him. Who did he think he was to call me a tramp-whore? Though they weren't his words, he meant it in those terms.

"Don't bother." He was out of sight at this point. "I've wrapped those ropes around rails and the legs several times. That means it'll take more strength than you have to break out of them. So you might as well save yourself the rope burns."

I screamed and ranted, throwing my head back in the pillows and pulling with all my might. Those fucking ropes wouldn't budge worth shit. Hell, I'd dislocate my arms if I knew it would free me. Then once I got free, I'd beat down the mother-worthless-fucker just like I had some of the drunks in the bar. I was the best damn stripper in the county. Everyone knew it, even that fucking cunt Tiffany.

The door opened and slammed closed. A few minutes later, a howl broke out in the woods. A slit in the curtain provided just enough room for light from part of the moon to spill across my bed.

I didn't like being tied to a bed when the only sound of life was the wind rustling the trees outside. That howl left me thinking that something evil waited just beyond those walls and I had no way of defending myself if someone or something broke in here. Damn.

Chapter Twenty-Five

Matt never came back. He pretty much disappeared most of the night and left me to pinch off my bladder. Fucking jerk.

Just before dawn, the front door of the cabin cracked open. My eyelids parted in time to see the top of his head come through the entryway. When the door closed, I relaxed on the pillow. If he wanted to talk, then he had best buy himself a parrot to answer back.

Constant tossing in my sleep and an ache declaring war across my forehead had left me worn out. Something was wrong. My fiery anger had disappeared. I stopped caring and all I seemed to want to do was sleep. Sweat glued my hair to my head and more drenched my back and armpits. My arms and legs ached from the ropes with the simplest toss or turn. Every part of my body hurt. Even my teeth.

Footfalls thumped up the steps. Matt had his arms raised above his head, letting a T-shirt slip over the span of muscles throughout his chest and cobblestone stomach. I turned my attention back to the ceiling before he caught me peeking. He didn't need to know I cared because I didn't.

Matt stopped on the side of the bed. He blinked. His nose wrinkled with a whiff. "Shit."

"Did not! I might be pissed at you, but not enough let you change my underwear." Damn. So much for not talking.

"That's not what I meant." He lowered himself to the mattress and pressed the back of his hand to my forehead. "You're feverish. You probably caught a bug or something."

"Well, if it's not too much trouble, can I *bug* you to let me go to the bathroom? Five more minutes and your worst nightmare will come true."

He reached for my ankles and began untying them first. Once he finished freeing me, I planned to kick him in the face. No such luck. I had lost all the feeling in my legs and couldn't move them two inches without help. Hell, he should've just strung me up on the rack and stretched me from limb to limb.

Once the tension loosened on my wrists, I rubbed the raw, stinging skin. When I tried to sit up, what little strength I had bled out of my body and my headache intensified. It wasn't just lying in one position that hurt. This was something else. Maybe what he'd said about me catching something wasn't too off the mark.

Matt stood there with his hands on his hips and brow arched. "You're not moving."

"Wait a minute, okay? I fucking hurt—no thanks to you."

He scooped me off the bed despite my squealed protests and started down the stairs. "Looks like we're going to have to do this the hard way. Can you at least sit on the toilet or do I have to help you with that too?"

I scowled. "Can I piss on your lap?"

He chuckled. "There's only one chick I'd let do that and even then I'd probably curse her out. Sorry, babe, but you're not her."

"You're one of Robert's clients, aren't you?"

His eyes narrowed. "What if I am?"

I shook my head. "It figures. If you think you're gonna get a fortune read or something like that, you've got the wrong psychic whore."

"And which whore would you be?"

"The bouncer, jackass."

He kicked the bathroom door open. "Can you handle this on your own or do you need help?"

A wicked thought came to mind. Grinning, I ignored the ache in my face. "Would it make you happy if I said yes?"

"No."

Jerk.

It took some maneuvering, but I managed to get where I needed to be. Sitting up made it easier to breathe, but exhaustion riddled my body.

I dragged myself toward the window and gave the pane a thrust. Either that guy had nailed it shut or the dirt caked on the glass was a sign it hadn't been opened since the cabin was built. I gave it another bump with the base of my wrist, but it wouldn't budge.

"Is that what Robert does? Reads fortunes?"

"No." I didn't care that I sensed his presence standing in the doorway watching me. Weird, yes, but it was just one of those things I did. My senses seemed to be very acute when it came to my personal space. "Robert doesn't read fortunes, fool. The strippers do. Some of them, anyway. The others are sensitives. All of it is done at private parties though, so you're shit out of luck if it's insider information you're looking for. Ask a bitch who cares because I don't."

"Funny you should say that." Matt reached around and grabbed my hands.

Searing pain cut through my raw wrists. I jerked my elbow into his ribs and yanked away. "You asshole! Thanks to you I was lucky that I could wipe mine."

Smoothing his hand along his ribs, he chuckled. "I'll fix them up as soon as I get you back to bed."

"I'm fine."

"Not with that fever, you aren't."

"Oh yeah?"

"Yeah." He grinned right before tossing me over his shoulder and carrying me out of the bathroom.

Boy, did I hate this motherfucker.

Although, there was one interesting piece that made me stop and think. The angle of his butt as it moved underneath his sweats. Lord help me, it was tempting to touch. It's not every day a woman sees something interesting enough to snatch her attention away from wallowing in anger. It was nice, tight and perfectly rounded. I loved the way it moved with each step.

By the time I thought of a way to hurt him, he'd lowered me onto the bed. I wanted to scramble across the mattress to the other side. In theory. In reality, it didn't happen. Damn whatever this bug was.

I got to the other side with my back to him, but I had a feeling it had a lot to do with Matt gawking at my ass from behind. His fingers wrapped around my ankles and hauled me to the other side of the bed. Using a piece of rope, he tied my wrists together and finished off with my ankles.

I wanted to fight. I wanted to rake his eyes out for trussing me like a roasted chicken, but I just couldn't do it. This flu thing had come on hard and fast.

"Now." Matt shoved a wavy tress behind my ear. "I'll fix us some breakfast. When I'm finished, I'll see what I can do about those rope burns. Sound good?"

Whatever. I turned my head away, refusing to look at him. Unfortunately, my growling stomach gave me away.

Matt smiled and left the loft.

He turned out to be very slow with the feeding. It felt like days since my last meal and he pussyfooted around with the food. The more he fingered through the newspaper, the slower his forkfuls of omelet came. Ire aside, I had to give him props for being one hell of a cook. There was a reason why cereal was my number-one breakfast choice. Well...that and French toast. I knew how to do French toast because Flora—

I jerked my head away from the fork.

No, I didn't. Where the hell had that thought come from and who was Flora? I was a lousy cook. My roommate Joy had told me so. It must have been a stray thought. *Yeah. That was it.*

I watched as Matt flipped through the newspaper and came to a stop. So did my omelet feeding. I growled to get his attention. Without lifting his head from the article, he held out a forkful of omelet again. With my hands and ankles tied, I had to worm my way toward the prongs to get to the food. If he had trusted me with utensils, this wouldn't be an issue. Then again, we might have a bigger one if he gave me the knife.

I finally got my lips in place to swallow the fluffy egg with bits of a salty ham, soft green peppers and onions, and a pinch of tangy salsa. Everything slid down my throat, the last of the deliciousness fading from my taste buds. Damn was that good.

"You mind handing over the orange juice?"

"Mm hm." He didn't move. His attention remained glued on an article.

"Excuse me. Hungry and Tied over here would like something to drink before she chokes."

"Uh-huh."

Dammit. Angling my feet closer, I pinched his thigh with my toes.

He yelped.

"Serves you right. I'm hungry and you're slacking on the meals. Either feed me or untie me to do it myself. But don't leave me hanging when it comes to food."

Matt blinked. I thought he would rifle something back, but he didn't. "Do you know a guy by the name of Avery Wells?"

"No," I lied. The first name sounded familiar, but the last name was a blank.

"Well, perhaps you should." He folded the paper in half with the story he had read on top. He tossed it onto my thighs. "Wells was shot outside the sheriff's department during a drive-by shooting. From what I understand that's not very common in a town of less than two thousand people."

My gut wanted to scream even though it never reached my lips. Why this guy meant something to me, I couldn't explain it. My instincts said I should be jumping out of this bed and running for the door to be at his side. Not sitting and pretending not to care.

"You know him, don't you?" Matt tipped his head, eyes studying me.

I shook my head and put deny-deny on my face.

"Okay, then." He cut into another sliver of omelet and held it to me. "More?"

Again, I shook my head. My appetite went from starvation to nothingness. After hearing that news, I didn't want to eat anymore. I found it easier to lie on my side, close my eyes and imagine none of this was happening.

Chapter Twenty-Six

Several voices held scattered conversations throughout my mind, making it hard to settle on just one. The group of people in my dreams had had enough of discussions to last a lifetime. One particular chat started overpowering the rest. We were in the woods just south of Boston.

"Perfect shot, Lex. Center mass." Dane slung the rifle over his shoulder before crouching to inspect the furry corpse.

I did the same with my metal crossbow and smirked. "You wouldn't have it any other way or you wouldn't have put me in the treetops."

Dane took out a switchblade and sliced a tuff of dark brown fur off the wolf. "At least this one won't be terrorizing any more of the campers. You should've told us about this before taking matters into your own hands. The Boston Pack will skin you alive if they catch you in the area."

My best guess said a small group of wolves had broken ranks and started hunting humans. After four teens had disappearances in five weeks, it had started gaining some attention. Even as a half werewolf, I knew how dangerous it would get if humans discovered us. Someone had to put a bullet in this bastard. Dane and his Hunting Club were busy chasing down bounties on other supernaturals when I had called them to handle this one.

I wasn't an official member of the club because I didn't normally go after preternatural troublemakers at the drop of a couple thousand dollars. I usually kept to my own and used my crossbow for self-defense. Dane must have been okay with that because he never asked me to join their group either.

I went with them this once because I had read the

headlines about the brutality of the slayings, which were too close to my territory. Parry didn't seem to give a damn or he would've dispatched his own wolves to handle this. He hadn't.

Many thought a wild animal had gone after them, so they started putting up notices to campers and even closed the state park. That didn't stop the last two deaths at another park about sixty miles away. Whether or not this wolf and his missing friends belonged to the Boston Pack, I couldn't say. Werewolves didn't carry pack ID.

The bushes rustled. Riley, a club member, emerged through the copse in human form with a blond wolf loping beside him.

Seeing Riley in the nude was nothing new, though I had to give him props for having a nicely toned body. Most women drooled at the sight of him. Not me though. I was more intrigued by the wavy black hair he liked to wear hanging halfway down his back. Whenever he changed, all of it would retract back in his hide while his soft pelt thickened in his pores. It was no wonder it always took him longer to change than anyone else.

There wasn't a day that went by where he didn't have a sexual innuendo for me. Why I put up with that man and his antics, I couldn't say. Even worse, he had a libido equal that of a dozen Chippendales in one room.

Dane stood and dropped the rogue's fur inside a plastic Ziploc bag. "Aren't you supposed to be in wolf form?"

Riley shrugged too late and not very convincingly for the story he was about to relay. "We heard voices. I changed first, and I didn't want to take the chance of some damn soldier of misfortune stumbling across us."

"Where are Chris and Jocelyn?"

Before anyone answered, the mated pair emerged from the shadows on the trail where the hunters had chased two more wolves. In human form, Chris was African American with a beautiful glow on his medium complexion. He had the soft eyes of a model and closely shaved hair. Next to him, strode a female wolf with dark brown fur and hazel eyes. In human form, Jocelyn was a shade darker than Chris. If anything, she reminded me of a goddess who'd descended down from Mount Olympus. She kept her hair short and stylish with golden highlights. Knowing how much they loved each other pricked me with a hint of jealousy, but in a good way. They were the most perfectly suited couple I had ever seen in my life. Chris's hand brushed over his wife's head and along her back as she sauntered closer to inspect the dead corpse.

"The other two are dead." Chris watched the lovely lines of his wife before turning his attention to Dane. "No time to change though. Joss and I had to lose a couple of hunters on our tracks. We hid the corpses in a cave not too far from here."

Riley folded his arms over his chest. "I know this is stating the obvious, but we need to get out of here. These woods are crawling with militia wannabes. Not to mention, if the Boston Pack finds us here, our asses are toast. I'd rather they think their wolves ran away than us having picked them off."

I thumbed at Riley. "Mr. Adonis here is right. We don't have the wolf power to fight the local pack with a maniac at the helm. If they—"

"Point taken." Dane hoisted the dead wolf up and slung it across his shoulder. "We'll take this one and come back for the other two later."

Riley kicked a mound of dried leaves. "Shit. What about the money we could fetch off the black market for these guys?"

"I'm not taking a chance that one of our wolves gets shot by some dumbass human who wants to play GI Joe. Now either move your ass or I'll move it for you."

No one said a word as Dane steeled us with a glare, daring someone to challenge him. We either lowered our gazes or looked away. Meeting his glare would mean a challenge and Dane didn't like anyone who challenged his authority when his main purpose was to keep us alive. He was our leader and that was the end of it. Anyone who thought otherwise would end up getting shot in the thigh and carried off. One would think stupid Riley should've learned his lesson from the last time. We respected Dane's authority. Even the few human hunters we worked with understood that without question.

A clap of thunder bolted me awake. Sweat covered my back and front. My hair was glued to my face.

That dream remained fresh and raw like an open wound oozing with puss and blood. We were in the woods hunting the Boston Pack. When, I couldn't say. Dear God, for all I knew Matt could've been the target. But why? What would make us—

Lightning streaked across the sky. Thunder rumbled a second later. I didn't know if I was ever afraid of storms, but the bad omen that came with this one left me shaken.

"Matt. Where are you?"

A grumble answered me.

"Matt!" I began wriggling my way toward the edge of the bed. It would hurt if I hit the floor, but I had to know if he was okay.

I swung my legs over the edge. The rest of me followed through with less grace. My hip landed first, followed by my chin and teeth clacking together. Stars twinkled in my vision before I opened my eyes. Feet thudded across the room and flew up the stairs. I saw Matt's head, then him diving for the floor.

"Shit." He helped me to sit up. "You okay?"

"No." I had to mumble because my achy jaw wasn't ready for a full-blown conversation.

Sliding his arm around my back and under my knees, he lifted me onto the bed. "At this rate, I'm going to need railings to keep you put. What would you do if you fell down the stairs?"

"Lie there and hope I didn't break my neck in the process."

"That's what I'm talking about. You have to be—" He stopped and stared at me. His eyes squinted. "Who's in there?"

I stared back. "What kind of question is that? And why am I all tied up?" Realization hit me. This man had left me bound in a bed in a log cabin out in the middle of nowhere. "You perverted pig. What the fuck do you think you're doing? If this is how you treat all of your girlfriends, then you're lucky you still have mobility from the waist down."

A half smile bowed his lips. "You haven't told me who you are yet."

"How about I take my fist upside your head and knock some sense into you?"

"I'm still waiting."

"For a wallop?" I let a growl simmer while closing my eyes to let my temper simmer. "Just tell me one thing. Did you rape me? If so you're better off leaving these bindings in place."

Matt lowered his eyes to my front. His finger traced along the oversize tee until he came just below my breast. He stopped. Just when I thought he wouldn't go any further, he flicked my nipple.

"Why you son of a bitch!" I bent my knees and began kicking him the best I could despite my tied ankles. My tied fists went straight for his face. If this jerk planned to assault me, then I'd put up such a fight that he'd have to burn my body to get rid of the DNA evidence.

Matt grabbed my wrists and tackled me onto the mattress. His body covered mine. I continued to kick and scream while he remained calm. There wasn't an ounce of lust in his eyes, but rather nonchalance. The more I fought, the more I wore myself out. Matt was strong enough to hold me down without breaking a sweat.

"I had to know." He held my glare. "I've been dealing with your alter ego for the past few days."

I stopped. "Days?"

Matt hauled himself off me. Taking hold of my wrists, he began loosening up the rope. "Sorry about this. But only the real Alexa would want to crack my skull for touching her like that. Your alter ego was another story."

The last few days. What the hell had happened to me? There were bits and pieces, but something about a fever clouded most of it. "How...? What...?"

He loosened the last tie. When I opened my mouth to speak, he raised his hand. "I'll tell you everything. But first, let's get you a fresh change of clothes. You haven't had a bath for a while. As cute as you are, my sense of smell can only take so much."

Good Lord. I had really stunk up the place. My clothes smelled like days-old sweat that had undergone periods of "refreshed perspiration" during my mental absence. One more day of this tee and it would take a paring knife to get me out of it. A thick coat of ick covered my teeth. It wouldn't surprise me if I had a couple of cavities hidden under there. There was no telling what my hair looked like.

"By the way..." Matt helped me up. "You were tossing and turning in your sleep. Something wrong?"

His dark eyes swallowed me under their spell, but it wasn't enough for me to part my lips. I wanted to tell him about the dream, but I couldn't. Suppose my "bounty hunting" group possibly wanted him dead? Until I figured out if they were after those particular werewolves or all of Parry's people, I didn't want to bring trouble down on Dane and the others. They did a good thing by getting rid of those monsters, so why add extra unnecessary trouble into the mix? Besides, for all I knew it was my job to hunt his people whenever they stepped out of line...which would make him my enemy.

Chapter Twenty-Seven

While standing outside the bathroom door, Matt told me everything that had happened at the cabin. Just like those two guys who had approached me at the saloon, he had followed me there too. As it turned out, Avery Wells was my father and Wesley Dane was his close friend. Both names sounded familiar, though my heart held very little feeling for them. It was nice to know I had a father, but it sucked that I lacked any memory of a father-daughter relationship.

While soaking my body in the heated garden tub, I dug through my memories. Flora and Charles Hill came to mind, along with a bed and breakfast whose name I had forgotten. Matt filled me in on that too. Some of it I had remembered on my own, but he had to help me with the rest. That was the problem with my recollection. It turned into a jumbled mess more mixed-up than before. At least he had an email I had sent him to help me figure some of my life out.

"How long has it been?" I tucked the corner of my plush towel to my front.

Matt opened his mouth when I stepped out of the bathroom. No words came out. For a werewolf, he wasn't used to seeing a woman wearing a towel. Perhaps if I dropped it, my full monty might untangle his tongue.

"Uh..." He blinked and smiled. Before saying another word, he turned his back to me and began stoking the fire. "Too long. Your court date has come and gone and a warrant was issued for your arrest."

"*What?*"

"I'm guessing that's how your father and that Dane guy found you. The police probably contacted them. Anyway, Robert was smart. He kept you hidden away for a month before putting you back on the stage again. He probably thought nobody would stick around long enough to think you were still here."

"A month?" One whole fucking, hellish nightmare of a month?

I gulped. There was no telling what that bastard had done to me in all that time. Even more sickening was I had no recollection of it. Just the thought of his filthy hands all over me, I wanted to jump back in the tub and pour scalding water all over my skin.

"Hey..." Matt came forward and placed his hands on my shoulders. "We're gonna figure this thing out, okay? I've been in touch with Monica and told her that you've been suffering from a nervous breakdown." When I opened my mouth, he shook his head. "It's imperative that we establish some sort of mental condition with you. It's the best chance we have for staving off these charges."

"But I'm not—"

"I know you aren't. Monica doesn't and neither does anyone for that matter. But it's better this way. At most, you'll have to sit through some boring therapy sessions, but that's better than going to jail. The only problem is that we need to get you somewhat certifiable by a licensed psychologist. I have a feeling that'll be easy."

I folded my arms and did my best not to pout, although I knew I had failed. "That's not funny."

"I know it's not." He stole a quick kiss to my forehead. Apparently that was commonplace for him because it never broke his rhythm. "Look, this might also work in our favor. If we can find someone who's a hypnotist, they might be able to dig up some of your memories. No more living in this fog of uncertainty."

"Or it might spell doom when I start blabbering about werewolves and witches. This is dangerous stuff you're talking and you know it."

"Yeah, but you don't change. That's why I think it's best. I'd never recommend this to a full blood. But we'll handle all that as soon as I get you back to Boston."

I shook my head. "Not without my father. If he is what you say, then I have to know he's okay."

"Already beat you to it." Matt took my hand and guided me

across the room. "You up for hanging out by the fire or would you like to go back to bed? It's about two in the morning, you know."

I smiled. "That has exactly *what* to do with my father?"

"Can I at least have a kiss first? I'm still trying to woo you, ya know. And, you have no idea how happy I am to have the real Alexa back. I swear, I could freakin' explode right now."

"Uh-huh. Maybe if I found some clothes, it would help you focus."

"Now why you want to go ruin the mood with a crazy idea like that?"

I wrinkled my nose at him. It was that or give him the finger. Besides, I was in a playful mood, not a hostile one.

Making my way up the staircase, I continued the conversation over my shoulder. "You were gonna tell me about my dad."

"Oh. Right. Well, he's okay, if that's what you want to know. At least that's what I think. He checked out of the hospital against doctor's orders. From what I understand, he took the bullet in the side. It missed any major organs, which is good. Considering he's half werewolf too, it makes sense."

I barely got a fresh tee shirt over my head when I stopped. "Like me? How did that happen?"

"Genetically speaking, it's impossible. I did a background check on your mother and found out she's human. But there's this story about a five-year-old who was attacked by her werewolf grandfather and...well... The point is, the way the newspapers reported it, a timber wolf had broken inside your home and bitten you. The hospital said it was a strange form of rabies. Since you already had the werewolf gene, your grandfather exacerbated it. At least, that's the theory from the werewolf side. That's why you're more half than a quarter. I'm guessing it was a territorial thing where he thought your father had intruded on his land. That's why he went after you guys."

I stopped digging in the drawers for clothes and walked to the edge of the loft so there wouldn't be any question in my mind as I braced myself for something I probably didn't want to hear. "You mean he attacked more than just me?"

Hesitant, Matt lowered his gaze. "I—uh—don't know how to tell you this, but..." He lifted his head. "Your older sister Genevieve survived, but your baby brother died in the attack."

I dropped to my knees and clutched the invisible kick to my stomach. Tears blurred my vision and spilled down my cheeks. I had no fucking memories of the kid, but it didn't stop me from feeling like someone had ripped out my intestines. My baby brother was dead and I couldn't remember it. Damn Robert. Damn him to hell. Although I was sure it was a memory many people would rather live without, I didn't want to. Whoever he was, he was a piece of me gone forever.

Footfalls thumped up the staircase. Matt dropped to the floor and gathered me in his brawny arms. I would've liked to swear up and down that I didn't need his comfort and push him away, but I couldn't. The words never came out. I'd be lying to myself if I said it. Sniper, huntress of rogue werewolves and strong woman that I was...even I needed a shoulder to cry on. Matt's just happened to be there. He must have held one hell of a torch in his heart to come this far and stay this long for me. Yeah, I wanted to cry in his arms more than anyone else's at the moment.

Matt held me tight, stroking my hair in silence. Thank God he let me have my cry.

Once I worked my way through the ordeal, I pulled out of his arms and wiped my wet lashes. "Now I know why my father would come this far to look for me. How he knew..."

"I think Flora told him. You left that journal with her, remember? You said you had emailed a copy to the inn. You're a very smart woman. I'm glad I know how to pick 'em."

I smirked before slapping him on the arm. I needed that chuckle. "Smart ass."

Matt helped me to my feet and led me downstairs to the fireplace. "I don't know where your father is. It's like he and his friend went to the hospital then vanished. Considering how much this small town hates them, it doesn't surprise me. The newspaper implied he was shot in retaliation for the bar fight he and Dane started."

"I have to leave them a breadcrumb once we get back to Boston. To let them know I've left this godforsaken hellhole."

"You mean you don't want to tell them face to face?"

I shook my head. "Not if they're going to lock me up for safekeeping. After seeing the lengths they'll go to get me back, I have this weird feeling that they're extremely protective of me. I'd rather stay a step ahead of them if it means I stand a better chance at figuring this thing out. I love them, but..."

"Say no more—I get it. Besides, I don't think I'm in the mood to come between you and family. There's only—"

Whining wood just beyond the cabin walls caught our attention. Both our heads turned toward the far wall facing the front of the house. If Matt's hearing was anything like mine, he knew that noise was out of the ordinary. To a human, it might sound like the wind playing with the storm door. To our keen senses, that was the weight of a foot creeping across wooden planks.

Before I moved toward the steps, Matt darted to the window. I followed him. My fingers clutched his thick shoulder to help balance me while I stood on tiptoes and peered over him. A half grin dotted his mouth, but only for a second.

"See anything?"

"Nope." He turned and eased me away from the window. "You might want to put some pants on. We're leaving. Tonight."

Travel was the last thing on my mind. I would rather we grill our intruders for information and then leave their bodies at the bottom of a lake. Brutal, I know, but I was tired of people kidnapping me off to faraway places and brainwashing me into doing dreadful things. Nothing wrong with a little brutality to make my point. Besides. Matt had probably rented this cabin, thus making it our temporary territory. We would guard it as such.

Whoa. I'd even started thinking like him. Scary...but a little cool too.

My sharp hearing had picked up a voice that mumbled something about going around back while another said he'd take the front.

I knew those guys. They were some of Trixie's bouncers. I couldn't say for sure if Sammy or Paul was with them. If we moved the curtains they'd know we were on to them. Still, I refused to let those bastards take me back.

I ran for the loft, taking the stairs two at a time. Matt said he had bought some clothes, so hopefully he remembered my pant size. I yanked open the drawers and started searching.

"I'm going out back," Matt said in a loud whisper that echoed from below.

I found a pair of sweats that were a size too big even with the drawstrings. I had one leg in when I hobbled to the edge of the loft and leaned over the railing. "Are you nuts? What if they have guns?"

A wicked grin pressed dimples into his cheeks. "I've got something better."

Before I lodged another protest, he pulled his shirt over his head and let it fall to the floor. His zipper went next. Reaching for the waistband, he pushed his jeans down to his thighs.

Oh. My. God. The man went commando, and with an ass that round and smooth, he was certainly within his right. I wouldn't peel my eyes off him even if the cabin walls were in flames. I gulped to keep my saliva from dripping down my chin. Had someone told me I'd get my chance to have his butt cheeks in my hands, I would've dropped to my knees in thanks.

The back door clicked open. While copping a visual feel, I hardly noticed he had made it across the room. I opened my mouth again to voice my disapproval, but he stepped out.

Gunfire exploded outside.

My heart stammered to a stop. Dear God, if anyone hurt him, I swear I'd go through with that bottom-of-the-lake plan.

I grabbed the railing and leaped from the loft. I landed in a crouched position with a thump. My eyes scanned the surroundings like a cat checking the area for danger.

The knob turned. Someone wanted in.

I flew to the other side of the room and pressed my back against the wall. They might expect me standing and aim high enough to blow my head off. However, they wouldn't aim low. I crouched close to the floor.

The knob twisted and the lock clicked. The fireplace was the only thing that shed light into the cabin. My heartbeat pounded in my ears when the door opened. No creaking sounds or anything that would bring me to the edge of panic. It was as smooth as butter on glass.

Carrying a gun, the stranger stepped inside. He pointed the barrel around the edge of the door, aiming just above my head. He shoved the door away, probably for a wider view. Too bad, his eyes found me before his gun did. Boy, was that a mistake.

My fist flew upward, crushing his manhood back to newborn length. The man crumpled to the floor with his hands between his thighs and scrunched into the fetal position. Poor thing. I would've felt sorry for him had he not wanted to hunt us down. I grabbed the gun and pitched it across the hardwood floor. Guns made me uneasy, though I couldn't remember exactly why.

Squatting next to him, I fisted his hair and pulled his head back to see me. "What the hell do you want?"

The man's face remained contorted in pain. "Paul called. Said he wanted me and the boys to check this place out. He had a feeling you might be here."

"How did he know we'd be here?" When he wasn't forthcoming with an answer, I put him in a headlock. That got his attention.

His pulled one of his hands from between his legs and grabbed my arm. "Keish! What the hell's got into you, girl?"

"Answer me."

He gagged. "Some of the folks here in Livermore recognized your bail-bondsman boyfriend. Thirty-eight miles away, but still a small town. Not too many stores with women's clothing. Tiffany used her psychic mojo to find you."

Psychic mojo. Matt said my alter ego had implied Gamboldt had a psychic whore on staff.

Pieces of speech began to replay in my head. Some woman—Elaine—had tried to read me. Then there was Paul who had mentioned a banker and using mind tricks on him. Where was all this coming from?

Unfortunately, I didn't have time to torture this guy for more answers. Matt was out there running around with a maniac gunning for him.

I fisted his hair and slammed his head into the hardwood floor. This guy had wasted enough of my time.

The door slammed open again.

This time another intruder barreled through with his gun pointed at me. I should've been scared, but I wasn't. Matt remained at the forefront of my mind. That was all the motivation I needed to put an end to this. Besides, I would rather die than go back to Trixie's.

"Up, Keisha." The man lifted the gun, signaling for me to do as he said. "I don't want to have to hurt you."

"Good. I don't want to beat you into a wall."

He laughed. "Shoot, girl. I don't think for a second you're lying either. Now, let's go."

With blink-you'll-miss-it reflexes, I shoved the barrel of the gun away and thrust the heel of my hand across the bridge of the man's nose. The gun fired, but the bullet hit the floor to my left. I'd chalk that up to fast, damn good instincts...even if they were hybrid ones.

Still holding the gun, I slugged him with a right cross. The man stumbled out the door and into the porch railing. I hit him with a roundhouse kick to the stomach. He bent in half, but the force was enough to shove him over the railing and into the bushes lining the front of the cabin.

Enough wasting time. I went back into the cabin, found a pair of cheap sneakers and headed out the rear door.

Matt's wild scent came through like fresh cologne. I smelled him all the way over the railing and into the bushes where he had disappeared.

Woods enveloped my surroundings. I leaped over large boulders and rotted stumps, following his trail. Strange that I honed in on it among the woodsy scents. I could even pick out the fresh rabbit trails and deer that had left crisscross paths along the ground. When I came to a small ravine, I slid down the incline and splashed into the frigid brook at the bottom. Matt's scent had disappeared, but I continued in a straight line anyway. There was no reason why he'd head downstream unless another animal was after him and he wanted to lose the scent. Grabbing a thick root, I climbed up the opposite side of the hill.

I stopped and whiffed the air. Still, no male wolf smell. Damn. Maybe my senses were wrong after all.

Stupid as it sounded, my instincts urged me to go down on all fours. It was a good thing I was in the middle of the forest or I'd never have lived this down. After dropping to my knees, I pressed my face close to the earth and sniffed around for a scent. I must have looked like a wild woman raised by dogs, pushing my way through leaves and twigs.

A smell hit me. On the smooth surface of a small rock, I found a piece of Matt. Excited, I continued searching, picking up more and more until I found the right direction again. I hopped to my feet and darted through a thick copse.

Branches and twigs snagged my sweats and pricked my calves. Twice, I tripped on rocks and thick roots, but they didn't stop me. I needed to find him before that maniac hunter put a bullet in his ass. I was sure he wasn't hurt or I would've smelled blood on the air.

Something about this experience brought back pieces of my dreams with me running through the woods. I half-expected a pack of wolves to filter out of the shadows and run with me. They didn't, of course, but in a way, I wished they had. At least those shadows were friendly. Heaven only knew what awaited me out here.

A black wolf leaped from a band of thick foliage. I stopped and threw my back against the nearest tree, cold bark biting into my back.

Matt—my gut said it was him—growled. His ears flattened on his canine head and his lips peeled back to reveal a set of serrated teeth. The only signs of his human half were in his mahogany eyes. However, with the searing hatred burning through them now, I couldn't be a hundred percent sure about that.

He lunged.

I ducked to the right and threw my fists in front of me, ready to fight him off. I guess I was wrong about anything human behind those eyes once he had turned into a wolf.

Matt landed somewhere behind my tree. A man screamed and stumbled backward. The wolf's powerful jaws remained clamped around his assailant's arm. Jerking his head from side to side, he hung on until bones cracked like a person biting into an apple. The yanking had turned into a pull as he tore the arm off and let it fall to the ground. Matt lunged at the man's throat, silencing his horrific screams.

The savagery of his kill bothered me, though I knew it shouldn't. If my dreams were correct, I had killed a few werewolves of my own, only I didn't have sharp teeth to do it with. However, that cute butt and those adorable dimples didn't seem cute anymore. Part of him was human, but full acceptance meant choosing the beast inside him too. That scared me. I didn't want to be a savage like that.

Matt stumbled away from the unmoving body. In fact...he stumbled a lot.

Any doubts I had left me. I ran to him and dropped to my knees.

A whine came through his closed muzzle as he walked with a slight limp. Whenever he stopped moving, he lifted his left paw off the ground or barely let it touch.

"Come here, you big baby." I snatched him by the scruff of his neck and buried his head between my breasts. That might be just the thing he needed to calm down. "Let me see."

He groaned and pulled away. I got rough with him this time. Matt tripped into me, so I wrapped one arm around his neck and held him still. He was a powerful animal, but I held my own and examined his shoulder. Maybe this was the best way to respect the wolf side of him. Through power and strength, seeing as he seemed to understand that most.

Blood matted his fur. At first, I thought it was from the man he had killed, but even after I cleaned it with my fingers, more appeared. Jagged pieces of skin about the size of a quarter kept pooling with blood. It looked like a graze, which meant he'd be okay. If he were human. Being a werewolf, I couldn't be sure.

"You need to change," I said. "You up to it?"

This time, Matt pulled away and settled down on his belly. His head lowered between his front legs and he closed his eyes.

His fur rippled. Seconds later, something began slithering underneath his bubbling coat. Several cracks jolted his legs and back. His tail was the first to go. It began receding into his tailbone until it disappeared. His face broke in several different spots just as his pointed ears began to round off and shrink back to where they were level with his eyes. Clawed paws elongated into fingers, thumb pressing out on the sides. With the exception of his head, his black hair had thinned out like a man balding on a time-lapse camera.

Minutes later, a naked man lay on the ground with one leg bent and the other one sticking straight out at me. Had the circumstances been less urgent, I might have sat there and admired the view.

I got to my feet and hurried to his side. The graze on his shoulder was just that. Although it looked like a nasty burn, at least he'd live. The sissy. He was probably faking just to get my attention.

I combed my fingers through his sweaty hair. More sweat covered his body, glistening under the half-moon sky. Human or werewolf, the man was gorgeous. Not only that, he had saved my life.

Matt mumbled something. His head lifted and he looked at me with a lethargic gaze.

I looped my hand under his arm. "We need to go. Can you

make it?"

Matt nodded. He pushed off the ground and got to his feet, leaning his slick, muscled body on me. Good thing I lifted more than the average guy.

"We have to leave." A series of huffs and a gulp overtook him. "You still up for a road trip?"

"Honey, you're asking the wrong person. I'm so ready to get out of this town that I could start walking now."

He chuckled. "Let's not. I don't want to get arrested for indecent exposure."

"Who says this is indecent?" I slapped him on his heated rear for good measure. Boy had my comfort level jumped a notch.

He chuckled. "I knew you couldn't resist. And I'm gonna make you pay for that the first chance I get." That silly grin on his face said he meant every word of it.

Chapter Twenty-Eight

Flying would've been a better choice, but we couldn't chance it as long as we remained in Arizona. We didn't know the extremes that Robert would go through to get me back, and he had already made an appearance at the airport the last time I was on the run. Plus, it gave Matt a chance to fill me in on the whole psychic ring that Robert had under his thumb. Although Matt had received his information from my alter ego, we had nothing else to go on. Gamboldt used his mind control to get other entrepreneurs to sign over their business to him, but it didn't explain why he needed me for my assassination skills. He had something else going on, and I had a feeling that what he told the strippers and me was only half the story.

"There was a medical technician. A witch you told me about." Matt drove with one hand on the bottom of the steering wheel and the other lying in his lap. "You don't know if she destroyed your records, do you?"

"What does it matter?" I stared out the window as we zoomed past a thick forest.

"It matters because whatever is on that report might help Monica with her mental-illness defense."

"I haven't spoken to Pippa since that time I cornered her in the subway."

He shook his head. "It doesn't matter. I called Monica and had her subpoena the hospital for a copy of your records. Whether or not she went through with it, I don't know. She hasn't called back."

An image of Luz flashed through my mind. "You don't think someone... She's still alive, right?"

"Lex, she'll call when she calls. Just do me a favor and play like we're boyfriend and girlfriend around her, okay? I don't want her thinking I'm here to step on her toes or anything. She's good at what she does. In fact, she's already lined up a psychiatrist for you to see when you get back. He's going to—"

"Can we not do this right now?" I tried to keep the irritation out of my voice, but it came out anyway. "I don't want to think about having to share a jail cell with anyone and certainly not in Boston. Been there, done that."

"It won't happen. I'll put up your bail money again after you turn yourself in to the Boston PD."

I shook my head. What did he want from me? A medal? My life rested in his hands and the only thing I could do was sit behind bars until someone let me go at *their* earliest convenience. I didn't relish going back to the city at all.

After our long drive to Houston, we dropped off the rental and boarded the earliest flight to Boston we could get. Once there, we did as Matt said. I turned myself in to the police before someone else could. Monica showed up at the station with my medical report in hand, along with a doctor's note recommending I have psychiatric evaluation due to amnesia...which was due to a virus. Weird. I didn't know there was any such thing as viral amnesia. My funny lab work had probably brought the doc to that conclusion.

Thank God, I ended up with a lenient judge. My jail stint lasted less than a day on the condition that I have a psychiatric evaluation in the next forty-eight hours or be in contempt. The judge even suggested a court-appointed shrink, but once again, Monica was a step ahead of him and already had my appointment lined up before the judge smacked the gavel. Damn, she was good. Unfortunately, the Assistant DA wasn't ready to drop the charges, which meant another court date. If Robert's people kidnapped me one more time, I'd end up in jail without any chance for bail and who knew what kind of trouble heaped on my head. We needed to put an end to Robert. The sooner the better.

"What now?" I crossed my arms against the chilly city breeze and tucked my head into my lapels.

"Tomorrow is your appointment with Dr. Manish Anri." Monica's heels clicked down the steps of the courthouse as she made her way to the curb. "He's a friend of Frank and Sonya.

I'm trusting you to get her there, Mr. York."

I didn't like the way she sniped at him like that. I touched her arm to get her attention from hailing a cab. "Monica, please don't blame him. It's not his fault. If there's anyone you should be pissed at, it's me. I should've—"

"It's not that." She shook her head. "Look, I know there's more going on and I wish you guys would level with me. I'm your lawyer, for heaven's sake. I'm not out to get you."

Matt stepped closer. "What makes you think we're hiding anything?"

Monica reached inside her briefcase, pulled out a folder and handed it to me. "Keisha Walker's last known address was here in Boston. Prior to that, she was a student at New Mexico University and worked part-time as an entertainer at a bar and grill the locals refer to as Jasper's Jungle. This was prior to your disappearance. Both Jasper's and Trixie's, unofficial names by the way, are owned by Llewellyn Gamboldt who's ninety-seven years old and living in a nursing home in Cambridge. I have a hard time believing this man has a clue of what's going on, but someone who's using his name does. I think you do too."

My stomach knotted tight enough to cut off everything below my navel. If she'd found out all that information, then she might have drawn a target on her back. Damn. This was one more complication we didn't need.

Matt slipped the folder from my hands. "There's nothing going on other than what we told you. Alexa went back to Battle Rose to find some answers and got caught up in a mess there."

"I tried to visit this guy at the nursing home, but they acted like they didn't know who I was talking about and wouldn't let me in to see anyone unless I was related. Family wishes and all. Anyway, the orderly who escorted me out said I would have had to repeat my questions several times because Llewellyn's memory span lasts about two minutes, if that. While I don't have all of the facts, I'm pretty sure fraud is going on here. If it's more dangerous than—"

Matt held up a hand to stop her. "Whatever the connection, I'm sure we can handle it."

Shaking her head, she stepped away and folded her arms over her chest. She stared at us like a mother at her wit's end with her children. "I don't know if I can do this. Whatever you two are hiding, why I'm even a part of it. You're a lawyer, Matt. Maybe you should take the case."

While I didn't mind Matt taking charge because he understood the supernatural challenges we were up against, my stomach nearly crapped on itself at the thought of that. I liked having Matt by my side and trusted him to watch my back more than anyone else. He even took a leave of absence to fly halfway across the country and put up with the bullshit of my alter ego to get me back. If he handled my case, he might have to spend more time in the office instead of doing the footwork with me. Who would watch his back if something bad happened to him while he was there? I trusted nobody but myself to look out for his best interests. Selfish or not, I wanted him right here where I could see him. He meant too much to me. Maybe more than I could've imagined.

My God. Was this the wolf or the human inside me talking? Either way, these foreign feelings scared the hell out of me. Was this how I felt about Matt all those months ago? Why he staked out the inn after my disappearance? Holy shit.

"He's not." Matt's mouth was open when I cut him off. This was my problem, so it made sense for me to handle it. "I need him to help me figure out the broken pieces of my memory. He doesn't have time to worry about my case too. That's what I need you for. But since you're asking, I'll be straight and to the point."

"Lex—"

I held a hand up to stop him. Monica had stuck her neck out by going to that nursing home. For all I knew, she might have invited trouble on herself and not realized it yet. The more she knew, the better to protect herself. I owed her that much. I didn't want her to become another dead body on a slab.

I cupped Monica's arm and guided her into the nearest bar, which turned out to be more of a nightclub. While I didn't drink, her listening to what I had to say might go down easier with a few beers. To my surprise, she didn't protest.

About a hundred people jammed to the thumping hip-hop beat while waitresses managed to carry their trays of Jello shot and test-tube drinks stretched above their heads and out of the way. We should've picked a quieter place, but this was as good as any if we didn't want someone to hear us. Hell, we hardly heard ourselves.

Matt finished off his beer before I yelled over the alternative rock blasting through the speakers at the opposite end of the building. Monica only had half of her Sam Adams down because she spent more time fidgeting with the cap. I settled for lemonade, though I wished for once that I had the stomach for at least hard lemonade.

"Robert Gamboldt owns both Jasper's Jungle and Trixie's Tricks." I slid a finger along the sweaty side of the glass. "That crap about Jasper's being a bar and grill, and Keisha being an entertainer sounds just like that. Crap. If what you said about Llewellyn was true, then I'm guessing Robert is using his relative's name as a front."

Monica lowered her gaze. "For what? Money laundering? Drugs?"

"I don't know, but I have a feeling my lost memories hold the key. Until I can unlock them, we've got nothing to go on other than hearsay."

"Not to mention, we don't know how dangerous these guys are." Matt flagged down the waitress and pointed at his beer for a refill. Once he got the word out, he shifted in his seat and knitted his fingers together on the table. "They kidnapped Alexa and followed her here to get her back. There's no telling what these people are capable of. You need to know in case..."

"Oh my God." Monica sucked in a breath to steady her nerves. "They're going to come after me too, aren't they?"

"In all honesty, I don't know. But I'd feel better if you stayed with someone. Anyone. Until this mess is cleared up. So, if you still want to drop the case, go ahead. I won't blame you and I certainly won't stop you. But you need to know the facts."

Monica sat in silence. Even after the waitress brought over Matt's extra beer, the quiet at our table continued while something along the lines of punk and hard rock played in the backdrop.

Despite the gulp bobbing in her throat, resolve filled Monica's face. "I can stay at my fiancé's condo and I'll continue to do the case. But if something comes up, you have to promise me you'll let me know. No more secrets, Alexa. I can't work like this. Especially since this thing has a mob undertone to it."

Matt's head whipped up. His nose wrinkled with a sniff. I watched as something in the distance caught his attention like a piece of fresh kill hanging on a string.

"You guys have to leave." He shoved his hand in his pocket and pulled out his wallet.

I stared at him. "What are you talking about?"

"Pack members."

"Huh?" Monica stared between the two of us. "Pack of what?"

I knew what that meant. If we both had to go, then she needed to go first to get away from my strong werewolf scent. Something about Matt's pack dug a fork into my craw. If they were anything like he said, they would start trouble with me and might finish it with Monica since we had come together. She was a human and a nuisance at most. Me? I was a dangerous nuisance because I lived between the wolf world and the human one. I was a freak in their minds. An abomination.

Grabbing my coat, I scooted out from behind the table. "Let's go," I said to Monica.

"What? What's going on?" She snatched her purse from the seat next to her and stood. "If we're in trouble—"

"You're not." Matt tossed some cash on the table. "But I will be. Some friends of mine just walked into the bar and they're the kind of people who like to start trouble whether you're looking for it or not."

Monica narrowed her eyes. "What kind of friends are we talking about?"

"The gangster kind."

I loved how that just fell off his tongue like some everyday word he used in court. No big deal. This is just business. Of course, based on the frown on Monica's face, I was sure his nonchalance didn't sit well with her.

"Unbelievable." Of all the nights for his stupid pack members to visit, why did it have to be this one? I sure as hell wasn't in the mood for a fight, but knowing his crew, they'd probably be the first to start one.

Matt mouthed a curse. "If they see me here, they'll want to discuss business. After all, I've been avoiding them like crazy these last couple of days to spend time with you. To help you through your ordeal and all." He glanced at Monica.

That last part was to feed her a line—I was sure of it. She didn't understand pack business, and neither did I for that matter because I didn't know what it was like to really be with one. However, my instincts had my nerves on end. They said we were about to step in a pile of shit if the pack caught me here with their wolf.

"Come on. It's better this way." I cupped her elbow and started into the crowd.

"Wait!" Matt caught up to me just as I shoved her into the thickness of the gyrating horde and was about to start in another direction. He tipped his head down to mine and delivered a kiss deep enough to take my heart with it when he came up for a breath. Gosh, I loved the way that man kissed. When he pulled away, his eyes met mine and he slipped a piece of paper in my palm.

"What's this?" I was about to open it and see for myself.

He closed my fingers over it. "It's the name and address of a friend. Get in touch with him. Before I went after you, I told him all about what's going on. I didn't want Monica to see you with it or she might have started asking questions. Anyway, Tate said he'd help. He's cool and I trust him with my life."

"You're asking me to trust a stranger with mine. Are you nuts?"

A large smile bowed his lips, sinking dimples into his cheeks. "Just trust me, okay? I don't want to leave you high and dry without someone watching your back. Tate's a good guy. I'd never lead the woman I've fallen in love with astray."

"M—"

A hand touched my arm before the words slipped out. Had I heard him right? Too bad I didn't have time to analyze that because Monica had made her way back and given me those questioning eyes before she opened her mouth.

"Are you coming?" She planted a hand on her hip. "I'm not in the mood to get mixed up with trouble. You're giving me enough of that as it is."

And I bet her bill was going to reflect it too. "Yeah. I'm right behind you." I turned her around and shoved her into the crowd, aiming her toward the back door.

I followed, but my gaze never left Matt. Sentiment wasn't my strong suit, but Lord knows the heaviness weighed down my chest with each step. Both of our eyes were on each other until I no longer saw him among the waving hands and bobbing heads on the dance floor. I just prayed that wasn't a sign it would be the last time I'd see him. If so, there wasn't a crypt his pack could hide in where I wouldn't hunt them down to get him back. He didn't belong with them. He belonged with me.

Chapter Twenty-Nine

I waited with my fingernails digging into the edge of a brick building more than a half a block away, and the wind blowing in my favor. Not theirs. Their scents drifted across my nose among the smell of gas and oil from the traffic roaring down the street. Add that to the delicious grilled-steak aroma from the restaurants and the sugary pastries from the bakery and my scent was secured. The back-door exit helped too.

Watching those bastards flank Matt on both sides as they escorted him away from the club dug at my soul. I wanted to rip him from their hands. He was mine dammit! Not theirs. Parry had lost his claim on his wolf. I was sure of that.

A brown minivan pulled to the side of the curb. After hailing a cab for Monica, I chose to stay. Actually, I had a feeling my instincts chose for me. I pressed my back against the brick wall in the alley and made sure my body remained in the shadows.

Two more people exited the van to greet him. Despite the smiles, thumps to the back and jokes going around, something in Matt's empty eyes made it forced on his part. Twice they settled on me as though he saw through my dark cover and longed to be with me instead. At least, that was what I told myself.

A slinky woman stepped out of the open side door. She was more legs than anything else. She had curly blond hair that stretched the length of her back and wore a crop top with a striped mini skirt. If she bent over, all of her business would be out. Hell, the thing barely covered the lower curve of her ass. Perfect Trixie material, if you asked me. When she wrapped her arms around Matt and molded against his body, she planted a deep, sultry kiss on his mouth. Why that fucking whore. That bitch had better be glad I had purposefully glued my feet to this alley. I'd snatch her to baldness and push her skank behind in front of a tour bus. How dare she—?

This wasn't helping. I needed to keep my cool.

Matt hugged her back with his arms slipping around her rail-thin waist. Although the kiss didn't look like much, his holding her said enough. Perhaps I needed to rethink what we'd started back at that cabin. Or at least lay down some parameters, assuming he'd go along with them. A guy who claimed to be falling in love with someone didn't kiss or hold another woman like that.

A deep breath cleaned my brain. I needed to sort out my lost memories first. Love, or any hints thereof, had to wait.

Reaching into my pocket, I pulled out the piece of paper Matt had given me. It had a phone number and the address of his friend. Once everyone got into the minivan and it pulled away from the curb, I stepped out of the shadows and hailed my own taxi.

Going to Tate's house wasn't at the top of my list. I preferred hitting up the older Gamboldt at the nursing home and cutting off his breathing tube until he gave me some information. Unfortunately, my cruelty hadn't reached that point yet. It was a fleeting thought at most. Besides, the fatigue clawing at my bones convinced me otherwise. I needed a safe place to crash for the night and Matt had suggested his friend who he trusted with his life. I wasn't sure I trusted this guy with mine. But it wasn't like I had much of a choice. Most likely, someone had twenty-four-hour surveillance on the Crescent Inn by now.

I arrived at an old brownstone not too far from the Theatre District. I double-checked the address on the slip of paper with the numbers on the small window above the door. This was the place. After hiking up the steep concrete stairs, I slid a finger down the names listed by the entrance and found Tate's. As a guy exited the building, I grabbed the large metal door and hurried inside.

About a minute later, my knocks echoed down the hall. Doors were the same chestnut brown as the floor. Everything else was painted paisley blue. It would've looked nice had it not been for the scratches mucking up the paint job and dulling the floors. At the end of the hall, someone had parked their bike in front of the window leading to the fire escape. A thick, musty scent corroded my nose. I bet months of mold and mildew lived in and around the AC vents.

Tate wasn't what I expected. He stood about an inch or two taller than me, but it made getting mesmerized by his startling sky-blue eyes easier. They sparkled like a Siamese cat's. He was bald, but with a sexy appeal. His warm smile made me smile back. Although he wasn't much in terms of height, he bulked up pretty well underneath his green scrubs. When he took my backpack, I noticed muscles roping his upper arms.

"Matt told you I had a girlfriend, right?" Tate carried my backpack down the hall and entered a room near the back of his apartment.

"No." Did he want me to follow him? I stood facing the living room with the hallway and kitchen on my left. "Is that a problem?"

After exiting the room, he sauntered down the corridor smiling. "Not unless you're turned on by this beautiful body."

I went blank, unsure of how I should take that. "You're trying too hard."

Laughing, he playfully slapped my elbow. "I'm just kidding. I wanted to see the look on your face. Relax, okay?"

I nodded and let go of the breath I'd been holding.

He tipped his head to meet my eyes. "Everything's going to be okay. No worries." Slipping around me in the somewhat tight living quarters, he entered the kitchen and went straight for the fridge. "You hungry? When Matt called from the van, I ran downstairs to the grocer and picked up some food. I don't know what you like, but I pretty much got the basics."

"No thanks."

"You know, there's nothing in the rule book that says you have to stand there like a statue. Have a look around. It's good to see Matt hanging out with someone outside the pack for a change."

I managed to lift my head over my shoulder before the rest of my body followed through in that same direction. Something about his place made me nervous. Although Tate hadn't given me any reason to agonize, I couldn't help the touch of anxiety coursing through my gut. I just didn't want to be here. This was another wolf's residence. His den.

Setting my preternatural instincts aside, I sat on the chestnut brown couch. The thing molded to my body, fitting like a glove. I noticed a spread of JAMA and NIH magazines on the coffee table.

"You're into medicine?" I picked up a magazine and flipped through it.

The refrigerator door closed. Tate stood behind the counter pouring something. "I'm a pediatric RN at Mass General. For some reason, my Alpha seems to think that makes me close enough to being a doctor. So, I study up on things whenever I get a chance. And before you ask, I've never heard of Pippa the witch. Matt asked me to ask around just in case."

"You're not a real doctor? I mean—don't get me wrong or anything. I'm sure you're smart like that."

He chuckled. "Lex, if you had any idea how many times our pack likes to pick fights among themselves you'd understand why. Besides, it's not like we can go to doctors. Unfortunately, my Alpha doesn't care that I would rather work with kids than a pack of wolves."

Hearing him use my nickname was weird. Still, I didn't correct or ask why. Matt must have talked a lot about me.

"Tell me something." Tate entered the living room with two glasses of what looked like orange juice. "You and Matt an item? 'Cause with your scent alone, I can see why."

"Don't you start too."

A huge smile splayed his baby face. "Come on. You smell like a delicious steak with a little wolf seasoning on top."

"Coming from a man I hardly know that sounds wrong in every sense of the word."

"Only to human ears." He handed me my drink. "Matt suggested I give you something to help you sleep since you've been sleeping like shit lately. So, I slipped something in your drink. He means well and all, but I've got this thing about drugging people against their wishes." Tate sipped his drink before plopping down in the matching chair. "He filled me in on your amnesia. And if it weren't for you being a werewolf I'd—"

"Half," I interjected.

He chuckled. "Half then. Anyway, I'd send you both to the hospital for psychiatric evaluations. He made me write a bunch of information about him and you in case you both went missing. But, I understand where his concerns are coming from. Working on a few hours sleep isn't going to fix anything."

"Can you...?" I had a problem with asking a complete stranger for help, but Matt trusted this guy with my life. If I couldn't be real with him, then what was the point in my being here? "Is there anything you can do to help me get my memories back?"

He shook his head. "Nurse. Not a therapist. He also gave me the time for your appointment with that Dr. Manish Anri guy and reminded me to tell you to tell the truth. About being half werewolf and all. Just don't show him anything that might prove who you are. If that doesn't win you a get-out-of-jail-because-I'm-a-nut card, then nothing will." He pointed at my glass. "You gonna drink that or would you like something that isn't spiked?"

A sip brought a delicious coolness down my throat. It was orange juice, but there was something slightly medicinal about it. Keeping the nightmares away was the only reason I drank it. Enough of them had plagued me on the plane ride. Twice I woke up with a start and got an eyeful from the passengers. Something mind-numbing would be great right about now.

I set the glass on the coffee table. "I need my memories back."

"I'm sure you do." Tate threw back the rest of his orange juice before placing his glass next to mine.

Eventually, whatever Tate put in my drink would take hold and I'd succumb to sleep. There were still some things I wanted—needed—to get off my chest. "What do you know about psychics?"

"Psychics?"

"Some of my memories had to do with psychic women, I think. They worked with me at a strip bar. There was also a rich banker, but I have the feeling he wasn't the only one. Maybe I'm reading too much into this, but I can't get the word 'scam' out of my head every time I think about it."

Tate sat in silence with a finger tapping his bottom lip. He concentrated on an invisible spot on the other side of the room a few seconds before he spoke. "I don't know about psychics and stuff like that, but I'm at your beck and call to find out."

Good. Come morning we'd start at that nursing home.

Chapter Thirty

Soft light broke through the sheer curtains and landed across the bed. Tate must have tucked me in because a knit blanket covered everything up to my shoulders. What kind of guy kept a knit blanket around? The room was small with only a full-size bed, a closet and a chest of drawers by the wall. Several picture frames lined the surface. One of them was a photo of him and Matt holding up their catch after what looked like an enjoyable day of fishing.

When I pushed the blanket back, cold air whooshed against my legs, inciting a round of gooseflesh. He had taken my pants off too. I'll give him the shoes, socks, and pants but for his sake, those had better be the only things he had taken from me.

Light shone across Tate's face from the door I had opened. He lifted his arm to block it out. He pushed off his sleeping bag and placed a gun on the floor next to the flattened pillow.

I blinked. "What are you doing?"

"Watching you." He picked himself off the floor and stretched his arms over his head. His baggy shirt and mismatched pajama bottoms shuffled with him as he walked down the hall. "You hungry?"

"You left your gun on the floor."

"Oh yeah. Bring it with you. I usually keep it in a lockbox on the fridge." He disappeared into the kitchen.

Something about that didn't sound right. Why would a werewolf keep a gun handy? Then again, it was probably faster to grab it than to change to his four-legged form. But that begged the question of why he needed it in the first place.

Doing as he said, I picked up the gun and met him in the kitchen. I placed it on the granite top while he measured out dark coffee grounds.

Upon first glance around the apartment, I couldn't find a phone. "I need to call Matt. I want to find out if he's okay."

Tate filled the pot with water at the sink. "It's by the window, but you can't call him."

"Why not?"

"Because if you call the den from my number and ask for Matt, there'll be hell to pay. Parry will think I've given the number to my human girlfriend. I'm not angling to be on that bastard's bad side. Three-quarters of the pack are ass-kissers who'll be more than happy to rat me out. It was hard enough to convince everyone that my lover was just my plaything."

I planted a hand on my hip. "How can you let your best friend go with those maniacs? Why don't the two of you just get the hell out of town? Start elsewhere?"

Tate emptied the pot of water through the vent on the top of the coffee maker and pressed the button for brew. "It's complicated. Our brains are genetically wired to follow an Alpha wolf. Perhaps not to our deaths, but close enough to it. That's the way it is with a pack."

I must have lacked that werewolf gene. "Now *that* sounds more like brainwashing to me."

He laughed. "If you want, I'll call Matt for you. But I'm pretty sure he's doing okay. If not, I would've been down there nursing his wounds instead of in this kitchen with you."

"Call him. In the meantime, can I use your cell phone? I have to call my inn to make sure everyone is okay there. Then, I want to see what the visiting hours are like at the elder Gamboldt's nursing home." I glanced at the clock. "All while hoping I can keep my appointment with the shrink." This was going to be one hell of a day and it had only begun.

Between phone calls and filling our stomachs with breakfast, we touched base with everyone we needed to talk to. Not to mention, I got sidetracked when Tate handed me the phone to talk to Matt. Nothing filled me with relief more than to hear his chuckle and imagine those cute dimples with every happy gesture. God help me, I just wanted to hold him in my arms again. Was that asking too much?

I called the Crescent Inn last to make sure Charles and Flora knew I was back in town and okay. Having been away all this time, I couldn't bear their not knowing.

Dane answered the phone. "Angel?"

My heart caught in my throat at the way that name rolled off his tongue. My hand shook, ready to press the button to hang up. I couldn't bring my thumb to cut us off. For a family friend, as Matt called him, he had a certain power over me that implied I would be breaking some sort of unsaid vow if I disconnected. Perhaps this was the wiring thing that Tate mentioned earlier. If so, I didn't like it.

I gulped. "Dane?"

He sighed. "Thank God. Where the hell have you been?"

How dare he take that tone of voice with me? "It's not important. But if you spoke to Flora, then you probably know about my amnesia. Do me a favor and at least fill me in on a few things before you decide to chew me out. Starting with that guy who claims he's my father. How is he?"

As it turned out, Dane had sent him down to Charleston with my sister, Genevieve, and my mom for safekeeping. He and my father had it fixed in their heads I'd be safer with my family until this thing blew over and suggested I come back to the inn so he could escort me to them. Like that would happen. I already had miniature panic attacks thinking he'd probably had the call traced. There was a part of me that said I should do everything in my power to make sure he and Tate never met. Two wolves from two different packs and both vowing to protect me. Not a good combo at all.

"When are you coming back to the inn?"

I switched my phone to the less sweated ear. "When I know you're not going to hide me away with the rest of my family. Whether you like it or not, I have to figure this mess out."

"We can figure it out together."

"No, we can't. You made that much clear when you sent everyone away. My mother didn't raise stupid kids."

"How would you know? I thought you had amnesia?"

Smart ass. I clenched my teeth until my annoyance with him settled down. "Look, buddy. Don't play with me. I'm not in the mood. I've got crazy Romas who are probably out there looking for me as we speak. Not to mention a lunatic venture capitalist who has psychics on the payroll and some sort of—"

"Venture capitalist? Who?"

I paused. "His name is Robert Gamboldt. Why?"

Dane muttered something under his breath. He cursed several times before coming back to the phone. "I know the guy because I'm a businessman myself. Remember? No—wait! Don't answer that. Anyway, I've been keeping an eye on this area ever since I invested my money in your bed and breakfast. That guy has a reputation for being a slimy-ass bastard, but he's also untouchable. He has figureheads, but that's about it. If what you say is true about psychics on the payroll, that would explain his amazing luck for picking investment winners."

"Did you know he's able to control minds?"

Dane grumbled his frustrations over the earpiece. "No. But if I had to guess based on what he did to you, I'd say he's more powerful than his crystal-ball-reading staff. Not many people can manipulate a werewolf's mind like he did yours. Assuming that's how this whole amnesia thing started. From where I'm standing, it makes sense."

I lowered my gaze in shame, though not feeling the heat that usually flooded my face. This was more like frustration for being so weak. "He got to me, didn't he?"

"But the way I look at it, he'd still have you if you weren't half werewolf, stubborn as hell and one heck of a fighter."

His compliment softened my mouth to a half smile. I never thought I'd see stubbornness as an asset. Unfortunately, that didn't change the fact that Gamboldt had gotten to me.

"Angel..." Dane paused. "If this is about him, you need to get out of the city. You need to walk away until we can—"

"Screw that!"

"Look, I know you're scared—"

"This bastard is the reason why I lost my memory to begin with. He knows me. Whether I'm hiding in Charleston or Guam, he'll find me, Dane. That's what he does and he's damn good at it. My memory's filled with more holes than a beehive. Hell, I don't even know if you and I are lovers or not."

"Oh God." His voice teemed with disdain. "Have you lost your freakin' mind? As much as I love you, I'm not *in* love with you. You're like a daughter to me. Not to mention your father would blow my head off with a shotgun." His voice became distant as he spoke to someone in the background.

The bedroom door creaked opened down the hall. Tate stepped into the living room wearing a pair of jeans and a sweatshirt. He mouthed something to me and thumbed at the front door. I waved my hand over my shoulder. I had no idea what he wanted, but it was time to end this call.

I pressed the phone closer to my ear. "I have to go. There's a lead I need to check out."

"Not alone you don't. It isn't safe."

"I won't be alone." I hung up before he fished a clearer answer out of me.

"You okay?" Tate's heartbreaking blue eyes searched me.

"Fine."

But I wasn't. We were about to tangle with a supernatural who had unknown powers. Not only that, I was dragging another innocent into the fight. Note to self: *call Monica sometime today and make sure she is still alive.*

I stopped off at a pawnshop to see if there was a weapon small enough for me to conceal while walking the streets of Boston. I found a knife with an ankle strap and a belt holding a horizontal sheath that fit around my waist for hiding a blade at the small of my back. Since it was cool enough to warrant a jacket, nobody would see it. The shop owner tried to get me to buy a gun, but my gut balked. In my flashbacks, my weapon of choice was a crossbow. I'd stick to that and knives until I remembered otherwise. And since walking the streets with a crossbow was probably against the law, the blades had to do.

"What now?" Tate zipped his jacket and shoved his hands in his pockets.

I stared. "Don't you have a job or something? Really. As much as I like you, I don't want—"

"I do." He grinned. "But Matt asked me to stick to you like glue. Besides, I'm in love with your scent."

"Great. A talking shadow who has his mind on my body odor. That sounds enticing." My eyes rolled.

I continued down the street, hoping to figure out a way to lose him. Tate wasn't a bad guy or anything. Unfortunately, anyone who tried to help me had this habit of disappearing or dying. Look what had happened to my father. Not to mention Matt's personal assistant, Luz. In a way, maybe I should be thankful that Parry had summoned Matt back to their den. On second thought, *not!*

A car pulled up to the curb just as we stepped off. A second or two later and it would've taken us out. Tate looped his arms around my waist and pulled me back onto the sidewalk.

Tinted windows lowered on the black town car. Ignoring the blaring horns, the driver slowly inched the car the remainder of the way around the curb. He stopped when Tate and I were in view of the back open window.

A middle-age guy lowered his head toward us. Except for the thick black hairs around the edge, he was balding. A real horseshoe head. He slid his glasses up on his hooked nose and smiled with crooked teeth.

"Ms. Wells." A slight Slavic accent came across with his charm. "Would you do me the honor of stepping inside? Please. It's seems we're not the only tails you and your friend have picked up."

My head shot over my shoulder. Dozens of people sauntered down Berkley Street and I couldn't tell one from the other. The only danger in the area was the drivers gunning through red lights.

A familiar head ducked behind a poll, back turned to us. Could it be...? Noooooo. There was no way it was—

Sammy glimpsed over his shoulder. I knew those eyes and that brown hair anywhere. Through some sort of divine prophecy, he had tracked me down. Wherever he was, Paul wasn't far. Though I doubt they'd start trouble in public, I didn't want to chance that they might have more of Robert's goons with them. So much for going to that nursing home.

Our choices were simple. Either Tate and I go with Sammy and Paul, because I doubt Tate would let me go alone. Or, I got in the car with the old fart who I knew nothing about. Even worse, there was a humungous chance he worked for Robert and wanted to offer me a nice ride back to Arizona as a doped-up piece of luggage.

Not much of a choice, if you asked me. I glanced at Tate before I stepped off the curb.

The werewolf grabbed my arm. "Are you nuts? You don't know who this guy is."

"You're right." I freed my arm and pointed at Paul who was marching up on Sammy's left side. "But unfortunately, if those two guys reach us, they're going to offer me a one-way trip back to Battle Rose. I've been through that door. I'd rather try this one."

Again, I started for the car. This time, I reached under my jacket as though it were in the way and curled my fingers around the leather hilt of my knife. If anyone was about to deliver a surprise, I'd rather it be me.

I sat on the expensive seat, but stayed close to the door in case the driver should think about speeding off. Tate lowered his head and shoulders to look inside. He offered up a smile then turned his attention back to where Sammy and Paul stood. To my surprise, they stopped and stared like two hyenas waiting for their turn for a piece of the kill.

I brought my focus back on Horseshoe Head. "What do you want? Did Gamboldt send you?"

The man shook his head. "No. In a way, the Lennors gave me no choice after they tried to warn you about us. But that doesn't matter anymore because I'm sure you know all about my clan, the Garridans. Speaking of which, we would appreciate it if you'd return to Arizona where you'll be safe. No tricks this time."

"Uh-huh. So much for door number two."

I snatched the knife from the sheath and stabbed the old man in the thigh. No more games. No more lies. No more dicking around. My beautiful wolf was gone and there was a chance I might not get him back until this whole thing blew over. Far be it from me to hold back now. When it came to survival, the wolves had it right. Survival of the fittest. I was about to act on mine.

The knife stuck out of his expensive black slacks with blood oozing down the side and leaking onto the leather seat. I wondered if he thought his white upholstery still made a statement. While shocked gasps tortured him, I continued to drown him with my glare. When he grabbed the knife to yank it out, I slapped his hand away and wrapped my fingers around the hilt. With my free hand, I snagged his fragile throat. His eyes bulged as he sputtered in agony.

When the driver lifted a gun over the seat, Tate was on him. He grabbed the man's wrist, squeezing until his fingers loosened around the handle and trigger. The gun dropped to the floor by my feet. I rested my foot on top of it. Tate refused to let go, growling a warning to the terrified man. Good thing I hadn't tried to lose him after all.

"Careful," I warned Tate. "We'll need him to take a few

notes. I don't think the backseat driver here is going to be in the mood."

Tate released him and picked up the gun from under my foot.

I shifted in the seat to make myself more comfortable. Too bad I couldn't say the same for Garridan's messenger. "If your people want to talk, then take this number down." Thank goodness, I had invested in a cell phone. Tate handed the driver a pen and he wrote it on the back of his sore hand. "Tell the Garridans I'm nobody's property, including their buddy, Robert Gamboldt. If they want to talk me out of the massacre my pack and I have planned for them, now would be a good time."

I yanked my knife from his thigh and backed out of the car, bumping into Tate along the way. This was too sweet of a weapon to leave behind. I grabbed the door and slammed it shut, sad that I hadn't broken the window in the process. We watched the car speed off down the street, fishtailing and missing other cars by inches while bouncing in and out of potholes.

Someone had to break the silence between the two of us. The last thing I needed was Tate fearing little old me. Now was a good time to find out if he still wanted any part of this. "What's on your mind? Having second thoughts about me?"

"I think he's convinced you're one crazy bitch." A smirk curled the corners of his mouth. "I, on the other hand, believe you're insane for bluffing the guy like that."

I glanced over my shoulder, looking for Sammy and Paul. To my surprise, they had disappeared. Did they expect me to get in a car with a stranger and drive off on a road trip? Tapping Tate on the arm, I motioned with my chin for us to continue down the street. If those two were still waiting to make a move, why make it easy for them?

"I wasn't bluffing," I said. "I'm part werewolf and I don't have any attachments to the Boston Pack. But if what I've seen in my visions is right, then I have connections to other werewolves elsewhere."

Tate ran his hand across his bald head. "You don't want to go there, Lex. Trust me. Parry won't like having another pack in his territory. He's psycho enough to burn your B&B to the ground, if he has to."

"Relax. I'm not bringing anyone here. All I need is for the

Garridans to think I am. It doesn't matter if they think my fake pack is Parry's or not. I'm hoping the possibility alone will be enough."

I was about to sheathe the knife when Tate stopped me. I stared at him. "I can't walk down the street with a bloody knife."

Tate took the knife and slid the flat of the blade on the inside of his coat. "You can't put water on a nice piece of steel like this either. There. It's as clean as it'll get until we can pick up a can of oil or something."

"I know that. But do you see a can of oil around here?"

He slid his arm across my shoulders and laughed. "I still think you're insane. And what did you mean by having visions of other werewolves? Does Dane have a pack or something that you're part of?"

I stopped and stared. That question triggered at least a dozen more in my mind and the only answer I received was a combination of "I don't know" and "maybe". While I wanted someone to confide in, I wasn't sure if Tate was that person. "Dane is a werewolf. I think he has friends who are werewolves too. Whether or not they're a pack, I don't know."

We didn't make it to the end of the next block when I received a phone call. One of the Garridans took me up on my offer for a meeting.

Chapter Thirty-One

Ms. Garridan—not the old guy's wife unless he's into them that young—wore a black leather skirt with fishnet pantyhose. A matching, floor-length duster swept across the floor of Seekers Tavern. She wore a white blouse underneath with too many buttons loose at the top and enough cleavage to make a man drool to his kneecaps. Her black bob with the royal blue highlights stood out against her pale skin.

Her cat-like eyes picked me out of the crowd. Stalking toward the booth where I sat, she threw her coat out of the way before taking a seat across from me.

Two wrestler-sized men came in behind her. She nodded to them and they headed to the bar like good, obedient dogs.

I glanced over my shoulder to make sure Tate remained seated at the far end. He tipped his Samuel Adams to me. My eyebrow arched, alerting him to the two guys. Again, he tipped his beer. When he cut his gaze toward Garridan's bodyguards, I reached underneath the back of my jacket and looped my fingers around my knife. Just like her horseshoe-head father, grandfather or decrepit husband, I wasn't taking any chances.

Her finger stabbed at my face.

When her mouth opened, I cut her off. "You'll want to move that before I slice it off for you."

Garridan smirked, blue-lipstick lips shimmering under the light. "I could kill you right now, you know."

"So much for asking nicely."

The knife came out slicing across the tip of her finger before she realized what had happened. Blood oozed from a fine line, dripping on the table. The astonished look on her perfectly made-up face: priceless. She quickly replaced it with anger and began sucking on the wound to keep it from bleeding.

I feigned boredom with a sigh. "You wanted to talk? Talk. I'm on a schedule here. My shrink is expecting me to be on time for our session today."

From her deadpan stare to her knitted eyebrows, I knew she had trouble knowing whether or not to believe me. For once, this psycho thing just might work in my favor.

"Figures." The woman folded her fingers together on the table. A trail of blood seeped down the knuckle of her thumb. "You stabbed my uncle. By all rights, I should—"

I offered up an innocent smile. "Is that who that was? I thought he was a snake in the grass, so I was just doing some pest control."

She leaned back in the seat as the waiter showed up to take our drink order. Garridan requested a scotch on the rocks while I settled for lemonade. She tipped her head as if to ask why I wasn't drinking. If something went down, I wanted to be clearheaded enough to get my ass out of a jam.

"Do you want my help or not?"

Good point. It was time for me to rein in my condescension. If she wanted to help me after I'd just stabbed her uncle, then she was either desperate or stupid. From her stiffened back and perfect posture, I had a hard time figuring out which was true.

"Fine." I sat back. "Tell me something I don't already know starting from your guys' auction on the fairgrounds."

"When you went inside the tent, you and your friend were tagged."

"As in cattle for the slaughter?" Oooo, I didn't like the sound of that. But, I had to keep my cool if I wanted information.

She nodded. "That's how we helped to recruit those Gamboldt needs for his cause. We didn't want to do it, but we owed Robert money and he was hoping other supernaturals might come to our auction looking for magical trinkets or something of that nature. If so, then he would hit them up to join his ranks."

"And if you didn't give him what he wanted?"

She shifted in her seat, gaze lowering to the tabletop. "He'd go through all of us until he deemed our debt paid. He's a powerful man. So powerful, in fact, that it's best to be on his good side rather than his bad one. Until now, he scared me more. After all you're a hybrid werewolf. Your other half is human. Robert is neither. He's a monster even if he doesn't change into one. In fact, after he got his hands on you, he considered our debt paid in full. When you escaped, it became null and void again. Uncle Cam got nervous and did what he thought was best."

I clung to that part about the balance of fear shifting in my direction. I must have done something that had made them change their minds, though I didn't see my breaking Gamboldt's hold that big of a deal. Then again, he'd erased my entire life. That alone damaged me. Whether or not I was ready to forgive her for giving in to a bully was another story. I had a lot of fight in me growing by the second, but I couldn't say the same for the Roma. Until now, I hadn't met any and knew very little about their laws.

She continued. "My aunt, Tatiana, sensed who you were. She has the gift of seeing the muló. The evil spirits of the vampires and shapeshifters."

"I'm not evil."

She snorted and shook her head. "But you're part werewolf, which we see as evil regardless of your intentions. That's enough." Garridan slipped her hand inside her coat and pulled out a pack of cigarettes. I pointed at the *No Smoking* sign hanging on the opposite wall. Miffed, she shoved the cigarettes back in her pocket.

She settled for tapping her cigarette lighter on the table. "Aunt Tatiana is an old woman. She's my grandaunt really. Uncle Cam, her nephew, asked you to return to Arizona because he thought it would keep Aunt Tatiana out of Robert's sights. A trade, if you will." She stopped long enough for a small group of people to walk by before she continued. Once they were gone, she leaned closer. "Based on what Uncle Cam told me, it sounds like you're in a lot of trouble with the police. Robert can help you get out of it, but that means returning to him."

The waiter approached the table with our drinks and offered us menus. We declined, of course. This wasn't a social event. A semi-civil one, perhaps. The way we stared at each other, unwilling to give the waiter a glance, we both knew it. Meals you have with family and acquaintances. We were neither.

I sipped my tangy lemonade before sliding my finger along the cool surface of the glass. "That's not going to happen. I'm enjoying my freedom too much."

"But he can—"

I held up a hand to stop her. "Anything he can do to get my name cleared carries too high of a price. Not only that, I'm not a psychic like the rest of his whores. Why risk almost everything you have to get me back? Huh? Whether you realize it or not, he's got something else going on and he needs me to complete it."

"How can you be so sure?"

"I can't. Call it a hunch, because that's all I have to go on at the moment." That last part wasn't exactly true. I had a hunch about Gamboldt having psychics on his staff and them reading the patrons without their permission. Though it screamed scam and blackmail I needed her—someone—to connect the lines for me to be certain.

After gulping her drink, she slapped her glass on the table, rattling the ice cubes. "He made the Top Ten list of Boston's Most Profitable Entrepreneurs. I've seen this man's work. He's not afraid of anything, including you. I've seen him sit in a room and collect money or deeds from small businesses like they were handing over trading cards. If he's got something on the side that involves you, you can bet it has something to do with this. Those charities are nothing more than a cover."

I leaned forward with another question weighing on my mind. "What *is* his business exactly?"

She shrugged. "Nobody knows. As far as a building goes, that little office he has in Marshfield is about the only structure that has his name tied to it. He could be running whatever *it* is from his garage."

The image of my knife flashed in my mind. I clutched my sweaty glass to keep from sliding my fingers across my body to grab it. I had no reason to kill this woman as long as she gave me what I needed to know. I closed my eyes and rubbed them as though that would get the image out of my head. If anything, it gave me a headache.

"Do it."

My head shot up. I glanced around the bar to see who was talking to me. There was no one. Even the Garridan woman was looking at me strange.

Heat began seeping across my front, reaching up to my throat. I tugged at my collar. There wasn't any rash on the backs of my hands or arms, nor did they look flush. Could all of this be in my mind? It had to be. There was no way I'd outright kill someone and Garridan hadn't given me a reason to either.

"Kill her! Do it now!"

"No!" The word jumped out of me. I stared at the Roma with my heartbeat reverberating in my throat, hoping my outburst didn't signal my going crazy despite the voice in my head. But did that stop her scrutiny? Of course not. Those narrowed eyes said she was in the middle of drawing a conclusion.

"He's reading you, isn't he? I can sense it." Her breathing picked up as her gaze swept the room.

I shook my head, struggling to speak between pants. "He's not reading me. This feels like something different. Like..." I didn't know how to explain it. "There's a voice in my head. Telling me to do stuff. I don't want to, so—"

"He's trying to establish his grip on you again. He's been tapped into your brain for months because of the residue left behind. There might not be much for him to grab, but he's a persistent cockroach to try. And if he's telling you to do things while I'm sitting here, that means we've finally made his bad side."

I leaned across the table. "What kind of supernatural is he? If he can do this to me, I need to know."

She cocked her head as though surprised I hadn't figured it out. "Mind control. But you're stronger than I thought if you're able to stave him off while I'm sitting here. I should take that as a sign to leave."

Her goons moved, chairs scraping across the floor, but Tate was on them. One look of his startling blue eyes and I knew they went from dazzling during his calm mood to dangerous. Garridan's men must have noticed Tate's change in demeanor too, because they stopped, unable to take their eyes off him. If they didn't know who he was, they weren't about to take the chance to find out. Smart men.

I grabbed her wrist to keep her from moving. She couldn't leave as long as I had questions. While the voices continued to assault my brain, I ignored them and did my best not to cross the line from desperation to following through with stabbing her in the throat. After all, that was what the voice wanted me to do. *"Make it quick and easy"*, it said. *"Wednesday is a threat to you and everyone you hold dear."* There was no way in hell I'd walk away with that kind of blood on my hands. Not even if Garridan held all of the secrets of universe. They weren't worth a damn if I ended up in jail.

Garridan choked back a scream. When she realized it was about to jet out of her mouth, she clamped her lips together and scowled.

This was getting me nowhere. The more the voices egged me on, the harder it was to let go. Not only that, Garridan's men forgot about Tate and focused on us. The only saving grace I had was Garridan signaling them with a hand to keep their place.

I let go of her. "Sorry. I don't know what...happened. I just... Your name is Wednesday, isn't it?"

She rubbed her wrist. There was a momentary flinch at the mention of her name, but it didn't last. She went back to her stoic visage. "It is. The voices told you this, didn't they?"

I nodded.

She cleared her throat. "I must go. This place is..." Again, she cleared her throat. She fished one of the ice cubes from her glass and popped it in her mouth. "It's dangerous for us to meet without some sort of protection. God only knows how far Cam's—"

When she cleared her throat this time, I slid my lemonade across the table to her. I wasn't drinking it, so why not? Besides, I needed her to talk to me.

Wednesday grabbed the glass and gulped it down like a drunkard who'd failed detox. Juice slipped down her chin, but that did nothing to slow her gulps. When she finished my lemonade off, she clapped the glass on the table.

"Thirsty?" I asked.

After wiping the back of her hand across her lips, she rose from the bench and stared. "He knows we're here and we're talking. He'll do anything to protect his prized possession, including choking me to silence. The less you know, the easier it'll be for him take control of you again. My magic can only protect me for so long. I have to go."

I snatched her hand to keep her from moving. "You have to tell me where to find him."

A leer curled the corner of her mouth. "He'll find you if you sit still long enough."

"Please. I'll take anything. An address. Another lead. Anything." I couldn't plead with her any more than that. She'd said it herself. Gamboldt was most powerful when he kept me in the dark. I wasn't about to lie down and let this monster have his way with me ever again. "My friend Luz said people reported smelling or sensing earth magic around him. Does any of that ring a bell?"

Wednesday's eyes widened. When she opened her mouth to speak, a cough tore through her as though it had come from the depths of her lungs. Only smokers had coughs like that. She grabbed her throat and began wheezing. Redness flushed her cheeks. Regardless of the glares her people gave me, I remained steadfast in wanting information.

Chairs scraped the hardwood floors. Both of her bodyguards had left their stools and started for us. Tate approached them from the rear.

I stood and began smacking my hand on her back to loosen her choking fit. "Please. I need more information."

Garridan pressed her manicured fingers to one of her escort's chests. She tore the napkin from under her scotch glass—it remained in place like an old magician's trick. With a flick of her wrist, she produced a pen and began jotting something down.

Her fingers turned brown and began to shrivel around the pen. In seconds they looked like brown tree roots sticking out of her palm. She lifted her shaking hand to her face and stared in agony. Her head fell back and a high-pitched shriek belted from the depths of her lungs. I covered my ears to keep my eardrums from exploding.

The windows shattered throughout the bar. I ducked, but Tate pulled me to the floor anyway and covered my head and upper body. Screams broke out among the patrons as they dove for cover. The only person left standing was Wednesday. Even her bodyguards had dropped to the hardwood with their hands over their ears.

When she finished her tirade and the last of the glass shards clinked to the floor, I searched the bar.

Wednesday was gone.

Chapter Thirty-Two

Flashing lights and dozens of emergency vehicles brought the beginning of the rush hour to a standstill on Boylston Street. The police wrote the incident off as a drive-by. Although common in and around the Boston suburbs for chaos to break out, it was uncommon for something as odd as this in the middle of the day.

Detectives questioned everyone, including us. Running would have made it look like we had something to hide, so we stuck around. Plus, enough people had seen me with Wednesday, which made me the most obvious witness. Even Garridan's wrestler-type bodyguards—she'd left them behind—had agreed.

Our story: friends getting together for a few drinks when all hell broke loose. All of us stuck to it, including Garridan's people. To my shock, none of the patrons remembered Wednesday entering Seekers Tavern. Not even the waiter who'd brought our drinks. So, we never brought it up again.

Having to include Wednesday's two goons with us bothered the hell out of me. Tate's sideways glares and occasional grumbles at them let me know I wasn't alone. However, being supernaturals meant we had to put our bickering aside to keep humans ignorant of our business. At least they took it all in stride.

My cell phone rang loud enough to dislodge my erratic heart. A deep breath calmed my nerves. Stepping aside, I answered it.

"I'm watching the news," Dane said. "Where are you?"

"Probably on your TV." Ignoring a string of expletives in my ear, I glanced at Tate before stepping farther away from the commotion on the street. "Please don't tell me this isn't about staying safe. That piece of godfatherly advice is officially null and void."

"No shit. Look, I've got some information for you. Can you get away? Do you need me to pick you up?"

"Yes and no."

He chuckled. "There's a tea shop inside the Westin Hotel. It's a favorite of mine. I'll meet you there in a half hour."

I hung up. Looked like Dane and I would finally get a chance to meet. I hoped this one turned out better than the last.

A plethora of teas lined the wall behind the counter. A glass case with dozens of decadent desserts from ladyfingers to slices of seven-layer cake beckoned me. Not many people had frequented the teahouse this afternoon, which surprised me. I bet the uproar at Seekers Tavern attracted most of the crowd. It wasn't every day people had the chance to witness what the police deemed a "drive-by shooting" in downtown Boston.

Dane was on time. His dark hair was slicked back with a few waves running through it. He looked good in his blue shirt with a black leather jacket on top. He walked with a purpose, eyes on me that said I was the only thing on his mind.

Dane placed his hand on the back of the chair across from me. Before he pulled it out, he set his sights on Tate. My bald friend nodded and Dane sat. They must have shared some sort of unspoken language that I missed. In return, Tate excused himself to wait outside, brushing past Dane in silence.

I continued staring at his back until he stepped out of sight. "What was that all about?"

"Wolf business." Dane perused the dessert menu. "He respects me as your Alpha. But if he's leaving the premises, then I'm assuming he's not with you."

"Meaning...?"

He lowered the menu. "He's not your mate. It takes more than a beta wolf to tame someone like you."

I folded my arms. "How would you know?"

"Because I know you better than you know yourself right now." A grin tightened his crescent-shaped lips. He pointed at my half-empty cup. "How do you like the tea?"

"It's good. Now, you said you had information, so spill."

Dane reached inside his inner pocket and pulled out a piece of paper. After unfolding it, he slid it across the table. It was a printout of a newspaper article.

The *real* Keisha Walker had been killed at the tender age of twenty-seven around the time of my disappearance. Her body had vanished from the morgue before the autopsy. While the police still had it listed as an unsolved murder, they speculated the killer might have taken her to cover something up. She'd left behind a three-year-old son whose name was Tyree.

Holy shit.

My thumb touched her paper cheek as I read the article from top to bottom twice. She'd died from an arrow to the chest. The more I read, the more I knew her killer. For the last eight months, I had stared at the sniper every time I looked in the mirror.

My stomach sank to the floor and a tear rolled down my cheek. Another followed as I held my head and leaned on the table, desperate to grasp the situation and any meaning behind it. I had killed people and/or monsters before my memory lapse, and I was certain they'd had a reason to die. As far as I knew, this woman was an innocent single mom trying to make a better life for her child. She had transferred from the University of New Mexico to MIT to finish her mechanical engineering degree. Also, she'd worked as a part-time secretary and volunteered at her local church in Roxbury. I bet anything she'd left New Mexico to get away from Gamboldt. The jerk had probably promised to pay for her schooling in return for her stripping at his bar.

I was no better than the crazed werewolves I had killed. Amnesia or not, *I* did this. *I* had snuffed out someone as they were trying to turn around their life.

Dane held a napkin to me. Turning my head toward the window, I used it to wipe away my tears. I didn't want him to see me like this. I'd give anything to be one of those normal pedestrians walking on the street below us. Their lives were normal. Mine wasn't and would never be.

Dane folded his hands together on top of the table. "What the article doesn't tell you is that she was a telepath and worked for Robert."

That didn't come as a surprise, but it got my attention

anyway. "A telepath? Just like the other strippers."

Dane nodded. "That would be my guess. But I'm assuming you know more about that than I do. Whatever is locked away in your psyche, we need to get it out."

"Oh crap!" I glanced at my watch. I had fifteen minutes to get to Cambridge or miss my appointment with that psychiatrist, psychologist or whoever he was. After one last sip of my tea, I grabbed my jacket and stood. "I have to go. I have an appointment with a shrink."

"What?"

"It's a long story. Talk to me on the way."

"Hold on." He touched my arm. "What the hell are you seeing a shrink for? Your amnesia?"

"No, for my big toe. You just said—"

Dane shook his head. "No way, Angel. The last thing you need is some guy picking through your brain and finding out you're half werewolf. I won't allow it." He crossed his arms like his word was law.

I stared at him, fighting between laughter and giving him a few pieces of my mind about his so-called law and where to stick it. Instead of going for anger, I laid out the facts. "Look, I've got a possible murder charge hanging over my head. Not to mention a string of other problems that might result in me doing jail time. If I don't see this shrink to help me establish my insanity plea, the next time we have a conversation, there will be bulletproof glass and a phone involved. You still want to stop me?"

Dane studied my face for the longest time, as if he were memorizing the pimples or trying to summon one with his mind. When he stepped aside, I darted past him.

However, my bossy werewolf godfather wasn't leaving anytime soon. He followed Tate and me right down to the curb where we hailed a cab.

"Don't get me wrong." Dane leaned forward in the crammed backseat and addressed us. "I hope this doesn't mean you're in good with the Boston Pack."

Tate scowled. "Look, Mr. Dane. I know our Alpha has his issues, but you need to check yourself before you go any further."

I held up my hands to calm them both down. And here everyone thought *I* was the one who needed a shrink. "Whatever territorial problems you two are having, don't do it in this cab with me sitting in the middle. You two can take that shit outside." I paused. "No, Dane, I'm not a member of the Boston Pack. I'd rather slit my wrists before joining those asinine ranks. That's assuming Parry wouldn't do it himself. And Tate, before you ask, Dane's an intruder on your land just like me. He's from....?" I was thinking South Carolina, but I couldn't be sure about my memory anymore.

"Charleston," Dane finished.

Score one for me.

"And," Dane continued, "if you know what your maniac of an Alpha is like, why do you still hang with him? You look like an educated guy. From what I understand, your buddy Matthieu York is too. What gives?"

My mouth opened to answer for him, but I realized I didn't have one for that. Plus, it was a good question. Once again, the shoddy memory of mine had no recollection of my having a similar conversation with Matt.

Tate stared out the window. "Parry would make life a bitch for us if we ever left. He's spent years setting up alliances across the country. Not only to protect us, but to keep us prisoner. He has a good deal with me because I work in the medical field. Matt's a lawyer. We're like gold in his eyes, which makes him one of the most important supernatural leaders in the city. Crazed or not, our services are needed and people know they have to go through Parry to get them."

"You stay with him out of fear." Dane's even tone made it hard to gage the meaning behind his words.

Watching for a reaction from the driver, I leaned back in my seat in case a fist flew through the air. My face was too fragile to be the stopping force between two wolves gone wild in the backseat of a taxi.

"Knowing his history, I get that." Dane stared at the back of the cab driver's head.

I must have missed something. "You do?"

He nodded without looking at me. "You're stronger with a pack than without. Not many human families are in a position to truly seek revenge on your behalf. That's why most supernaturals are smart enough not to mess with a werewolf. It's better to align yourself with a pack than become the enemy of one. Because Parry is a psychotic bastard who believes in

Roman Coliseum brutality, stray wolves leave tasty little morsels like Tate alone."

Both Tate and I stared at him.

My eyes narrowed. "Good thing you're not looking for a fight, huh?"

Dane shrugged. "Not particularly. But don't get me wrong, Angel. I protect what's mine. Why do you think I bought that inn? You wanted to keep your lay-off a secret, so you got desperate and settled on the first job that came calling. *And* it just happened to be in another pack's territory. If you had told me where your new job was sooner, I might have stopped you from making the biggest mistake of your life."

"Thanks for jabbing me with the idiot stick, but can you wait until I get my memory back so I can mount a proper defense? And don't sit there like I went out purposefully looking for these guys. Memory loss or not, even I know I'm not that stupid. Did I know about the Boston Pack before I moved?"

"No. But like I said, it's a good thing I bought the inn when I did. It's harder to kick you out of the territory when you own a public business on it by human law. And just like I warned you pre-amnesia, Parry would have a fit if he discovered you, which he did. Eventually, he'll find a way to smoke you out. Count on it. I'm not in the mood to go head to head with someone else without a valid reason and you're walking that line. Thank God, at least Tate is minding his own business. Unless..." He turned his head to address me. "You're not sleeping with him, are you?"

"*What?*"

Tate's face contorted. "Are you out of your fucking mind?"

Dane's hands went up in defense. "Relax. Just making sure."

Yeah. Right. His quick reversal made me think twice about telling him anything about Matt. At some point, I'd have to get Tate alone and tell him not to say a word to Dane. If he and my father were tight, for all I knew my father had sent him to be my personal bodyguard in all facets of this word. Daddy might not take kindly to having his little girl devirginized by a wolf who had a maniac for an Alpha. Assuming I was a virgin when I did Matt.

Again, I glanced at the driver who rolled his eyes. He probably thought there was a nut in every bunch and he'd just happened to pick up three.

We showed up at Dr. Anri's five minutes early and with a game plan. I would go in while Tate stood by to bail me out in case I said too much. Chances were the shrink would think I was nuts and suggest a round of therapy. Since we didn't have that kind of time and I'd never see this guy again, what did it matter? Dane didn't like that idea. He wanted to come in with me and play boyfriend, but I vetoed him. He was still a stranger to me, and Tate had given me more than enough reason to trust him. Unwilling to get into another fight, Dane threw up his hands and said he'd wait outside.

Dr. Anri looked like a dork. The twig of a man stared at me through his black-rimmed glasses. His flat hair molded his head and he had a habit of rubbing his trimmed beard. He wore a peanut-colored jacket with a pair of brown slacks and matching loafers.

After about thirty minutes of talking about my feelings and the last thing I didn't remember before my time at Trixie's, Anri suggested hypnosis. I quivered at the idea, but if I wanted some clues to what had happened in my life, this was a good way to do it. Tate wanted us to leave. When he saw I wasn't budging, his eyes narrowed, but he stayed by my side. Matt had really good friends.

Anri led us over to a couch where I concentrated on a penlight. It took about five tries before he finally got me under. The first three tries, I had trouble keeping my giggles under control.

I became uninhibited and relaxed while in a state between awake and asleep. I would've been happy to stay like this for the rest of the day. It was calming and inviting, like floating on a cloud on my way up to heaven. I was free, flying across the night skyline with the wind ruffling my hair. My beautiful white gown glowed against the moonlight. Stars twinkled like little—

Crack!

My head slammed against the wall. Pain licked through the back of my skull.

When I opened my eyes, it looked like the subway had gone through Dr. Anri's office. A chair lay on the floor while another one rested in pieces on the other side of the room. Propped against the wall was the round top of the table. Who knew where the legs were? A sea of papers were scattered across the floor. Some had torn edges like they'd once belonged to books while others had patient names on them. On the far side of the room, cracked glass webbed from the edges of a windowpane.

Clothes disheveled, Tate crumpled to his knees. Three angry claw marks marred his cheek and neck. Next to him lay Dr. Anri. He rolled himself over and straightened his shattered glasses on his nose. He touched his temple and pulled back a blood-covered finger.

I blinked. "Do I even want to know what happened?"

Panting, Tate leaped to his feet and marched toward me. He grabbed my arm and yanked me to my feet. Questions marred his worried eyes and not an answer in sight. This couldn't be good.

"Don't." Holding his ribs, Anri winced while picking himself up off the floor. "It's not her fault."

"The hell it isn't." Tate turned his vehement scowl on Anri. "She almost killed us."

"What?" I pulled myself away from Tate and backpedaled until I bumped into the wall. "What's going on? What happened?"

Tate slammed both his hands near my head, trapping me against the cold ivory surface, his glare burrowing into my soul. I didn't want to be near him with that much fury in his eyes. Unfortunately, he didn't leave me much of an escape route.

"You fucking bastard." Tate leaned close enough for the shrink not to hear. "We'll tear your ass out of her, Gamboldt. That's a promise."

I blinked. On second thought, maybe ignorance was bliss...especially if he thought I was Gamboldt.

I lifted my head over his shoulder to see Anri making his way to his desk. I lowered my voice to a whisper. "What the hell are you talking about?"

Tate snagged my neck, crushing my throat. "Get out of her. You hear me?"

Gagging, I dug my fingernails into the backs of his hand. "You asshole," I wheezed. "It's me. Al—" Cough. Cough. "Alex...uh."

He blinked, but didn't release me fast enough. I brought my knee up, ready to mash his manly grapes. He grunted.

I glared at him. "Let. Me. Go."

"Is everything all right?" Anri tipped his head to the side for a better look.

Tate's eyes slid to the corners, following the shrink's voice. His attention snapped back to me. "Is it really you?"

A light knee-bump raised him up on his tiptoes. Anger tightened my face. "You want to ask me that again?"

"I asked if everything was all right?" Anri's footsteps started toward us.

Tate let go and lowered his arms to his side. I dropped my leg and grabbed my neck by the time the shrink finished closing the distance. We exchanged glares before turning our attention to Anri.

"Are you two okay?" He pressed a bloody cloth to the side of his temple. "Maybe we should all take a seat...somewhere." He looked around his devastated office.

I peeled my back off the wall and made my way to the couch. It was the only thing left standing, although it was askew by thirty degrees.

Tate didn't bother sitting. He leaned over the back of the couch, threatening to invade my personal space and obviously not giving a damn what I might think about it.

Anri sat at the other end. "Your boyfriend hit you against my wishes." He eyeballed Tate before turning his focus on me again. "I don't condone his violent solution. However, you were out of control."

Tate snorted. "Please. She was a fucking psycho."

Anri raised his hand to quiet the peanut gallery. "Do you know this man? Robert Gamboldt?"

I looked to Tate for a cue, but he remained too miffed to offer up a straight answer. I went with the truth. "Yes. I think he's responsible for me losing my memory."

"In that case, I think he did more than that." Anri turned the cloth over and refolded it for a cleaner side. "Are you familiar with the term brainwashing or programming?"

"Only what I've read and seen in the movies." *The Manchurian Candidate* came to mind, but why I remembered that movie and not what my family looked like, I couldn't say.

God, I hated this. It bugged me that I didn't know what it was like to give my mother a piece of artwork to stick up on the refrigerator. Or, when I rode my first bike. When Dad kissed my first strawberry to the knee. Hell, I'd give my left arm to know when my sister and I had our first fight. What did she look like? Who was her boyfriend? Did I ever catch her kissing one? Whenever I tackled my brain for the answers, I came up with crickets. Despite avoiding my family, there was no avoiding the small part of my heart that inherently belonged to them. And yet...they were as unreal as the people on the magazine covers scattered across Dr. Anri's floor.

Hate didn't begin to explain the rage inside me. Gamboldt had taken more than my memories. The bastard had taken my entire life.

"Earth to Alexa." Tate waved a hand in front of me. When I jerked back, a smile brightened his eyes. "You phased out a minute. Did you remember something?"

I hugged myself and shook my head. "Just thinking about the family I don't remember. Gamboldt's gonna pay for this."

Dr. Anri cleared his throat. "If this Gamboldt person is real, then he's somehow impressed his will on you. Turned you into something you're not. He has preprogrammed you to act out in a violent way if anyone tries to undo what he's done. In all honesty, I've never seen anything like it."

"Like what?"

The shrink stalled as he stared at an invisible point on the floor. He stood and made his way toward his unkempt desk. "I don't know. Or at least, I'm not sure. However, I'd like to prescribe some valium. To help you relax. Your friend said you weren't getting enough sleep anyway. Not only that, but..."

"But what?"

"Well... Things like this sometimes have a way of making themselves known. In other words, they might seem like they're a part of your own reality when your subconscious is sitting on the sidelines and someone else is in control. I'd like you to continue with therapy to help unravel more of this mystery. Going deeper next time might pull out more of your memories as well and..."

Something was wrong. Body language lacked a scent, but I knew uneasiness when I saw it. This guy's shifty eyes refused to settle on mine for more than a second or two at a time. He blubbered about things that made no sense, making me question his sanity in return. Or...maybe he realized he was out of his league.

I leaped off the couch and marched to his desk. He had better be lucky a piece of furniture stood between us or I'd yank his pencil neck across the top and drag him throughout this room until he told me. Then again, looking at the sight of this office, I might have already done that.

I leaned over the papers and smashed desk lamp and glared at him. "Level with me, doc. What else happened that you're not telling me?"

Anri finally lifted his head and met my eyes. "While you were under, your alter ego said something about not needing practice to put an arrow through our heads. That you had trained for it enough. I think you conspired to kill some people. Whether or not you succeeded, I don't know. The only thing I'm sure of is that I might have to refer you to someone with more experience with this kind of thing."

I *knew* it. Out of his league my ass. Unless he had a degree in supernatural psychology, there wasn't enough therapy in the world to help my cause.

Tate pressed a comforting hand on my shoulder. I shrugged him off. Enough people had touched me already. I didn't want anymore regardless of their innocent intentions.

"What happens now?" I continued to stare, demanding answers with my eyes instead of resorting to physical violence. Again. "Am I certifiable?"

Anri found a prescription pad underneath a pile of papers. "You need more help. Certifiable?" He folded his arms across his chest and leaned against the windowsill behind him as though he feared me without wanting to put on a show. "In your present state, no. When you had taken on this Robert Gamboldt persona, yes. Multiple personalities syndrome is something you don't want to play with."

"But you just said—"

"That's how it looks on the surface, Ms. Wells. The strange thing is that when you take on a new persona, you don't take on that kind of strength. It was like you had the power of two, possibly three men combined. Not only that, you referred to yourself in the third person, as though a self-centered person were using your body for their will. That's why I'm having a hard time trying to label the exact problem. I don't want to give you anything stronger than valium until I'm sure what the problem is."

Someone had to tell Monica. I didn't know if it would be me or him. Either way, I didn't care. However, if anyone outside of Anri's office found out about this, both he and Monica would become the next victims on my growing list.

When Tate and I left the office, Dane was nowhere to be found. He didn't strike me as the type to take off without telling someone or leaving a note with the receptionist. Not to mention, he had gone through a lot to make contact with me and refused to leave once he had.

I led the way outside onto the street only to have footfalls that didn't belong to Tate scraping the ground behind me. He was on my left. As I turned, something pressed against my right lower rib. A dark blue SUV pulled up alongside the curb and a gray car stopped behind it. The SUV's driver and the passenger I recognized as Garridan's goons who had disappeared earlier. Wednesday had said she wanted to continue this elsewhere, and it looked like she meant it.

With Dane already sitting in the backseat, we joined him. Not like we had much of a choice anyway.

Chapter Thirty-Three

The Garridans had gone from owning multiple stores to one two-story consignment shop a couple miles away in Northern Revere called Vujo Garments. From the large front windows, we had a great view to the boardwalk and some of the small taverns and restaurants. Lean a little ways out from the building, and there were large fishing boats tied to the piers with masts jetting up at the partly cloudy sky. Each breeze brought a fishy stench that corroded my nostrils.

The guards led us up to the second floor where we shared the same view as we did from the first floor. In the corner of the room near the panoramic window was Wednesday. She sat on a chaise lounge where another woman tended to her wounded hand. Sweat beaded her forehead, plastering pieces of her blue-black hair to her face as it scrunched in agony. We made it across the room filled with clothing racks, pushing some of the garments aside.

"Glad you could come." She winced again and pulled her hand away from the other woman.

I had never seen anything like it. Her hand was that of a woman at least four times her age. Red veins looked more like welts underneath the skin. Blisters pulsed on the back of it and near the fingertips. When she flipped over her hand, red cuts oozed blood from her palm.

Trembling, she used her injured hand to point Tate to the chair across from her. She forced a smile to her lips. "Sorry I had to leave like that. It was a battle of wills where more explosions were bound to happen." She turned her hand over to Tate. "As you can see, I lost. With all of the supernaturals on Robert's payroll, he has many eyes and ears across the city."

Wednesday motioned around the room. "This place is protected by Roma magic and has been for the last thirty years. Robert knows this, so I don't know how long it'll last. I'm sure he senses treachery in the ranks."

"And that would be...?" Dane shrugged.

She spied him. "Who is this? Your friend, I recall seeing at the bar. Even had him checked out before allowing you both to come. But this gentleman, I don't know him. There had better be a good reason why he's here."

I put on my best cheesy smile and stepped in front of Dane. "This is another friend of mine. He's harmless."

She wrinkled her nose. "Since when are werewolves harmless?" Wednesday winced and snatched her hand back from Tate. "You asked me about earth magic back at the bar. There are many forms of it. The best I know of are the wise women and witches. Wise women are a little harder to find. Not the case with witches, and I'm not talking Salem. There's a coven west of Boston."

"Where exactly?"

She shrugged. "I don't know. They move it all the time. But they're also like sentinels. In fact, I'm surprised they haven't made contact with you."

I glanced around. This was no time to keep my mouth shut, since I seemed to be the only one in the room with knowledge in that area. "There was one. Her name's Pippa and she's a lab tech. When I went to the hospital—"

"That'll work."

I arched my eyebrow to acknowledge her rudeness. "When I went to the hospital, she followed me. Said I shouldn't have come and let them take my blood. At the time I didn't know what I was or I would've stayed away." On that last note, I glared at Dane. After what had happened with Dr. Anri, he probably had another warning about hospitals and the dangers they posed. That reprimand would have to wait. "Anyway, I don't know how to reach her nor do I know where to begin."

Wednesday fought through a wince to speak. "There are sixty-seven Garridans around Boston and we have connections with other clans. While I can't promise anything because there are still a few Robert supporters among our ranks, I can start asking. It's the least I can do since you might be the only one who can put Gamboldt down."

I shook my head. "I'm nobody's hero. I'm just trying to get control of my life. I don't like some stranger holding the reins in their hands."

That's exactly what Gamboldt was doing and I didn't like it. Who knew where and when his hunger for power would stop? After all, he didn't seem the least bit intimidated by my half-werewolf status. Next thing you knew, he'd strike out on his own to control a full blood. If he succeeded there, Parry would probably be his next target. Switching the control of the Boston Pack from one maniac to another would only make things worse. Especially for Matt.

I closed my eyes to block the memory from coming through, but that didn't stop another idea from forming. One that kept slipping my mind. "How did Robert know about me? Did your Aunt Tatiana sense something about my skills?"

She shrugged. "Not that I know of. Her powers are good for sensing what kind of supernatural a person is. But even with that, it's not a hundred percent accurate or she'd know what Robert was by now. We don't. Even Uncle Cam doesn't. All he knows is that the man has a very charismatic way with people."

"Great, the guy just lucked out on my being a marksman."

Dane folded his arms and shook his head. "That's the thing. Only a few of us know that. I was the one who trained you. Your uncle helped too, but that's it. Your parents didn't like it at all. What about Flora and Charles? Could they have known?"

Perhaps, but he'd said something that bothered the hell out of me. If only Dane and my family knew about my archery skills, was it possible that Robert might have already gotten to them too?

I closed my eyes forcing those thoughts from my head. I didn't want to think about that monster having his hands on anyone in my family. Whether I knew them or not, they were mine, dammit. I'd gladly kill the bastard if he breathed in their direction. Knowing what I knew now, thank goodness Dane had taken it upon himself to put my loved ones in hiding. It was more reason to stop Gamboldt permanently.

"Headache again?" I opened my eyes to see Wednesday addressing me. "You shouldn't be feeling anything. There's a stronger protection spell around this place than the one I used around myself at the bar. If you feel—"

I shook my head. "I'm fine. Just thinking about my family."

"That's makes two of us." Dane gave my shoulder a reassuring squeeze.

Wednesday slumped back in her chair. "If they're anything like you, he might be trying to find them. You should warn them."

"Believe me, they've already been warned." Dane began walking around the second floor, checking out some of the antique furniture and the pictures on the wall. "His mind-control powers have already been established. What bothers me is how he's able to control a half wolf, but not a full blood. At least, none that I know of. Tate would've said something by now, I'm sure." He plucked a large painting off the wall and stared at it.

Tate nodded. "Good point."

Wednesday frowned. "Robert can't control everyone and he knows it. Why do you think the entire vampire world hasn't fallen under his spell? Or the werewolves haven't bowed down to do his bidding. Parry doesn't like him, but he respects him. Nobody knows what Robert's capable of. We might be sitting in our car when he commands someone to shoot us at the stoplight."

"Whoa whoa whoa whoa whoa." Dozens of questions mixed with worry and excitement clogged my brain. "Parry knows about this guy? The fucking Boston Pack Alpha?"

Until now, I hadn't thought Parry had anything to do with my nightmare. Given my circumstances, I didn't have that luxury anymore. Holy shit. It made sense Gamboldt would only go after me and not Matt. If the Roma had marked him, the bastard would automatically toss him out because he was a full blood and most likely one of Parry's people. Since everyone knew about Parry's disgusting disposition, Gamboldt probably had me pegged as a stray.

It wasn't that the madman lacked the power to control the werewolves but could've struck a deal to leave them alone. As long as nobody touched Parry's precious pack, that fucker was set. If Gamboldt got his hands on me again, he wouldn't let go. Given the supernatural population in Boston, who knew where that mind-controlling monster would stop?

Wednesday nodded. "They were once seen shaking hands outside. After one of our auctions."

"Parry might know how to find Gamboldt." I could've pissed a kidney for not thinking about this sooner.

Dane put the picture down to rejoin us. "Yeah, but if it doesn't benefit him in some way, he might not give a damn."

"We're gonna find out." Tate handed the gauze to Dane and leaped out of his seat. Before leaving the room, he had unclipped his phone and placed a call.

Dane took Tate's seat and began wrapping Wednesday's hand. He did it with the care and skill of a man who looked like he had done it at least a dozen times prior. When all of this was over, I'd have to ask him where he'd acquired his skills.

Speaking of which, he owed me some answers, so I tapped his shoulder. "Tell me about me. Who am I to you really?"

Dane sighed as though he had anticipated my question, but didn't want to answer it. "I taught you everything you needed to know about how to defend yourself. Being half werewolf, you needed an edge over a regular werewolf. Especially if you wanted to survive this crazy world of ours. About a quarter of our species is female and not everyone survives the transformation if they're bitten or their blood gets infected with ours. But my point is that your being part werewolf and smelling like a pork chop would only entice a rogue wolf to either rape or kill you. Your father and I weren't about to let that happen. And it wasn't like you'd spend the rest of your life living at home either. So, before you went away to college, he sanctioned me to train you. Like I did him."

Oh my... That made him... Could he be...? "How old are you?"

"Ninety. We age slower than the average human. And before you ask, I was bitten. Most of us were. To die of old age is a rarity in this life because we're always fighting over territory or whatever scraps we can get. There are packs in many major cities, so this day and age of modernization has made us more civilized. To some extent. There are more werewolves alive today than when you were born. Then you have packs like Parry's where they believe in the old ways of survival of the fittest and taking it to the extremes."

"But you taught me how to live among them. Didn't you?"

Nodding, he taped off the edges of Wednesday's dressing. "I had to. You're like the daughter I hoped to raise before she was killed by a werewolf. Once I fell in with your family, I swore I'd never let anything happen to you guys. In fact, I made a promise to your uncle."

"Uncle?"

"Graham. He's your grandfather's brother, to be exact. Anyway, we turned out to be very good friends. From there, his family became my family. After your grandfather had bitten you—by the way, is any of this news to you?"

"Some, but go on. I know about my grandfather going crazy and attacking me and my..." I gulped and shook my head.

Images of a little boy screaming in terror flooded my brain. I couldn't get it out of my head, his tiny arm in the mouth of a giant wolf. My throat tightened up, squeezing tears from my eyes. His screams wouldn't go away. Dammit, they wouldn't stop. They just kept going and going and going and—

"Hey hey." Dane was out of the chair and had both hands on my shoulders. He tilted his head, his concerned face studying mine. His thumb swept across my cheek, clearing away a tear trail. A timid smile inched onto his too-tanned face. "While I'm glad you're getting back some of your memories, Angel, that's not the one I was hoping for."

Shaken, I eased out of his hands. What in the world had I gotten myself into? Why did lycanthrope have to choose me instead of my choosing it? Things would have been better if I were a normal kid living in a normal world with normal parents. I'd be like everyone else in the rat race and not standing in some magical Roma's store with a werewolf looking for signs that I might break.

"You okay?" Dane asked.

I nodded despite another tear slipping down my cheek. Steeling myself, I wiped it away and turned my back to Dane. Under normal circumstances, I wouldn't turn my back on anyone in this house, but I had to do it to regain some composure. I hated crying in front of people whether I knew them or not.

Wednesday continued her story about her family's dealings with Robert. I tuned some of it out because the large window overlooking the boardwalk caught my attention. Right in front of the store, Tate stood talking on the phone. His lips moved, but it looked like he did most of the listening. Customers walked right past him and into the store. Below our feet, the bell chimed before a thump signaled the door closing.

More people crowded the boardwalk below. They moved like ants going back and forth without running into each other. Even Tate looked around with an annoyed look on his face. He stepped to the side, just barely in my sights, most likely to hide some of his preternatural conversation. The number of pedestrians doubled in the few minutes he had stood there. Cars and trucks began traveling back and forth along the main road on the north side of the building. The whole scene looked like we had gone from Revere to a busy New York City street.

Wednesday's attention shot toward the window. "Ohmygod. He's broken through. Quickly, woman. Where is your friend?"

I pointed at the window. "He's down there talking on the phone."

"Outside?"

I nodded. "Why?"

"Because our protection spells don't go beyond our front doors."

Aw shit!

I began pounding on the window to get Tate's attention. He lifted his head, smiled at me, and went back to his conversation. Surely, he must have seen me. I continued, smacking the glass, ready to break through it if I had to. Speaking of which, a chair caught the corner of my eye. I grabbed it.

"No!" Wednesday was on her feet. "The protection spell is in full force. You won't be able to break the glass."

I tossed the chair at the wall and ran to the backside of the long building. My feet pummeled down the steps until I made it to the ground floor. Racks of clothes hung everywhere and there were more customers clogging the aisles leading to the front door.

I pushed every animate and inanimate object out of my way. Clothes tangled around my arms. I jerked myself free. More clothes...shot out from the racks. Sleeves threw themselves at me, snagged my arms and trying to hold me back. They didn't have much strength, but they slowed me down. Shirts tried to stop me from reaching the front, but I flung them to the floor hangers and all.

By the time I made it to the front door, the traffic and the people had disappeared. Everything looked normal from the guy threading his fishing pole to the woman walking with her two children.

I yanked the door open, the force flinging the chime off the wall and clanging against the carpeted floor. Wind brushed across my face like an afterthought. To my right, Tate had disappeared. His cell phone wide open was the only thing left of him. Panic sent my heart thumping in overdrive. I picked up the cell and listened to the angry voice screaming on the other side.

"Answer me, dammit."

Throbbing nervousness clogged my throat while I continued to scan the streets. I put the phone to my ear just as Dane hurried out of the store and stood beside me. "Who's this?"

"Who the hell is this?"

Oh crap. I forgot he came down here to call Parry and probably discuss pack business away from us non-pack folk. "Your wolf's gone."

"You bitch. If you hurt one hair on my dog's head—"

"You stupid prick. Maybe if you'd stop being such an Alpha pussy and take some responsibility in your own hands, your so-called dog wouldn't be in Gamboldt's."

"You little cunt! I'll tear your mongrel, half-bred ass—"

"Fuck you. I don't have time for this."

I hung up in the middle of his rant. Alpha werewolf or not, I wasn't feeling his sense of entitlement. I couldn't mess around with stupidity like that when I needed to get my friend back.

Chapter Thirty-Four

Right in the middle of our crisis, Monica gave me a call and suggested I visit her at her office tomorrow afternoon. She had just finished speaking with Dr. Anri. Against our wishes about lying low and doing her job, she'd called the nursing home to inquire about Llewellyn, but again, no information was allowed to be given out without express wishes of the family. Even if the old guy knew something, there was no way to get it out of him. As if we needed more bad news on top of Tate's kidnapping. Sadly, the few people we questioned said he'd walked away with some so-called friends of his to have a drink. The Garridans speculated that a confusion spell was used as a diversion.

While Dane and I rode the subway back to the city, I tried to reach the Boston Pack's den again with Tate's cell. If they didn't call me a mutt bitch, then it was something worse. Dane took the phone and placed the fifth call as we stepped out of the subway tunnels. Good thing too. Dane's anxious pacing when the train was in motion had driven me nuts. He seemed a tad more relaxed being on the streets with hundreds of people and less of a chance for another kidnapping.

"I need to speak to..." He looked to me for the answer.

"Matt?" Really, he was the only one I cared about in that hellhole.

He frowned. "That's the guy you're dating, right?"

I rolled my eyes. This was no time to talk about my personal life or lack thereof.

Dane shook his head before going back to the phone again. "Matt."

He spent another minute or two enforcing his authority like a true Alpha who had some sense in his head. Unlike that jackass running the Boston Pack. It took a few tries and some running around before Matt came to the phone.

I snatched it from Dane just as we rounded the corner a few blocks from Tate's place. "Hello? Matt?"

"Thank God. Was that your friend Wesley Dane?" His voice was like heaven.

"Forget about him. Look, Robert used whatever powers he possesses to take Tate. I'm not talking the mind control either. This was something different. We were at a consignment shop in Revere talking to Wednesday Garridan when they used magic to swipe him under our noses."

"Where are you now?"

I glanced around, lifting my head to spot a street sign. "We're about two blocks from Tate's."

"Why are you there? Hell, Lex, you need to be in hiding or something. Get out of town while you can. We'll figure this out when Parry releases me."

"Releases you? I thought you were there because Parry wanted to keep an eye on you. Not hold you prisoner."

"This is his idea of holding me prisoner. I found out what he meant last night when I tried to leave."

Uh-oh. I did *not* like the sound of this. "What happened last night?"

Something like playing cards snapped together in the background. Glass shattered and it sounded like a screaming match had broken out. A door whined opened and closed with a thud. Crows squawked in the distance.

"Where are you and what was all that noise?"

"Had to go outside to get away from the foolishness." After a huff, he continued. "One of my stupid pack overheard me talking to Tate last night about leaving this place and they told Parry. The bastard broke into my room and..." A hacking cough seized his voice. "Sorry about that. I've got a cold, I think."

"That's bullshit and you know it. What's going on, Matt?"

"Nothing."

"Don't lie to me!" Whoa. My voice got a little loud on that one. Passersby stepped aside or looked at me like they didn't want any part of my explosion. Dane gave me a you-might-want-to-chill-out look and I agreed. I took a breath to calm down. "Talk to me. If you don't tell me what's going on, I'll find out even if I have to come down to Kingston to find you."

"Don't. Trust me on that."

"Then say something."

He paused. "Parry wanted to make sure I stayed put. A good beating usually assures that."

"What the—?"

I tossed the phone to Dane and grabbed hold of the nearest *No Parking* sign I found and strangled it. It was a good thing the Department of Transportation cemented these things into the ground. I wanted to throttle something just to get the anger out of me. A growl helped, though it was pitiful compared to that of a real wolf. It didn't matter. I just needed to get my frustrations out before I battered a storefront window instead. Helplessness and I don't mix. Boy, did I feel it big time.

Dane laughed and waved at the passersby who decided my tantrum was more important than where they were going. "Don't mind her. Just a little tension release."

Once I wore myself out, I pulled my clawed fingers off the signpost and flexed the pain out of them. Dane shook his head before handing me the phone.

Matt's voice brought me back to the conversation. "Look, I don't want you doing anything crazy."

A little late for that. Just ask the leaning signpost of Pisa.

Matt paused. "Parry's on a rampage. He jumped in the car and took off with a few of his cronies not too long ago. I have no idea where he's headed, but I bet anything it's either your way or Gamboldt's."

"What makes you say that?"

"He mumbled something like 'that damn Gamboldt' and 'not keeping his word' before taking off."

Call me crazy, but I had a hunch Parry had sold me out to Gamboldt to "get the stray" out of his territory. The only part that pissed me off was Parry taking his temper out on Matt. The more I learned about this guy, the more I thought the only thing standing between Matt and Parry was a pack of wild wolves who'd rather have a leader who'd let them run wild than one who demanded order.

Unfortunately, I couldn't do anything about the power struggles among the Boston Pack right now. But once I finished this, all bets were off.

I hung up with Matt and let a new resolve fill me. I turned to Dane. "How much money do you have?"

"Enough. Why?"

"I might need you to bail me out of jail."

When I started off, Dane snagged my arm and hauled me back. "Just a second, Ms. Death and Destruction. I know that look in your eyes. Where the hell do you think you're going?"

"The one place where I can get my own leverage. We're hitting that nursing home."

Haven Park was a beautiful nursing home that looked more like an elegant mansion situated on a mountainside in Waltham. It had a great view of the city and the highway below. A light breeze brought my attention to the setting sun just beyond the rustling tree limbs. Around the side of the tertiary-level building was a parking lot about five times the size of the Crescent Inn's, if not more. Reserved parking was left for the staff on call. We arrived as a medical transporter had pulled up to the front ready to hand off another patient.

When Dane and I walked inside, it wasn't anything like I had expected. This place looked more like a cozy hotel than a nursing home. There were flowers everywhere along with a rose pink pattern on the textured walls and matching rug liner. Hardwood flooring spread throughout the entire first floor. The cushioned furniture looked liked it had been professionally cleaned and the magazines lay in two fanned piles on the coffee table. If this was going to be the last resting place for your loved ones, they wanted it as comfortable as possible. One thing was certain. It took a pretty penny to keep your elderly relatives happy in a place like this. If so, then Gamboldt cared a lot about his uncle, meaning I had come to the right place.

The receptionist sitting behind the counter didn't look anything like a nurse and lacked a nametag to confirm it. Two more nurses stood behind her restacking a bunch of folders in the slots along the wall. I thought that was interesting considering this place probably had about fifty rooms at most.

I put on my concerned-relative face as I approached the counter. "Excuse me. I'm here to see Llewellyn Gamboldt. I flew all the way from Arizona because I just heard the news. Is he okay? Oh, God, please tell me he's all right."

The receptionist frowned at me. "*She* is doing fine. What did you say your name was?"

She? I thought Monica said Llewellyn was a guy. In fact, I'm pretty sure she did. *What gives?*

Dane smoothed one hand along my back and cupped my free hand with his other one. The sensuality of his gesture touched a nerve inside that made me want to ease awaybefore cooties crawled off his person. I stayed put. Though I couldn't recall, my body must have, because it settled into his hold without my having to think too hard about it. If it were Matt, the endearment would've melted off me. With Dane, it said play along. It made me wonder how many times before we had to do a play-along in the past.

"Please." His voice wasn't as urgent as mine, but he was sincere. "My fiancée and I have been traveling all day. She's been frantic with worry and hoping to see her aunt today."

The receptionist narrowed her eyes on us. "I don't know. We're very strict about who—"

I poured on my fake hostility. "Look, what difference does it make? I just flew thousands of miles to see my aunt because Robert said it wouldn't hurt to pay my respects. You can call him if you want, but he'll be pissed if anyone disturbs him while he's at the Children Come First and Second charity dinner at the Westin. I'm sure he's donated a lot of money to this place, since you guys have been doing such a great job with my aunt and all."

The woman's lips thinned, but she handed over two visitor's badges anyway. She certainly didn't put up much of a fight. Whether Dane had noticed it too, something told me we needed to make this a short visit. For all I knew that woman could be calling Robert right now and describing us to him.

Llewellyn was actually Louise "Lou" Ellen. Monica hadn't gotten it mixed up either. Dane picked up the old woman's chart and noticed it said male. Either the woman was a hermaphrodite, or Robert did it with the hopes of keeping her identity a secret from anyone who might have meant him harm. He certainly had enough money to pay them off for a little cover-up in return.

Lou Ellen shifted in the bed. She was a large woman who looked every bit of her ninety-plus years old. She had a large, bulbous nose with a wart growing beside it. I couldn't be sure, but I'd swear someone had put lip gloss on her. There was no way her lips were that juicy while the rest of her looked dried and wrinkly. Thin white hair covered her head with a slight curl on the ends and her fat fingers kept the quilt clutched to her front.

When she opened her eyes, I jumped back. They weren't just the white of a blind person, they were more like pearls. A thin ring around the middle of her eyes suggested she had an iris among the milky pallor.

"Who's there?" Her voice came across in an endearing, grandmotherly way. "Robert, is that you?"

So much for that vegetative state.

I glanced over my shoulder at Dane. He motioned with her chart for me to answer her. I didn't know what to say to the old woman. A plan had come to fruition on the way, and we'd even rehearsed it twice. Something about seeing her had changed all that. Call me a coward if you want, but I wasn't into rousting old women out of bed for information. Nonetheless, we needed it.

I leaned close, careful not to touch her. If she had powers like her son's, I didn't want her reading me. "It's not Robert. It's...Elaine. From Trixie's Tricks."

"Lainey!" She clapped her hands together and started reaching toward me. "Where are you, my sweet grandbaby? Say something."

Great what the f—? That meant my so-called friend at Trixie's was actually... Dear God. Gamboldt had probably planted her and concocted our friendship to make it easier for her to keep a close eye on me. Just when I'd thought maybe I'd had one friend in that place who I trusted. In reality, I'd had no one. They were all on Robert's payroll and parts of their jobs were keeping me down.

I clenched my teeth to prevent myself from saying something I'd regret later. Gulping helped me regain my friendly persona. "No way. I don't want you reading what's been going on in my mind these days."

Chuckling, she swatted the air next to my head. "Silly girl. You know good and well I burnt myself out a long time ago. If your father's not careful, he'll do the same. Tell me. Who else is in the room with you? I can hear him breathing. By the way, your voice sounds a bit strange. Don't tell me you've picked up smoking again."

I coughed. "I haven't. Just a cold is all. As for the person in the room with me, this is my fiancé, Herbert."

Dane shot me such a glare that I thought it would singe my playful grin.

Nonetheless, he stepped forward. "Nice to meet you, ma'am."

"You, too. I hope you've been treating my little girl well." Her wrinkled lips pursed together in a smile.

"I have. Well, perhaps I should leave you two ladies alone to get—"

"No." I flagged Dane to come closer. Now that I knew she was safe, I cupped Lou Ellen's pudgy fingers. "I need some advice. And I don't want to go to Daddy about it. You know how he is."

"You must be mad at him. The last time you called him that, he said he wanted you working at the nightclub. I hope it hasn't gotten rough or anything. He promised me it was for a nice lounge in downtown Boston. If any of those executives give you any trouble, you send your father to me. Understand?"

"Will do." A new plan formed. I had a good idea of where I wanted to go with this and how to get my answers. "You knew about Dad having a half werewolf working for him right? About him brainwashing her to do what he wants? It's scary."

All of the joviality fell off Lou Ellen's stiffened face. She retracted her hands from mine and curled them around her quilt.

That did it. The gig was up. She knew who I really was and didn't need any powers to give her a clue. In fact, she was probably the type who didn't have a problem with her life hanging in the balance because it had since the day they had wheeled her in here.

"He's making a name for himself in more than just one community isn't he?"

I frowned. "Come again?"

"You know what I mean. Your father thinks the best way to get what he wants is through intimidation. If he has the right people in his pocket, then they'll make it happen. If what you say is true, about him having a half wolf under his control, then he's on the brink of making it happen. How did he do it—do you know?"

I shook my head, but forgot she couldn't see it. "I don't. He doesn't tell us all his secrets. All I know is the other women and I pinch information off the execs at Trixie's and it's used against them."

"Good Lord." She threw her head back in the pillows and shook it from side to side. Her eyeballs might have rolled up to the top too, but I couldn't be sure. "I can't believe him. Why does that crazy son of mine have to be so damn greedy? His father taught him to take only a little and what rightfully belonged to him. Not take everything because he thinks he can. It'll be the death of him. Just like trying to control vampires and werewolves. Tell me, what's he doing with this half wolf? How far has he gotten with her?"

"He's used her to kill."

Lou Ellen closed her eyes and crossed the Holy Trinity over her chest. "He can't do it alone. Your father doesn't have that kind of power. Someone else must be helping him magnify it. It's the only thing that makes sense." She felt three buttons on the inside of her bed before she pressed the fourth one. A whirling motor came to life, raising the bed for her to sit up. "He told me he had necromancers, witches, and others who supported him in his mission. Fools, all of them."

"What mission?"

She stared straight at me. Her lips trembled, but no words came out. She wet her lips again. "The best way to make someone listen is to make them fear you. Thank goodness he hasn't taught you that lesson yet. Your father has been pushed around all his life and he's tired of it. Just when he thinks he's the big man on campus, he finds out there's always someone bigger. You want power in our world, then imagine what you can do if you have a Pack Alpha or a member of the Vampire Ministry under your control? That means you have a voice to be reckoned with. A voice that can upset the balance of power in your favor. If you need something, why ask when you can use your mind control to bend their will? Or at least make them fearful enough that they will concede to your whim."

"Werewolves are unpredictable. They're meant to be controlled by an Alpha wolf. Anything less and they'll rebel."

"True. But regardless of the species, all of them will respond to fear. That's just the beginning. Curbing it to suit your needs is the next step. Making it happen is the third. If your father has a half wolf under his control, then he's achieved step one. On to step two."

And it would tear the supernatural community apart. Nobody appreciated having a leash around their necks. Certain species didn't work well with one another and it had nothing to do with ancient rivalries or revenge. It had more to do with instinct. Just like flies would never join a beehive. Gamboldt was insane to think we'd give him respect just because he wanted it. Achieving it through fear was one way, but what he had proposed went beyond that. He wanted complete control over something that human laws had hardly contained for the last millennia. Even then, our laws superseded theirs because we lived in fear of being discovered. We'd be damned before we lived with a new kind of fear from some low-grade supernatural like him. Talk about a revolt. Robert would have one that would rival the Revolutionary War. Big time. Perhaps enough to spill into the human world.

Lou Ellen began fidgeting with the edge of her quilt. "If you're going to kill me, you might as well get on with it. The only reason Robert hasn't done it himself is because he's a good boy who respects his mother. He just gets a little confused at times."

I straightened and stared at her. "Elaine knew all along, didn't she?"

She half-smiled. "No. Robert doesn't tell his daughter everything for her own good. She's also very wide-eyed and naïve. You don't strike me as the type, if you're trying to dupe a blind woman. Are you the half wolf you spoke of?"

I gulped. "Yeah."

Lou Ellen nodded. "Then you know what's at stake. While I love my son, he can be a bit screwy at times. I don't condone whatever he's done to you. Not to mention, I know my time is near and all I want to do is make things right with the Lord to better my chances of Him calling me home. I don't want to be a wandering spirit like some of our relatives."

Dane stepped close to the bed. "Wandering spirit? You mean he can channel dead people?"

She shook her head. "No. But controlling someone else's mind means you can see through their eyes, too."

Yes! I punched Dane in the shoulder and grinned. "That's it. That's how he's been able to track me all this time. He can astral project his mind. Chances are, he probably knows we're here."

"Thanks to Ralph, the orderly, he does," a voice said.

Both Dane and I turned toward the door. As fate would have it, Paul was standing there and he wasn't alone. Frankie, my stripping nemesis, stood behind him and his gun.

Chapter Thirty-Five

I folded my hands over my chest, trying not to look intimidated despite the quake that seized my heart. With that silencer screwed on the tip, he could shoot both of us and nobody would ever know. The only problem was, he needed me alive. Dane, on the hand, was expendable now that Robert already had his hands on a wolf. After all, it only took one for him to experiment.

"You guys messed up royally by kidnapping the wrong wolf." I glanced at Ms. Gamboldt wondering what would happen if I used her as a shield. Killing had dropped off my list of priorities when she'd told me everything and then some. Besides, I wasn't in the business of killing old women no matter how prepared this one was for it. "Tate belongs to the main people you don't want to mess with."

"Yes, we do." Frankie closed the door behind them. "Eventually, he would've been a target. Might as well have taken him while we had the chance. Made you flinch, didn' it?"

"Why you miserable, bitch." I started around the bed for her, but Dane snagged my forearm before I got up in her face. "I'll do more than flinch if he comes back the worse for wear."

Paul laughed. "Then you had better get your boxing gloves on because that's exactly what we plan."

After nudging me aside, Dane wandered away from the bed and stood on the opposite side of the room. Perhaps he thought firing bullets around Lou Ellen wasn't a good idea either. "How do you plan on getting us out of here? Shoot us. Then get one of Robert's necromancers to bring us back to life?"

"We're going to walk out of here nice and slow."

"Good." Huffing, Lou Ellen folded her arms. "Because the

sooner you people leave, the sooner I can get my beauty rest before those other men come up here. Real meanies. Especially the redhead."

All of us stared at her, but I was the one who spoke. "I thought you said your powers didn't work anymore."

She smiled. "They don't. Except for when I'm really scared and get vision flashes. I might be wrong, but they're asking to see me about something. News about my son, I think."

Paul ran to the window and shoved the curtain out of his way. He pressed his nose against the glass.

Dane grabbed him and wrestled him around the room, crashing into the extra chairs.

They only distracted me for a second when I set my sights on Frankie. I jumped her from behind with a chokehold. Until then, I had no idea how hard it was to get your arms in the right place around someone's neck. Most of it required upper body strength, which was something I had in abundance. The only problem was her struggles didn't make the hold any easier and I had to be careful not to snap her neck in the process.

The gun went off. Despite the muffled sound, it was enough to get my attention.

Frankie sagged to the floor by my feet. At first, I thought she'd caught the bullet, but there wasn't any blood or an exit wound. She'd passed out from the pressure I'd applied to her throat. Gently—not sure why—I laid her down and looked up.

Dane remained in a crawl position with Paul sitting back on his knees and the gun shaking in his hand. A spot of blood dropped on the floor underneath Dane. Another drop followed from the inside of his jacket.

Rage boiled through me. That son of a fucking whore had shot my friend. Granted, though our friendship thing was still on the fence because my head needed more convincing, the hatred and anger swirling inside said otherwise. Messing with a woman's family would turn her into a madwoman. When Dane went out of his way to protect mine that sealed his status for me.

I flew across the room and kicked the gun out of Paul's hand. Before that same foot touched the floor, I whacked it across his face. Paul grabbed his cheek. My foot came up, ready to pummel him again. To my shock, not once did I lose balance.

I called off my attack. Nothing would have pleased me more

than to bash his skull against the wall. Watching that bastard squirm while he held his nose would have to be enough. At least there was some satisfaction with the amount of blood seeping through his fingers.

I left him and rushed to Dane's side to pull open his jacket. Blood had soaked into his blue shirt and over his black jeans. Thick crimson oozed from the bullet hole.

Dane touched my sleeve. A strained smile splayed his face. If he did that to comfort me or imply it wasn't that bad, it wasn't working.

"No." He nudged me away. "Just...go to the bathroom. Find a towel or something."

I did. When I returned, I balled it up and pressed it to his side. He grunted before batting my hands away with his bloodied ones as though he wanted control of the situation and didn't need my help. Then again, it could've just been the Alpha-in-charge in him talking.

I let him be without a hint of frustration or offense. If that was how he wanted it, who was I to stand in the way? Not that I didn't want to, but rather...it was on him to tell me what to do and I'd comply. Why this weirdness had come over me, I hadn't a clue. However, trying to fight it was like going against some sort of wolf programming.

"What's going on?" Lou Ellen remained on her bed, her fat fingers quivering while clutching the edge of the quilt up to her mouth. "Is anyone dead?"

"Not yet." I shoved my arms around Dane's chest and lifted him to his feet. Screw the wolf programming. He'd take my help and like it.

He shook his head and braced his arm between us. "We have to get out of here."

"We have to get you to a doctor."

He laughed. "You know of one? We are in a nursing home, after all."

Oooo, I could've smacked him for that smart-aleck comment. Luckily for him, he was already hurt. Dousing my rage, I started us toward the door before stopping and staring at Paul and Frankie. "We should beat Robert's address out of them, you know."

Dane shook his head. "No way. If the redhead she's talking about is Parry, we need to get out of here. Fast. My blood will leave a trail that his bloodhounds will follow."

Damn his common sense.

I peeked into the hall. Other than an old man in a wheelchair at the other end, it was clear. We hurried into the corridor, leaving blood droplets staining the polished hardwood floor. Just as we made it to the stairwell, I glanced over my shoulder and caught a horde of four coming off the elevator. A man with red hair led the way in the wrong direction. I shoved Dane inside the stairwell and quietly closed the door behind us.

Dane clutched his side and panted. "What gives?"

"Parry and his crew." I looped his arm around my shoulders and hurried him down the stairs again. They'd pick up that blood trail and Dane's scent any minute.

Just as we reached the bottom landing, the door on the third floor slammed open. I glanced upward and Parry glared down at me. His teeth formed a snarl through his thick beard while his eyes were livid enough to wish they breathed fire.

That was all I needed to get my ass moving. I threw open the door and stumbled outside onto the asphalt.

Flora stood on the opposite side of the check-in desk when we arrived. She set her eyes on me and shook her head, mumbling an "mmm mmm mmm".

Once she got over her momentary anger, Flora enveloped me in a hug so heartfelt and sick with worry that her D-sized breasts smothered my air supply. Pulling back, she did a visual inspection before crushing me again to her front.

I couldn't help returning the tight embrace.

Flora pulled away and planted her fist on her hip. "Girl, where on earth have you been? You scared the life out of us. Lord help me, I should smack the foolishness out of you." She glanced over my shoulder and noticed Dane for the first time. "Mr. Dane you look awful. What in the world have you kids been up to?"

Dane leaned against the wall with one hand hidden under his jacket. Sweat beaded his forehead and haggardness sank his eyes. I thought it funny that she'd call him a kid when he was old enough to be her father. That was slow aging for you.

Uh-oh. Blood dripped to the floor just to the side of his brown deck shoes. My wide-eyed glare told him to play it off. If he didn't Flora was bound to notice.

Smiling, Dane waved his free hand and straightened. "I'm fine Flora. Just tired and hungry. Any chance I can get you to rustle up some lunch?"

I rolled my eyes. Didn't he notice it was nighttime? I thought the slow cab ride with darkening skies beyond the windows might have been his first clue.

Grinning, Flora shook her head. "You two are a trip. Young lady, your father has been calling this place like crazy looking for you. I have half a mind to call him back and give you up."

"Where's Charles?" Dane blinked several times, though squinting on the last one.

"He's out running some errands for me." Flora arched her eyebrow again, studying Dane. "You look like you need some soup. Are you sure you're all right?"

Dane chuckled. "I'm fine. A little gassy perhaps. Those burritos are still burrowing through my stomach."

Oh. My. God. *Why* did he have to go there? A half smile trembled onto my face. I strode across the floor and looped my arm around Flora's good one. Turning her toward the dining room, I escorted her to the door. "You know how my dad is. Always worried for no reason. Which reminds me, you haven't rented out my room, have you?"

She patted the back of my hand and met my eyes. "Of course not, baby. And..." Her gaze lowered a moment, a slight flush filling her brown cheeks. "I'm sorry about all the trouble Charles and I caused you. You did a wonderful job with keeping this place running. But running off like that to set things right is no excuse. You shouldn't have to go up against the mob by yourself. In fact, you should be calling the police on these fools."

Huh? What in the world was she talking about?

Oh. She meant the last time I supposedly "ran off" to take care of business. Where she got the idea that the mob had something to do with this only left one person. She must have spoken to Monica. Probably wanted to know where I had disappeared or did she have any information on my whereabouts. I bet the police had a field day showing up at the B&B with a warrant out for my arrest and scaring poor Flora half to death.

"Let me take care of this." I squeezed her pudgy hand and cemented my plastic smile in place with the hopes it passed her scrutinizing gaze. "There's no reason why you and Charles have to go through this with me. That's why I canceled all of the reservations and have had next week's patrons shipped elsewhere for their stay."

Flora stared. "You must have hit your head again. That was a month ago."

"Oh." Damn, I hated this missing time. The hours, days, and weeks started merging into one clump without any sense of time. "Well...maybe we should think about doing that again. Just in case."

"You know that's gonna eat into our savings, right? We're barely above water as it is."

"It's a chance we have to take. I won't put anyone else in danger if I don't have to. In fact, I want you and Charles to—"

She shook her head. "We're not going anywhere. There are only a handful of guests and we're taking care of them just like we always do. You saw us through our rough patch. We're gonna see you through yours. This building will still be standing just like it always has. You wait and see. Now...let me go in here and see if I can rustle up some dinner for you two."

I wished I felt better about that, but I didn't. While I loved the Hills in the short time I had known them, I wanted to shove both of them on an airplane and fly them as far away from here as possible. They were too old and fragile to be caught up my mess. Dammit, they didn't deserve this. Unfortunately, that wasn't enough to keep Gamboldt away.

But that was the question. They were here and I was here. That bastard could've broken into the B&B at any time or used his mind-control powers on them to infiltrate our home. Surely it didn't take a lot of his power to muck up the minds of two senior citizens.

Dane coughed.

Good Lord, I had forgotten about him standing there. By the time I turned around, he had disappeared up the stairs without me. He moved fast for a guy who had been shot. I followed his scent, but stopped between the first and second floors.

The scent of blood had thickened the air. A red splotch on the burgundy Persian rug caught my eye. It was Dane's all right. He must be bleeding through the towel. Great. I hurried up the staircase after him.

Just as I rounded the end of the railing, I noticed the door to my quarters open. Once inside, I helped Dane take off his jacket while he sat on my bed. Blood soaked the folded towel to the point that there was no white left. If it hadn't been for Dane needing my help, I'd have backpedaled out the door.

I shook my head. "This isn't good. You need to see a doctor."

Dane chuckled and forced himself to sit up. "No. I need my bag from my room. I don't think the bullet hit anything major."

"It hit you, you nut ball. Isn't that major enough?"

A humble smile bowed his rubber-band lips. "That's my stubborn, demanding little Angel I miss. You're going to have your memory back, Lex. I swear." Dane reached inside his coat pocket and handed over his room key. "Go and get my black backpack. It'll have everything I need."

I did as he asked without having to search too hard. With the backpack slung on my shoulder, I exited his room.

Footsteps thumped up the stairs. Two flights down, Flora's arm poked out over the railing. It burned me that she would come up these steps at her age to tend to us.

I dropped the backpack on the floor and went down to meet her. Actually, I scolded her first and felt good about getting her back. Then, I thanked her for the giant wicker basket of food. She had better be lucky Charles was out picking up some supplies or he would've cursed her out, too, for pushing herself too hard.

With the backpack and picnic basket in hand, I entered my room. Dane wasn't there. Grunts echoed from the bathroom. I placed the basket on the table and brought him the backpack.

Dane sat on the edge of the bathtub holding a different not-so-fresh towel against his side. Thick crimson droplets had stained the white porcelain tub.

"It's not as bad as it looks." Engrossed in his cleaning, not once did he look up to acknowledge me. Not like I expected it either.

"Yes, it is." I lifted more towels off the rack and placed them on the floor for easier access. "Flora's going to demand an explanation first. Then she'll kill you."

"Can you reach inside and hand me the black pouch?"

I let my rant go and found the small bag in the bottom past a bunch of gauze, first-aid tape and other medical kits that left me scratching my head. "What's in it?"

"Drugs."

I continued to go through his things. Holy crap. He had all sorts of bandages, ointments, syringes and even a stethoscope. I lifted a blood-pressure cuff out of the bag and held it in front of him. "You mind telling me what this is for?"

"Measuring blood pressure."

Lord, if it weren't for him being hurt, I'd give him a reason to feel some real pain. But it was my own fault for not asking the right question. "You know what I meant. Are you a doctor?"

Confusion twisted his eyebrows. "What makes you think—? Oh. Never mind. I forgot you have the amnesia thing going on. But to answer your question: no. I learned my skills in a more unorthodox way."

"Uh-huh."

He tossed a bloody rag in the tub. "I killed people for the fun of it the first twelve years after I was bitten. I've learned a lot in the five-plus decades I've been a werewolf." He picked up the small pouch and fingered the clanging vials. When he found what he wanted, he leaned over—grunting—and pulled out one of the syringes I'd left lying on top of the bag. "Are you going to watch?"

"Not unless you need a hand. Flora brought us some food."

He grinned. "I know. The crab cakes and lobster bisque smell delicious, I'll tell you what. How about you set the table for two while I handle this? Otherwise, your hovering will only make me nervous."

An offer to leave? I'd take it. I didn't want to see him perform surgery on himself anyway. There were some things my stomach could handle, but I drew the line at causing pain to oneself. Besides, I had other things to do like check the roster and see if the new guests' names sounded familiar.

Tate's cell phone rang to life with a digital rendition of a U2 song. I didn't recognize the number and hesitated about picking it up. My fingers itched to press the green phone button anyway. Against my better judgment, I answered.

"Thank God." Matt sighed.

Hearing the care in his voice warmed me. "You're not going to believe—"

"Where are you?"

"What does it matter? I'm at the inn. But that's not what I want to—"

"You need to get out of there. Anything familiar to you isn't safe. I can call my doorman and he'll let you into my condo."

"If you're thinking someone's going to jump me, it won't be a first and you know it. The only difference is I'll be protecting my territory with a knife in hand, if I have to." I unsheathed the blade at the small of my back and held the sharp edge up to the dim light. Still some blood, but it would have to do until I oiled it down like Tate said.

"For a jackass, Parry can be a smart man. He had one of our members who's also a PI do a background check on Gamboldt. He found out about the nursing home. Until now, he didn't give a shit about the place. He caught wind of your delicious scent and that of another wolf."

"I know. Dane took Tate's place as sidekick after he was kidnapped. After tonight, he'll probably think twice about doing it again." I sat on the bed and stared at the food getting colder by the second. It didn't matter. I finally had a chance to take the load off and I did. "Matt...I'm sorry about Tate. I didn't mean to let my guard down or—"

"It's not your fault."

"It is if he dies. My God, why do I keep getting innocent people caught in my damn crossfire?" Tears blurred my vision. Blinking, I threw my head back to stave them off. This wasn't the time for a breakdown. Our race against the clock didn't allow for it. Eventually, Robert would catch up to me and when he did, I had a feeling there wouldn't be a third escape. He'd either kill me or hide me deep enough inside his twisted world that a pack of were-bloodhounds couldn't find me.

"It's not your fault. None of this is. You didn't ask to be kidnapped. The only thing you did was walk into an auction hoping to buy some furniture."

No matter what he said, I knew differently. More people were going to die unless I did something to stop this bastard.

"Can you do me a favor?" Matt asked. "Look outside your window and tell me if you see any cars parked on the street. And if so, what kind."

"Why?" I left the bed and hurried to the window. "If Gamboldt's going to do something, he's going to do it within these walls. Not from the outside."

"Who said I'm talking about him?"

Uh-oh. My belly knotted at the sound of that. I clutched the rod for the blinds, but didn't twist it. "You want to tell me what's going on?"

"Sweetie, you guys left a calling card at that nursing home. One that Parry wasn't happy about finding."

Oh man. He was talking about Paul and Frankie. Perhaps they were loyal to Gamboldt, but with enough pressure, they'd turn into squawk machines. I knew we should've cut off their air supply when we had the chance.

Chapter Thirty-Six

After a few more minutes with Matt, I said my goodbyes before I died of excessive nagging. Sure, I didn't take Parry or his antics lightly, but the deed was done. The fool had seen us, tracked us and wanted to kill us. Nothing we could do about that now. Constantly reminding me to "stay safe" was like using an umbrella in a category-five hurricane. The only way I'd be safe is buried six feet under with a stone slab on top to make sure I stayed put. Sorry. No can do.

Whether or not Paul or Frankie talked, I couldn't say. Unless the police got there before Parry, they'd spill. Even then, that wouldn't stop Parry from getting what he wanted out of them. The guy probably had a mole or two in the police department.

In all the chaos, I had forgotten about Dane. He had been in the bathroom a long time. I decided to check on him to make sure he hadn't died on me. That would be disastrous...considering he wasn't such a bad dude after all.

Dane remained seated on the rim of the bathtub, wrapping the last of his bandages around his waist. Papers and torn pieces of fabric littered the floor. Instead of picking them up, I offered to help him to his feet. He refused it in favor of using the sink as leverage and adding another trail of sweat down his face during the struggle. Biting back the pain or not, anyone who eased into the main room with the help of the wall and pieces of furniture was in agony.

I followed. How I'd break the news to him, I didn't know. But the sooner I did it the better. "We've got a problem. Not yet, but soon."

He sat on the bed. After lifting his feet off the floor to rest his back against a stack of pillows, he turned and waved his hand for me to spill.

"If Paul or Frankie talked, they'll lead Parry and his crew here. I have a feeling they didn't know where I lived or they would've toppled this place by now. They're probably—"

"—on their way. Believe it or not, that doesn't surprise me. You might as well tell me about this Matt guy you're dating."

"Huh? What's he got to do with this?"

He pushed away from the pillows and met my gaze. "Who's Matt?"

His demanding eyes and matching tone made it clear that he'd dig as deep as it took to get the answers out of me. I thought it best to just give in and save him the hassle.

"He's a member of the Boston Pack just like Tate. But he's been helping me because we were apparently an item before my disappearance and—" I stopped because I knew where he was going with this. "Look, if you think Matt had anything to do with this, you're nuts. I trust him. He never would've come all the way to Battle Rose to find me if he didn't care. What the hell did he have to gain by bringing me back into his pack's territory? Huh? Isn't that what you wolves strive to do? To keep interlopers off your land? You can't get anymore off than Battle Rose."

A huge smile curved Dane's lips. "You're in love with him."

"Bullshit. We're just—"

He threw a hand up to stop me. "Uh-uh. I know you, amnesia or not. You're in love with this guy, which brings new meaning to the Romeo and Juliet thing. His Alpha will never accept you into his pack. Parry has a reputation throughout the world and it's not good. Why do you think I was against you moving here when you finally—" He waved a dismissive hand. "Never mind. We already had that argument. I just wish you had listened to me in the first place about Boston."

"Who cares about that? If Matt and I want to get married someday, we'll—" I caught myself. Grumbling, I folded my arms and refused to look at him.

Where the hell had that come from? Sure, I liked Matt. In fact, I was deeply fond of him. He had a special place in my heart. One that screamed for me to burn Parry and his wolves out of their den for hurting him. That wasn't love. It was...something else. But nowhere near love. It was just my werewolf and human personas getting crossed. That was all.

Hypothetically speaking, if I wanted to start a family life, it made sense to find out where Matt stood. Seriously, how did I know if he wanted kids or not? Suppose he liked his pack more and refused to leave them? I certainly couldn't ask him to choose between us because that was unfair. He had known them for a lot longer than me and even formed bonds with them that a lowly half wolf could never break.

Dane's face lightened as fatherly mode slipped behind his eyes. "I didn't mean to go there. If you like this guy, then I'm sure there's a good reason. Sorry I teased you."

"Whatever. Right now, Parry's going to knock on that front door any minute and when he does, he's going to know werewolves have encroached on his land. Not to mention, we still have the problem with Gamboldt not having a problem with encroaching on *my* land. He's probably waiting in the wings for another attempt. If all hell breaks loose, the police will be handing out arrest warrants like flyers."

Dane folded his hands behind his head and stared at the ceiling. "Do you remember how to use a crossbow?"

"No."

"Well, hopefully it'll be like riding a bike. Go back to my room and find a black duffle under the bed. It'll have your name on it. Once you see what's inside, I'm hoping this will all make sense."

"What'll make sense?"

Dane pushed off the pillows with an excited look in his eyes. "You're a sniper, Lex. One of the best damn shots I've seen in a long time."

I crossed my hands in a T. "Timeout, buddy. I'm not killing anyone. That extracurricular activity has gotten me into enough trouble."

"Then get a pretty dress on and some makeup because you're about to get tossed off Boston Pack property in a body bag."

"This is a public place, for heaven's sake. He can't—"

"Trust me, Lex, you don't want to be bullied by a monster like that."

"What do you want me to do? Shoot him in the middle of the street? Oh, that makes a lot of sense. Detective Konoval won't have to dig up enough evidence to charge me with his murder too. It'll be lying at his feet."

Dane chuckled. "I'm asking you to stand your ground by scaring the hell out of him. That, Parry will respect. Otherwise, you're better off going the rent route."

"I'm not paying him shit."

"Then I hope you have lots of insurance."

I snorted before marching across the room toward the window. On the way, I tripped over the rug. So much for trying to make a graceful retreat. I kicked the ruffle out of the way and parted the blinds.

Other than several cars traversing up and down the street, there was nothing out of the ordinary. How long it would stay that way remained to be seen.

"Scare him, huh," I mumbled.

"Yeah. I'll go downstairs and field him."

I turned and offered my own warning gaze. "I don't want trouble around here, Dane. Understand?"

He chuckled. "Angel, the Hills are like saints for watching over you. I'd never let anyone hurt them."

Yeah right. Like he was in any condition to stop it. The only thing that would keep a rumble from happening was the human guests. Other than burning the place down, Parry wouldn't do anything that would give them a reason to call the police. At least, I hoped the arrogant bastard was that smart.

I found the duffle bag like Dane had said and what lay inside left me speechless. There was a sleek, black crossbow with the bow's arms folded down. There were several dials and latches, but something told me not to touch them because they had already been calibrated to perfection. The pulley system on the bow screamed the word "compound" in my head. A small scope lined up with the shaft.

The crossbow stirred my senses because my scent covered every inch of the smooth bow from the trigger to the middle of the bow. State-of-the-art came to mind. Uniquely crafted for someone with my expertise. A sniper's elegant weapon of choice. I loved this puppy.

Black quivers sticking out of the bag caught my attention. Pulling one resulted in black straps of Velcro and a pocket filled with arrows. It took me a few turns before my hands placed the pouch on my thigh and the straps fell to either side. No arrows hung across my chest in a sling. This was something new and specially made for someone on the move. It allowed me to get to my arrows faster.

That wasn't all. I put everything down and pulled out something that looked like a black bodysuit that bordered too close to kinky. There was no way in hell I'd wear that thing. Dane must've lost his mind.

Something else lay on the bottom of the bag. It was a vest with more Velcro for keeping things in place and... Holy Crap. I remembered this vest. The mesh pockets on the front and the secret zip pockets throughout.

I was more than just a sniper. I was *the* weapon of choice. Whose choosing, I couldn't say, but I had a feeling it was one of my own. It would explain why I didn't care much for guns when this was my trademark. But...I was missing something. I dug through my blocked memories for anything that would lend a clue to my gut instincts.

An image of me carrying a machete or...

I walked through the woods carrying a bowie knife. Twigs and dried leaves cracked under my footfalls. I glanced from side to side, anxiety flooding my system. Either something stalked me or I stalked it.

A reddish-brown mass lunged from my right.

I stepped aside and sliced down with the knife. Blood splattered across the trees. A giant werewolf lay on the ground with its side split open. Its front paw kicked a few times. When it stopped, the last of its breath exited, flattening its lungs.

Footsteps pummeled the underbrush from where the werewolf had lunged. The bushes rustled. Another werewolf stepped through the copse. His cold eyes locked on to me. A growl peeled back his black lips, exposing a set of sharp teeth. Spittle mixed with blood dripped out of the monster's maw.

I crouched low and met the bastard's eyes. "Come on, wolf. You afraid of a little ol' half breed like me?"

His growling lowered another octave. Pointed ears flattened on his furred head. His front lowered. Instead of coming straight for me, he stepped to the side in a ritualistic death walk, sizing me up for attack.

I brought my knife up and held it perpendicular to my arm. With my other hand, I motioned him forward. "Chicken shit."

The wolf lunged.

My reverie stopped. The most I recalled from that scene was I wore these clothes and fought with the knife. Seeing as I was here to remember the tale, I had won. But like Dane said, I knew what I was supposed to do now. It was like it had been bred into me...and of my *own* choosing. I needed to make up for what I lacked in werewolf skills if I was to survive this world. My instincts demanded it. Whether Dane had chosen to train me or not, the wolf inside me would've found another way.

I gathered everything in my arms and headed back to my room. If Parry wanted a war, he was messing with the wrong soldier.

Chapter Thirty-Seven

The tree across the street had a perfect vantage point. I spied everything from here, including the front door to my inn. My black spandex kept me well hidden about twenty feet off the ground. The thick leaves and branches helped too. The occupants of the large home behind me never saw a thing or they would've raised holy hell by now. Thank goodness, these people weren't night owls.

Parry had arrived with an entourage about fifteen minutes ago. Yeah, that bitch Frankie had sold us out. What they had done with her was anyone's guess.

Dane said to stay put and don't do anything unless he gave a signal. I kept my crossbow aimed at the window in the library. Several people moved about, but Dane remained seated by the window in front of the lace curtains.

He promised me he wouldn't move from that spot. If he did, then I was to fire an arrow through the window. That would be a warning sign. If he made a motion to get up deliberately, then he'd straighten the curtains first.

Movement in the blue pickup truck caught my attention. Parry and troops had traveled here in two vehicles. Five people entered the inn. Still, the five of them could've fit in one car. But they took two vehicles.

Blond hair flashed from the backseat window. I could be wrong, but my gut urged me to act. Best to know the enemy and where they stood than to wait until they got an edge on us.

Taking up the crossbow, I dropped out of the tree. Dane was sure Parry wouldn't do anything crazy, but I didn't trust that. If they had something or someone hiding out, then I wanted to know about it.

I crept across the street, approaching the truck from behind. My eyes continued to scan the area, making sure nobody saw me. If they did, hopefully they'd know the crossbow wasn't for them. If they thought otherwise, I'd find out after the cops read me my Miranda Rights.

Creeping up on the side, I recognized Frankie in the backseat, but Paul was nowhere around. Surely Parry had seen him lying on the floor where we'd left them. Why in the world would Frankie go with them and leave her buddy behind? Something wasn't right.

I needed that guy in the front seat out of commission. Might as well get to it.

I pulled the handle.

The door wouldn't budge. Damn. That would be my luck.

When the driver turned his head and growled, impulse took hold. I flipped my crossbow up and rammed the butt through the glass, shattering it. It butted him square in the face. When I pulled back, the man shook his head. Shards pierced his cheeks and nose. Blood began to ooze.

He wasn't down yet. Stunned, perhaps, but not out like I wanted. So, I slugged him a second time to make sure.

His scent touched my nose. The guy definitely smelled like a full-blooded werewolf.

He slumped against the seat with a red spot swelling his cheek and blood trails lining his face. I had taken a full-blooded werewolf down. Speed had won over strength in this case. I rocked.

Hands clapped.

"Bravo!" Frankie hung out the window smiling and offering up her applause. Lethargy filled her eyes like she had had a few beers before jumping inside the enemy's truck. "I never saw that coming."

I whiffed the air. Not that I would know what drugs smelled like, but she didn't smell inebriated either. I brought the crossbow up to her throat. Her laughter stopped, but the smile remained in place.

"You're good." She stopped clapping and remained slumped against the door. "Very good. That's why I wanted you. Everyone has a special talent that I can't resist. You're all like little puppets whose strings are mine alone to pull."

My feet backpedaled. Stunned, I stood in the middle of the

street without realizing it. A car headed straight at me with lights beaming and horn blaring brought me back to reality. I jumped to the side of the truck—threw myself really.

Had I heard what I thought I heard? This wasn't the Frankie I knew. Something had changed her. She was a born bitch, but this wasn't normal for her. Parry hadn't drugged her up. Something had possessed her.

"Gamboldt," I seethed.

Her smile beamed. "In the flesh. So to speak." She popped the back door open and stepped onto the street. "I planned on staying with the wolves until I found another prize. They're hiding your lover, you know. No, scratch that. You *do* know, don't you?"

"You son of a bitch." I knew what he wanted and it wasn't just me anymore. After all, if he took one wolf, why not take a chance with another? One who was just as valuable as Tate. I'd be damned before I stood here and let him put one filthy finger on Matt.

She laughed. "That wolf of yours is a prized hound. A supernatural lawyer? Come on. What are the chances of us coming across something like that in our world? He's special to say the least. As it turns out, I need his services. Just for a short while though. I'll return him to his rightful owner when I'm done. The same goes for the cute little nurse."

"Fuck you."

Frankie rolled her eyes. "Really, Alexa. I thought you had advanced beyond crudeness."

Anger hooded my eyes. I stepped forward ready to hit the stripper with my crossbow, but I decided against it. Although there was hardly anyone on the street, I didn't know if one of my neighbors might have caught the scene in front of my inn. There weren't any sirens yet. Why press my luck again? Besides, haughty morons like him liked to talk. *I* needed him to talk. Talking might lead to leaking important information.

I slipped my hand behind my vest and gripped my sheathed knife. "I hear you had other jobs for me. Any chance on my finding out what they might be?"

Frankie smirked. "Why? You interested?"

"No. Not really. Just curious. I figure if I'm going to go to jail because of you, it wouldn't hurt to have an idea of why."

"You can level the playing field where I can't. If anyone

crosses me, you eliminate the competition. Simple as that. You kill quick, fast and unassuming. Just like a predator. I like that."

"Thanks. But you're avoiding the question."

"Tell you what." Frankie shifted while leaning her back against the door. "If you're worried about Keisha, don't be. In a few minutes, those murder charges will be off your back."

I didn't like the sound of that, but I didn't have time to debate it either. Another car traveled toward us. I lowered my folded crossbow to my side and out of sight. However, my hand never came off my knife. When the car passed, I brought my attention back to Frankie.

She was gone.

Damn that bitch! Where did she—he—go? I looked in the truck bed, but it was empty. There were some rusted gardening tools and an old tire, but nothing more.

A finger tapped my shoulder. I whirled around while drawing the knife. Frankie stood beside the truck, her bent arm propped on top of a side mirror and leaning her cheek on her knuckles.

"Wonderful trick, don't you think?" That same maniacal smirk splayed her face.

"Would you like to see a better one?"

Frankie raised her hand. "Please. I'd prefer not to have this pretty face messed up. She's such a wonderful lay."

"What did you mean by Keisha would no longer be my problem?"

"I'm shocked you're not asking about your friend Tate. I assumed he means something to you. Just as much as the werewolf lawyer to be exact."

I lowered the knife, keeping a tight grip on the leather hilt. "You're not going to tell me anymore about Tate or Matt. So, unlike you, I'm saving my breath."

Chuckling, she straightened and stepped around the mirror. "I have another party coming up. I'd like you to attend. You see, the people coming to this one are rich execs on the verge of hitting Boston's list of elite. I want to make sure I'm on their good side. Sometimes it takes more than a good game of poker to ensure that. Especially when they're the kind of people who can shape local laws in my favor."

"And my exact role?"

"As it's always been. A demonstration. Ms. Walker was more like a demonstration for me to get an idea of what you were capable of. She wanted out and failed to read the fine print about nobody simply running away. If I had paid better attention, I would've seen that couple walking their damn dog down the street at the time. Then again, you fought my control. You're stronger than I thought for a half werewolf. But in the end, you killed at my command. Luckily, no one saw. You even escaped before the police came. To be on the safe side, I had to stash you away and Trixie's seemed like the perfect place. After all, that's where I keep many of my special treasures."

"Wow. You're nothing more than a supernatural leech, aren't you?"

For the first time, her smirk drained off her face. The look went beyond stolid. She focused all of her bland hatred on me as if she willed me to have an aneurism. "As much as I appreciate your snarky bitch-ousness, you've got other problems. In fact, she's waiting for you on the third floor."

A scream radiated through the inn. Flora's face leaped to mind.

Frankie laughed. "Oops. Looks like someone misjudged Keisha's rising. I'll have to have a talk with my necro about that. Great skills, though, if I do say so myself."

I darted around the truck and headed for the front door.

Chapter Thirty-Eight

I slammed the door open, smacking it against the wall. Several people—werewolves—stood in the lobby. Dane froze halfway up the first landing when his attention landed on me. His shoulders relaxed as if disappointed I had disobeyed him. He'd just have to scold me later. Based on the mumbles and whispers coming from the other floors, I wasn't the only one who'd heard the commotion.

Pushing through the thick clog of snarling werewolf bodies, I passed Dane on the staircase. "Keep everyone off the third floor."

"What the hell is going on?"

This came from a guy who looked like a redheaded version of St. Nick. A thick beard stopped at his sternum. His waist disappeared under his distended stomach and he was mostly legs from that point on. Shoving one of his minions out of his way, he looped his thumbs through the belt links of his jeans. A show of authority, though it was more a show of potbelly. His narrowed eyes settled on me and his nose wrinkled with a whiff. Rage creased his middle-aged, freckled face.

"You're the half bitch, aren't you?"

I opened my mouth for a quick comeback, but decided against it. I needed to get upstairs.

One of Parry's wolves hunched their shoulders and started for me.

I flipped my knife over once and hurled the blade at him. It spun end over end and struck him in the shoulder. At first, nothing. He stood there with his jaw hung in disbelief. Just when I expected a scream, he let out a loud exhale and tore it out. By the time he poured his rage on me, he was looking at the tip of my crossbow. Perhaps he'd forgotten I had it. I hadn't. If he wanted to finish this, I'd be more than happy to put him out of his misery.

Dane didn't interfere. Instead, he stood by my side with a smirk on his face. "To answer your question, she's someone who'll be more than happy to whoop your ass. Any more?"

"I've got one." I held the werewolf in my sites. "Why are you idiots hauling Robert Gamboldt's ass around town in your truck?"

A tick worked in Parry's cheek like the information shocked and pissed him all the same, but he refused to show any more emotions than he had. "We'll finish this later...Mr. Dane." He turned and his people followed him out the door.

"Good." I tore away from the herd and hurried up the staircase, taking the steps four at a time. "Everyone back in your rooms. Now!"

Did they listen? Of course not. Perhaps a few did, but they didn't close their doors.

When I arrived at my room, I found Flora cowering on the floor in front of a toppled table. Tears streaked her eyes. Keisha Walker stalked across the room like the walking dead with a faraway look in her eyes. I expected them to be gray or white by now, but they weren't. They were normal. Her dark skin looked blue from lack of oxygen or something, and her teeth had turned varying stages of brown like pieces of wood smudged out. Clumps of her hair were matted with leaves and mud as though she had just crawled out of the grave. Eight months down there hadn't rotted her away like I had suspected, unless Gamboldt's necromancer was good at preservation too.

She reached for Flora, but stopped. Her head swiveled more than 180 degrees until her chin rested above her right scapula.

My fear of the Linda Blair zombie didn't last long. Fury seized me. How dare this monster attack an old woman? Flora had come up here to check on me, and this was the thanks she got? No fucking way. Not in my house.

I yanked my crossbow to my shoulder and pulled the trigger. An arrow slammed into Keisha's neck. Her head flipped back and she staggered. When she regained her balance, blood seeped through her growling teeth. She started for me.

I had another arrow mounted without thinking about it. I wanted this devil's reject put down.

The second arrow slammed center mass into the dead woman's chest. Had she been human that shot to the heart would've killed her. Time to go for the next best thing.

I mounted another arrow and aimed for her head. The arrow hit home, causing Keisha to stumble toward the window. I ran across the room and planted a jump kick square in her chest. She fell, smashing through the glass.

Instead of checking to make sure she was dead, I hurried to Flora's side and crouched in front of her. It broke my tough-girl in half to watch her tremble in terror. I prayed to God her fear wasn't on my account. Slowly, I reached for her, but she jumped. I pulled back. Damn, it hurt to see her like this. God knows I'd never meant to scare her.

After a swallow, I steeled myself because I needed to talk to her. "Flora. The police will come. I can't be here when they arrive. Do you understand? People's lives are at stake and this is something the police can't handle."

"Th-th-that." She swallowed and closed her eyes. "That demon. She wasn't... Was she...?"

I shook my head. "I don't know what she was. But I'll be damned before I let her or anyone else hurt you or Charles."

Dane hurried into the room. Sweat covered his face and he held his bloodied side. "Cops. They're only minutes out."

I stood and rechecked my crossbow. "I know."

"You can't be here."

"I know." I glanced at Flora. "Dane, I need you to stay with her. Please. I can't..."

My throat closed and tears took me by surprise when they flooded my vision. I refused to let that happen. There wasn't any time for this. I blinked them out of my blurred sights and met Dane's face.

He handed me the keys to his rental car. "I've already started taking care of it. But right now you need to go." Reaching in his back pocket, he pulled out his wallet and handed me a credit card. "Just be safe. Don't worry about the cost. Lay low until things blow over."

I shoved the card back. "I've got my own money. I won't—"

"You'll take it and you'll like it. Do I make myself clear? Besides, in case you haven't noticed, it has your name on it too."

I snatched the card from him and held it up. Sure enough, there was my name. My *real* name. "Now I know you've lost your mind."

He laughed. "Not really. After all these years of being a werewolf, I've learned how to prepare for almost everything. That's why I took out joint accounts for everyone under my wing, including your family. And before you ask, there's an extra ID for you in the glove box. Now get out of here. I'll take care of the rest."

"No you won't." Flora reached up with her good arm. Both Dane and I helped her off the floor. She took a few seconds to catch her breath. Dane watched her with a careful eye. Once she got a second wind, she walked across the floor to the end of the bed. "I can take care of myself. And if I have to, I can take care of both of you too. Now you give me that bow and arrow whatchamacallit and you do as Mr. Dane says. Get your behind out of here. I won't have you going to jail for saving people from demons like that. Between the two of us, we'll come up with something. Now get!"

All this time I'd worried about her being able to deal with my situation and here she was taking control of it. I wanted to argue, but she had snatched the crossbow from my hands with this I-dare-you look in her eyes. She meant what she said about taking the blame and that was it. Now if that didn't call for a tear or two, what did?

A smile tickled my lips, but the sirens hollering in the distance put a stop to it. They were probably audible to human ears by now.

I couldn't help giving Flora a hug and kiss before I left. Dane didn't need it. He offered me a nod while waving his hand for me to get gone. I wanted to hug him, but time was of the essence.

Darting through the crowd filing into the hall, I made my way downstairs. At the front door, I stopped. Glancing over my shoulder, I hoped and prayed I'd see this place again. More important, I hoped I'd live long enough to see my friends and family again.

I found more than just the black rental car parked on the street. Pippa, the witch from the hospital leaned against the passenger's side door with her arms folded across her chest. She pushed away from the door with her red curly bob waving across her cheeks. Seriousness marred her face.

"You're the human hybrid who set up a business on Boston Pack territory." She shook her head. "You should've told me instead of letting me hear it from Wednesday Garridan."

"Come again?" I glanced over my shoulder and noted the sirens drawing closer. In all honesty, I didn't have time for this, but I wasn't going anywhere until I got rid of her.

"The hybrid. A year ago, word spread that a hybrid was found on Boston Pack territory. An extremely rare breed. Anyway, Parry is known for a lot of things and boasting is one of them. He wanted to make it clear that no wolf, especially a half breed, was allowed on his land. Word spread among the supernatural underground about your mysterious disappearance a few months later. The gossip didn't last long, of course, because there were other things going on at the time."

"What does this have to do with you being here now?" I stalked around to the driver's side door while keeping an eye on her. "And you might want to talk fast because the cops are on their way. I'd like to be gone before they arrive."

Pippa leaned against the car, folding her arms on top. "There's a reason why Robert hasn't been able to touch your innkeepers' minds. It has to do with those witch's ladders hanging around the house, the mobiles with strings, feathers, and sticks? Anyway, it's part of a protection spell. The problem is it's breaking down, which means we're running out of time."

"You put it there?"

She shrugged. "Not me, per se. Others in my coven. Right before we officially met in the subway, I didn't know who you were and I destroyed your records before I copied the address. Out of sight out of mind, so to speak. I can tell you more on the way, but that means you have to trust me."

"Look, don't take this the wrong way, but everyone who's been around me has met a horrible demise. Are you sure you want to put your neck out like that?"

She pulled the handle, but the door didn't open. Her eyes fixed on me. She'd meant every word. While I wanted to throw up another argument, I had used up my best one.

Against my better judgment, I triggered the automatic locks. "Enter at your own risk."

Pippa thought it better that I go to a protected place instead of a one-star hotel where criminals choose to hide and raids were sure to follow. While I assumed most witches called Salem home, she took me to Pine Bridge, a small town outside of Worchester. As she put it, any witch worthy of their craft wouldn't live in the so-called witching capital of the world where there were too many human eyes around.

After Pippa had reported her first meeting with me, one of her coven sisters did some checking around and found out the human hybrid, me, had returned. I was the first person to make it back from Gamboldt's stronghold with my life intact. Those like Keisha Walker weren't as lucky because the snake wouldn't take no for an answer. When you joined his ranks, you joined for life because you knew too much.

That was the case with Pippa's former leader. Sarah Jenkinson had been a powerful witch who'd earned the right to lead Boston's Western Coven. Unfortunately, her power went to her head. Robert happened to be there to sate her appetite. She went against the teachings of her coven by seeking personal gain and justifying it as the best for her people. In doing so, she opened up their *Book of Shadows* to an outsider and used its spells for wrong. Her people feared an outsider might trace Sarah's power back to their coven and put all of their lives in danger. Now, it made sense why Gamboldt had upped the ante by wanting Parry's wolves. He had a powerful witch on his side to amplify his mind-control powers.

Witches were moving up in the world. I parked in front of a large cabin that looked more like the kind of vacation home several people would rent based on seasonal activities. Golden light shone through the first-floor windows, illuminating the glazed wood interior. The second floor was as large as the first. I stepped closer to the edge of the house and looked down into what I thought was a cavern. It was the finished basement with an outdoor Jacuzzi, shower and sauna. Through a set of glass doors was an indoor pool. Now I understood why these guys didn't live in Salem. Their extravagant lifestyle would stand out among the shacks I'd expected to see.

There wasn't anyone around. According to Pippa, they were out getting ready for Samhain, the witch's holiday. Pippa showed me to a room on the second floor. It was simple with a single dresser, a wicker bed and one lamp on the nightstand.

I called Dane to get the scoop and return the favor with

what I had learned to this point. Surely my patrons had given the police a wonderful description of me leaving the scene of a crime when I was there to protect them.

To my shock, Flora played it up like an Academy Award Winning Actress. She claimed that while she was checking on one of our guests, she noticed the door open to my room. When she went to investigate, Keisha attacked her. They wrestled for the crossbow, but Flora got the upper hand and shot her in self-defense. The bruises on Flora's shoulder and arm from her hitting the wall were all the evidence they needed for a scuffle. Dane backed up her story by saying he had arrived just as Keisha fell out the window. Fingerprints worried me, but Dane said not to worry about that. Easy for him to say.

Detective Konoval bought it...for now...but he confiscated my crossbow as evidence. Whether they'd put Flora in jail was another story. So far, no charges had been brought against her. A senior citizen fighting for her life wasn't the kind of honor badge a police chief wanted on his arm as a fight against crime. Right now, Detective Konoval needed to look into bringing charges of fraud against someone for faking Keisha's first death. While there were some extenuating circumstances involved, like the state of her body just before she died, it was hard to argue that she'd been dead to begin with.

That was what Robert had meant by taking care of my possible murder charge. I had a feeling there would be more questions than answers when all was said and done. Like how and when the body went missing from the morgue. Where had Keisha been all these months? Whether or not Robert had an answer for that, I didn't care. I was off the hook and that was what mattered. Well...not entirely off the hook. I still had to deal with Billy the bum's assault and battery charges among other things.

After a hot shower, I ventured back to my room and noticed another one of those witch's ladders hanging from the upper part of the windowsill. It was on a smaller scale with feathers, knots and different color beads all tied into a loop, but it stifled the room nonetheless. My stomach churned and nausea began to travel up my throat. I lunged for the trashcan sitting in the corner just in case.

"Alexa?" Pippa stepped into the room and smoothed her hand along my water-beaded shoulder. "Are you okay?"

I shook my head. If I opened my mouth, I couldn't be sure of what might come out. I pointed at the ladder and waved it away, hoping she got the idea.

"Oh." She went to the window and unraveled it from the lock. She rushed it out of the room and returned to open the window. "Sorry about that. I didn't think the ladder would bother you."

The fresh air did wonders for my nausea. It was swept away like the sun breaking through a morning mist. "Those things make me sick. Or at least that one does. The others just…they make me uncomfortable."

She cocked her head. "They're used for protection sort of like a rosary. You don't mean me any harm, do you?"

"You haven't given me any reason to."

Her head lifted with a light-bulb-moment gesture. "Oh, I get it. Robert still has a hold on you. A weak one because he hasn't been able to influence you. But it's there. There's also the possibility that your heightened senses are picking some of it up too. Although for a hybrid, I never would've thought your senses would be that sensitive. You sure you're not psychic yourself?"

My eyebrow arched. "Are you serious? If I were psychic, I'd be more than just Robert's personal assassin."

"You're an assassin?"

I waved a hand to stop the questioning and approached the window for some clean air. Despite the chill on the breeze, it was a welcome freshness to my lungs. "That's another story, but yes. Apparently, I'm a damn good shot with a crossbow. I had to be in order to survive. Werewolves see me as an intruder, regardless of how much wolf there is in my blood. So, my family took measures to make sure I had a fighting chance. Self-defense is one of them."

Pippa whistled through her teeth. "It sure came in handy if you survived Robert."

I shook my head. "Not yet. When this is over and I'm still standing, that's when I'll call it surviving."

Pippa didn't stay. She left me alone to my thoughts, but the only thoughts I had were for Matt. This was the first time I'd had a chance to call him since all hell had broken loose. The way things were going these days, we both had our own personal battles. I prayed we'd come through in one piece.

Chapter Thirty-Nine

Even though it was late, I took a chance and used Tate's cell to call Matt. For once it didn't take a series of threats, insults and hang-ups to get through to him. The person who answered sounded too out of it for a basic hello, which was probably why he handed the phone over to Matt without question. From what I understood, those Parry left behind spent part of the night snorting cocaine and drinking. Come morning, they would be nursing headaches, black eyes and various cuts and abrasions. A night of drugs and drinking always turned out the same way, which was why Matt had a condo in the city, far away from these maniacs.

"I'm getting out of here. Even if I have to change and sneak off into the night, I won't stay. I've got a stash of clothes and money in a hole just off the highway in South Weymouth."

"Matt, if you leave, they might hurt—"

"This is bullshit, Lex. Parry has people following me around all the time and watching everything I do. He doesn't want me anywhere near you because he thinks you've infected my brain. That I should've killed you the first chance I got."

"Why didn't you, by the way?"

He chuckled. "I thought we discussed this already. I've never smelled a werewolf like you and it seemed a shame to let a delicious latte morsel go to waste. Not to mention, you weren't causing any trouble. You were acting like a normal person, which is weird for a stray wolf, half or otherwise. Your parents must have been a strong influence in your life."

Heat flooded my cheeks. I was still stuck on that part about a latte morsel. "They were very influential. But right now we've got more important things to worry about and I'm not talking about your escape either. Can't you just sit tight and let me handle this? After all, I'm the one who Gamboldt wants. Once I finish with him, I'll come down and break you out."

"Good Lord, Lex, you make it sound so easy and it's anything but. What happens if that maniac snatches you away from me? I'm scared..." He took a breath. "I'm scared I'll never get you back if it happens again. We both know I'm right."

That we did. In fact, I was sure I'd had this same conversation with myself not too long ago. "At least I've got a place to stay for the night. How safe it is, remains to be seen."

"Believe it or not, it's pretty safe. Witches believe in doing no harm and it's a rule they live by to the fullest."

"Yeah, right. Tell that to their coven leader. She's the one who fell in with Gamboldt and gave up their craft secrets."

"You're beginning to sound like them, you know that?"

"Is that a bad thing?"

"Not necessarily. But I have a feeling Pippa is setting you up to have an alibi. I'd highly suggest calling Monica and giving her the latest on what happened at the inn. Just keep the supernatural stuff out of it if you can."

"I know the drill."

"And don't forget about your appointment tomorrow with Dr. Anri."

"I won't."

"And make sure—"

"Geesh! Would you stop nagging me?"

"Nagging you?" Matt laughed. "You make it sound like we're an old married couple. I'm just—"

"Nagging."

He laughed again. God, it felt good to hear his laughter despite his circumstances. If I helped him do that while living a nightmare, then I was doing a good job. *Selfless pat on the back.*

The following morning, a knock at the door jolted me from the trenches of sleep. Flora still had my crossbow. That left only my bowie knife for defense. After a few blinks around the room, how I ended up in a strange bed and in a strange house trickled back to me. Since there were no bindings on my wrists or ankles, that meant I had made it through the night in one piece. That was a plus. Did it mean I'd drop my guard? Of course not.

I reached for the knife on the nightstand, unsheathing the blade from the leather case. Keeping my foot planted on the floor a few inches behind the door, I opened it.

Pippa wasn't there. Instead, it was another redhead who looked somewhat like her, only longer wavy hair and rectangular glasses on her rounded face. She smiled, lightening up the freckles on her cheeks. She held a cardboard box in front of her with the address of the house on the *To* section and the address of my inn on the *From* and a Founding Fathers Courier Service label where the postage would normally be.

"I'm Pippa's older sister, Claudia." She handed it to me.

I tossed the knife on the bed and took it with both hands. I doubted my hosts would appreciate my reaching for a knife in the morning instead of a cup of coffee.

She started to walk away, but stopped and turned. "Um...don't take this the wrong way, but this house isn't ours. I mean—it belongs to Nora, our new coven leader. The house passes down from leader to leader and has been in our coven for the last seventy years. Anyway, it's a meeting place for us. It's also our sanctuary. We don't give this address out to anyone and—"

"It won't happen again." I knew where she was coming from, but they needed to understand a few things. "The Crescent Inn was my sanctuary and someone turned it into the devil's nest in my absence. So I understand why you guys don't want any part of my mess. You want your anonymity."

"Good. As long as—"

"You need to understand that this has become your war too, when your former leader switched sides. You can't just wash her under the rug and hope that her betrayal won't came back to haunt you. Gamboldt will walk over anyone to get what he wants. If he's bold enough to kidnap a werewolf, then what's to stop him from having others bow to his whim?"

Claudia approached with her fingers kneading themselves to knuckle whiteness. When it looked like she had gathered all of her thoughts, she met my eyes. "That's why you're here. We've gone through years of persecution because we're experts when it comes to power going to our heads. That's why we avoid Salem and only a few of us have contact with the supernatural community. Too many ghosts and stigmas of our past are up there. We're a shunned group by choice. But my point is this. We don't know how to fight Robert when he's got us at a disadvantage. We're willing to get our hands dirty to set things right, but we won't open this house up to any dangers. Not when we have the next generation learning their craft on the bottom floor."

"Next generation? As in kids?"

She nodded. "Their ages range from five to sixteen."

"Damn." This was getting more complicated by the day.

"Sarah knows. We'd be fools not to think that Robert does too. Our little ones' minds won't be able to stand up to his brainwashing. That's why we need help. *Your* help. If we had approached the Pack Alpha or the leaders of the Vampire Ministry, we'd have ended up dead and perhaps our entire race at the bottom of the Charles River for being stupid enough to open up our teachings to this monster."

I shifted the box on my arms. "I'm just one person. I can't hold the fate of the supernatural balance in my hands without some help."

"We're here if you need us. Unfortunately, Pippa's participation might be iffy at best. She was called to the hospital this morning. With a schedule like hers, nothing is guaranteed." She clapped her hands together and brightened her freckled smile. "I'm going downstairs to get some breakfast started for the students. You're more than welcome to join us. I'll steep some tea, unless you're a coffee drinker."

"Tea's fine. Thanks." I retreated inside and closed the door.

The package was from Dane. He'd wanted to know where I was when I called last night to report in. Of course, he'd given me an earful and thought I'd learned my lesson by now about talking to strangers. Pippa wasn't a real stranger because I'd met her before. She wasn't a real threat either, as I recalled. Dane didn't care. He'd gotten all Alpha wolf on the phone, asserting his authority and stuff. So, I'd hung up.

Inside, I found a pair of brass knuckles in a beige drawstring sack-purse and a metallic telescopic baton wrapped in bubble wrap. The leather holster I assumed strapped to my thigh. Gee, and here I had hoped for some cookies and fresh brownies. The last item was a red dress with a pair of matching strappy heels. Did the man think I was headed to a thug picnic? Heaven knows the dress and the baton alone would make an interesting conversation piece. At least the black thigh-length jacket was a nice bonus.

A tiny red, white and blue striped flag on the upper part of the heel caught my attention. When I touched it, a sharp metal blade sprang out. A grin lifted my cheeks. Now that was my kind of a shoe. Prada, eat your heart out. Although I'd rather have something that was no more than an inch and half off the ground, I'd take these three-inch daggers of death any day.

Underneath everything was a note. Dane didn't think it was a good idea for me to show up at the inn wearing my sniper gear and thought this looked more ladylike and harmless at first sight. I couldn't understand why he'd think I'd show up there, until I read down further. Both he and Flora had agreed to relocate everyone to other bed and breakfasts and pay for their first-night stay for the inconvenience. They cleared the house for my "pretend" return. Considering everything that had happened, he knew it was the last place I'd show up because too many enemies had intruded upon my den. However, those outside our community wouldn't know that. They'd assume I'd go back home once the coast was clear. In all honesty, I wasn't feeling the werewolf thing and wanted my den back just like any other human. I owned it. Enough said. Anyone in their right mind would want their possessions back.

I finished putting five perfect arrows in the center of a target. The bull's eye was at least a hundred feet away.

Acres upon acres stretched across the massive estate. Vines crept up the side of the granite wall. A wrought-iron fence surrounded the property. Small mounds of snow sat untouched throughout the brown grass. It was winter and cold as hell with the condensed air fogging from my mouth. To my left sat a garden house that looked like a smaller version of the one behind me. I turned and looked up, counting the three floors and an attic that could've passed for a fourth floor.

From the large deck, Robert stepped down the stairs clapping his hands. "Well done, Ms. Wells. I'm impressed."

Robert reminded me of a younger version of Milton Burroughs. His dark eyes settled on me, bags sagging underneath. He had a long head, making it almost too big for his narrow shoulders. Gray peeked along his temples and reached back into his ink-black hair. The man wore a black sports coat with a dark blue turtleneck underneath and slacks that matched the shirt. Smoke billowed from the end of his cigar, digging into my sensitive nostrils.

I said nothing. In my mind, he hadn't said anything that required a response.

He leaned in and engulfed my mouth in a kiss. His tobacco-tasting tongue slicked across mine, demanding to dominate me. The scent of expensive cologne and his sweet cigars continued to assault my senses.

When his hand cupped my ass, I pulled out of the kiss.

My instincts screamed in outrage at this fucker's invasion of my personal space. I didn't want that mongrel touching me. As much as I wanted to claw out his throat, something stopped me. Robert wasn't Alpha enough, although he thought he was, but I knew better. That bastard would never make me his mate. I'd end up bashing his skull before he came up for a breath.

"Leave her alone, Robert." A woman spoke just out of my view. "If you try to get her to go against her instincts, it'll break our hold. The potions I made will only open her up so much to your will."

He snorted, eyes roving up and down my front. "I'll have her once we're done."

"Not unless she wants you. She's part werewolf. Her Alpha heart is for an Alpha mate. One who's her equal, not dominant. Unless you can prove you're her mate, the wolf inside her will fight you. It sleeps right now, which is the only reason we have her under our control. I can't guarantee what will happen if that wolf should wake."

Robert turned to the woman out of my view and took a long puff of his cigar. "Then we need to make sure the bitch stays down."

"She will if you leave her alone."

No matter how much I tried, I couldn't force myself to see the woman. My head struggled to turn. That damn unseen force had every inch of me in its grip. All I did was look straight ahead at Robert's repulsive face.

"What do you plan to do with her?" the woman asked.

Robert puffed his cigar again. He started strutting around me, his vile breath filling my nostrils. When he opened his mouth, he blew cigar smoke in my face. Entranced or not, it didn't stop me from biting my bottom lip to keep my churning stomach in place. Whoever the woman was, she was right about my senses and instincts overriding his control. Eventually it would happen and I'd be more than happy to twist his head off in return.

He flicked his wrist. I pulled the state-of-the-art bow back, aiming the tip of my arrow at the small red target in the center. "She's the perfect weapon. Wherever she goes—wherever she strikes—my enemies will know that I've sanctioned it. They'll know by her trademark."

Robert stepped in front of me. His chin was about an inch away from the sharpened tip. Another puff of smoke blew from his mouth, billowing toward my face. I struggled not to release the taut bow and kill him. My fingers refused to follow through. While I screamed inside to be set free, my body held me prisoner by not doing what I asked.

When Robert paced to the other side of me, I released the arrow. It pierced the target dead center, slicing one of my previous arrows to pieces.

"The arrow." Robert's smile was all teeth as he turned to the anonymous woman again. "She's a clean killer. The perfect assassin. No torn bodies or blood on her hands. Between your potions and my brainwashing, we'll be able to command more like her. The Romas did well with bringing her to my attention. Consider their debt wiped clean, but make sure they know my eyes are on them. I have no problem with using them as target practice for my hired gun."

"Then you had better teach her to wear gloves."

Grass rustled just behind my ears. Someone approached, threatening my personal space. Again, I tried to turn, but my body was against it.

Hands covered my eyes from behind. This time the invisible force persuaded me to mount another arrow on my bow and fire again. I followed through. The bow snapped. The undulating kickback left the weapon quivering in my solid hand. When the person's hands came away from my eyes, I noticed the new arrow less than an inch from the last one I had fired.

"Bravo!" Robert clapped his hands.

"Not so fast." The woman's voice traveled across the back of my neck like fog on a moonlit pond. "As good a shot as that is, if her fingerprints are on that arrow, you can kiss your new toy goodbye. Remind her to wear gloves and always use a different arrow with different markings. Make her kills untraceable in every sense of the word."

My personal space lightened up with the sound of the footfalls retreating.

Sarah Jenkinson. The mention of potions had given her away and Pippa had already confirmed one of their own had sold them out. However, there was one good spot about this new development that I should've thought of before. If it took a spell to do this to me, then perhaps they knew another spell to counter it. I'd have to ask Claudia when I got downstairs.

Though Dane had good intensions, there was no way I could return to my inn anytime soon. No thanks to his witch, the Romas, a necromancer and whoever else he had in his back pocket, Gamboldt had made my sanctuary unsafe for me. My wolf side wanted to mope around the neighborhood for as long as it took to make sure it was okay to walk through the inn's front door again. To my human side, that was unacceptable. I wanted my home back, dammit. The only way for that to happen was to start making some waves. I'd start with another trip to the Garridans.

Chapter Forty

I parked Dane's rental across the street from Vujo Garments, the Garridans' store, and probably the only one they were able to salvage from the auction block. After flipping the keys around on my finger, I shoved them in the pocket of the jeans I had borrowed from Claudia. Showing up in the dress that Dane gave me was a little over the top. The baton hidden under my coat and the knife sheath against my thigh were enough. People gave me funny stares on my march down the boardwalk. At least they stepped out of my way because they knew I meant business. Let's just hope the Garridans thought so too.

When I shoved open the doors, the only thing familiar was the chiming bell above the threshold. Everything looked different somehow, like there were more clothes and trinkets than before. The musty odor I remembered wasn't from the old beams running above our heads, but rather incense burning in the corner. If I had my guess about it, I'd say they had strengthened their protection spells—not that I blamed them.

I forwent the clothes shopping and went straight to the counter. An old woman with more wrinkles than an elephant's butt lifted her sagging eyes. She pointed a gnarled finger at me and began trembling. I hoped that wasn't Aunt Tatiana because I had a bone to pick with her once this was over.

"M-m-muló."

A mild tremble clacked the feet of the old woman's chair against the hardwood floor. I had to do a double take on that one because her legs were too short to touch anything. There was nothing moving that chair except her anxiety and the waving of her finger. From a physical point of view: impossible.

From a metaphysical one: highly probable.

"Muló." She dropped her knitting on the floor.

I stepped forward and picked up her knitting needles and latest creation off the floor. When I went to hand it to her, she shrank away.

"Aunt Tatiana."

Great. This was the old woman I wanted. What was up with these old people having a hand in this foolishness? Shouldn't they have known better at their age?

The voice came from a woman standing at the other end of the counter. She finished up with a customer before hurrying to where Aunt Tatiana sat quaking in her chair. The young woman's long blond hair flowed about her shoulders, waves of curls that reminded me of a fairytale princess. Taking the corner of her long skirt in one hand, she moved it out of the way to crouch next to her aunt and rub the back of her pustuled hand.

I couldn't help thinking of everything I had touched in the shop on my last visit with Tate and Dane. I just hoped whatever the old woman had wasn't catching.

"Please, dear aunt." Worry etched her tender face. "Calm down. It's all right. The muló knows this place is protected." She poured her ice blue eyes on me. So much for looking delicate. "And if she doesn't, she'll find out the hard way."

I snorted and handed the blonde the knitting. "Don't even think about it. The witches gave me a protection spell. One that'll also block Gamboldt's mind control."

Okay, I didn't have all that. The best Claudia had offered me was a pentagram pendant for good luck and some prayers of safety in my quest. In fact, she'd used it as a teaching point to the younger witches and even had them casting spells on my behalf. I had my doubts that any of it would work, but it was the thought that counted. Whether the Garridans believed that or not was up to them. I just hoped I was good enough to bluff my way through it.

The woman rose, but kept a suspicious eye on me. "You're Alexa, the half wolf, aren't you? My cousin Wednesday had a feeling you'd return. She said we should be ready."

"I'm not looking for a fight, Ms...?"

"Summer." She handed the knitting back to Tatiana and went behind the counter again. "I hope you're not here for the old woman's blood."

I offered a final glance at Tatiana before turning my attention to Summer and following her down the front of the counter. "I'd be lying if I said I hadn't thought about it. But given the choice, I'd rather save my energy for someone who really deserves it."

"Gamboldt, I presume." She smiled at a patron and started ringing her items up. "Uncle Cam has caused us enough trouble that our council cast marimé on him. You won't see him again any time soon."

"What's marimé?"

"It means banishment due to impurities. Just as we had washed our hands of Gamboldt, he dirtied himself by falling behind him again. We are serious about not wanting anything more do with that man." She handed the customer her change and thanked her for shopping. The smile remained on her face until the bell chimed above the door upon her exit. "If you're here, that means we have more washing to do."

I couldn't tell if that was a snipe at me being dirty or how they handled all muló like me. I let it go.

"Before we exiled him, he left something. Said if someone came here looking for him, that I was to give them this." Summer reached under the counter and handed me an envelope. "He said he would make things right again. At least right with his soul."

I tore into the envelope and pulled out an invitation to a high-stakes poker party with an address and formal dress code. It was a good idea Dane had sent the dress after all. Another piece of paper slipped out of the invitation. To my shock, it was an apology. It was also the key to how they had managed to track me all this time. Sammy, my love interest back at Trixie's, was also a telepath. With us having formed a physical connection, it made it easier for Robert to keep tabs on me.

I didn't want to think beyond that "physical" shit. It was time to focus on setting my life right. Whether I got my memory back or not didn't matter. Protecting my family and friends did.

Life went on around me regardless of my current state of affairs. I still had to catch up with Monica and make my appointment with Dr. Anri. One toe out of place would have both of them thinking I had skipped town again. I couldn't afford to lose Monica as my defense attorney while Matt remained behind bars with Parry.

My appointment with Dr. Anri was pretty much the same old crap. This time, I refused to let him put me under without someone I trusted in the room. He understood because he still nursed the knot on his head. So, we talked about stupid stuff like feelings and my relationships with friends and family. He challenged me to call my parents and tell them how everything had turned out. As long as I came out of this in one piece, he'd have his answer at our next meeting.

Monica was another story. I tried calling her three times but had to leave a message either on her voice mail or with her secretary. The only person I reached was Dane and that was to fill him in on my plans for his red dress and how they involved a poker party. He didn't like it, of course. I hung up when he started in with asserting his authority again. I'd make an awful pack wolf. It was a good thing I didn't feel the need for one.

Come nightfall, I had my knife in place and the retractable baton in the passenger's seat. With my dagger heels strapped to my feet and the brass knuckles in my purse, I set out to find Gamboldt to finish this.

The house was the same one I had seen in my vision. It looked old and just as stately as ever with more vines having crept up the sides. There were lights on in every window and my heightened hearing picked up classical music coming from somewhere within the house.

Even though I had an invitation, I wasn't sure if going through the front gate was the best idea. The guard would probably announce my arrival and have the whole house waiting for me with guns and potions pointed.

The stone wall surrounding the property wasn't colonial-fort high. Plus, there were ways over it with the giant trees growing from the corner. I slung my shoes over my shoulder, tied off the flowing length of the halter dress and started climbing the tree. By the time I reached the ten-foot drop at the top, I had only one smudge and it came off with a little spit. I leaped off the wall and landed in a crouch. It was like my body was built for agility along with strength. I'd need them both tonight.

Instead of putting the heels on, I crept across the cold

lawn, making my way from tree to tree for coverage. I ducked into the woods on the side of the house. Fresh loam was like a taste of mint bursting inside my mouth. The scent of pine and earth filled my nose. Deer hooves thumped across the ground less than a quarter of a mile away. My mind's eye pictured rabbits scampering through the underbrush. Here, my senses amplified with the wilderness around me.

An opening at the other end of my hike brought me a few yards behind the guard's house. Another car, a blue truck, approached the gate. The window lowered and my stomach fell with it. Oh. My. God.

Charles sat behind the steering wheel staring straight ahead while Flora remained emotionless in the passenger's seat. He handed the guard something before the gate slid open and allowed him through. Right on the bumper of his truck was another car. I didn't recognize the driver. More important, I couldn't take my eyes off Charles's truck pulling away from the wrought-iron fence, heading toward the large Tudor mansion.

Several more cars pulled into the driveway, each stopping at the front gate for the guard to check off their names. I didn't recognize any of the people behind the steering wheels.

I continued across the lawn. Instead of going for the front door where a butler greeted those coming in, I headed around to the side to a window. Whatever was going on, I didn't want them to see all my cards just yet. Besides, a little fear never hurt anyone.

Standing on my tiptoes, I pressed my face close to the glass. Books lined the walls. A series of pictures sat on a small table by the door. Closest to the window sat a desk with a small Tiffany-style lamp in the corner. Several pieces of paper lay strewn across the desk with a magazine on top.

Tossing all caution aside, I smashed the window with my baton. Using it, I traced the metal bar around the edges to knock out the rest of the shards. No alarm. That didn't bode well for my breaking and entering. Either Robert knew I'd do this or he was a fool. A man this careful didn't strike me as the latter. I put my bets on a silent alarm. It wasn't like I had a chance at getting in unnoticed anyway.

After crawling inside, my sensitive hearing picked up footsteps thudding across the floor just beyond the closed door. I flattened myself against the wall ready for it to open. When one of the butlers stepped inside, I slammed the baton across the back of his head. He crashed into a small side table.

One of the collapsed pictures tossed across the floor caught my attention. My eyes refused to leave it. I picked up the silver frame and studied her face to be sure.

The woman stood next to a horse wearing a jockey's hat and a pair of beige slacks. A black braid with apple-red highlights caught the breeze at just the right time, blowing across her face. A smile lifted her crow's feet and brightened her blue eyes. Although she appeared a few years younger than Gamboldt, I knew that face.

Random images began bouncing back and forth in my brain.

Sarah Jenkinson lurked in the background at Robert's house. She paced back and forth while I loaded an arrow onto a compound bow for target practice. My target was a man who'd created his own software company out of his apartment and refused to sell it to Gamboldt. I released the bow and planted the arrow through the center of his chest without remorse. I had silenced the man's cries. Another innocent death on my hands.

A second image of Sarah came to mind. She stood over me while holding a smoking poultice at breast level. Her thin, wrinkled lips moved to the sounds of a meaningless limerick. Robert waved his hand in a circular motion about my face. Though I couldn't make out his words, I had the feeling he had issued orders without moving his lips. Sarah sauntered around me mumbling something nonsensical again. Robert's invisible clout stretched beyond his voice. It was like Sarah projected his will, intensifying whatever hold he had on me.

It was just as she said in one of my earlier vision. Sarah amplified his power. I was nothing more than their guinea pig. Eventually, they'd work out the kinks to control species that were more powerful than little ol' me. In fact, I bet they took Tate not only as bait, but as the next step in their mystical research.

I whipped the picture at the wall and marched out of the room.

Chapter Forty-One

Golden wood adorned every inch of the mansion, from the floors to the high ceiling. A line of small chandeliers lit up a path toward the music piping from around the corner. A navy blue Persian rug ran the length of the floor like a red carpet. Fresh flowers adorned side tables every few feet. Large family portraits hung on the walls with their pinched faces and pursed lips. The only ones who seemed to be smiling were the children.

The low hum of the crowd forced my footfalls to slow. I didn't want these people knowing where to find me. Not yet anyway.

Angry voices jarred my nerves. I hurried back the way I had come, entering a large room filled with various coats of armor, a Samurai statue in the corner with his forked helmet and a Viking carrying a large ax on his shoulder. The stupid doors refused to slide closed and there weren't a lot of places to hide. I pressed my back against the wall and waited for them to pass.

"Nice place."

Wait a minute. I recognized that voice. Turning to my front, I inched to the edge of the door and peeked into the hall.

"Glad you like it." Dottie strutted to a stop wearing a low-cut blouse barely covering her sagging, mega-sized boobs. "Too bad you were all Sarah delivered to us on such short notice. It would've been better to include your entire coven, since we're celebrating your holiday and all."

Pippa stood next to her. What was she doing here? I thought she had to report to the hospital for something. She had obviously gone there at some point because she wore a pair of blue scrubs with her hospital ID clipped to the breast pocket.

"I know," Pippa responded in a robotic manner like she

wasn't all there.

"That's okay." Dottie patted the back of her hand. "We'll work something out to bring them into the fold. In fact, Sarah's working on it as we speak."

I bet she is. I launched into the hall.

Dottie gasped and stumbled back. "Keisha! N-n-now wait. You have to let me—"

I wound my hand back and bitch-slapped her into a wall. When her head bounced off the wood paneling, I was on her, fisting her hair in my hand. I yanked her around and plowed my fist into her jaw. She hit the floor of the showcase room and slid to a stop. Her head most likely bounced into a concussion because she lay on her side, unmoving. I prayed I hadn't cracked her skull because I didn't know how to do dead-body disposal yet.

Pippa was another story. I didn't know if slapping her or snapping my fingers would do the trick. Then again, if it were that easy, surely someone would've broken me out of my trance a long time ago. But I wasn't a full-blooded anything. Maybe she didn't need as much of a jolt as I did.

I grabbed her shoulders, shoved her into the showcase room and gave her a dose of shaken-baby syndrome to snap her out of it. When that didn't work, I remembered the scented poultice and put her in a headlock. She scratched and clawed at my arm, anything to prevent cutting off her air supply. I didn't want to kill her, but I needed whatever junk was in her lungs to get the hell out. Maybe forcing her to take in some oxygen after being deprived of it might help. If it didn't, perhaps the shock to her system would.

"Alexa." After a series of gasps and her eyes rolling back in her head, I let go, letting her drop to the floor. Her hand rubbed her reddening throat, lethargy clouding her half-closed eyes. Frowning, she blinked at me and adjusted her crooked glasses. "Head hurts. Can't focus. What...? What happened?"

"You were under Robert's control just like me."

"Then how...? What...?"

"You're a full-blooded witch, right?"

She opened her eyes and stared. "Full blood? There isn't any such thing among witches. Our powers aren't necessarily hereditary. With enough training and perseverance any human can do them."

"Anyone?" This was news to me. If anyone could be a witch, then... "Ohmygod. Does Robert know that?"

Still holding her head, she offered me her arm to help her off the floor. It took a few deep breaths before she answered. "They've solidified their partnership in a way I'd rather not think about. Besides finding the right witch and someone who's powerful enough to teach you without draining their own power, it takes years to master the level that my coven sisters and I have. Sarah could do it, but that means she would've had to have started teaching him about ten years ago. She was a different woman back then. Her personality didn't change until the last two. Gamboldt had started gaining recognition a few months before that."

I bet anything Sarah had been feeding him secrets to stay on his good side. Even if she swore she'd done it for the safety of her coven, I wouldn't buy it. Not once did she flinch when it came to drowning me with those stinking potions.

Pippa grabbed my arms, eyes pleading. "Please, Alexa. This information can never get out. If people know about the kind of power we harness, there's no telling what it'll do to the rest of the supernatural world. It's taken us centuries to have order among our community. It would take millennia to set it straight if humans knew."

While this was news to me, it was something I planned to store away for future reference. It wasn't like I wanted to study witchcraft when I had enough problems of my own as a hybrid werewolf.

Pippa touched her fingers to her forehead. "I have to think. Have to get in touch with my coven to warn them about the Festival of Darkness that Sarah has planned for tonight."

"This is a powerful night, isn't it?"

She nodded. "There's a poker game going on upstairs, but I can't recall which room."

The only other people I knew in this house were the Hills. They wouldn't do anything to sabotage my plans, at least not under their own volition.

I took Pippa by the arm and led her to the door. "Show me."

Leading the way, she peeked into the hall before stepping into the corridor. I followed, ducking in and out behind large planters and tables. It wasn't much for cover, but it would have to do. Besides, if things went awry, I wanted to make sure I was near enough to something to either throw or use as a shield.

Pippa forced me back behind a bushy plant growing straight up from a large urn. It wasn't an ideal spot, but it kept the two men from seeing us. I leaned forward just enough to recognize one of them. It was Sammy.

When they'd finished passing, Pippa motioned me to follow her up the stairs. At the top, we rounded the corner where a familiar scent caught my nose. I didn't stick around long enough to pay any attention, but there was a lingering memory that tried to poke free. I recognized that smell because it belonged to the monster who held Matt captive.

Son of a bitch. I grabbed Pippa to stop her.

"What do we have here?"

Aw shit. Too late.

Parry stood behind us at the far end of the hall with two growling wolves by his side like sentinels. Pippa screamed. I grabbed her by the arm and threw her behind me. Witch or not, I trusted my survival skills more than hers.

He planted his hands on his hips. "I'd send my wolves to tear a chunk out of your mutt hide, but I've got more important things to do. Like the next round."

We watched as he and his wolves stepped into a far room. Laughter and a little light music floated from behind the doorway. I didn't want to go in there, but I knew that was where everyone would be. That was where I needed to be too.

"Robert," Parry shouted. "Your bitch is here."

So much for the element of surprise.

Pippa clutched my sleeve, panic reeking from her pores. "I don't want to go down that hall. I'm scared."

No reassuring words came to mind. She wasn't the only one who wanted to go in the opposite direction.

Nevertheless, I steeled myself and started down the hall. If she wanted to leave, then I'd make sure she left in one piece. Pippa caught up to me but clutched my upper arm like a small child entering a haunted-house attraction with their parent.

Nothing prepared me for what lay in that room. Parry's ferocious wolves laid their ears flat against their heads with spittle dripping from their snarling mouths. The black one stepped forward with his head hung low to the floor. His dark eyes bored into me. The chocolate one followed his lead.

I knew those wolves by scent, but I didn't want to believe it.

"Call off your dogs," a voice said. "I see my lovely prize has arrived."

When Matt and Tate backed off, I continued inside.

Hardwood floors covered every inch of the room with its tan and beige décor. A coffee-bean-colored leather couch and chairs sat in the center of the room before a large entertainment center. Two men who I didn't know sat watching the game on TV while feeling up the thighs of the whores on their laps. One of them was busy with a deep, sultry kiss, her long hair kept me from seeing both her and her lover's faces. On the other side of the room, five men played cards at a dealer's table. Several of the strippers from Trixie's either danced around the table or slithered up next to their man of choice. They smiled to me, some offering their hellos and calling me by that horrible name. The entire room stank of sex, alcohol and some sort of incense.

Charles and Flora were nowhere in sight. Anxiety gnawed my empty gut. *Dear God, please tell me they're okay.*

A stronger whiff of the incense dug into my brain. I glanced around the room. Not one window was open. In fact, it was rather stuffy. What better way for the witch bitch to drug everyone. If she kept it up long enough, nobody in the room would be able to withstand Gamboldt's mind control.

Including the strippers. Good Lord. All this time I thought I was the only one under his control and everyone else was acting on free will. The smoke at the strip bar was thick and choking just like this, and it seemed to follow us into the dressing room. Or was it always there? Anyone who walked into that place wasn't immune to Gamboldt's will.

Speaking of which, the man himself stood next to Sarah Jenkinson, admiring the large fireplace burning on the opposite side of the room. He cut his dark eyes at me as though he stared into my soul and wanted to tear my heart out with a single thought. A perfect smile flexed his mouth, happy to have his wayward star pupil back.

"Trixie's was your Petri dish." I took my time heading straight for him and his witch. "Once you had their minds softened up, you used them to dance on the stage. To do your bidding. Except for Elaine and Frankie. You used them to keep an eye on everyone."

He poked a finger at me. "You see that. I knew you were a

smart one. The only problem is I'm still trying to figure out how you broke my will."

"You've underestimated me as a hybrid. Even the werewolves don't know what to do with me because I'm not exactly human or like them."

He brought a cigar up to his mouth for a long drag. "I'm not buying it. Something else caused you to blink."

Other than being dressed like a cop and—

Werewolves hated cops. In fact, we detested anything that had to do with possibly exposing our people to the human world. Could that have been enough to snap me out of my mental slumber? That and the combination of doing something that normally went against my will. But surely I had stripped other times on that stage. Dressed as what, I couldn't say. There was also the possibility that werewolves only responded to Alpha likenesses. A strong witch? Maybe, though the species might give me pause. A strong wolf? Every time Dane had tried to assert his authority, I cut him off. Whenever I was in his presence, my wolf instincts dictated that I at least listened to his commands. Nevertheless, Dane couldn't cancel out my free will completely.

But Robert? He was nothing more than a chump trying to be a champ. Calling him the equivalent of a beta wolf was an insult to all betas everywhere. He was a pretender. A charlatan. A wannabe trying to belong to the club. He was beyond pathetic. He was nothing more than a rat trying to get a crumb.

"Blink this." I grabbed one of the leather chairs, yanked it off the floor and hurled it at the panoramic window.

Everything moved in slow motion. Robert and Sarah screamed. They hurried to stop the chair, but it was too late. It took out the entire pane.

"You bitch." Sarah snapped her fingers at the wolves then pointed at me. "Attack!"

Oh shit.

Matt started out ahead of Tate, both their ears flattened against their head and readying themselves for ass-chomping mode.

While Parry closed his eyes and steadied himself as if waking from a dizzying spell, there was nothing to stop his wolves from attacking.

With the baton in one hand, I unsheathed my knife. God

knows I didn't want to hurt Matt, but I'd defend myself at all costs. I stepped in front of Pippa and shoved her backward. "Go. Now!"

She took off.

The wolves started after us.

Pippa bolted out of the room first. I followed close on her heels, refusing to look back. She hurried down the stairs while I leaped over the railing to the first floor. We started for the front door, but stopped. Sammy and the other bouncer from the bar blocked our exit. I grabbed Pippa by the arm and circled us around to the back of the house where we found a door leading to the backyard. I threw it open...and stopped.

Now, I knew why I wasn't able to reach Monica. She, Flora, Charles, Frank and Sonya from the hotel, Dr. Anri and several others I didn't know, stood in front of a bonfire burning on the lawn. Their lifeless eyes stared straight ahead. They were like pieces on a checkerboard, waiting for someone to move them.

They weren't alone. Six nude women stood around the fire wearing flowers in their hair and dancing with their hands held high...until I came along. They stopped and stared, lost looks marring their faces. If I had my guess, I'd say Sarah had converted a few members of the local coven.

Glass crashed behind us. I ducked my head and dodged aside. Pippa did the same.

I brought the baton around just as a black furred mass leaped for me. I cracked it against the side of Matt's head. Both of us went down hard.

I rolled away and scrambled back to my feet. Matt lay shaking his head. I noticed the swollen eye and the blood dripping from his nose. I hadn't meant to hurt him that bad, but he needed someone to snap some sense back into his skull. My heart crumbled as I watched him struggle to get to his feet. Man, I'd hated to do that. Surely, he understood. I prayed he'd come to his senses before he retracted his muzzle with another snarl.

I searched out Pippa. She lay face down on the lawn with Tate growling over her.

"Kill her." Robert leaned over the balcony looking at us.

I pulled my knife up to my chest ready to defend myself.

He wasn't talking about me.

Parry hopped over the railing from the second floor. He

marched across the lawn and yanked Pippa up by the back of her neck. With his arm wrapped around her chest, he grabbed her head.

"No!" I started for her.

Crack.

He snapped her neck and let her limp body slump to the ground.

Oh God. No. Tears welled into my eyes. Not her. Not another because of me.

I screamed at Parry. "You lowlife piece of shit! She never did anything to you. You're gonna let that weak-ass human bend you like a twig? He says jump and your big, bad furry ass waits for him to say how high. What kind of Pack Alpha are you, you psychotic prick? You're not even fit to lead a group of cockroaches."

Parry closed one of his eyes like he was going through a migraine. He grabbed his head as if in pain and dropped to one knee.

I stared at Gamboldt. Heaven knew I wanted to smirk, but I couldn't. I knew the weakness with his mind control and there weren't enough potions in the world to break down a werewolf's survival instincts. We only answered to Alphas. Parry, on the other hand, answered to no one. Gamboldt didn't even fit *that* category. Judging from the anger coursing the idiot's face, he knew it too.

Gamboldt tore away from the balcony and hurried back inside.

A body hit me hard, throwing me to the ground and snapping my head back on the grass. Growling had filled my ears, but the dizziness and the pain burrowing into the back of my skull took precedence.

By the time I finished blinking the stars from my vision, Tate stood with his growling muzzle a few inches from my face. When I lifted my arm, pain shot through my left shoulder. Something snapped back in place in the joint. Searing hell shot through my bones. That motherfucker had dislocated my shoulder. Friend or not, he was in for a hurtin'.

I wound back my fist and slammed him across the jaw with a right cross. When Tate stumbled backward, Matt snagged him by the scruff of his fur and dragged him away from me.

I turned onto my stomach and began searching the ground

for my baton and knife. I had lost them when Tate hit me.

Something shiny caught my eye. I scrambled toward it.

A foot came down hard on the back of my right hand before I reached my baton. Sarah stood above me, grinding my palm into the ground with the heel of her shoe. She gritted her teeth in a maniacal grin, growling as she tried to punch a hole through the back of my hand.

She wasn't the only one with a pair of swank shoes. Only, mine were better.

I whipped my limber body around in a cool martial arts move and kicked in the side of her knee. She screamed and hopped around on one leg until she collapsed in agony.

I picked up the baton and smacked her across the back of the head. I noticed the leather hilt lying on the ground with the blade under Sarah's shoulder.

"Attack!" She pointed at my friends, family and strangers, ordering them to come after me.

I lifted my foot up, pressed the flag on the side and rammed the bladed heel of my shoe into Sarah's stomach. She grabbed my leg, but it was fruitless. I twisted my heel enough for life to leave her hands and her body to fall to the grass.

Robert burst through the back doors and onto the deck. "Noooooooo!" He dashed across the lawn and dropped to his knees beside his witch's body. "You cunt. I'll kill you for what you did to her."

"You'll need another army, asshole." I retracted the stake back into the heel of my shoe. "Yours is waking up."

A heavy gust of October winds doused the flames from the bonfire to half its blazing glory. Coldness settled into the backyard.

The growling and grunting from Matt and Tate had stopped. Tate stood on shaky legs while Matt stood above him with his head cocked to the side. When he lifted his canine face to me, I returned one hell of a grateful smile.

I looked to Gamboldt still mourning his dead witch. He poured his fury into a single scowl when his eyes met mine.

"Bitch." He jumped to his feet with my knife in his hand, winding it back to fling at me.

A body tackled me to the ground, one hand covering my head while the other cuddled me close.

Dane took most of the impact. I stared, questions pummeling my mind. The loudest: *Where the hell did he come from?*

Hitting the ground hard for a third time wasn't any more pleasurable than the first. It fucking hurt when your once-dislocated shoulder cried out in agony again.

I pulled away from Dane to see Matt standing above Gamboldt with his shoulders hunched and blood dripping from his mouth. The maniac lay on his back with his dead eyes looking at me. More than half of his throat was a mass of bloody muscle and tissue with an artery squirting off the last of his life. Blood seeped into the ground. More tissue and bone lay exposed to the air.

"Let's get the hell out of here." Dane eased to his feet before helping me up. "This is Boston Pack territory. Let them be the ones to tend to the humans."

"Where the hell—"

"I followed Charles and Flora. They were acting strange when they left the B&B. Like something had come over them. I think the migraine I had earlier tried to sucker me in too. Anyway, they stopped in the middle of what they were doing and got in the truck."

Never in my short, forgotten life had I been so happy to see him. Then again, his timing could've been a little better.

Like Parry, most of the people, including my friends, had dropped to their knees or lay on the ground. They grabbed their heads and moaned in pain. Flora worried me most because of her high blood pressure. There's no telling what Sarah's control might have done or would do to her.

I shook my head and started for the Hills. "I can't leave them. They're like family to me. Everyone I touched, that bastard used them to bait me. If anything happens—"

Dane silenced my tirade with a finger to my lips. His stern look demanded my attention. "We need to leave. Now. They'll be fine."

"He's right." I didn't recognize the voice or the man standing beside him. He had shoulder-length, wavy brown hair and eyes as blue as topaz. The only thing familiar about him was he had sat at the end of the poker table upstairs.

I looked him up and down. "Who are you?"

"My name is Noah Windham. I'm a liaison to the Vampire

Ministry and probably your only friend here. As long as you're not friends of Parry's, that is."

"More like intruders on his land." Dane motioned him to lead the way.

Together, the three of us left through the woods.

Chapter Forty-Two

Two weeks later...

My memories started coming back the night I killed Sarah. With each brain-shattering migraine, I recalled certain events in my life. The most important—and painful—ones to return were those regarding my family. I knew my mother, my father, my sister and Uncle Graham. In a weird sense, I included Dane and his ragtag group of bounty hunters as family, although I didn't hunt with them on a regular basis. Only when I needed their help with a problem in or around Boston, like the rogue werewolves haunting my visions.

The one memory I wished I hadn't gotten back was where my rogue grandfather had attacked both my baby brother and me. Avery Jr. had died because of his wounds. I hadn't because I was a little older and perhaps a little stronger. At least that was the theory. That bite changed me from a quarter to half werewolf.

I sat at the desk in the study trying to figure out how to recoup some of our losses. It had crossed my mind a dozen times to march right up to Parry and demand reparations. After all, if it hadn't been for my insulting his ass right out of his brainwashing, he might still be a limp rod following behind Gamboldt like a puppy looking for treats. Not knowing how many minions he had under his thumb kept me from following through with it. The splints on my fingers were good deterrents, too.

Large snowflakes fell beyond the windows and hadn't stopped since Pippa's funeral a few days ago. I went, but I kept my distance. When the ceremony ended, I stepped forward and left my own white rose on her grave. I begged God to forgive me if I had done anything to cause her death. Better safe than sorry.

Sweat beaded down the side of my glass of lemonade, enticing me. I lifted the cool drink to my lips and savored the sweet tangy flavor.

"Knock knock." Flora stuck her head in the room. "Are you still worrying over nothing?"

Putting the glass down, I leaned back in my chair. "Someone has to. I lost my job at the university. The only thing I'll be using the computer for these days is to keep the bills and the registry in order."

Flora sauntered into the room with a hand on her hip. "This place can hold its own, you know. In case you forgot in your amnesia craze, we've been in business for the past few years."

"But it takes at least five years to—"

She flipped her hand at me. "Stop reading those foolish business magazines. You take pride in this place. Respect the business because that's all you'll need to carry us through. Besides, we're not in the hole yet."

That we weren't. I couldn't help thinking my heroics had earned the mysterious check that had showed up on our doorstep the following day. It wasn't much, but it certainly helped. Of course, Flora wasn't happy to see the dried flowers and funky symbols drawn in chalk on the sidewalk or on our white picket fence. She said it looked too much like witchcraft. Gee. I wonder where she got that idea.

The bell rang from the hall.

Flora waved a hand. "Hush up, you old fool. Can't you see I'm trying to talk to the boss woman here?"

My jaw dropped. "Flora. You can't talk to our guests like that."

I pushed away from the desk with nothing more than my sincerest apologies on my mind and shook my head at Flora as I passed her. Here we needed the patronage and she wanted to scare the customers off.

My heart slipped to my knees when I stepped out of the room.

Matt stood there drenched from his black, glistening hair to his slush-infested black shoes. That beige wool coat he wore hardly did him any good. He let his duffle bag fall to the floor and placed his laptop bag on top of it. A huge smile pressed into his cheeks, creating two adorable dimples. They were like mother's milk to my eyes.

My parents had spent the last ten days with us. Mom and Dad had helped clean up and get things ready for our grand reopening. They thought I should take some more time off, considering everything that had happened. We had lost enough money, no thanks to Gamboldt. Letting another dime go would only set us back further. Since I was one arm down and hadn't seen them in months, hoping they would go home was just that. Hopeful. Not probable. Thank goodness Dane didn't tell them about Parry possibly gunning for me or they'd never have left. Of course, that didn't stop him from sticking around too. Only yesterday, had they finally headed to their home in Albany, New York, allowing me to settle into a normal routine. All three promised they'd be back next weekend to check up on us. I rolled my eyes.

Sure Parry worried the hell out of me, but this was also a very commercial place. If we had guests, then they would be enough to keep the furry boogieman away. I was sure he'd prefer not to kill me in the presence of witnesses.

I straightened up and put on my business face. "You got a reservation?"

Matt grinned. "Yeah. One right up there on the third floor. The corner room."

"It's filled."

"Then how about one next to it?"

"That's filled too."

"Oh for heaven's sake." Flora marched out of the library and began flipping through the book on the podium. "That room is free and you know it. Stop giving the man a hard time and let him sign in." Grinning, she held the pen to him. "Your room is free."

"*What?*" I scowled at her.

Matt licked his tongue at me as he reached for the pen to sign in. When he finished, he pecked Flora on the cheek and picked up his bags.

I glared at him.

"Don't stand there like you've got mud in your shoes." Flora pointed at the stairs. "Show the man to his room. It doesn't take two arms to do that, you know."

"Fine. Can you handle your own bags or do you need a forklift?"

Glowering behind her glasses, Flora swatted me on the rump as I passed her. "You be civilized to our guest now, you hear? He's planning to get me off on self-defense tomorrow, which is more than I can say for you, Ms. Insanity Plea."

Good thing she was my elder or I would've had some choice words for her. But like she said, Matt was sure the court would either drop the charges or acquit Flora for having anything to do with Keisha's second death. There was just too much evidence in her favor and too much unknown. We knew most of the facts were impossible to human eyes, but the coroner wasn't apt to put zombie as cause of death on her second certificate. Not to mention, Flora's age, bruises and witness accounts helped. All of the sketchy details left the DA completely confounded about her case. At least Claudia and a couple of the other witches had provided an alibi for me. Although, Detective Konoval still thought someone was out to ruin my name and business. I wanted to give him Parry as a suspect, but once again, our laws superseded others.

Matt followed close, breathing his sauna breath across the hairs at the nape of my neck. If I had known it would leave me tingling, I would've worn my hair down to shield my bare neck instead of in a French twist. We arrived at the middle landing when Flora cleared her throat. Both of us stopped and turned.

She wiggled her finger at us from below. "And I don't want to hear any frolicking around while you two are up there. They have motels for that kind of mess."

"Flora!" I wanted to stick my head in a hole in the ground.

She smirked. "Maybe you two can fool each other, but I know that look when I see it. It got me into all sorts of trouble when I was your age."

Matt chuckled. "Like what?"

"I married him." She walked off still waving her finger at us. "You two will end up just like us. Mark my words."

Matt and I stared at each other. Our lips fluttered until smiles burst through.

Without warning, he dropped his bags and slammed his mouth into mine. We kissed like two animals warring for the last drink of water. How had I forgotten something this good in my life? His body heat warmed every inch of me despite his soaking coat. My fingers combed through his wet hair, fisting a few tufts along the way. Our heavy breathing probably echoed up the stairwell.

Matt moved me from one side of the boxed staircase to the other. My leg had hooked around his. I pressed my pelvis into his heated bulge. My body burned, wanting him like it knew it had to make up for lost time.

"What did I say about that frolicking?" Flora shouted from downstairs.

Matt and I stopped and laughed. He lifted me in his arms and carried me the rest of the way up the stairs. He promised to have me for his mate. We'd just have to see about that. When he put me down on the third floor in front of my door, I pressed a finger into his chest to stop him from going any further.

"One thing." I folded my arms, clutching the key so he couldn't get it. "Remember when your friends practically snatched you from the bar?"

"Yes." He leaned close, desire bleeding into his predatory eyes. "Although, they weren't exactly snatching. More like accompanying me back to our den. But semantics skemantics. Who cares?"

"I do. You kissed another woman and now you're standing here ready to make me your mate. You care to comment, counselor, before I unlock this door? Because I assure you, the wrong answer will have you sleeping in a dog house instead of a bed and breakfast."

Matt stepped back with this look on his face like I had just shattered his world. He ran his hands through his hair and paused as if to figure out how to explain. "Her name is Astrid and she's nobody. And as for the kiss, it was just a greeting. Many pack wolves greet their fellow wolves with a kiss or a thump to the back. Astrid isn't the thumping kind."

"Some kiss." My brow arched for him to continue or perish. Though I loved Matt, I needed to know for my own peace of mind. No way I was letting someone into my heart if there was room for a mistress or harem on the side.

"Aw, Lex. Don't do this. Honey, I promise you, it was all for show. When you're a single guy in a pack who has money and a good career, you make one damn good piece of breeding material. I don't mean to sound all egotistical, but the females are always throwing themselves at me. No matter what I say,

Parry encourages it because he doesn't want any outsider staking claims on me. *His* prized possession."

I looked toward the hall window, wishing I could go to their den and beat Parry upside the head with a sharp ax. "He's not going to make this easy for us, is he?"

Matt closed the distance and took my hands in his. "No matter what happens, you're the only woman I want. You're alpha and lady enough for me. I'm ready to stake my claim, if you are. And if Parry and the others don't respect that, then I have no place with them. My place is with you. My happiness is with you."

"You'd give up the only pack you've known for a half wolf like me?"

He shook his head and tipped my chin closer to his lips. "From where I'm standing you're all woman. And yes. Corny as it sounds, I'd give up the entire world for you."

Oh man. What does a chick say to something like that? Luckily, I had the answer in my hand in the form of a key to *our* room. After a sultry kiss with the man I wanted in my life more than anything else, I unlocked the door to 3-A...and invited a wolf into my heart.

Epilogue

Months later, Matt and I picked out a spot in Martha's Vineyard for our wedding. It would've been sooner, but my father demanded he be allowed some time to get to know his future son-in-law. It only took a few weeks for my father to start treating him like a second son. Although Dad had issues with him being a werewolf, he knew Matt would never forsake me. I was his for life.

Of course, Parry gave us hell. He remembered my string of insults and that was what mattered. Forget that I saved his sorry ass when I should've killed him for accusing me of stealing his wolf. Still, our days were numbered in Boston because Matt had defied his Alpha by choosing to take a hybrid for his mate.

We didn't care. Matt and I had plans for our future and they didn't include the Boston Pack as long as they continued to threaten me for being a half breed. I promised Matt if they ever came near me or my family and friends that I'd go through with my plan of setting their den on fire. For once, my lovely mate didn't object.

We tackled a lot of things like most newlyweds...and flipped a lot of coins to kill off the arguments. The biggest one turned out to be where we'd live. In the end, the living arrangements worked out better than I had thought by moving where Matt's pack wouldn't find us. The peace ended three months later.

With numerous phone threats, wolf piss at our door, and Parry's thugs following me on the streets, the Pack Alpha bastard made it clear what he thought of me. Sadly, it came to a head when a dozen of Parry's pack members checked into my bed and breakfast while I was away on a business trip, and trashed their rooms to the tune of ten thousand dollars in damage. Matt had to choose between his pack and me. Luckily, my husband was smart enough to come to that conclusion without my having to point out the obvious.

It would take some time, but eventually, we'd find a place safe to live, love and raise a family. Until then, we traded in Matt's SUV for a different model Parry's people wouldn't recognize, stockpiled our money and kept emergency suitcases packed in case we needed to make a quick getaway. It was only a matter of time before Parry would try to kill me and reclaim his wolf by force. Our only hope was to find a safe haven where Parry couldn't touch us. A place like that *had* to exist. If necessary, I'd spend the rest of my life searching. After all, our hopes for having children depended upon it.

About the Author

Paranormal author Marcia Colette is always hard at work on her next novel...assuming her day job doesn't get in the way.

Ever since her first book opened to fantastic reviews and became a Fictionwise bestseller, she hasn't looked back. She can't write a story unless there are paranormal aspects or a certain level of creepiness involved. When not crafting novels with twisted plots and supernatural thrills, she's diving into her massive DVD collection. Marcia is a member of the Horror Writers Association, Paranormal Mystery Writers and Romance Writers of America.

The best place to find her is at http://marciacolette.wordpress.com where she loves connecting with readers and other writers. Conferences/conventions where sci-fi, fantasy and horror reign supreme are a good bet too, along with the occasional romance conference.

To learn more about Marcia Colette and her other works, please visit her at www.marciacolette.com.

One choice means heartbreak.
The other, death.

Run, Wolf
© *2009 Keith Melton*

Nightfall Wolf Clans, Book 1

Leah Kendrick is guilty of only one crime: loving her human mate, Tom, enough to give him the gift of The Bite. The Pack council is merciless, and the punishment swift. In an instant everything she's ever known is ripped away, and they're turned out into the long winter with nothing. No money, no car, and no protection from a variety of creatures who'd like nothing more than to take down a lone wolf.

Friendless and broke, they form a daring plan to take back what's theirs and chase safety north. But the Pack has other ideas. And with time running out it's about to call their bluff...

Warning: Contains savage werewolf combat, defiant love, graphic violence/language/sex, kangaroo trials and unrepentant criminal havoc.

Available now in ebook from Samhain Publishing.

Enjoy the following excerpt from Run, Wolf...

We drove in silence, Tom at the wheel, on our way to steal back the money the pack had stolen from me. The weight of the quiet seemed to crush down around me in the truck, as if I were a mile underwater instead of driving through Somerville toward Cambridge. We headed south down narrow Prospect Street with its triple-decker houses that pushed right up against the road, looking faded and a little tired in the midday sun.

The shotgun lay beneath a blanket near my feet on the passenger side. Unloaded, but I was careful not to touch it. Respectful. Under my coat, I wore a polyester summer robe and nothing beneath it, in anticipation of the Change. I'd wrapped myself in one of those space-age thermal blankets that looked like a big sheet of aluminum foil and cranked the heater to keep my legs from freezing.

The office was a rundown one-story brick-fronted building. A wide, plate-glass display window took up most of the scarred façade, but I couldn't see inside through the bleary glass because of the blinds. A sign that said *Chockley Real Estate Management* had been painted on the glass, though the letters were now nicked and chipped. Weeds grew out front, poking up through cracks in the sidewalk.

The street was mostly empty, with only a few cars parked here and there. Frost still lingered in the shadows where the sun hadn't reached. Tom pulled the truck over to the curb just before the front of the building, trying to keep our getaway vehicle as close as possible and still stay out of the view of anyone who might be inside.

He looked at me. His eyes were steady, no trace of any fear, just a clear focus. "Ready?"

I nodded. My heart was beating—not fast—but with a strange weighted force so I could feel the thump reverberate through my chest and into my throat. I just wanted to get this done so we could go. Could go somewhere and live in safety. Not so goddamn much to ask.

Tom reached down and gently lifted the shotgun. He loaded it with shells, one after another, and then he pumped a round into the chamber. The sound was all business, a dead-serious *click-clack* that raised goose bumps on my skin, despite the fact that I knew the gun would be largely useless. My eyes strayed to the small, corded leather bag tossed in the console's drink holder. *That* was what would make the difference. My mother's sterling-silver shrimp ring was wrapped inside. I'd put it there with salad tongs first thing this morning, and I had the wounds to show for it. When I'd been unwrapping it, I'd brushed a little too close to the silver and my left hand had a line of blisters along my index finger that would be a long time healing. I could still feel the dull throb of pain.

Tom set the shotgun across his lap and lifted the bag, his face a mask of disgust at the feel of the silver's hateful aura. The ring seemed to send out a pulse—like a woofer pushing air for bass—that repelled us both. He slipped the leather bag over his head, careful to have it lay against the outside of his jacket. It was vital that the werewolves be able to smell the silver—just enough to make them unsure if the shotgun was loaded with silver pellets.

Tom looked at me and nodded. I shrugged off my coat and the silver gray blanket, pulled the door handle and stepped out onto the street. I kept my arms wrapped about me, though it did little to fight the cold. A powerful yearning swept through me to Change immediately and revel in the warmth of my fur, but I fought the urge. I couldn't shift until I was inside, otherwise the world would be treated to the first armed robbery that started with a naked woman on the sidewalk, and ended with something sporting a sharper set of teeth.

We hurried toward the glass door. Tom kept the shotgun as concealed as he could by his jacket. I clutched the robe around me, but the cold bit right through it and the cement froze my bare heels. My heart kept up that heavy thud.

Tom reached out and pulled the door open. A hot sizzle of adrenaline pumped into my veins, and an electronic sensor sang out an artificially cheery *deeeng dong*.

The woman at the high counter looked up at us as we pushed inside. I recognized her immediately. Her name was Nora something. She'd been here the first time I'd come with Hannah to sign up for my car loan. Her eyes widened and her hand paused, hanging in the air only a few inches from a beige mug giving off the smell of Dunkin' Donuts coffee.

Tom swung the shotgun up and stared at her along the iron sights. "Don't twitch." He pushed deeper into the office and

I shadowed him. "Can you smell the silver?"

Nora's lips pulled back from her teeth in a disgusted grimace. "Yes."

"This is loaded with silver buckshot. Don't make me use it."

Nora's gaze jumped to me. I could see the emotions in them—the hate, the *offense* that I'd do something like this. The smile I gave her dripped all kinds of nasty.

"Leah," Tom said. His voice was so calm it even helped settle me down some. "Do it."

I shrugged out of the robe, letting it puddle around my feet. Doubt flashed across Nora's face as I stood there naked. I closed my eyes, reached deep inside of myself, touched the wolf and Changed.

Pain. A tractor-trailer's worth and more. It burst within me like an explosion, as heat and jagged agony ripped through me. My bones broke, realigned; muscles tore, re-knitted; tendons snapped, reattached. Fur pushed from my skin. I felt my mouth tearing away from my face, my cheek and jawbones shattering as it stretched into a muzzle and filled with deadly fangs. The suffering stopped all at once, as completely as if it had never been. I stood there as wolfbreed, feeling the strength coiling through my muscles, reveling in how alive the world smelled, how crisp and deep the sounds were now.

I leapt forward, and I loved the powerful spring and release of my leg muscles as they launched me toward the counter. When I landed on it, a brass nameplate and a fake spider plant crashed to the floor. I crouched down, my arms dangling between my legs with my long claws curving out of my fingers. The snarling growl I gave Nora was low, but she flinched backward all the same.

"This isn't—" Nora began.

"Is there anyone else here?" Tom kept the shotgun aimed at her.

Nora shook her head. Her hair brushed against her face, lagging a half second behind the motion of her head. I lifted my muzzle, sniffing, tasting the air.

"She's lying." I sent my thought to Tom across our Bond. I could smell another werewolf in the back offices. The scent was faint but undeniable.

"I know," he sent back. Then aloud to Nora: "Get him out here. *Now!*"

Fear scent began to bleed out of Nora's pores. I could smell it mixed with fresh sweat. "I don't know what—"

I growled again, giving a menacing glimpse of teeth. Nora glanced at me, and then looked back toward the offices. I smelled the Change as the were behind the door shifted into wolfbreed.

"He's gonna fight," I sent. *"We don't have much time. They've already alerted the pack."*

We'd anticipated their communication across the Bond. If we moved fast, we'd be long gone before any help arrived. The more savage part of me felt regret. Already my heart rate had slowed and my wolfbreed body felt limber, powerful, almost aching for a contest. The wolf urge to battle seethed in my muscles, but I kept it on a double-wrapped chain.

The other werewolf hammered out from the back room, sending the cheap, hollow door splintering off its hinges with a massive hole dead center. He leapt into the hallway, his eyes blazing amber, fangs bared. I'd seen him before, I recognized that bark-colored fur and that swath of black beneath his chin. His smell was familiar, but I couldn't remember that damn name.

"Handle him," Tom sent. He kept the shotgun on Nora, whose gaze remained flat and far away. I recognized the look. She was talking across the Bond to the entire pack.

The brown wolfbreed dropped down on all fours and shot out of the hallway. My claws dug into the fake panel counter as I gathered myself and launched at him. Tom never moved the barrel of the shotgun—never even glanced at the oncoming snarling freight train of fur and fangs.

LaVergne, TN USA
13 January 2011
212354LV00001B/44/P